BOOK SMART

WORK FOR IT BOOK #3

AMANDA PENNINGTON

WWW.SMARTYPANTSROMANCE.COM

COPYRIGHT

This book is a work of fiction. Names, characters, places, rants, facts, contrivances, and incidents are either the product of the author's questionable imagination or are used factitiously. Any resemblance to actual persons, living or dead or undead, events, locales is entirely coincidental if not somewhat disturbing/concerning.

To Gregg, for always believing in me

CHAPTER 1

MEL

Cameron: Who's excited for yet another meeting that could've been an email?
Mel: I'm arming myself with extra snacks to share.
Ivy: It's not even 7am yet. Stop ruining my vibe with reminders about how miserable this workday is going to be.
Mel: We'll make it up to you with extra coffee from the Bluesy Bean.
Ivy: You're forgiven.

It is a truth universally acknowledged that faculty and staff meetings are soul destroying.

The color in my vision gradually flattened into black and white. I felt the marrow seeping from my very bones, draining away. Soon I would be an empty husk, my insides all withered to the point of blowing away at the slightest puff. The meeting would never end. All of us were destined to die in this conference room.

Yes, it's melodramatic. It's also 100 percent true.

At the urge to feel something—anything—I typed my passcode across my phone screen. My Meetings Binder, complete with a printed cover and colored tabs (all of them empty), served two purposes. One, I could look studious to anyone important enough to matter—as long as they didn't look too closely. Two, with my phone tucked behind my binder, I could discreetly tap on a few apps without goody-two-shoes Clarice ratting me out. Large scrolling motions with my fingers were a dead giveaway, so it was best to only tap, and only occasionally. I wouldn't want to be called out like Vernon was last week.

The colorful Instagram logo blinked. When the app opened, of course the first image in my feed was a book cover. I swallowed. I should've known better. No, I did know better. I just enjoyed the pain. We were all about to die in this conference room anyway. Might as well die for a cause better than Keith's endless PowerPoint presentation.

BIG REVEAL! Read the Instagram post from Always Cheerful Lisa. *So thrilled to be sharing my new book cover with my favorite followers! Love you all so much! Hope you love my new characters as much as I do!*

How many heart emojis was that? Eleven? That was too many. Someone needed to make a law to limit how many times the same emoji could be used in one post. If it was wrong to use multiple exclamation points, it was also wrong to use multiples of the same emoji.

My fingertips lingered on the screen. The novel's cover was beautiful, the light hitting the glossy book jacket just right. Feelings of genuine happiness for Always Cheerful Lisa conflicted with an inner voice reminding me that I hadn't achieved anything even remotely like she had. I felt jealous, okay? She was yet another of my college classmates publishing a book, or getting married, or having babies, or finding an agent, or winning a writing award, or getting a promotion at work. Okay, so the writing and book successes rankled the most, but still.

How did my fellow English major graduates manage such achievements, anyway? In the same amount of time it took them to find success, all I had done in my twenty-nine years was rent an apartment, buy a car, and keep working as a writing tutor at the university, all while I waited for my own big break in the writing world.

A text notification snagged my gaze.

Cameron: All PowerPoint software across campus will die a slow, agonizing death as soon as this meeting is over. Not that you heard it from me.

I fought my smile. It paid to have an inside source in the IT department. I tapped out my reply as discreetly as possible.

Mel: Please tell me you can actually do that.

Cameron: I can. And I will. Even if it means breaking into the dean's office.

Mel: Tell me again how many studies show that meetings like this make us less productive? A bazillion?

Cameron: Yes. Precisely a bazillion. What an exact statistic. But by the time I'm done, these pointless meetings will also be PowerPointless. Get it?

I twisted my lips to hide another smile and shot a look at Cameron across the table, where his tall body slouched low in an uncomfortable office chair. His ever-present chestnut cowlick stood defiant against his efforts at tidiness, and his face was expressionless—but his blue eyes were gleeful behind the dark frames of his glasses. Behind him, the floor-to-ceiling conference room windows offered a barren view of winter in New England.

Mel: If you have to ask if I got it, it's not a good joke.

Another text notification popped up, this time from a group thread.

Ivy: You two are being too obvious.

Cameron: Your mom is too obvious.

Ivy: You don't even make sense.

Cameron: You do realize you just handed me another mom joke on a shiny silver platter, right?

Ivy: NO.

Leaving my two best friends to argue on our thread, I switched over to Facebook. At least Always Cheerful Lisa wouldn't be posting about her new book cover on there. She was too hip for Facebook. She was too cool for Facebook. Too awesome for—

My attention caught on an article in my News Feed. "Advice for Women Seeking Husbands—in the 1950s." Perfect. The headline promised countless gems to fuel my righteous anger against everyone pressuring me to date, marry, and make babies. Nothing like the patriarchy in its purest form (the good ol' 1950s) and modern-day snark (social media comments from modern feminists) to boost my mood. Not much made for better entertainment than an internet showdown.

This faculty and staff meeting just became tolerable.

I scrolled through the article, glimpsing a few goodies: Stand in a corner at a party and cry quietly. Take a class about making toupees. Paint or draw or knit outside an engineering building. Sunburn your skin to stand out.

I forwarded the article to our group thread. Cameron and Ivy would appreciate it. *Mel: Enjoy the laughs, my friends. Enjoy.*

Fair-skinned Ivy replied almost immediately, exactly with the response I expected. *Ivy: Get a sunburn?! Yeah, that'll get a man's attention all right. Because I'll look like a tomato and then die of skin cancer. Ooh la la.*

I was typing my reply when Cameron's message came through.

Cameron: Turning to the fifties for dating advice...feeling desperate, Mel?

My fingers paused. Was I feeling desperate? My inner feminist cried a valiant "Never!" My inner fan of Masterpiece romances sobbed into an embroidered pillow.

3

But husband hunting wasn't the point. The point was not that I had only dated four people in my life and had Instagram and Facebook to thank for some serious comparisonitis. The point was not that even my Facebook account was trying to give me dating advice. No. The point was that the list was archaic and ridiculous and stupid. The point was the humor.

This called for deflection Cameron-style.

Mel: Your mom is desperate.

Ivy: BURN.

Cameron: And so the student becomes the master. Well done, my young Padawan.

We didn't die in the meeting after all. We escaped the valley of the shadow of collegiate death—barely. The three of us—Cameron, Ivy, and I—agreed to meet for an early lunch. It would take us a little while to recuperate from Keith's Presentation: Edition Infinity, so why not eat our feelings through the recovery process?

Ivy and I plunked our cafeteria trays on a table, easing into the humming background of student life. Unlike the uncomfortably quiet faculty and staff lounges, the cafeteria was the hub for the same youthful, academic energy that kept me at my job. I already felt a little better.

"Thanks for sending us that list of sexist dating advice, because it's the only thing that got me through the meeting," Ivy said, her chair screeching across the floor as she pulled it closer to the table. She tucked a wayward blond strand back into her messy bun. "Our grandparents were alive then. Or maybe even our parents. I'm not sure. I can't math."

"We never would've survived the fifties," I agreed.

"The same way Keith would never survive a meeting if he didn't have his precious PowerPoint?"

"Have no fear," Cameron said from above us. "There won't be a Power-Point next time."

"Hiya, Cam." I pulled out a chair for him.

He returned our standard greeting. "Hiya, Mel." Tucking his messenger bag under the table, he sat and stabbed his fork into the cafeteria food. "I'm serious though. My cousin just outlawed PowerPoint presentations at his business because they make meetings last so much longer. Why can't we?"

Ivy frowned. "You're going to outlaw PowerPoint? You don't run this college yet, Cam. You're an adjunct computer science professor who unofficially leads the IT minions. You have no sway in administrative decisions."

She stopped him when he opened his mouth to speak. "Do *not* make another mom joke. I've had it."

He smirked and shrugged without making eye contact. It was a distinctly Cameron gesture that he pulled off with a quiet, laid-back confidence that left me guessing every time.

"I agree," I mumbled around my sandwich. "The mom jokes aren't that funny, so you can stop those. But the puns? If you stop making puns, I will be genuinely worried about you."

Cameron grinned and muttered about his talents finally being appreciated, but Ivy feigned a glare. "Don't encourage him."

She looked back to the napkin and pen she was using to sketch an outline of the people sitting two tables away. It never failed—every free moment, Ivy would find a receipt, gum wrapper, anything at all, and whip out a pen to start doodling. Or that's what she called it. Her doodles were better than any masterpiece I could draw.

As they bickered, I watched Ivy doodle and mentally congratulated myself for bringing together such wonderful people. Being the glue in our three-way friendship was my favorite role. I gained the benefits of friendship with two coworkers who were also extraordinary human beings and who jokingly argued about mundane nonsense. They were equal parts inspiring and entertaining. My lunch hours couldn't get much better than this.

Cameron turned to me. "So, you're planning on snagging a man 1950s-style, huh?"

Ivy frowned. "Don't even joke about that. It's horrifying."

"Not true." He pointed at himself with his fork. "I, for one, would love to walk outside the computer science building and see an eligible damsel knitting. It would be comforting, I think, to know I would always be warm thanks to her cozy knitting."

Ivy's frown hadn't left. "Laugh all you want, but I feel bad for the real-life women who actually tried some of those things. How sad and desperate do you have to be to make wigs as a way to find a man?"

I grinned at their reactions. "It's not like I'm actually going to follow the advice. I thought it was funny. Don't you think it's funny?"

Cameron shrugged. "It's horrifying, and funny, and sad, sure, but I do know some people who would be desperate—no, *lonely* enough to try some of those suggestions. Because that's what it really comes down to. Loneliness."

I nodded. "Right. It's about loneliness. You just get tired of living alone and watching everyone else look like they're having a great time, you know?"

My eyes drifted over Ivy's shoulder to settle on a couple clearly smitten with one another. She was petite and beautiful, and he was tall, with glasses and an oversized, ugly sweater. They sat as close together as possible, his arm draped over the back of her chair, their heads close together as they talked.

Yep. They were definitely having a great time.

Cameron cocked his head at an angle. "It makes you wonder whether advice like that would work today. How much has society really changed? Is love life advice really outdated, or is it timeless, like the original *Jurassic Park*?"

"Of course it's outdated!" Ivy scoffed at him. "We live in the twenty-first century. I certainly hope I'm seen as more than a potential housewife or a baby-making machine."

"I'm just saying," Cameron continued, "playing devil's advocate here, if love is timeless, then wouldn't the basic principles of finding love also be timeless, no matter the century?"

I tuned out their chatter, my mind stuck on an inkling. It was a whisper of an idea, hovering at the edge of my mind. But it might be interesting. And it might be fun. And it might change my life.

Cameron and Ivy stared at me.

I frowned. "What?"

"You sat up straight," Cameron said. "You always slouch when you eat, but when you have an idea, you sit up straight like you're afraid the thoughts might fall out of your head if you move the wrong way."

"No, it's because you have that look." Ivy gestured at my face with her fork. "You're thinking about something crazy. Like that time we filled the campus fountains with soap."

Cameron laughed. "That was you two?" He grinned and then shook his head. "Never mind."

"No, just hear me out." An irrational fear filled me that if I listened to any more conversation, my idea would float away—or fall out of my head, as Cameron so eloquently put it. "Cam's right."

"Thank you very much." He preened at Ivy and then turned to me. "I just love being right about…?"

"What if someone used 1950s dating advice in our modern dating world and then wrote a book about the experience? Like the pros and cons, ups and downs, goods and bads. Dating today is a nightmare. Nobody can deny that. All this swiping right or left and texting, sexting, ghosting—it's a mess. We act like we know so much more about being men and women today than they did then. But do we? What if some of the 1950s dating advice is still applicable?"

Ivy stared at me. "You can't be serious."

6

"I said *some* of the 1950s dating advice." Excitement bubbled up in my voice now. "Because if love really is timeless, then the basic principles of pursuing that love should be timeless, too, right?"

"So *that's* what I was right about," Cameron muttered, sounding less than enthusiastic.

Ivy pointed her fork at me accusingly. "So this someone is going to take advice from the 1950s into our twenty-first century dating world. Get a sunburn in New England. Cry in a corner at a club full of gyrating twenty-year-olds. Learn how to make a wig in a world that has Rogaine. Pose with a flat tire when roadside assistance is a cell phone call away."

I nodded. This idea was priceless. I knew it.

"And who's this 'someone' going to be, huh?"

Her question stopped me. I hadn't written anything of my own, in earnest, in a long, long while. None of my projects had ever taken off like my college classmates' had. I'd never be able to write an entire book about dating using tips from the 1950s. Would I?

My phone vibrated on the cafeteria table. I imagined yet another notification about yet another post from Always Cheerful Lisa, marketing the glossy, professional cover for her new book.

I swallowed. I took a deep breath. "I'll do it."

That's when Cameron spewed his mouthful of coffee across the table, and Ivy dodged away from the spewage with a shriek, and this chaos solidified the statement in my mind. I could do this.

CHAPTER 2

CAMERON

Mel: Who wants to join me on our first 1950s experiment?!
Ivy: Me! What's the plan?
Mel: Advice #11: get lost at a football game. But let's exchange it for the exhibition basketball game at our home gym tomorrow night. Cam, be prepared to talk us through what's happening in the game. #notsporty
Cameron: You two are killing me. You know it's not called a gym, right?
Mel: It's a gym. What else would it be called?
Cameron: It's an arena, and it's called Goldner Arena.
Ivy: But it's a gym.
Mel: Arena shmena. Same difference.
Cameron: I have so much to teach you.

For people who have experienced traumatic events, life splits into before and after. Meaning, in everyday terms, people change after trauma. Before his accident, so-and-so was carefree. Before her broken heart, so-and-so was on the right track.

Life before my stroke was carefree and spontaneous. I was the king of last-minute surprises. Life after the stroke? Not so much. Losing the entire future I'd built for myself, spending two years in intense physical therapy, relearning how to walk and hold a fork...this meant I quickly subscribed to the "prepare for the worst" mindset.

A "prepare for the worst" mindset also meant keeping at least two spare sets of clothing in my vehicle at all times, because disaster could strike at any moment. Like a spilled drink. This came in handy because now I could throw away the shirt I ruined when I spewed coffee all over myself and the cafeteria at large because the woman I've loved for five years suddenly announced a ridiculous scheme to find true love using dating advice from the fifties instead of looking to her left and thinking maybe her true love had been sitting right beside her all along.

That's right. My Mel (who would probably never be My Mel at this point, who was I kidding?) had decided to run around the city, following outdated advice, putting herself at the mercy of total strangers, sadistic serial killers, and —the horror—Celtics fans.

The entire concept blindsided me. No way would My Mel ever think of doing something so rash. Her spontaneity was one of the many qualities I loved about her, but this? Not My Mel.

I could potentially fix this whole conundrum by telling her how I felt, but if she didn't feel the same way, and it changed how she looked at me...

I couldn't handle it if Mel ever looked at me differently than she did now, like lifelong friends, even though one friend regularly wondered how her lips would taste against his. No more sharing lunch hours in the cafeteria, where she would steal chips or fries or baby carrots from my plate. No more knowing smiles over idealistic freshmen who had yet to take a college-level exam. No more ducking into the tutoring center just to see how her day was going.

The truth is, I'd worked hard to rebuild my life. It wasn't the life I'd originally wanted as a college athlete. But it was still a good life. I'd remade my mind and my body through physical therapy and a new career. My friendships were part of that (possibly the most important part). I couldn't risk losing her.

When we first met as two new hires at orientation, I had fallen laughably head over heels for her. She'd walked through the door with a friendly smile and a braid over one shoulder. I just knew.

I'd bided my time. I'd spent three weeks casually getting to know her better, making sure she felt comfortable around me and wouldn't label me as a creep for asking her to dinner moments after meeting her. But then, at lunch one day, Ivy had asked her point-blank about a boyfriend. Mel had teared up over the last guy who'd broken her heart just a few weeks earlier. "I'm taking a break from the dating scene," she'd said. As much as I'd obsessed over every time her foot bumped my shin under the cafeteria table, I'd known it wasn't the time. I couldn't be her rebound guy. So I'd waited.

And waited.

Until she'd decided she was ready to date again, and apparently I didn't get the memo until she showed up to the university holiday party with a boyfriend. She'd dated him, and then he'd broken her heart, and she'd been miserable. Again I'd worried about being her rebound guy. Again I'd waited.

The cycle repeated itself a few more times. And here I was, still waiting, unsure whether she felt anything for me but friendship, unsure whether she was over the latest scumbag until I was too late and she was with someone new. We were so close now that I worried about risking our long, comfortable friendship.

I'd resorted to dropping hints (extremely obvious hints, in my opinion) and watching for signs that she had feelings for me, too. I wanted her to notice me, I just wanted a signal from her before I jeopardized our friendship.

Now, clearly over her last relationship, she was on to something new. This dating experiment could ruin any chances I had left of being with her someday. What if she met someone serious? But the way her brown eyes had lit up over her writing idea had me hesitating. How could I bring myself to do anything to erase that expression on her face?

I braced my hands on the roof of my car, closed my eyes, and breathed deeply. Just focus on the task at hand: change my shirt. I opened my eyes and stared at my mottled reflection in my car window.

(Another before and after: The droop on the left side of my mouth, the last physical reminder of the worst years of my life. My sister, Samantha, said it was barely noticeable. But *I* noticed it.)

I focused on the cold seeping from my car roof into my palms. This 1950s Dating Debacle was no reason to regress to bad habits. I could already hear Toby, my physical therapist turned best friend, ribbing me.

No self-pity.

No catastrophic thinking (like Mel meeting a sadistic killer or converting to Celtics fanhood).

No worrying about things beyond my control (like Mel meeting Prince Charming and living happily ever after, her long, dark waves and pretty smile just beyond my reach).

Thinking this way was a waste of time and energy—time and energy that I needed to focus on what I wanted most.

Mel.

Well, yes. I wanted Mel. But I also wanted to be the new full-time computer science professor, finally moving beyond adjunct life. I needed to focus on that. I would earn the job. I would earn it through my own hard work, and I would mentor students, and I would live a fulfilling life regardless of any obstacles. This was what I really wanted.

I opened my eyes, changed my shirt, and turned back toward campus. Time to get to work. Pep talk: check. Up next: corrupting PowerPoint without leaving a trace.

CHAPTER 3

CAMERON

Mel: Cam, do dirty stories bother you? The list says I shouldn't share dirty stories with men.
Cameron: I guess it depends on the girl, the number of dates we've been on, and the dirt.
Mel: Fair enough.
Ivy: Cam, you're always telling dirty jokes.
Cameron: Dirty stories are different from my dirty jokes. My dirty jokes are delightful innuendos of genius. I wouldn't want you to miss out.

Monday night at Mel's apartment meant too many throw pillows (complete with tassels dangling from the corners) and too many fluffy blankets tossed across chairs and sofas. It meant vanilla-scented candles. It meant a patchwork of furniture from thrift stores. In the winter, it meant hot tea and Moscow mules; in the summer, icy lemonades and margaritas. It meant cozy. Comfort. Absolutely Mel. Absolutely lovely.

It also meant Mel in leggings. Let's not forget the sight of Mel in leggings.

But for now, I grumbled to myself in my car. I'd just seen Ivy walk through the main doorway. She was there first, so I wouldn't have Mel to myself for the few precious, bittersweet moments I craved.

At first, it amazed me how quickly it became second nature, this equal parts eagerness and nervousness to spend any fraction of time with her. It became automatic to look for her each moment I was on campus, to watch for her at odd times even when I knew my chances of seeing her were slim. (I knew her schedule inside out. Not that I was a stalker. Not at all. I just kept track of her every move so I could see her smile as often as possible. Totally normal.) I purposely went out of my way to walk through the lobby of the library, since she worked in the tutoring center there. It should have bothered me how much my mood depended on whether I was with Mel: if we carpooled together and ran late (like we did to that conference last year), I loved traffic; if I was on my way to see her and ran late (like tonight), I hated traffic.

Collecting my bags of chips and jars of salsa, I walked to the building and made my way up the main stairwell.

Moments after I knocked, the door opened, and there she was. Bare feet. Fuzzy sweater. Hair in a messy knot. And leggings. Sweet, blessed, sent-from-above leggings.

"Hiya, Cam." She smiled.

My breath caught. "Hiya, Mel."

She opened the door wider, keeping eye contact. I'd heard students complain that she was intimidating when they went to the tutoring center. Sure, her eye contact was direct. Sure, I'd been a bit intimidated when we first met, too. But I liked her steady gaze. (Another before and after: I never understood the value of eye contact until people spent a few years avoiding looking at me.)

Mel took my offering of chips and salsa. I nodded to Ivy, who was already curled under a blanket on the couch, a steaming mug cupped in her hands.

"We were just debating the merits of dating apps," Mel said. "Tell us your thoughts, professor."

I hung my coat by the door, inhaling the faint sweetness of the glowing vanilla candles. "What about them?"

"Ivy says it's the only way to meet anyone these days."

"What happened to meeting at work, or bars, or the gym?" I took a seat on the far left of the couch, with Ivy at the far right, hoping Mel would sit between us, close to me. I accepted the chilled copper mug Mel offered. Moscow mule. Extra lime. She always remembered.

Ivy raised an ink-smudged finger. "That's exactly the problem. What if you don't like going to bars? What if you can't afford a gym membership? What if you're career-focused, or you have other"—she waved her finger through the air—"responsibilities? If you don't meet someone at random or at a work event, you're a goner."

I shrugged, watching Mel put my chips and salsa on the coffee table.

"I believe that fate finds a way," Mel said.

Ivy smirked at Mel. "Yeah, sure. Fate finds a way. Is that why you're doing this dating experiment? You got tired of waiting on fate?"

I stilled. Mel's 1950s Dating Debacle was not what I wanted to hear about. I'd filed it away in the box labeled "Things Not to Think About," right next to the folder of "Peeing My Pants on Stage During the First-Grade Spelling Bee," and I'd shoved it in the back of my mental attic, next to the other cobwebby boxes.

Mel shrugged. "I'm not forcing fate, if that's what you mean. I'm doing it so I can write a book about it."

"Right." Ivy didn't hide her skepticism.

"You're actually doing it?" I managed through a mouthful of chip and salsa. I knew she wanted to write books, had known that since she told me within my first week of knowing her, but this was what she chose to write about?

"Of course."

"I thought you were joking."

She shook her head and curled her legs underneath herself in the armchair across from me. (Not on the couch next to me, but at least I had a good view of the leggings.)

"I wasn't joking," she said. "It's the first writing project I've been excited about in a long time. And I think it's a timely topic, you know? Feminism, the disaster that is modern dating, that kind of thing."

I stared at the ice cubes floating in my mug.

"I can't believe you're doing this." Ivy smiled and shook her head slowly. "Are you planning to do everything on the list or just pick and choose?"

A laptop materialized in Mel's hands. "That's something I wanted to talk to you two about. I need your help."

My fingers tightened around my mug to the point of whitening my knuckles. Help? No. I wasn't helping with Mel's Dating Debacle. Never. Absolutely not.

Mel continued. "I don't think I can follow all of the advice on the list—and I don't want to, honestly, because some of that advice just doesn't fit me or doesn't translate well into the twenty-first century. So I need your help figuring out if I should follow the advice to the letter or make adjustments, just general brainstorming. And then I need help actually following it. You two are my wingmen. Er, wingpeople." Mel smiled. "Consider yourselves voluntold."

Ivy shrugged in a "whatever" gesture.

I did not shrug. I scrambled. How could I stop this without being obvious? Desperation slowed any quick-thinking abilities I may have had just minutes ago. "So no more game nights on Mondays?"

"Well, I was thinking we could postpone game nights or maybe do them every other week, at least while I'm working on this," Mel said. "We could use Monday nights for brainstorming or trying out the list. But it might take us a while." She squinted at her laptop screen. "This list is really long. Are you two okay skipping a few game nights?"

I sent telepathic messages to Ivy. *Stick with me here. Tell Mel she's crazy. We don't negotiate with terrorists, and we don't negotiate with game nights.*

"You know we'll always support your dreams, Mel," Ivy said. "What's on the list?"

I nearly dropped my mug when Mel moved to plop onto the middle couch cushion, laptop in hands. Maybe I could spill my Moscow mule on her laptop. Or put a virus on her laptop. Or—

"I copied the list into a document so I could take notes," Mel said, focused on her screen.

Ivy leaned closer to look at the document. I leaned closer to breathe Mel's shampoo. (Don't judge me and my unrequited love.)

I skimmed the tidy bullet points.

Painting your phone number on your roof, or adding it to a billboard? Breaking down on the side of the road? Loitering in sporting goods stores?

Mel and Ivy were talking about ways to revisit old relationships to see if they could be saved, or maybe it was the likelihood of an elderly neighbor's grandson being single, when I interrupted.

"Are you sure this is safe?" I spoke without thinking, and they both swiveled to look at me. (So much for subtlety.) I cleared my throat. "I mean, you're physically going to these places and trying out this advice. What if some scumbag tries to take advantage?" I lost my nerve and ended on a less-than-convincing "or whatever."

They both stared until I began to worry that I'd misspoken more than I thought. Then they erupted into laughter.

"He's serious!" Mel exclaimed.

"He has no idea!" Ivy gripped a tasseled throw pillow to her stomach.

"It's very nice of you, Cam," Mel said, patting my forearm, "but welcome to reality. Scumbags are a part of life. Women meet them everywhere, whether or not we're trying out decades-old dating advice. Not everyone is sweet like you."

My cheeks warmed, both from the compliment and from the condescension. "I know that. My point is, won't sexist psychos be more attracted to sexist old-fashioned dating strategies than they are to our standard twenty-first-century dating strategies?"

Ivy paused. "That may be a good point."

I mentally high-fived her. *Way to have my back, Ivy!*

Mel nodded. "It is. But that's part of why I'm doing this—exploring whether 1950s dating advice is applicable today. We can add our notes about playing into the hands of the, er, 'sexist psychos' in the book."

Well. That backfired.

"What about advice number twelve?" Ivy pointed to the laptop screen.

My fingers twisted around the now-empty mug. I had to do something. I needed a minute to think. To make an argument she couldn't out-plan.

Mel and Ivy didn't notice when I stood from the couch. "I'm making another drink. Either of you want anything?"

Not waiting for their replies, I made my way to the kitchen. Focusing on my mug, I took a minute to tune out their voices a few steps away, instead listening to the ginger beer fizz around my half-melted ice cubes.

Just because she was following this advice didn't mean she would meet anyone. It didn't mean anything would happen, good or bad. It didn't mean she would be unsafe (since they so clearly pointed out to me that creeps are every-where, not just in dating scenarios, which I already knew—I had a sister, after all). Was there anything else I could say or do to stop Mel?

"Cam?"

I jerked to attention at Mel's question. "Yeah?" My voice rasped with guilt over my saboteur thoughts.

"Could you bring more salsa? It's on the countertop."

"Sure."

My lungs filled. She was still Mel. We were still friends. Her 1950s Dating Debacle was just a phase. Everything would be okay. Life would go back to normal soon. The normal where she laughed at my puns, and I beat her at Monopoly, and she beat me at Scrabble, and I watched Google traffic patterns to maximize my time with her. Perfectly adequate normal life.

CHAPTER 4

MEL

Mel: Am I too fussy?
Ivy: In what context?
*Mel: Women in the fifties weren't supposed to be too "fussy," but that's such
vague advice. How much fuss is too much fuss?*
Cameron: If you have to ask...then you're probably too fussy.
Mel: You're no help.

I loved my boss. I really did. But he wasn't like other bosses.

Other bosses might occasionally talk about their personal life, but they
mostly talk about work, keeping clear boundaries between professional and
personal. Other bosses probably wear suits, or at least button-downs and
khakis. They comb their hair. They shower.

Not Dr. Curtis Schaaf. Our tutoring center meetings were more about the
latest conspiracy theory he was obsessed with—or his ex-wife, or his house-
plants—than they were about work. He didn't comb his hair. I doubted he
showered on any regular basis at all.

But he was a genius. I'd never before known anyone so brilliant. He could
tutor any student on any topic—the most advanced levels of number theory,
anatomy, philosophy, literary theory, astrophysics, history, anything.

His genius was one of the things I reminded myself of when his staff meetings went overtime because he was ranting about chemtrails. Or now, when he slouched into the tutoring center, the middle of his lumpy sweater splattered with a mystery stain.

He greeted me the way he greeted everyone—last name, monotone, no facial expression.

"Hirsch."

"Good morning, Dr. Schaaf."

He sighed when he walked across the room. He sighed when he sat at the small conference table wedged into the main waiting area in front of the receptionist desk. He sighed when he cleaned his glasses on his lumpy sweater.

I knew his most likely answer, but I had to ask anyway. "How are you today?"

He sighed when he looked at me. "Hirsch. It's morning. Please."

It was 11:00 a.m. Definitely late enough that he should be functioning better than this, but yes, technically, it was still morning.

Trying not to smile, I turned back to my desk.

The tutoring center was a corner space that straddled the library and the library lobby. The center itself was one large room with cubicles dividing it into various "office" spaces, each with a table and two chairs. The main area had a small conference table and a desk from the seventies, where we kept an information sheet for students. We'd started using online scheduling a few years ago, much to Dr. Schaaf's disdain.

Administration had recently tried to rebrand the tutoring center, which had glass for all four walls, as "the atrium." But we still called it the Fishbowl.

There were only a few staff members present for the morning meeting. Since the tutoring center hired mostly students who would be in class at this time of day (or who would claim to be in class), only a few lucky staff members were present for the morning meeting. Dr. Schaaf greeted each arrival with his customary monotone, expressionless greeting.

Seeing it was almost time for the meeting to start, I ripped out a notebook page and scribbled a note to leave in Cameron's office after the meeting. *Flaxen (Freisen). Spilled cologne (Schaaf). Good luck with your classes this afternoon!* It was a game we played each day, trading goofy notes about the color of Dr. Freisen's bowties (today was a yellow day) and guesses about Dr. Schaaf's clothing stains (an ongoing mystery). After wearing out normal adjectives like green, blue, and purple, we'd moved on to more obscure words, like verdigris green, smalt, and cattleya. As for Dr. Schaaf's stains, our guesses ranged from standard, like coffee, to outlandish, like acid rain. Not that we would ever ask him, especially after Cameron once joked, "Do you prefer wearing your coffee over drinking it?" and Dr. Schaaf blankly stared at him before walking away.

Lauren sat next to me, patting my shoulder as she set a container of home-made candies in the middle of the table. As a stay-at-home mom, she was always making something sweet; as a part-time tutor, she was always mothering tutoring staff and students alike. Basically, everyone loved her and wanted to be like her. She was the best thing that ever happened to the Fishbowl—the stale snacks stayed stale for the next meeting, but her candies would be devoured in mere minutes.

Dr. Schaaf sighed again. "Today's agenda."

That was my cue. I read through the general update about the tutoring center. I gave a special kudos to Lauren for talking with the anatomy tutor about staying professional even if he was teaching students about the reproductive system. Then I moved on to two points that needed to be addressed. First, we needed a new science tutor who could handle the advanced geology students. Second, we needed a policy about friends or significant others of the staff being disruptive during tutoring sessions.

Dr. Schaaf nodded for me to continue.

I gave him the list of potential students that Lauren and I had interviewed for the replacement geology tutor, explaining our rationale for each candidate. At times like this, I missed Holly Dolinsky, who used to handle the interviews for hiring tutors. She could always tell who would be a good fit.

He skimmed the list. "Let's go with Samuel. I've heard good things about him."

Snagging a candy, I waited for him to bring up the disrupted sessions. I didn't mind pulling most of the admin weight, but there were some things that he, as the director of the Fishbowl, needed to handle himself.

Veronica saved him the discomfort and brought up the loitering herself. "So, like, I can't let my boyfriend hang out with me between classes anymore?"

Dr. Schaaf's voice was flat. "No."

Other bosses probably had people skills to go with their combed hair.

"But he's a commuter." Her voice took on a plaintive tone that wouldn't earn her any points with this crew. "He's got like three hours to kill every day."

"Library. Cafeteria. His car. A dark alley. Lots of other places he can kill some time."

Her lower lip stuck out in a literal pout, and she ducked her head to continue scratching off her chipped nail polish.

"Anything else?" Dr. Schaaf said.

Lauren spoke up. "My kids have dentist appointments next week. I'll let you know the times I'll be unavailable."

"Good. Let Hirsch know."

Of course. His favorite phrase to use during meetings.

"Anything else?" He sighed.

I pushed a paper across the table toward him to start our age-old debate. "I've been doing some research, and I found some new punch clock options that I think would make us more efficient—"

He sighed.

I ignored my instinctive apology and need to overexplain how many hours I wasted on timecards each pay period.

"We keep the punch clock we have," he said.

"But—"

"Budget cuts are always in the works. The more the administration forgets any of us are even here, the better it is for all of us."

Monique, our physics tutor, barked a bitter laugh. "And the more likely it is that we don't get raises."

"You're a work-study tutor. You don't get raises." He turned to me. "Is the punch clock acting up?"

Did I ever smack it to jog its memory so it would start working again? Every single day. But that didn't qualify as "acting up" to Dr. Schaaf. "Sometimes," I hedged.

He pointed at Trevor, our linguistics and Spanish tutor. "You're handy. Can you fix it?"

Trevor stared down at his clasped hands. "Well, I need to check the mechanics and see if any parts are broken, because if they are, then I need to see if they're available, and how long it would take to get them here, and then—"

Dr. Schaaf sighed. "Yes or no."

"I mean, I'll try my best, but—"

"So yes. Anything else?"

Nobody answered. He leaned back in his chair, shifting his weight to slouch even more. No, no, no. Not the conspiracy theories—

"The real reason we need to keep that punch clock running is because I want as little government interference as possible. They can't watch us if we don't give them anything to watch…"

An hour and several monologues on black helicopters and bioweapons later, the meeting ended, and we bolted away before Dr. Schaaf could launch into another topic. Lauren left to pick up her kids from her dad's—I wished I felt as carefree as she looked. Veronica moved back to the receptionist desk, nail polish flakes sticking to her fingers. Monique and Trevor left for class.

I was prepping for a tutoring session scheduled to start in a few minutes—with Esther, a sweet foreign exchange student from Hungary—when Dr. Schaaf noticed my notebook.

"Going old school with paper and pen?"

Before he could launch into the benefits of paper and pen in our AI world, I explained the list. "I'm working on a new writing project. It's a social experiment of sorts." I placed my hard copy of the list in front of him on the conference table. "I'll be trying out this dating advice to see what happens, and then I'll write a book about it."

"To see what happens," he muttered, studying the list for longer than I expected him to before handing it back to me. "What exactly do you expect to happen on these, er, mancounters?"

Mancounters. What a turn of phrase. Too bad he uttered it with such skepticism. But that wouldn't stop me from using it in my book. *Book note...*

Ignoring his tone, I shrugged. "Anything could happen." Some awkward but hilarious experiences. A bestselling book that could launch my dream writing career. True love. I could hardly wait to find out.

Veronica straightened her posture so quickly she nearly fell out of her chair. That could only mean one thing—a Cameron sighting. He was in the lobby. When he turned for the basement steps that led to the computer science department, Veronica let her posture droop. Not that I could blame her for her reaction.

Watching Cameron walk away, I thought of my first workday here. He was one of the first people I'd met. I'd noticed him immediately. He was tall, dark-haired, blue-eyed, and handsome, making him impossible to miss. His good looks had been intimidating. Like I hadn't already been on edge about making a good impression on my first day.

But, Cameron being Cameron, he'd made me feel welcome. The words his students wrote in his reviews—"approachable," "easygoing," "down to earth"—fit him exactly. He'd put me at ease. At first I'd thought his attention was because he was interested in me, and even though I'd been on the mend from a recent breakup, I would've jumped at the chance to be with him. But then it'd been obvious even on that first day that Cameron was kind to everyone.

So I'd told myself not to be an idiot and start imagining a workplace romance before I'd even finished my first day at my new job. He didn't see me as anything more than a friend, and I shouldn't see him as anything more, either. *Friends,* I'd lectured myself. *Just friends.*

Looking at Veronica, who was now striking a pouty-lipped pose for a selfie, Dr. Schaaf sighed again. "Hirsch. I don't care what you do. Just as long as you still work here. I don't know anything about"—he gestured at the Fishbowl around us but still looked at Veronica, who was texting while spinning in her office chair—"any of this stuff."

I smiled. Another one of his favorite phrases.

"But I'll tell you what I expect to happen," he said, "with the latest about George Soros…"

CHAPTER 5

CAMERON

Ivy: How do you plan on getting lost at the basketball game?
Mel: Not sure. Maybe on my way to or from the restroom?
Cameron: It's not a large arena. It would be hard to get lost there.
Mel: If it's not a large arena, does that make it a gym?
Ivy: Lol. With your sense of direction, it won't be difficult to get lost, no matter the size.
Cameron: If I ran into a girl who got lost at our arena, I'd question her general sanity. Just saying.
Ivy: Then start questioning Mel's.
Mel: Hey!
Ivy: Kidding! Love you, Mel.
Cameron: Not kidding but love you anyway.

My last text echoed in my head. *Not kidding but love you anyway?*

What an idiot.

I kept my hands steady, spotting Toby as his arms shook with effort. Our friendship may have started with him as my physical therapist, when he gradually shaped me into a functioning human again, but now it was based on outdoing one another in reps lifted and miles run.

Too bad Toby always tried to be my emotional therapist, too. I wished I could forget how he teared up after I "graduated" to walking on my own two feet.

Toby paused for a rest between sets, breathing labored. "This'll be the first basketball game you've been to since the stroke, right?" He grimaced, his white teeth bright against his brown lips.

I nodded.

"Does Mel know this?"

"No. I don't want her to know. She'd try so hard not to make a thing out of it that it would definitely be a thing." I could picture it now, the well-meaning tiptoeing around me, just like my family had done for far too long. I would do almost anything to avoid a repeat of those months.

"Mel must be some girl—"

"You know she is."

"You didn't let me finish. What I was going to say was, she must be some girl for you to escort her on her way to meet some other man. And especially to meet some other man at a basketball game."

I shrugged.

"How're you taking it?"

"Like the champ I always am."

"Sure you are."

I grinned. Toby always thought he could call me out. Most likely a professional hazard from always pushing his patients to do more than they thought they could. Also because he was good at it—that tactful kind of friend who pushed and supported at the same time.

But we both knew what he really meant. After the stroke, I wasn't myself for a long while. And not just physically. Toby had been a big part of pulling me out of the depression, no matter how much I kicked and screamed. No matter how much I made fun of his pep talks.

"Just text or call if you want to talk," Toby said. "It's the same as always. You know the drill."

"Yes, sir," I mocked.

He positioned himself on the bench for his last set. "We'll run a few laps after this."

I frowned, mentally clicking through his spreadsheet of our workouts. "That's not in the plan you emailed me for this week."

"You need the endorphins."

I watched as he lifted the bar from the rack. "You keep getting physical therapist and psychotherapist confused. But it's okay. I won't sue you for malpractice just yet."

But he was right. (Not that I'd tell him that.) I'd already started running every morning before work, needing the extra boost to avoid slumping into old habits that inevitably led to downhill slides, namely because of the upcoming basketball game. I had a lot to be grateful for. My life was good. It was just that sometimes the goodness could feel more like a background tab I left open on my browser while I was busy with other work.

While I waited for Toby to wipe down the barbell and bench, I checked my messages. My brother-in-law had texted about when I could visit the family again and if I could fix his laptop when I was in town. Typical Derek.

There were also new messages from Mel and Ivy.

Ivy: We should meet at the Bluesy Bean for coffee/snacks before the basketball game.

Mel: You don't enjoy stuffing your face with greasy food served by sweaty students?

Ivy: At their outrageous prices? No.

Cameron: The price is for the mystery. Is the food greasy? Is it sweaty from the students laboring over the kitchen grills? Will we ever know?

Shoving my phone back into my pocket, I strode after Toby toward the locker room. We mopped up our sweat in silence and pulled hoodies over our heads on our way outside. I watched the dark pavement for ice patches. I'd learned the hard way to always be on the lookout for winter in New England. The sound of our steady footfalls set a good pace and began clearing my head after a few minutes, like always.

Toby dodged a shallow pothole. "So when you're at the arena, what do you do?"

"I know what to do."

"I know you know. But I still want to hear you say it."

"Deep breaths. Focus on physical sensations to stay present. Keep moving, even in small ways."

"And when you get home after the game?" Toby said.

"Call or text you if I need it. Ask you to make me a grilled cheese sandwich."

The latter was a jab at Toby's miserable cooking skills, but he ignored it.

"And?"

"Go for a run, preferably outdoors, no matter the time of day or night. Tell you to stop bugging me."

"Good."

We ran in silence until Toby spoke again. "You've made too much progress to go backward now."

"I don't plan to go backward."

"Nobody plans to go backward. It just happens."

I couldn't be annoyed when his tone was so kind. From anyone else, the words would feel like a lecture. But in our friendship, Toby could say just about anything.

"I'm done ribbing you to ask out Mel," he said (which was always what he said right before he ribbed me about asking her out). "But I think you should be careful. Helping her with this dating project could backfire."

Did he honestly think I hadn't been obsessing about all the ways this could end badly for me?

"Yes, Mother." Just because he could say anything didn't mean I'd let him live it down.

He huffed a laugh in his exhale. "I care, man. That's all."

I knew he did. "Thanks."

"And I think asking out Mel is your next step to moving on with your life," Toby said. "It's the final obstacle you haven't overcome."

"She's not an obstacle. I just don't want to ask her yet. I'm biding my time. Enough about me. What about you? What happened with Yvonne?"

He sighed. "Just didn't work out."

"Why not?" If I had to put up with his pestering, he had to put up with mine.

"She's just... We wanted different things."

"How so?"

We reached the end of our first loop. It sounded like he needed this run almost as much as I did, so we kept going, even though my joints were starting to ache, given that this was my second run of the day.

"Someone told me once," Toby said, his sentences choppy with the effort of our pace, "that when we ask for someone to love us, we expect, say, twenty-five cents' worth of love. A quarter. But that person, for whatever reason, only has a nickel of love to give us. I guess in some relationships, like family, you accept that nickel, and you learn how to live with it." Now Toby's voice was so quiet I almost didn't hear him over the sound of our footfalls. "But I want a girl who can give me a quarter's worth of love, you know?"

I paused, thinking it through, picturing Toby asking Yvonne for a love that was bigger and deeper than what she could give him. Toby, with his bottomless heart. I thought of me, asking my family and friends to love me the same way they always had after my stroke. "Yeah," I said, also chopping my words. "Makes sense."

"I just need to make sure I can give the same quarter's worth of love that

I'm asking someone else to give me, you know? Like I need to make sure I'm not cheap about it. Or shallow when the time—and the girl—is right."

I blinked at him. "Where's all this coming from?"

"I have thoughts sometimes," he said.

"And not just feelings? You must be sick. Here's your prescription for a daily run." A thought hit me. "Why not come with me to the basketball game? Meet some new people. Make new friends."

"While your girl is on a husband hunt? No, thanks. I'll keep my distance until she chills out a bit."

"Good idea." I laughed, but I also eyed his tall frame and wondered if Mel had a type that I didn't know about, or if Toby fit all types.

"Or maybe I should meet her," he said. "Woo her. Lure her into my arms. Make you fight for her."

Even though I knew he was joking, jealousy stabbed at me. I ignored it. "'Woo her'? Who talks like that?"

"Race you to the next block. Loser asks out Mel."

We raced. I lost. But we both knew I wouldn't ask her out.

CHAPTER 6

MEL

Ivy: Cam and I are at Goldner Arena. Where did you park, Mel?
Mel: I'll be there in a minute. I'm stuck at a traffic light.
Cameron: Sure, sure. Just admit it. You're already lost, aren't you?
Mel: Very funny.

"Fine. You two were right. Our gym is smaller than I remembered."

"Arena," Cameron corrected around a mouthful of nachos.

The three of us stood at the top of the bleachers, surrounded by a crowd of people in red and white. The gym—excuse me, *arena*—itself was huge. Our team did well enough, and people came to see our biggest games from a good distance away—or so Cameron said—but the actual building? It had the basic food, restrooms, paraphernalia to buy. And not much room for getting lost.

"You'll just have to get creative to lure some stranger into your wily schemes." Ivy sighed happily between bites of hot dog and slurps of milkshake. I had treated them both to their greasy/sweaty food of choice since they were my wingpeople. So much for Ivy's complaints about the food.

Cam shrugged. "You could always just enjoy the game like everyone else."

The usher pointed us to our seats. As we made our way through the crowd, Cameron chatted with university staff and students he knew as we passed by them. Had Maureen heard about the new volumes coming to the library archives from the northwest? Did Lewis's grandson enjoy his tenth birthday party last month? How about the coffee pot in the art department still being broken after all this time—could you believe that?

What I couldn't believe was how Cameron knew all these details, remembered them, and then used them to connect with people.

I glanced at Ivy. She had her own charm, just in a different way. Like now, when she smiled at a man and touched his shoulder, making his cheeks flush and effectively edging us closer to our seats.

I had none of Cameron's charm, none of Ivy's flirtatiousness, but at least I had tenacity. Or that was what Dr. Schaaf said when I brought up the punch clock again yesterday. Tenacity that had me following outdated relationship advice.

We settled in for the game. Or at least tried to settle in. Ivy was uninterested in everything but her food, and Cameron, eyes on the court, crunched on some nachos and cheese. Now that we were seated, my friends' silence felt loud compared to the noisy voices around us.

I waited what felt like forever before I elbowed Cameron. "What's wrong with you tonight?"

"Nothing." He narrowly caught a glob of nacho cheese from landing on the front of his university shirt. "Does it seem like something's wrong with me?"

"There's definitely something wrong with you." I pointed past him to Ivy. "She's practically making out with her milkshake, and you're not cracking any jokes."

Ivy mumbled something around her milkshake straw.

Cameron turned back to me, grinning. "She's too easy of a target."

Since when did he ever consider a target too easy?

Ivy leaned over Cameron to stage whisper at me. "You have any idea what just happened?"

"Incredible." Cameron's mutter sounded less than impressed. Louder, he said, "That's called a shot clock violation. When a team has the ball, they have thirty seconds to hit the rim or get a basket, and if they don't, that buzzer sounds and the ball automatically goes to the other team. That's for college basketball. In the NBA, the team has twenty-four seconds. It stops teams from stalling at the end of a game."

I'd already known that, but I didn't want Ivy to feel alone, so I played along. "Look at you, being a wealth of information." I stole one of his nachos. "So how good were you when you played basketball?"

"I had a basketball scholarship to college."

"So you were really good."

"I was the best on our team." He said it with the quiet, laid-back confidence that I loved about him—the confidence of someone who had nothing to prove. He stated it as fact, like I could google it, and the search results would read: "Cameron Whitacre, Best on Team."

"Why don't you play now?"

He was so focused on the game that I thought he hadn't heard me at first. When our team scored a point, he cleared his throat, mumbled, "I don't know. Just needed to move on, I guess," and shoved another nacho in his mouth.

I dropped it. I knew the gist of his stroke, the months—maybe years?—he'd spent in physical therapy. Of course I was curious. He was one of my two best friends, and I knew almost nothing about this part of his life. But I also respected him enough to give him space when he clearly wanted it.

Ivy leaned over again. "Why is the ref whistling? And do either of you think he's cute, or am I hallucinating from the toxic food?"

Cameron wrinkled his nose. "He's old."

"Ageist," she shot back at him.

I shrugged. "He's okay. He's not quite George Clooney or Kevin Costner, but he's aging pretty well. You know, the barista at the Bluesy Bean is always checking you out, Ivy. You should—"

The buzzer interrupted me, and Ivy frowned at Cameron for an explanation.

"Another shot clock," he said.

I turned back to Ivy. "You should—"

She shook her head. "Never happening."

"Why not?"

"Have you seen him?"

"Of course I've seen him. We go there all the time, and he never upcharges you for the extras like he does to the rest of us. The whole time we're at the Bluesy Bean, he stares at you."

She shook her head with more energy than I'd seen from her in a long time. "No. He's not attractive."

Clearly surprised, Cameron glanced away from the game. "Even I think he's attractive."

She rolled her eyes and then noticed my stare. "What?"

I leaned across Cameron—why was he sitting between us anyway?—to make sure she heard me. "Your brain has bumpers, Ivy. Like a bowling alley.

You see a guy you think is too gorgeous for you, and your brain panics and instinctively pushes you back into the lane of average good looks. Your brain doesn't even let you consider him."

Ivy rolled her eyes again. "That's worse than Cam's jokes. You've seen me flirt. Nothing stops me."

Cameron pressed a palm to his chest. "My jokes are outstanding. Your flirting is passable."

I didn't let her distract me. "Prove it," I challenged her. "Flirt with the barista. See what happens."

Ivy scowled. "Aren't you supposed to be lost by now?"

Knowing I could only push her so far, I snagged another of Cameron's nachos as I settled back into my seat. "So, tell me. When is the best time to get lost at a basketball game in hopes of meeting an eligible bachelor?"

His eyes darted between the court, me, and his nearly empty nachos container. "Maybe halftime?"

"Lots of people leave their seats, upping my chances. Right. Watch my bag, will you?" I shoved my wallet and phone into my jacket pocket. "I don't feel like lugging around all my paperwork."

I reached for the second-to-last nacho, but Cameron's warm hand caught my wrist. This close, I could see his top and bottom lashes touching at the corners of his eyes as he smiled at me.

As always when I touched Cameron, I fought against the desire to move closer. His touch was gravity, and I fell, every single time, into a feeling that I struggled to label. His skin was smooth and warm, so I felt oddly grateful when he leaned in instead of pulling his hand away. I felt grateful for his warmth, not his closeness or my front-row seat to his crinkling eyes. Definitely not.

"You know," he murmured, "if you want nachos, I can go get you some."

Just friends.

I forced a laugh. "But then I couldn't steal yours."

The halftime buzzer went off—what a horrible noise—and I stood, focusing on my task and not the way my wrist still felt warm from his touch. "All right. Off I go, into the great unknown to hunt a husband 1950s-style. Wish me luck."

Hoping to look confident and nonchalant, I made my way down the bleacher steps. I joined the crowd, following their steady crawl through the bleachers and past the food counter. I meandered to the gift store. Mindlessly shuffling through clothing and hat racks, I noticed a keychain my dad might like. I hadn't seen him in months because of his work schedule, but his birthday was soon.

By the time I waited in the long checkout line to purchase the keychain, most of the crowd had returned to their seats. Disappointing. But I still had a mission.

Intentionally heading in the opposite direction of our seats—take that, Ivy and Cameron, I did have a sense of direction after all—I found a few offices and broom closets. The farther I wandered, the emptier and darker the corridor became. Hopefully all of these office doors were locked. Anyone could break into the rooms and find private documents about students, grades, policies, who knows what, and nobody would see them or hear them with the background busyness of the arena.

Eventually, I turned around to go back to the arena, when a wobbling shadow darkened the floor next to me.

"May I help you, ma'am?"

It was the elderly security guard I occasionally saw around campus. Apparently someone else had thought about the dark offices, the private files, and the potential for theft. Good on you, elderly security guard.

"Um, well—" I hesitated.

He wasn't the eligible bachelor I had in mind. What would he do in an actual security situation? Threaten to call the offender's grandma?

I looked down the hallway toward more offices, then back toward the arena. Should I keep trying for a man within two decades of my age, or should I be polite to someone I considered a coworker? And how should I explain why I was in this empty hallway? Did he even recognize me?

"I—well—it's just—"

"Are you lost?" he deadpanned.

Who would've thought sass would be his secret weapon? I instantly felt self-conscious. If only Cameron were here to charm the guard for me.

I laughed nervously. "I just got a little turned around. You know, the crowds, and"—I gestured with my hands and noticed my plastic gift shop bag—"and the lines at the gift store, and—"

"I already called for backup," he said. "They're on their way. You'd best start figuring out your story while you can."

Um. What?

I blinked. "You called the police?"

He straightened. "We have policies for when we see a stranger nosing around private offices in the dark."

Sweat dampened my palms. "But don't you recognize me? I've worked here for years."

He squinted at me in the semidarkness. "No, ma'am, can't say I do."

"Here, I have my university ID." I reached for my work bag. But my ID was attached to my lanyard, which was in my bag, on the seat next to Cameron, who was probably inhaling a second helping of nachos and cheese.

He shook his head and stepped aside, sweeping a wrinkled hand down the hallway. I felt like I was nine years old again, my grandpa shaking his head at me over a broken lamp.

We walked only a few steps—more like shuffles for him in his black Dr. Scholl's—before I started nervous-rambling. "I didn't expect you back there, popping up out of nowhere like that."

"It's just my job, ma'am."

Again with the sassy deadpan.

"Right. Well. Good job—" Too bad I didn't know his name. I gestured like I would jokingly punch him in the arm but thought better of it.

We rounded the corner to the restrooms. In the hallway, two younger security guards made eye contact with my elderly escort and strode toward us. The tension in my stomach eased, even as I slanted a look at the guard shuffling next to me. How ornery of him to let me think he'd called the police when "backup" meant other campus security staff.

The elderly security guard nodded to them. "She was in the east wing, near the offices, just like I said."

The other guards gave me a once-over.

"What was your business in the east wing?" the female guard asked.

"It's a misunderstanding," I said. "I was just heading back to the arena, and I got a little turned around."

The three of them exchanged looks as they glanced up and down the relatively small hallway of the relatively small Goldner Arena, doubt obvious in their grim mouths.

"Look, I'm harmless," I explained. "I work at the tutoring center. My university ID is in my bag. It's at my seat in the stadium. Just let me go get it, and—"

"We'll come with you," the elderly guard said.

Come with me? I mentally walked into the arena, through the bleachers, to my seat, next to Ivy and Cameron, all while being followed by three very official uniforms...

I took in their stances, the two younger officers with their feet planted shoulder width apart, the elderly security guard with his squinting frown. I nodded.

I did my best to ignore the looks as the four of us walked through the arena, passing row after row. I noticed Clarice from the registrar's office; Victor and his girlfriend, Emily; Vernon from IT. Was it too much wishful thinking to hope they would be kind enough to never bring this up?

At the sight of us, Ivy's eyes widened, and Cameron stood from his seat.

I grabbed my bag and dug through it with nervous hands. Of course my lanyard and ID were buried under folders and chewing gum wrappers and—

"What happened? Are you okay?" A tidy line creased Cameron's brow, his eyes darting between me and the security guards.

Nodding, I smiled with relief and held up my lanyard.

The security guards passed my ID between themselves, inspecting it more carefully than seemed necessary—until Cameron spoke up.

"Good to see you, Harold." Cameron grinned and offered a hand.

The elderly security guard squinted at him before breaking into a smile. "Always good to see you, Dr. Whitacre."

"Since when do you have night duty?"

"Since my wife watches the grandkids after dinner." Harold laughed. "These days, I get more peace on the job than I do at home."

"Or at least you did until you found Mel." Cameron nodded in my direction. "She didn't get into too much trouble, did she?"

All signs of sass gone, Harold shook his head. "No, not too much. Just needed to make sure she is who she says she is."

Finally, the guards nodded dismissively, all business as they returned my ID. With one last squint at me and one last grin to Cameron, Harold shuffled along behind the other security guards toward the exit.

I slumped into my seat, wishing for an invisibility cloak to avoid all the curious stares.

Ivy leaned across Cameron. "What did you do?"

"That old security guard found me. He thought I was up to something, so he called for the other two. They didn't believe I wasn't causing trouble, so they wanted to see my university ID. Like I look like trouble." My laugh sounded strained even to me.

Their lips twitched with suppressed grins before they started to laugh.

"That didn't exactly go according to plan, did it?" Ivy teased.

"Try not to enjoy it so much." I turned to Cameron. "How do you know Harold?"

He shrugged. "I know everyone."

Of all the times for him to know a random security guard. "Well, the next time you and Harold are having a heart-to-heart, ask if he questioned my sanity."

He nodded. "Sure, I can do that, but more importantly, did you get his number?"

CHAPTER 7

CAMERON

From: Keith Freisen
To: Cameron Whitacre
Subject: Morning Meeting

Good morning, Dr. Whitacre,

Please stop by my office this morning. I have an opportunity to discuss with you.

Thank you,
Keith Freisen, PhD
Academic Department Chair
Computer Science and Information Technology

From: Cameron Whitacre
To: Keith Freisen
Subject: RE: Morning Meeting

Be there in 10.

Thanks,
Cameron Whitacre

Computer Science Mind-Bender (Adjunct Professor) and IT Department Wizard (Director)

Keith's email had to be about the full-time position. What else could it be? It was the only "opportunity" around, and Keith knew I wanted it more than anyone else.

In the restroom of the computer science department, I straightened my collar and tie, re-tucked my shirt, and pulled the comb from my messenger bag to quickly run it through my cowlick. I pushed my glasses up my nose. Short of a tuxedo, this was as good as I got. (Would a tuxedo help my chances? Because I would do it.)

I let the restroom door slam behind me, and I didn't miss a step as I distractedly returned students' greetings in the hallway. I could only think about getting to the department chair's office as quickly as possible.

Dr. Keith Freisen's door stood open at a precise thirty-five-degree angle. Knowing him, he had a formula for the exact door position that showed approachability but formality, friendliness but professionalism. He probably kept a single lint particle on the carpet to mark the spot.

At my knock, he stood and smiled, automatically straightening his bowtie. I mentally tagged its blue-green color as *skobeloff* for my note to Mel later today.

Dr. Freisen pulled at his sweater vest. "Dr. Whitacre. Good to see you."

We shook hands and went through our usual exchange of, "Likewise, Dr. Freisen," and "Please sit down, Dr. Whitacre," and "Please call me Cameron," even though we both knew he would still call me Dr. Whitacre.

I sat.

He sat.

I waited.

He wasn't one for small talk, and I only wanted to talk about the full-time position, so that was fine by me. I'd more than earned the job. Working extra hours, countless great reviews from students, good relationships with my peers, and the go-to technician for any IT job. The only thing standing between me and that full-time position was politics.

And now I'd overcome those, too.

Dr. Freisen cleared his throat. "As professors and leaders in our community, as academics, sometimes our professional lives and personal lives...intersect."

I blinked. This was...strange. "Intersect?"

"Yes. Our physical and mental lives are connected, and, to an extent, our emotional lives, if you will. As such, it is only natural that there are times that one influences the other."

What an unusual way to offer someone a promotion. But I nodded anyway, slowly, to look thoughtful, as you do in academia.

Seeming pleased with my response, he steepled his fingers into a pyramid. "Sometimes that intersection, that influence, is most apparent in our present day, and other times it is more obvious in our past. We must continue as professionals, of course, regardless of circumstances, and keep education forefront in our minds. There are rules in academia for a reason."

Circumstances? Rules? I tried to follow the tangle of his management speak. If a student had accused me of being inappropriate (which was laughable) he needed to say it straight. "Dr. Freisen, I'm not sure I follow."

Sighing, he stood and closed the office door.

I'd never seen his door at anything other than that precise thirty-five degrees. Maybe a student accusation wasn't so laughable after all.

He returned to his seat. "Please know that I am looking out for your best interests. I hope you take this as a good thing, as the best possible thing. This is an opportunity, really."

Yes, it was in my best interests to be offered the full-time position, please and thank you. But he was trying to be personable. It was a weird look for him, a bit too big around his shoulders.

I fought the instinct to shift in my seat. "What exactly is this about?"

"You know our university publication, *The Courier*, is an integral part of our campus and our local community."

I knew of *The Courier*. A generic name for a generic student paper. So what?

"People from all around read it every month," he continued. "Our student and faculty reporters usually focus on events, activities, etc. But this year they decided to feature profiles of various faculty and staff. They think it will show the community that we have strong leaders in place, and they think it will make us more relatable to students."

Now I could feel where this was going. No. Absolutely not.

"They want you to be their first in a series of faculty profiles. They have assigned a student to interview you for the piece. They think you have a...er, 'human interest' aspect to your story."

Panic clawed its nails into my throat, making my voice sound strangled.

"No, thank you. Please extend my regrets that I cannot be interviewed for a profile."

He leaned his elbows on his desk, throwing off his bowtie alignment. (I itched to point it out.) "If you concede to this interview, it will put this department, and you, in a favorable light with the deans, assistant directors, and president in terms of future opportunities."

He was asking me to dredge up my pain to give myself a better shot at the full-time position. He was asking me to use the administration's pity to get this job. Hadn't I earned it on my own merit? All the hours, all the students, all the IT support. I would have laughed if I didn't feel so broken.

"Thank you for the opportunity," I said, "but I need to decline."

He opened his mouth to speak, but I continued, "We have a lot of incredible faculty and staff. I can give some recommendations. Luca Kroft is doing amazing research and writing with Russian literature and history. Dr. Clark's psychology studies look at the biological effects of love on brain chemistry—"

"I regret that I need to insist on this," he interrupted. "The administration has already approved the list of faculty and staff to be featured in the profiles. They specifically requested that you be the first profile. They are very concerned that the image of the college be set in a positive light. They have already assigned a writer, and she will be reaching out to you shortly. I asked you to come here today so that I could give you notice beforehand. As a"—he straightened his bowtie—"gesture of goodwill."

"Is this blackmail?"

"Excuse me?"

"Is this blackmail?" My initial panic was fizzling down to anger, but even more quickly it was morphing into sadness and resignation. "If I say no to this, will I get fired?"

He blinked several times. When he spoke, his voice was soft. "No, this is not blackmail. But it is strongly recommended by people above me. I have no sway in this matter."

In other words, if I wanted any future for myself at this university, I needed to play along. I needed to leverage their pity into a full-time position.

"Thanks for letting me know," I said, mustering some professionalism. "I'll watch for the student's email."

He was visibly relieved. "Thank you for understanding. I hate being put in this predicament, just like you do."

His "predicament" was planets away from the one I was in. "Always happy to be the human-interest piece to represent the real tragedies in the world. Like genocides and Holocausts. We 'human interests' need to stick together." I stood and bowed slightly, mockingly. Maybe I was a little angry after all. "Happy to be of service."

His laugh sounded uncomfortable, and his smile looked strained. "Right, well—"

I didn't wait for his parting words. I intentionally left his door at a forty-degree angle because I could.

Walking away from his office, I made a decision. I would never do that interview. And I would earn the job without that article.

CHAPTER 8

MEL

Cameron: The list says "Sew loose buttons for bachelors." I have several shirts with loose buttons. How about I drop them off at the Fishbowl and pick them up next week?
Mel: No.
Cameron: Not even for me, your incredible, brilliant best friend?
Mel: No.
Cameron: For cupcakes?
Mel: You already give me cupcakes.
Cameron: I hate when I foil my own plans.

After the failed mancounter at the basketball game, I decided that I needed to think this through better. The list was big. I needed to break it down, figure out the items that I would adjust, choose the items that I'd leave out. I needed to lifehack this decades-old advice.

I also needed to have a structure for my writing process. I always researched well before I started even thinking about writing. In this case, research meant mancounters, so I would need to keep organized notes for each mancounter as I went, so then I could refer to them when I finally began writing later on.

Alone in the Fishbowl, I sat at the small conference table, tapping a pen against my list and absently watching students walk past. It was the perfect people-watching hideout thanks to its glass walls. With the other tutors at lunch, the quiet was perfect for brainstorming.

I ran my thumbnail along the side of my laptop. Breaking down the list and organizing mancounter notes wouldn't do any good if I didn't nail down a purpose for these mancounters. I needed a research question.

My fingers tapped across the keyboard. *Is true love timeless?* I typed, echoing my initial conversation with Cameron and Ivy.

I would have fun going on these mancounters, taking notes, having a writing purpose. There would be plenty of awkward moments, like having three campus security guards inspecting my ID in our packed arena, but maybe there would be some sweet moments, too. I would meet some scumbags, to use Cameron's term, but maybe I would meet some nice guys who would prove that not all men in the dating pool used women like commodities.

Several adorable, quirky meet-cutes, all choreographed as part of the experiment, ran through my mind. Each scenario starred a handsome man who was charming and kind and looked a lot like Cameron, but I didn't let myself dwell on that detail. In one scene, I followed the list and just-so-happened to drop my purse, and he rushed to help me pick up my scattered belongings. In another, I asked a handsome stranger for advice about what was best on a restaurant's menu, and we hit it off with our mutual dislike for peas. Then he would ask me on a real date and then—

Wait. What if I really connected with someone on a mancounter? Would I be obligated to stop the experiment? I wouldn't want to give up my writing idea—this was too important to me. Would I actually *need* to tell him? Would the mancounters affect our relationship or my writing ethics? Would he feel like I'd set him up or used him for my own personal gain? *Was* I using people?

I frowned at my laptop. What did I hope to gain from all this? Of course I wanted to write a book. Of course I want to see how the dating advice would play out. But I would be lying to myself if I didn't admit that, next to my ambition and curiosity, I felt a small, quiet hope that maybe I would find true love, too.

Telling myself to stop with the daydreaming and deliberate over my ethics later, I refocused on the dating advice. Some of the items on my list was stuff I could do from a distance, comfortably slouching at my desk on a slow day at the Fishbowl—like today. A specific line caught my attention: *Check out census reports for places with more single men than single women.*

Don't let me down now, Google.

The results were disappointing. Women accounted for more than half the population in New England. My chances didn't look good.

Was I willing to move for this experiment? Definitely not. But were other singles willing to move to improve their chances of meeting someone? I knew of some who might.

I thought of my quiet, empty apartment, and I thought of the social media posts from my friends with significant others. Cameron was right about loneliness. There was a strong appeal to starting life over where the dating pool had a few more fish swimming in your circles.

I turned back to the list. More advice, only this time, it recommended scouring obituaries for new widowers.

Now that was just outright insensitive. Not okay, 1950s.

Bicycle through Europe. On my salary? And at my below-average fitness level? No.

Work at a job where you're surrounded by men. So I could marry my coworkers or boss? No, thanks.

Carry a hatbox. How was that supposed to help? And what was the point of a hatbox in general?

There had to be things on this list that I could actually do. If I wanted to prove whether true love was timeless, surely there were some points I could work with, even if I had to make some adjustments along the way.

An hour later, a knock on the doorjamb had me looking up from my laptop and scratch paper.

"We had cupcakes at the department meeting this morning." Cameron stepped forward, pulling a handful of carefully folded napkins from his messenger bag. "I snagged you a couple."

Now was not the time to let my mind wander back to those imaginary meet-cute Camerons, even if he did look especially tall, dark, and handsome in his wool coat.

Smiling through any lingering daydreams, I unwrapped three large red velvet cupcakes. They were layered with cream cheese icing and probably filled with it in their gooey centers. They were perfect. I set two aside to share with Ivy when I saw her after work today.

"My favorite!" I grinned at him and bit into the first one. "You always remember."

He smiled. "Of course I remember."

"Thank you. I'll make this last...well, probably just a few minutes, if even that. But still. Thank you."

His fingers toyed with the buttons at the cuffs of his sleeves. He ambled closer, peering at my scribbled paper. "What are you working on? A student's paper?"

"It's the dating list. I'm trying to figure out what's actually usable or not."

He nodded. "Ah. The dating list."

I flipped the paper around so he could see it more clearly. "Some of it isn't applicable at all, like the three of us have talked about. But I'm going through the list line by line to try to make a plan, figure out next steps."

"Hm."

"Any ideas?"

He considered for a moment. "Not at first glance."

I frowned at him. "You know, we need you to start having a few opinions. You're our token male for this. I'll need to know what you think about things like"—I squinted at my laptop screen—"'men consider themselves experts on perfume.'"

"I don't know about that one. Perfume makes me sneeze."

"All perfume?"

"Yes."

I had a sudden mental picture of Cameron interrupting a romantic moment with a woman because of a perfume sneeze. It was a funny mental picture and not something to feel jealous over. Definitely not.

I cleared my throat. "Okay, then what about...should women wear sweaters more often?"

He shrugged again. "Wear whatever you want."

"Seriously, too much diplomacy and not enough opinion."

"Hey. I brought you cupcakes. That should give me immunity from interrogations about the list."

"That's true. The snacks from your department meetings are much better than ours."

He feigned a dramatic shudder. "Yours are stale before the meetings even start." Tapping a fingertip against the list, he said, "I'd better get going. Cupcakes don't smuggle themselves, you know."

I laughed, carefully wrapping the two remaining cupcakes. "Fine. Take your diplomacy with you when you go."

I watched him leave, his long strides pausing only to greet students or hold the lobby door for a coworker. He was good people. And the cupcakes were nice, too.

CHAPTER 9

MEL

Ivy: Mel, do you still need to borrow my car?
Mel: Please and thank you.
Ivy: You can have it Sunday afternoon. Just stop by to pick it up whenever.
Cameron: Car troubles, Mel? You can borrow mine, too, if you need it.
*Mel: Thanks, Cam, but I'm borrowing her car for my next scheduled
mancounter.*
*Cameron: Still not a fan of the term "mancounter," but which part of the list
are you doing?*
Mel: I'm going to fake breaking down on the side of the road.
*Cameron: Please tell me you're breaking down on a very public highway in
very broad daylight.*
Ivy: Of course she is. She's not stupid.
*Mel: Thanks for worrying about me, buddy. I'll be fine. I have it all planned
out.*

If you're anything like me, sometimes you make a bad decision, and because
you know it's a bad decision, you make a plan to try to smooth over all the
worries in the back of your mind.

For example, deciding to pretend that my car—or, more accurately, Ivy's
car—was broken down while I hoped for help to come along. Not the best idea

unless you're hoping to be mugged or kidnapped. So, to make it a little bit less of a bad decision, I chose a wealthier neighborhood, the parking lot of an upscale grocery store, and a sunny afternoon.

Those good decisions would cancel out the bad of pulling such a stunt in the first place—right?

Now I just needed a knight in shining armor to rescue this damsel as quickly as possible. It was so cold that I was tempted to call it quits just to start the faux-broken car for some heat.

I stood outside Ivy's old, discolored Toyota, hood propped open, stomping my feet to stay warm, swiveling my gaze around the parking lot to make it obvious that I was looking for help from a generous someone. My only company was a mob of four children who looked to be under seven years old, screaming and chasing one another. They wove between parked cars and occasional grocery carts, nearly skating across the slushy pavement.

My phone vibrated in my pocket.

Cameron: Has Donald Henry Gaskins found you yet?

A quick google confirmed what I suspected—Gaskins was also known as "The Hitchhiker's Killer." Thanks for that, Cameron.

Mel: I'm not a hitchhiker, and I'll text you if I feel unsafe. Plus I have pepper spray in my purse. Please stop worrying.

I couldn't stand out here, looking distressed when I was actually texting someone about serial killers. Jamming my phone back into my pocket, I blew warm air onto my fingers. Would this go better or worse than the basketball game? Maybe it would give me at least one detail for my book.

Or maybe this will give you romance, a thought whispered from the back of my mind. I told it to hush, even as a bit of hope rose in me. *Maybe.*

A tall, rosy-faced man strode across the parking lot toward me. With his wool coat and bearded jaw, he looked like a promising prospect. For the book, of course.

"Do you need help?" he asked.

"Do you mind?" I gestured toward Ivy's car. "It won't start."

He lifted his hands apologetically. "I admit I'm not very handy, but I can give you a lift if you need it."

I could hardly feel my lips on my face—hopefully I smiled, but I couldn't be sure. "Do you know where the closest auto-parts store or mechanic's garage would be? If it's not out of your way, I would really appreciate it."

"No trouble at all. I'm parked just over here."

We crossed the slushy road. I pushed my hands deeper into my pockets and tucked my chin into my scarf, already imagining his car heater on full blast.

Rounding the corner of an SUV, we paused in front of a minivan. The four children I'd seen running wild through the parking lot were lunging in and out of the backseats. They pulled hair, flung mittens, and pushed slushy snow down the necks of each other's coats. A woman was trying to coerce them into their seats, but given that she looked to be about eight months pregnant, her energy was no match for theirs.

"We run a bit of a madhouse," the rosy-faced man said, "but we're happy to help you on your way."

This was his car? I glanced at the children, the pregnant woman, the groceries in the trunk. "Oh, I don't want to be a burden—"

"No, we insist," he said, looking to the woman for her vote. She blinked at him, blinked at the kids, sighed, and ambled toward the backseat of the minivan.

An eight-month-pregnant woman was not sitting with a bunch of hooligans in the backseat of a minivan because of my fake breakdown.

"And I also insist," I said, backing away. "You already have your hands full."

He looked like he was about to protest again, but one of the children chose that moment to lunge from the van and faceplant onto the slushy pavement. Screaming erupted. The woman shook her head. The man took charge, ordering the kids into their seats and picking up the little one from the pavement.

I backed away, grateful they'd forgotten me. The youngest child, whose massive snowsuit covered everything except a pair of large green eyes, blinked at me several times. Even at such a young age, he knew I was making a bad choice.

Judge someone else, kid. I had a good reason to be out here. Sort of.

Back at my car, I checked my phone. I'd give it a few more minutes and then call it quits. This failed mancounter wasn't worth the icy pins and needles in my feet.

The souped-up truck that pulled in front of Ivy's Toyota looked like it had tried out for *The Fast and the Furious* but hadn't quite made the cut. It was huge, with those oversized tires that made the truck so tall that the owner had fastened extra steps outside the driver and passenger doors so people could climb in and out.

But what really caught my attention was the truck's engine, humming nicely and promising a heated cab. I rubbed my hands together and stomped my boots harder against the slushy pavement.

The driver door opened and my knight in a shining truck climbed out. He had shaggy blond hair and smiling eyes. Standing a few inches taller than me, he was no tall-dark-handsome Cameron, but he was still attractive. "Need some help?"

"Yes," I said. "I can't get it to start."

Because I'd unplugged the thingamajig from the other thingamajig, like YouTube had shown me, but he didn't need to know that.

"Want me to give it a try?" He smiled. "I don't want to overstep."

I tightened my jaw to keep my teeth from chattering. "Please do."

Taking the keys, he sat in the driver's seat and tried the ignition. Ivy's car sputtered and spat but didn't turn over.

Good.

Unless he was Donald Henry Gaskins with a shiny truck. A shiny, warm, heated truck.

He stood. "Well, I want to offer to help, but again, I don't want to overstep."

"Help like...?"

He lifted a finger for each option he listed. "You could wait inside the grocery store where it's warmer until a tow truck comes. You can stand out in the freezing cold a little longer. Or I can drive you to the repair shop just a few blocks away."

Three fingers. Three options.

I'd made several questionable decisions to get to this point—the car, the setting, the broad daylight—and now there was just one more. I could do this. Because otherwise, what would I say? "No need to help. Just give me your number if you're single"?

As it was, the only option that would qualify as checking off this particular piece of dating advice was the repair shop. And he was leaving the choice up to me. He wasn't forcing me into his truck.

I could already picture Cameron's text: *Donald Henry Gaskins probably made it feel like the victim's decision until it was too late, too.*

Shoving Cameron out of my head, I said, "What's the fastest option?"

He was jogging in place in the cold now, too. "The repair shop. But again, I don't want to push—"

"Repair shop it is." Caution: Who needed it, right? Cameron and Ivy were on speed dial if I needed them. And this humming truck probably had heated seats.

Opening the passenger door, he offered me a hand into the cab. Soft leather seats, immaculately clean, and, most importantly, warm. My skin tingled as it began to thaw out. Surely Donald Henry Gaskins hadn't kept his vehicle so clean.

Cameron needed to stop putting awful worries into my head. This guy seemed perfectly normal, perfectly nice.

He climbed into the driver's seat.

"Your truck is so warm," I gushed.

He smiled. "Soon you'll be able to feel your hands and feet again. How long were you out there?"

"A little while." Fifty-seven minutes, but who was counting?

"Do you have 'find my phone' turned on?"

Even though I smiled appreciatively, I only thought of Cameron's reaction. He'd probably nod in mock approval. *At least you found a decent one to leave your dead body in a ditch, Mel.*

He pulled his wallet from the console, opening it to show his driver's license. "Take a picture of that. Send it to wherever you want." He winked. "I'm not the big bad wolf."

Definitely not. I glanced at his license. Joshua Blake. Of course his name was the model of wholesomeness.

When I returned his wallet and introduced myself, he shifted the truck into drive. "The repair shop is just a few minutes away. I'll have you there in no time at all. Unless you need to stop anywhere first? Need a coffee or something to warm up?"

"You really wouldn't mind stopping for that?"

"Of course not. You're practically blue with cold."

Well. He just became more promising. "Sure, I'd like a coffee, if you really don't mind."

"There's a local place around the corner, and they have a drive-through. You won't even need to unbuckle." He pushed a button below the radio volume.

Heated seats. I knew it.

I couldn't believe this mancounter had not only produced someone kind enough to offer to drive me to the repair shop but to also ask if I needed something hot to drink. Joshua Blake wasn't just a knight in a shining truck, Joshua Blake was good people. Maybe the list was onto something. Time to think of a flirty quip and see if we had any chemistry between us.

Peeking at him across the truck, I decided he was good looking in a subtle kind of way. His face was nice, he was nice, his truck was nice, and as he hit the gas—

I immediately knew this was a horrible decision.

The pavement was messy with half-melted snow, slush, and road salt, but none of that gave wholesome Joshua Blake any hesitation. He pulled away from Ivy's Toyota, racing down the line of parked cars in the lot, not even looking both ways before he turned onto the main street.

He wasn't a serial killer. He was a serial driver, and his shining truck was a hearse.

This was it. Joshua was my grim reaper.

"You're lucky it's not sleeting now like it was yesterday," he said. "You think you're cold now? That would've been the worst day to break down."

All of the warmth I'd felt in the cab turned icy from fear when he crossed the lane of oncoming traffic without braking.

"Worst day ever," I echoed.

"You're lucky I came along to help before some creep showed up. My sister's car broke down a few weeks ago, and a real weirdo offered to help her. She was completely freaked out."

The truck edged into the other lane. I squeezed my eyes shut, opening them just enough to see that we narrowly missed sideswiping another vehicle traveling in the same direction.

"That's why I was so careful about your phone and giving you my driver's license," he continued. "My sister said this guy was pushy. She gave me a whole lecture about it. It's at the front of my mind, I guess."

He turned to smile at me even as he blew past a stop sign, and I managed my own trembling smile in return.

"Your sister sounds like she has good common sense." Unlike me, who thought broad daylight would protect me from anything bad happening on this mancounter. I felt for my phone in my pocket, but the thought of texting during such erratic driving made me cringe.

He veered around a curve and slammed on the brakes. We'd stopped at a drive-through speaker.

He smiled at me. "What would you like?"

Steadying my voice, I mumbled something about a coffee with one sugar. He placed his own order—large coffee, black—and we lurched toward the pickup window.

"Feeling better?" He adjusted the heat vents, temperature, and fan. He really did seem concerned, like a nice person would be.

"Yes, much better." I reached for my purse. "Here, let me—"

"No, I insist."

"But you're already doing me a favor—"

"And you've had a rough day. Maybe a no-strings coffee will help turn it around, huh?" He turned toward the window to speak with the barista.

My chest felt tense. My day was rough because I had made it so on purpose. It was all a fake. *I* was a fake.

I stared at the back of his head. How was it possible for someone to be so genuinely kind and yet so murderous on the roads? It wasn't road rage. It was plain old cluelessness. I pulled my phone from my pocket and texted Cameron.

Mel: I'll be at the repair shop on McKinley Avenue in a few minutes. Meet me there ASAP?

As kind as Joshua Blake was, the last thing I wanted was for him to drive me any further than the repair shop. If we didn't end up in an accident first, my heart would give out.

I'd put myself in this situation. I'd inconvenienced Joshua Blake, and now I was inconveniencing Cameron, all in the name of an experiment and the chance of romance. What a disaster. If nothing else, maybe I could salvage this by turning it into a funny story for my book.

Book note: Trust his driving skills at your own risk.

Joshua handed me my coffee, a beaming smile on his face. "Here you go. To heated seats!" He pretended to clink our cups together.

I managed one sip before we bumped over a curb and onto the road, again without stopping to look for traffic.

My original challenge since I climbed into his truck—step one, stay alive —now had a friend—step two, don't spill the coffee on myself or his spotless leather interior. I tried to become a shock absorber, keeping the coffee safe from all lurches, swerves, or other unforeseeable events.

"Has your car given you trouble like this before?"

"Um, no, this is the first time it's broken down." Or at least Ivy hadn't complained about it other than "My car is the worst-looking one on campus." So that made me only partly a fraud, right?

"It's the worst when they don't give you any warning, you know? They just die on you when you need them most…"

I had to say, his truck had excellent brakes for stopping at a red traffic light on such short notice. Kudos to the manufacturer.

"My aunt owns a repair shop across town. It's too far to take you there now, but if you want a second opinion, or if you want to borrow a car from her until yours is fixed, I'm sure she wouldn't mind."

Such a nice man. Such an aggressive way to tailgate the Buick in front of us.

"Thanks," I said. "I'll see what they say here and keep your offer in mind."

He made a left and then another sharp left into a small parking lot. A neon sign, dusted with snow at odd angles, advertised the auto repair shop.

We'd made it. I was alive. My coffee was intact.

He walked around to open the passenger door and help me down the steps. "You want me to come in with you?"

"Oh, no, I've already been enough of an inconvenience for you today."

"It's not an inconvenience at all."

"I'll be okay. I can't tell you how much I really appreciate your help." I lifted my coffee. "And this, of course."

Pulling a pen and the coffee receipt from his pocket, he scribbled a note and handed it to me. "Let me know if you need anything, or if you want my aunt's info. We're happy to help. Tell her I sent you."

I tucked the receipt into my purse. "Thank you again."

He gave a little wave, still smiling at me as he climbed into his truck. When he backed out of the lot, he set off a cacophony of horns from other drivers around him.

One of the drivers was Cameron, parking next to me as Joshua Blake's tires spun out and he disappeared down the road.

"Did you see that guy?" Cameron said as soon as I opened the passenger door. "He almost got into four different accidents in mere seconds."

I settled myself into the passenger seat and watched Cameron, feeling grateful as he looked both ways before pulling onto the street. I could kiss him for being so quick to drive across town for me and my disastrous mancounter. Not that I would actually kiss him. I would just think about it for far too long.

Just friends.

"Thank you for doing this," I said.

His blue eyes gave me a once-over. "Safe and sound from Gaskins, I see?"

I leaned my head against the seat. "Barely."

He stilled. "Meaning…?"

I glared at him. "Don't laugh."

He lifted a hand. "Scout's honor."

"I'm serious."

"Fine. I'll do my best not to laugh. Pinky swear." He wiggled his pinky finger at me until I laughed and linked my pinky around his.

"The guy who almost got into four different accidents in mere seconds?"

Understanding spread across his face. "No way. You survived...that?"

"Like I said, barely."

His laughter filled the car until I couldn't help laughing, too, happy that this bad decision was amusing now that Cameron was my real rescuer of the day.

CHAPTER 10

CAMERON

Mel: Who's up for a two-hour road trip? The list says I need to go back to my hometown to visit "the boy next door because he might've grown up to be Prince Charming."
Cameron: Isn't that why they invented the internet? So we can stalk while sitting on our sofas and stuffing our faces with Cheetos?
Ivy: Considering people like you invented the internet...this explains so much.
Cameron: You're welcome.

My condo was the exact opposite of Mel's apartment. Where she had throw pillows and fluffy blankets, I had bare surfaces. No vanilla candles in this bachelor pad, just the odor of expired takeout containers seeping from my refrigerator. Her patchwork of thrift store furniture felt cohesive (probably because of those pillows) but mine felt Spartan. The only personal touches were a few framed photos my mom and my sister, Samantha, had scattered around. My condo wasn't exactly a prime destination for anyone in my life.

So understand my surprise when Toby and I first became friends and he'd insisted that we regularly meet to play video games at my condo. I'd tried to tell him my only seating was a miserable, lumpy couch and my kitchen always smelled stale. Then I'd learned how messy his house always was, and I'd agreed to host our game nights rather than battle his cluttered surfaces.

When I came home from work, Toby was waiting for me. He crouched on the stone steps at the entryway, the glow of his cell phone reflecting on his face and eerily highlighting each puff of his warm breath hitting the cool air.

He stood when I came closer, shoving his phone in his pocket.

"Hey, Toby, how are you?"

"Excellent." He grinned. "One of my patients is finally getting some range of motion back in his shoulder. I thought we could celebrate with a relaxed night instead of going running—but only if you already worked out this morning, of course."

He was restless with the accomplishment, nearly bouncing up the stairs behind me. Sometimes I envied the way he lived so openly, putting his heart into his work and helping people the way he'd helped me. All I'd done with my workday was install some new software for the biology department, give Mel cupcakes, and wonder over that perfect curl that always fell to the left side of her temple.

My keys jingled between my fingers. "I don't have much food or drink to offer, but I do have an electric blanket to thaw you out."

"Only eighty-year-olds have electric blankets," he said, slapping my shoulder blade.

We trudged up the stairs, not speaking, as the college-age women who lived on the floor above me started down the steps, peering at Toby through their heavy eye makeup. He nodded and grinned at each of them like he was a celebrity.

I smirked at him as I unlocked my door. "What happened to the whole 'quarter's worth of love' speech you just gave me the other day?"

He shrugged. "A man has to let people know that his quarter's available, you know?"

"Right." I laughed. "Make yourself at home."

He did, dropping onto my cheap sofa like he was sitting on a cloud. Compared to the stone steps outside, it probably was.

I was in the kitchen, grabbing us a couple beers when he spoke. "How'd everything go at the basketball game?"

I handed him his beer and sipped from mine. "The game was fine. We have a good team, and we won by six."

"Team stats. Exactly why I'm sitting on the proverbial edge of the worst sofa in the state."

"I was fine, okay? I did the breathing. I kept my hands busy with nachos and sodas. It almost felt good, watching the game and feeling the team's energy when they won."

He nodded. "Good."

"Mel got lost to try to meet some guy—"

"What?"

"For the 1950s Dating Debacle."

He shook his head. "Wild."

Laughing, I told Toby how Mel had been accosted by campus security.

Toby grinned. "So she's done with it now?"

I stopped laughing. "No. A few days later, she pretended her car broke down in hopes a charming good Samaritan would help her out."

"Did she meet a charming good Samaritan?"

I thought of her in that truck, with the driver's blatant disregard for anyone's safety. My fingers twitched. "No. She caught a ride with a terrible driver who could've gotten them both in a serious accident."

He downed the rest of his drink. "I'm glad she's okay. If you do something weird to meet someone, you're probably going to meet a weirdo."

"My thoughts exactly." I shrugged. "But it's her thing. Once she grabs on to an idea, she doesn't let go. I can't talk her out of it."

"I disagree, because you could talk her out of it by telling her you're in love with her. I just wanted to make sure you're okay."

Ignoring half of what he said, I thought of telling him about *The Courier* article. I'd looked up the student writer, Alma Torres, in the university directory, and on Facebook, and in all my rosters to make sure she hadn't been in my classes. I'd memorized all the information I could find about her. You know, basic reconnaissance so I could avoid her as much as possible. I was giving the journalism department a wide radius and had taken to avoiding the mail room when I learned that was where she worked. So far I'd successfully dodged her and her emails and calls. I could keep dodging her as long as needed.

But knowing Toby, if I told him about the article, he'd make some big talk about picking a fight with Dr. Freisen. He never would, but if he did, Toby would win. Freisen's sweater-vest and bowtie would cry at the sight of my workout buddy's hard-earned muscles. Just imagining it cheered me up.

But Toby solved the dilemma for me when he gestured to my entertainment center. "Want to chill with video games for a bit?"

Now that was one thing my condo had over Mel's. She had one laptop that was always on the verge of breaking (and that she always brought me to fix). But I was in computer science. Of course I had several laptops and monitors, multiple gaming stations, one TV on the wall and a second in a box in my closet.

Thinking of my closet, I stood and rummaged through some boxes. "How do you feel about going old school? Like Super Nintendo?"

I turned, still holding the box. Toby was looking at a picture Samantha had left on the end table. It was a photo from the last basketball game I played in college. She didn't mean anything by it—she probably didn't even know it was from my last game. My parents had their arms around me, and Samantha crouched in front of us with a goofy grin. My face looked...triumphant. Ready for anything.

Little did that Cameron know that a few months later, everything would change.

"That was a long time ago," I told Toby.

"Memories like this are good to keep around though."

I walked past the end table to plug in the Nintendo, turning the frame face-down as I went. "Hope you're ready to show off your Street Fighter moves."

CHAPTER 11

MEL

Mel: Should I forget discretion and call him?
Ivy: Who?
Mel: A random guy I met at the grocery store. He gave me his number but hasn't texted me since we met last week. Per the list, I should make the first move.
Ivy: Are you going to text or call? People don't like calls anymore. They feel too invasive.
Mel: But texts are less risky. Less commitment. Shouldn't I just go all in?
Ivy: If you want to scare him off, sure.
Mel: I've got nothing to lose. Calling now just to see what happens.
Ivy: It's been a few days. What happened?
Mel: I left a message. Now it immediately goes to voicemail when I call.
Cameron: You've been blocked. Serves you right, stalker.

The only constants in life are death and taxes, and the fact that Ivy never knocked on my door. She just strolled right in and made herself at home as if she was part of the furniture. Her entrances were never grand but were natural, like she considered my home to be hers, too. I loved it.

My throw pillows and blankets could be scattered everywhere, and she'd never comment that my apartment didn't look Pinterest-worthy. If I forgot to light my vanilla candles along the windowsill, she did it for me without asking. It was like having a convenient co-host to make up for my scattered habits.

Tonight Ivy was wearing her signature all-black and large hoop earrings, her blond hair twisted on top of her head when she walked into my apartment. No matter that she worked at the registrar's office, to me, she'd always look like an artist at a gallery showing.

She silently closed the door behind herself, sat on my sofa, and wrapped up burrito-style in a blanket, curling her long limbs into the fuzzy throw.

I broke the silence. "Want a Moscow mule?"

"This is why you're my best friend."

I frowned at the dark circles under her eyes. "Are you okay?"

She nodded and sipped from the copper mug I handed her. "Just tired. Been busy."

"Registration for spring semester opens soon, doesn't it?"

"Yeah. And you know the registrar. Nothing like waiting until the last minute to reinvent a terrible new process for something we do every single year."

I sat in the armchair across from her. "You know you're always welcome to stay here overnight. You can cut some time off your commute."

"That's okay. I need to go home."

Why? To babysit her empty house? "Are you sure—"

A knock sounded at the door. Just as Ivy was constant in never knocking, Cameron was constant in always knocking. Every. Single. Time. No matter how often I left the door unlocked and hollered at him to "Come on in."

I opened the door. "Hiya, Cam."

His glasses fogged as he stepped into my warm apartment, making him fumble as he handed me his usual bag of chips and jar of salsa. "Hiya, Mel."

As I put the chips and salsa into bowls, I listened to Cameron and Ivy make small talk in the other room. I stepped over his long, jean-covered legs to get to my seat.

Cameron blinked. "You're all dressed up."

I laughed. "Should I be worried that I so rarely wear makeup that it's worth commenting on?"

Ivy filled a plate with snacks. "You're just wearing more than usual, that's all. I noticed it, too, at work today."

I shrugged. "The list said to wear more makeup. I figured I should probably be putting in more effort anyway."

Ivy's tone was noncommittal. "Do what you feel comfortable doing. Don't start making everything in your life about the list."

"The makeup thing needed to happen regardless of the list." I waved a dismissive hand in the air. "I'll turn thirty this year. Soon I'll be a wrinkled prune."

"You look good whatever you wear," Cameron said, eyes fixed on me.

His blue eyes, unblinking, showed he was sincere. But he was as likely to compliment me as he was anyone else, so it didn't mean anything. This was Cameron, after all: charmer extraordinaire.

I smiled. "You're sweet. And totally biased. Anyway, I find certain parts of the list unclear. It said to 'use my eyes to my advantage.' Should I bat my eyelashes like a cartoon?"

"Men just have bizarre expectations," Ivy said.

"Hey," Cameron protested. "Not all of us do. Most of us aren't sleazy."

She winced. "Sorry. I mean *people* have bizarre expectations."

He nodded his thanks. "That's better."

"Like, remember that last date I went on?" She stabbed some veggie dip with a celery stick. "He seemed perfect. Tall, dark, handsome, successful job." She emphasized each adjective with a jab of her celery, steadily growing more aggressive. "He paid for dinner at a fancy restaurant. He told me he didn't live with his mother. All good things. And then, when he walked me to my front door"—the celery stick was a gnarled mess at this point—"he told me I owed him a striptease because he paid for my dinner and listened to me talk."

Cameron muttered something under his breath. I couldn't hear his exact words, but I felt sure I agreed with whatever he said.

I grimaced. "How could I have forgotten about that?"

She pointed her mutilated celery at me. "Because you don't really date."

"I do too."

"Do not. You meet a guy, you like him, you date him. You don't blindly go out with guys like I do."

Ivy had a good point. She knew my system. Historically, I didn't date Ivy-style—going to bars, trying out dating apps. The way the list had me diving in headfirst was completely new territory for me.

She chomped on her celery. "Anyway, he wouldn't have been worth it."

But her tough-girl act didn't cover up the way her eyes stayed focused on her plate, her grin not quite wide enough.

"I'll tell you my secret for the perfect striptease," I said.

Cameron choked on the cracker he'd just popped in his mouth. I reached over to absently pat his back and hand him a glass of water. Ivy eyed me skeptically.

"You've got to start with a flannel nightgown. You know the kind, like a grandma wears? Underneath that, wear footy pajamas. When you take those off, all slow and sexy, your next layer is the ugliest thermal underwear you can find."

Ivy snorted a laugh. Cameron was still recovering from his cracker mishap, but he gave a watery smile.

"What should be under that?" I wondered aloud.

Ivy managed to speak. "One of those uniboob sports bras."

Cameron shook his head, his voice raspy when he spoke. "I don't think I want to know what that means."

"Yes, a uniboob sports bra. One that has sweat stains on it," I told Ivy. "That'll teach him never to ask for a striptease again. Take that!"

By now both Ivy and I were wiping away tears, picturing the hapless man who dared to ask either one of us for a striptease. Cameron barely recovered from choking.

"I'm sorry," Ivy said to him. "Sometimes I forget you're one of them."

And sometimes Ivy came across a little too harsh on Cameron.

My laughter sobered quickly at that. I was about to stand up for him when he frowned at us over his water glass. "Just because I'm a man doesn't mean I'm 'one of them.'"

"You're right." She sighed. "There are just so few of you good guys out there. Especially on dating apps."

"The good ones are easy to overlook, I get it," he said. "But sometimes guys feel the same way about girls. Women use people, too, you know."

I nodded. "You're right, Cam. Next time we're being idiots, tell us. And we'll tell you the next time you're being an idiot, too."

"Deal." He reached out his hand to shake on it. "Even though you two already bruise my ego on the regular."

"Deal," I agreed, fitting my palm to his.

His skin was smooth and warm, heating my always-cold hands. I wished I could lean closer, absorb a little more of him...

When he spoke, his voice was so soft I almost didn't hear him. "You're wrong about the secret to a good striptease, by the way."

I blinked. This wasn't where I'd expected the conversation to go, but maybe he was a more valuable source of mancounter information than I'd given him credit for. Better yet, would asking him for a demonstration be too much, or...?

He leaned closer. "The secret to a good striptease"—he paused to glance at Ivy and then back at me—"is to wear swimming goggles and flippers over your footy pajamas."

Ivy snorted. "I can see it now!"

He grinned, clearly pleased with himself. "Just remember me the next time you need dating advice. I'm full of surprises and endless wisdom."

CHAPTER 12

MEL

Cameron: "Buy him a gift, but nothing too expensive." Like that coffee mug you bought me a few years ago, Mel. I thought for sure it was a marriage proposal.
Mel: That's understandable. Anyone would confuse "World's #0 Programmer" with "Will you marry me?"

Balancing in heels, carrying a pie tin covered in aluminum foil, juggling my work bag and purse, I precariously made my way through the computer science and IT department, the smell of still-warm apple pie pluming behind me.

The delicious smell was a big improvement for the hallway. Tucked into the basement under the library, the department didn't see any daylight to speak of. The stereotypical computer geniuses probably wouldn't care, but I did. I wished Cameron didn't work in what felt like a dungeon.

I nodded to two TAs I didn't recognize. "Is Cameron in this morning?"

The shorter student nodded. "Dr. Whitacre? He's in the adjunct office down the hall."

"Just saw him walk past a minute ago," said the girl next to him, never lifting her eyes from the screen of her tablet.

I thanked them and continued down the hall, pausing in front of a bulletin board with department announcements, flyers for thesis presentations and internships, and motivational quotes.

A shoe squeaked on the floor down the hall, and I turned to see Cameron, openmouthed, staring at me.

"Hiya, Cam," I said. "I need you to taste-test something."

"Hiya, Mel," he said, still staring at me, or, more accurately, at my legs. "Are you wearing heels?"

I glanced down. "Aye aye, Captain Obvious."

"I've never seen you in heels before."

Considering how much my feet ached, I wished he still had never seen me in heels. "I prefer comfy shoes. But, well, the list. You know. I'm trying them out for today. I don't think they'll last long." But if heels made men look at my legs the way Cameron was looking at my legs, I might change my mind. Actually, who was I kidding? If heels made *Cameron* look at my legs like this…

His cleared his throat. "You usually don't come down here. Are you looking for someone?"

I laughed. "I already told you I need your taste-testing skills."

He cleared his throat again. "Right. Step into my office." He gestured dramatically to a doorway, and as I stepped closer, I remembered why I didn't come down here more often—it was more of a coat closet than an office.

"I've always felt a little sorry for myself that I don't have an office," I said, crossing the threshold, "but then I see your office and always feel a little better about myself."

He laughed. "I know, right? Check it out." He edged past me into the small space, bending to open a lower cabinet along the far wall. "There are cleaning supplies in here. You know, because this office has so much extra room, we might as well keep the Windex in here."

"Maybe they're hinting that you're a slob?"

"That's fair. And they'd be right. But by that logic, they're also hinting that I need to decorate for Christmas year-round." He opened the second cabinet door and tinsel fell onto the floor.

I laughed as he shoved the tinsel back into the cabinet. "There's no explaining that one. This office is terrible."

There was barely enough space for Cameron to tuck his long legs underneath his small desk, and even less room for the unlucky student forced to sit in the sad folding chair wedged between his desk and the wall. Cameron's computer and mess of paperwork and books covered all other surfaces. How could he possibly work in this room?

Given the size of his closet-office, I should've stepped into the hallway, opening up the space for him to walk around his desk and to his chair. But I didn't.

Instead, we went through the awkward dance of trying to shuffle out of one another's way—until Cameron placed his hands on my shoulders and we circled one another correctly. "Circled" is too generous of a word. Squeezing between the folding chair and his desk, we maneuvered ourselves through the tiny strip of space left.

"Sorry," he mumbled, his knee bumping into me.

"Oops," I muttered, stepping on his foot.

"It's really the worst office ever," he said, his elbow poking my side.

I laughed. "It really is."

I tilted my head to look up at him but wound up bonking his chin. His teeth audibly clanged together.

"I'm so sorry!" I cupped his jaw in my free hand that wasn't balancing a warm pie. "Are you okay? Did you bite your tongue?"

"I'm okay." He rubbed his chin. "Just a little surprised. I'm not used to you being this tall. The heels, I guess."

"Are you sure you're okay?" My chest tightened with the fear that I had hurt him, even accidentally. I studied his teeth, chin, and lips when he spoke, checking for any signs of injury, because if he had bitten his tongue thanks to my clumsiness, he would be too nice to tell me.

"I'm fine," he murmured. "Honest."

I felt his cheek move when his mouth quirked into a smile, and I felt the hum of his voice in my hand when he spoke. The sensations in my palm absorbed me until the fear tightening my chest shifted into an entirely different feeling.

I blinked and dropped my hand. His office was the wrong setting for this, for these emotions, for feeling his voice vibrate into my palm. My hand tingled. This was Cameron. I was being ridiculous. The list was getting to me.

"So I made some apple pie," I announced, gesturing to the dish. "Want to try it?"

"You know I'll never turn down apple pie."

I set down the dessert on his desk and pulled some paper plates and plastic utensils from my bag. "I made it last night and reheated it this morning. Hopefully it's not dry."

"I'm sure it's great." He folded into his chair on the opposite side of the desk. "You're a good cook."

"Cooking is easier to fake without a recipe. Baking requires recipes, and it requires me to follow those recipes. Which I don't always do well." I could hear my voice rambling in an attempt to push aside lingering emotions, but I didn't bother stopping myself. "I actually didn't follow this recipe perfectly either. It called for pecans in the crumb topping, and I didn't have any, so I used walnuts." I pushed his plate and fork toward him. "So you're my first taste tester."

He shoveled a large bite into his mouth and sighed. "This is amazing."

I took a bite of my own slice and echoed his sigh. "Maybe I should follow a recipe more often."

He smiled. "My vote is yes."

We shared our pie in silence for a few moments. I tried not to stare at his office. Or at the dark circles under his eyes. Rumor had it the administration would be filling the full-time computer science position soon. Was it really stressing him out that much? He needed to relax. No need to burn out before he even got the job—and I knew he'd get the job.

"Are you really okay?" I said. "I don't just mean your face. Even though I really am sorry about that. I mean your schedule must be hectic right now. You know you can talk to me if you ever want to vent about the grinder they're putting you through."

He spoke around a mouthful of pie but kept his eyes averted. "I'm fine. Just a lot going on."

I frowned at him. Something more than "a lot" was going on. But, like with basketball or the stroke, he'd slammed the proverbial door in my face.

"So what's the occasion?" he asked. "It's not pi day."

"Pie day?"

"You know. March fourteenth? 3.14? Pi?"

"Oh, that. No, it's not pi day. I made it because I know you've been stressed, and apple pie is your favorite, so I was hoping it would cheer you up."

His smile glowed. "You made this for me?"

A warm cotton filled my chest. I wanted to say yes, that this pie was all for Cameron, that Cameron deserved all the pies in the world if he would just keep smiling at me like that. But I couldn't lie to him.

"Partly. It's also for the staff meeting this morning. I made two other pies to share with everyone. Like the heels, this is for the list. It said I needed to learn how to bake an apple pie and bring it to the office for eligible bachelors to taste."

His smile dimmed, and he blinked down at his empty plate. "You've worked here for years. Do you think there are any eligible bachelors at your staff meeting?"

I laughed. "Definitely not. But that's not the point. The point is to see if an apple pie really makes that much of a difference in how potentially eligible bachelors treat me." I shrugged. "I thought making a pie would be harder, but Pinterest makes finding good recipes way easier than they had it in the 1950s."

"Well, it's a good pie, so consider this marked off your list."

His tone echoed my boss's when Dr. Schaaf first heard about my experiment. I shifted in my seat, willing myself to ignore how vaguely unsupportive Cameron sounded, when I remembered how much my feet hurt. I reached into my bag for my socks and Converses.

"What are you doing?"

"These shoes are killing me. I'm glad I brought others with me just in case." My annoyance with unsupportive people at large—and Cameron specifically—made my voice too sharp when I spoke next. "I know you think the list is unsafe or creepy. And I respect that. But I want to do this. I think it'll make a really interesting story."

He stared at me, laser-like focus only on me. "But what if you're losing yourself, Mel?" His voice was gentle. "What if you follow the list so closely that you aren't even yourself on these dates?"

I waved away his worries with a smile. "I'll always be me. Why do you think I packed my Converses in my bag? I knew these heels wouldn't last."

He didn't smile back. "I'm also worried that if you do meet some guy, he won't know the real you, because you'll be this list and not yourself. And then you'll be stuck with a guy who doesn't know you."

"That's sweet of you, but it's honestly not something to worry about." Irritation coiled in the pit of my stomach. Why did he feel the need to ask these questions? Why did he have to toss his worries onto my own pile of doubts—doubts that I refused to think about or say out loud?

Worse still, what if he was right? I already felt conflicted about how I interacted with men on these experiments. Now I would worry about my own authenticity, too.

He paused, and I could see him picking through his words before he spoke. "You're not actually hoping to find a husband in all this, are you?"

Despite my frustration with him, despite the fact he'd said everything in kindness, I struggled to keep eye contact with him. Instead, I stared at my pie.

He'd asked real questions that deserved real answers. But I didn't want to admit the truth, because now that I was faced with Cameron's well-meaning logic, my daydreams of real connection through the mancounters seemed silly. I couldn't bring myself to admit that I hoped to meet someone.

But that didn't mean giving up. I would follow the fifties advice, even if

Cameron asked irritating questions about my authenticity. I would make a show about the experiment being for the book. I would never fully admit my secret hope for romance. Nobody needed to know but me.

Feeling resolved, I looked up at him. A tidy line creased his forehead, his eyes pleading with me. The frustration in my stomach dissolved into longing. If I did meet someone, he would need to be exactly like Cameron.

Picking up my pie, I stood and slung my bag over my shoulder. "If I don't find a man, maybe I get a book." Shrugging, I kept my tone carefree. "If I do find a man, maybe it'll be a nice surprise. Either way, I've got nothing to lose."

CHAPTER 13

MEL

Mel: I refuse to go on a diet.
Cameron: Who told you to go on a diet?
Mel: The list is very opinionated about women's bodies, but I refuse.
Ivy: Yeah, twenty-first-century dating won't tolerate dieting like that.
Cameron: You don't need to diet.

Ivy let her bag fall to the floor and slumped into a chair, barely glancing around the empty tutoring center to make sure we were alone. "Please tell me you have some leftover pie."

"Rough day?"

"Everyone realized that this was the last day to drop a class if they're failing. So of course they all swarmed the registrar at the same time. And of course Clarice managed to disappear for all of it. Who knows where she was all day. It was just me, barely fighting off panicked students and irritated professors while I earned my puny salary."

I slid a timecard into a file, about to begin the next stack. If Dr. Schaaf had to process these timecards like I did, he wouldn't cling so hard to his conspiracy theories about the government watching our every move. "I saved you a piece of pie, but it's cold and probably congealed by now."

"I'm not picky."

I passed her the pie dish and my last plastic fork. "I'm out of plates, so you'll have to eat from the—"

Ivy was already digging in.

"Never mind."

She moaned at the first bite. "This is amazing. Anyone who didn't propose marriage to you after eating this pie is insane. I'm ready to propose to you myself."

I grimaced. "No proposals. Just a medical emergency, complete with an ambulance ride to the hospital."

Her fork paused halfway to her mouth. "What?"

"Apparently Vernon from IT has a walnut allergy."

Her eyes widened. "Oh, no."

"Oh, yes. He came to our staff meeting to fix a software issue. He devoured a whole piece of pie and then his throat swelled up. He couldn't even breathe enough to tell us what was happening. Someone called 911. An ambulance and team of EMTs came for him."

"Is he okay now?"

"Haven't heard yet."

"So...you almost killed a guy?"

"How was I supposed to know?" I said. "I've worked with him for how many years, and I never knew he had a walnut allergy. How did it not come up in conversation?"

She lifted an eyebrow at me. "Right, because walnuts are an everyday topic that people bring up all the time?"

"I'm serious. There should be some sort of public service announcement that goes out when anyone new is hired, letting people know about food allergies."

She scraped at the now-empty pie pan and licked her fork. "Sounds like a HIPAA violation to me."

"Well, if it is a HIPAA issue, food allergies should be an exception, because we had to spend our staff meeting watching Vernon get pulled back from the edge of death and then get driven away in the back of an ambulance."

Her laughter was small at first, but soon it bubbled up until she snorted. Ivy always tried to contain her laugh, to keep it quiet, but it never took long to explode into tears beyond her control. It was completely at odds with her chic black clothes and poise, and it was one of my favorite things about her.

She wiped her eyes. "You realize what this is, right? You're trying to find a husband and instead you poison somebody."

I fought my own smile. "It was an allergy. Not a poisoning."

She waved a hand at me. "Same difference. You're working so hard on this list, and it just blows up in your face. Or, more accurately, blows up Vernon's throat. Sounds like you should make him a walnut-free apple pie as an apology."

I scoffed. "I'm the last person he wants to see right now. I tried to give him his coat when they put him in the back of the ambulance, and you should've seen the look on his face. Like he thought I was trying to smother him with a down-filled North Face jacket."

She doubled over in laughter again. "Because you did almost kill him! With pie!"

"Not on purpose!"

I threw a highlighter at her and missed by several inches. She snatched it from the floor and threw it back at me, hitting me on the shoulder.

A soft knock at the door stopped our antics. My posture straightened. If it was Dr. Schaaf stopping by for these timecards, it would be just my luck. He didn't need to see me acting like a child while I was still on the clock.

"Excuse me. Do you know where I can find Dr. Whitacre?"

I blinked at the student, who had a long black braid over her shoulder, scuffed black combat boots, and an enormous bookbag that looked heavy enough to pull her backward at any moment.

"His office is downstairs in the computer science and IT department," Ivy said.

"I haven't noticed him leave through the lobby doors," I said, "so he's probably still there."

The student shifted her bookbag on her shoulders. "I've been waiting down there for him for over an hour."

"Have you emailed him?" Ivy said. "Maybe—"

The student interrupted, nudging the edge of the doorjamb with her boot over and over. If she used a little more force, she'd be kicking it. "I've emailed him several times, left memos with the receptionist and TAs, left voicemails on his office phone. It's been weeks of this."

"That doesn't sound like Cam—er, Dr. Whitacre," I said. "He's usually the best professor about getting in touch with students. Is this about a midterm coming up?" I turned to the office computer and opened a new email to Cameron.

"It's for *The Courier*. I'm writing an article profiling him. It's part of a new series to show the community what our leadership here is like." She shrugged a shoulder and her entire bookbag heaved, threatening to capsize her, but she calmly shifted her feet and rebalanced.

"I've been asking around because my deadline for the article is coming up," she continued. "One of the librarians mentioned that he's over here pretty often because he's friends with you. So I thought it wouldn't hurt to ask."

"I didn't know they were doing profiles," Ivy said. "Guess they're just featuring professors and not us lowly staff, huh, Mel?"

"Tell you what." I turned to the student. "We're both friends with Cam and see him at least once a day. We'll start hassling him about getting back to you. We can't give you his personal number, but we can text him for you. What's your name?"

"Alma Torres."

"On it." Ivy was already tapping on her phone.

Alma smiled for the first time. "Thank you both so much. Really. I'm stressed about this deadline. I can ask for an extension, but the editor is stingy about moving publication schedules around."

I smiled at her. "We'll do our best."

"Thanks." She gave a little wave and turned toward the door of the library, hunching under her bookbag, braid swinging.

"How many books do you think she's carrying?" Ivy whispered, her eyes following Alma out the lobby door.

"Too many for her to be waiting around on Cam for more than an hour."

I'd just started my text to him (*What are you doing ignoring students like Alma? Don't you want to be campus-famous?*) when movement in the main lobby caught my eye. Cameron had just emerged from the IT basement. "And there he is. Too bad Alma just left."

He stopped in the middle of the lobby to talk with a student. Cameron removed his glasses to clean them on his cotton button-down, his blue eyes sharper without the shadow of the dark frames. He was completely focused on their conversation. Something the student said made him laugh—his shoulders shook, and he tilted his head at an angle.

I shoved back at any feelings at the sight of Cameron being, well, Cameron, and I focused on the facts. He consistently had some of the best student reviews of any of the professors, with students always raving about his willingness to help them succeed. He had more open office hours than any other professor I knew of. Which made even less sense to discover that he was ignoring a student, that Alma had waited for him outside his office for so long.

"Cam is awfully handsome."

I startled at Ivy's voice. "You think so?" I said, even though I didn't need to ask. She'd echoed similar variations of that statement multiple times over the years.

She nodded. "Definitely. He's objectively perfect. Symmetrical features"—spoken like a true artist—"the classic dark hair, blue eyes, tall. Girls who aren't computer science majors practically fight to get into his gen ed classes because they've all heard that he's hot." She set the empty pie pan and plastic fork back on my desk. "Don't you think he's good looking?"

My eyes went back to the lobby. Now Cameron angled his body toward the tutoring center, still talking with the student but smiling at me when our eyes met.

"He's the best-looking guy I know," I said.

"So why not ask him out?"

I sighed. "Not this again."

"Yes, this. I've told you before, and I'm telling you again: He's smitten with you. All he needs is a little encouragement."

"A guy like Cam doesn't need any encouragement. If he were interested, he would've done something by now."

"How very 1950s of you."

I frowned. "What's that supposed to mean?"

She shrugged nonchalantly, but I could spy an Ivy challenge when I saw one, and that's exactly what this was. "It means you don't think you should be the one to make the first move. You think it should be the man."

I bristled. "That's not what I think."

Cameron and the student parted ways and he began walking toward the Fishbowl.

"I just think," I said, "that if Cam were interested in me like you keep saying, he would've given some hint about his feelings. And he hasn't. So I'm not going to act on your terrible advice and embarrass both me and him over nothing."

"It's not nothing," she said in a singsong just before Cameron came into hearing range.

He stopped at the threshold of the tutoring center, still grinning at me. "Any more pie left?"

"Sorry," I said. "She just ate the last piece."

Cameron blinked at Ivy like he'd just noticed she was there. "Isn't it the best pie you've ever had?"

She nodded, pouting at the empty pie pan. "I just wish there were more."

He smirked at me. "Almost worth dying for, huh?"

I groaned and slumped in my chair. "Who told you? Is nothing considered private anymore?"

He laughed. "You know how news travels around here. It's impossible to keep anything quiet for long. Plus Vernon works in IT, so I heard the news early on."

Ivy pointed a finger at him. "The real question is, did you know he was allergic to walnuts?"

"Of course. Everyone in IT knows about it."

"Did you get an email about it?" she pressed. "Or did it just come up in conversation?"

He shrugged. "Conversation, I think."

She grinned at me. "See? An email is a HIPAA violation."

I laughed. "I stand by what I said. But, more importantly"—I swiveled my chair toward Cameron—"a student named Alma has been trying to hunt you down. She was just here asking about you. Where've you been?"

"She's here?" His head whipped around to look over his shoulder.

"No, she just left. But she waited for you downstairs for over an hour."

"And she's left you emails." Ivy began ticking items off on her fingers. "And voicemails. And memos. You garner very persistent fans."

"Of course I do." His fingers tugged at his cuffs. "I should probably get back to her on those emails. I never thought she'd resort to tracking you two down."

"She started asking around since you never replied," I said. "Her article deadline is coming up, so she's freaking out a bit. As a fellow writer, I get it. Deadlines are nonnegotiable."

His fingers stopped mid-tug. "She told you about the article?"

I nodded. "I think it's great they want to feature you in *The Courier*. Awesome teachers like you should get more recognition."

He didn't reply, just stood there, half-smiling but staring at me with a strange look on his face. It almost looked like a case of nervous stage fright, but no way did Cameron have stage fright. Was he uncomfortable because I complimented him? Surely he'd read his own student reviews and knew how everyone on campus adored him.

Ivy stood, slinging her work bag over her shoulder. "All right, friends. It's been a long day. I'm heading home." She pointed a finger at me. "Those time-cards are dumb, and you should go home, too." She swept the same finger over to Cameron. "Email Alma."

"I'll walk you out," Cameron said, glancing at me. "You coming?"

"No, I think I'll finish up here. See you both tomorrow."

I watched them walk through the lobby, another room made completely of glass, creating distorted, dark reflections against the night outside. Ivy walked with elegant strides, eyes on her phone. Cameron held the door open for her, tossing one last smile over his shoulder at me.

I swallowed and tried to force my thoughts back to my last work tasks for the day. Cameron was all the things Ivy had said. But he'd never given a single hint of wanting anything more than friendship with me in the half-decade we'd known one another. And that was that.

CHAPTER 14

CAMERON

From: Alma Torres
To: Cameron Whitacre
Subject: RE: Interview Request – The Courier

Dr. Whitacre,
Hope you're doing well!
I'm following up on my earlier emails, memos I left with the department recep-
tionist, and visits I made to your office about scheduling this interview for the
article I'm writing for The Courier. My deadline is just a few weeks out, so I'd
like to meet with you as soon as possible.
Just in case my earlier email got lost in the shuffle, I'm available at the
following times:

- *8:30 a.m. – 10:15 a.m. (MWF)*
- *3:00 p.m. – 6:30 p.m. (MWF)*
- *11:00 a.m. – 2:00 p.m. (T/Th)*

If you prefer, I can email you the interview questions ahead of time so you can
prepare your answers. I understand not everyone is comfortable with inter-
views (I'm always relieved to be the interviewer and not the interviewee!) but I
promise I'll make this as easy as possible for you.
Please let me know when you're available for our interview.

I look forward to hearing from you!

Thanks,
Alma

I tried to clear at least some of my weekends to spend with my family. The full-time position wouldn't do me any good if I didn't have any loved ones after all that extra work. (And I needed a break from the fun new pastime of dodging a particular student for a particular interview.)

I sat next to Great-Aunt Olive on the enclosed back porch of my parents' house in the late-afternoon sunshine, watching my family and their antics.

Dad emerged from the kitchen, ambling his way to the garage, his tone patient. "I'm telling you, they need to recruit players who are better at defense."

Derek, my brother-in-law, followed him with a greasy rag clenched in his hand. "They just recruited McKnight and Suarez last year."

Great-Aunt Olive sipped her lemonade and smiled at me through oversized glasses that magnified her eyes like a cartoon character's. "Are you still in school, Cameron?"

"I'm teaching college students, actually."

"You're taking chemistry?"

I spoke louder. "No, I'm a professor."

"Oh, you're a performer. So you went to theater school, then? That's nice. I was quite the actress in my day, you know," she said confidentially. "That's how I snatched up your great-uncle Laurence before that no-good Cindy Haywood could grab him for herself."

"I never did like that no-good Cindy Haywood." I matched my facial expression to my words, knowing she read faces better than she read lips. Great-Aunt Olive may not hear you, but her stream-of-consciousness conversation made her more random entertainment than Bill Walton's basketball commentary.

I took her empty glass, gestured that I would refill it, and went to the kitchen. I found the kitchen crew prepping lunch. And by prepping, I mean my mom half-heartedly stirring some pots as Aunt Cynthia gossiped.

"...but you didn't hear it from *me*," Aunt Cynthia whispered to Mom.

"Hear what?" I asked.

Aunt Cynthia, ever reliable, said, "That new city official is having an *affair* with his secretary. I saw a notification on her phone yesterday, and it *said—*"

"Why were you looking at her phone?" my sister, Samantha, asked, waving away her two kids and pushing them toward the TV in the basement. "That's an invasion of privacy."

Aunt Cynthia ignored her. "I just knew she was up to *something*. She only gets giggly like that when she's infatuated with someone new." She poked a manicured finger into my little brother's side. "Speaking of *infatuation*, Trent, I heard you have a new coworker."

Trent's blush instantly spread from the collar of his shirt to the roots of his hair. Samantha and I exchanged a sympathetic look. Poor Trent.

Mom paused with the whisk in her hand. "You've met someone, Trent?"

"I heard she's *very* pretty," Aunt Cynthia probed.

"No," he hedged, "not exactly. We—"

Aunt Cynthia's voice drowned out his. "Her car ran out of gas last week, and I heard that someone saw *you* helping her out. *Very* gallant of you." She flashed a Cheshire cat grin at him.

Dad and Derek charged into the room, carrying the scent of motor oil and sweat into the house.

Mom beamed at Trent. "You should bring her around. It's been a long time since you brought a girl home."

"Who's bringing a girl home?" Derek asked.

Aunt Cynthia's audience had grown. Samantha and I shared another look.

Trent opened his mouth, but Aunt Cynthia beat him. "Trent. He has a *pretty* new coworker, and he helped her when she was *stranded* on the side of the highway."

Dad nodded. "Good job, son." He clapped my brother on the back and returned to the garage.

Aunt Cynthia blinked. Nothing like practical dad advice to squelch her tittering.

Derek winked at Trent. "I'll only tell you 'good job' if you get the girl." He pulled Samantha in for a flirty kiss.

Samantha blushed. Even after five years of marriage to clueless Derek and having three stubborn children, she still managed to blush.

Something tugged at my shoelaces. I looked away from the entertaining drama to see sticky hands gripping at my sneakers. The sweetest green eyes in the universe looked up at me. Even the drool dribbling on her chubby chin couldn't make Skylar any less perfect to me.

I stooped to pick her up. "Who let you crawl around by yourself? Are you missing all the excitement?"

After leaving the fresh lemonade with Great-Aunt Olive (who asked me yet again whether I was still in school and studying chemistry), I carried Skylar into the living room. The room was already littered with blocks and balls and an assortment of the odd plastic toys one-year-olds love so much. I settled onto the floor and Skylar sprint-crawled for the closest stuffed animal. She made a game of putting random items in a plastic grocery cart and pushing the cart along the rug, stopping to add or remove items at her whim. Impractical. Unrealistic. Adorable. Seeing her add a plastic cookie to her grocery cart reminded me of Mom's fresh brownies in the kitchen. Propping Skylar and a few stuffed animals in my arms, I meandered to the now-empty kitchen to snag a corner piece.

I was crossing the threshold back to the living room when I heard my name drift in from the enclosed porch. My brain did that age-old trick of instantly snapping to attention.

"Shame on you!" my sister hissed.

"What?" Derek protested. "It's true."

"It's still not something you say out loud. I can't believe you."

"I didn't say anything wrong. All I did was ask when Cam last brought a girl around."

Apparently the topic had shifted from Trent to me. Great.

"It's been a while," Mom admitted, "but that doesn't mean anything."

A while? It'd been since before the stroke. Girlfriends hadn't been a priority when I was spending all of my time in physical therapy. Then I was in grad school. Then I met Mel.

"Like I said, that's because it'll take someone really special to be with someone like Cam," Derek said, "and I'm telling you, Cheyenne is special like that. We should set them up."

My sister's voice was sharp. "Special like what?"

"Like, well, you know, she adopted a stray cat, and she has a grandma in a wheelchair, so she's used to, you know, sad stuff."

Silence.

"Or whatever," Derek half-heartedly muttered.

A solid thwack hit something hard (meaning Derek's hard head).

Derek protested. "Hey! I'm trying to help! Honest!"

"Your help sucks," my sister growled at him, adding some colorful language that normally would have me grinning.

"Cam has baggage," Derek insisted, ever slow to realize he was in a losing battle. "Cheyenne is good with baggage. That's all I'm saying. They might be a good fit."

Dad cleared his throat. "Thanks for your concern, Derek. We know you mean well. But Cam will bring a girl around whenever he's ready. That's his business. Not ours."

I could've kept listening, but Skylar was squirming in my arms. Or that's what I told myself. Honestly, I didn't want to hear what else Derek would say, even if he meant well.

Moving back to the living room, an image came unbidden to mind: bringing Mel home to meet my family. Pretending Great-Aunt Olive could hear her. Answering Aunt Cynthia's endless nosy questions. Standing by and watching poor Trent squirm under unwanted attention. Maybe Derek would indulge her in one of his many rants about the engine he tore apart last week, or Samantha would go into too much detail about changing diapers.

I'd thought about this many times before. Just like I thought about asking her to dinner. A more-than-friends dinner. It felt about as attainable as winning the NBA Finals.

Maybe I should ask Derek about his coworker. I'd act casual, like I hadn't overheard them. Maybe she would be nice. But the thought of becoming the human equivalent of a stray cat? No.

I set Skylar on the carpeted floor, and she crawled over to place a gnome doll, complete with a tuft of hot-pink hair, into her plastic grocery cart.

My phone vibrated with a message from my group thread with Ivy and Mel.

Mel: Is it normal for a man to only have eyebrows?

Ivy: Happy weekend to you, too. I need some context here. Are we talking facial hair?

Cameron: Or are we talking he has no eyes, no nose, no mouth. Only eyebrows on a blank face?

Ivy: Thanks for putting that horrifying image in my head.

Mel: Like he has zero hair anywhere on him except his eyebrows. No hair on his head, no facial hair, no arm hair, no chest hair.

That didn't sound right. I frowned.

Cameron: How do you know he doesn't have chest hair?

Mel: I went to the poker room across town. It gets the best reviews online. I went in broad daylight, so it was safe, no need to mother me, Cam. I sat down at a beginner's table and said I wanted to learn to play. The guy who offered to teach me was bald, and I didn't think anything of it until I noticed he didn't have any hair on his forearms, either.

Cameron: Definitely a Terminator from the future.

Mel: Then I noticed that his shirt was halfway unbuttoned, and he didn't have any chest hair. He must've caught me looking, because he said, "I like the smooth look."

Cameron: Ignore the hysterical laughter you're hearing from my parents' neighborhood right now. It's just me, in their living room, dying from hilarity.

Mel: He said it so casually, too, like he was talking about the weather.

Spirits lifting a little, I grinned at my phone and at Mel's Dating Debacle, which hadn't produced any potential relationships to worry me.

No, I wouldn't ask Derek about Cheyenne. One of these days, all my efforts with Mel would pay off. My timing would be right. She would see the cupcakes and laptop repairs and attention for what they really were. She would see *me*. She was worth the wait.

CHAPTER 15

MEL

Cameron: I hate to break your heart, Mel, but you'll never get anywhere with this "smooth look" guy.
Mel: Agreed. He's just too weird.
Cameron: No, I mean your legs are way too hairy for him.
Mel: Hey!
Ivy: Lol! He's right! Remember when the three of us did No-Shave November? Your legs were hairier than Cam's.
Cameron: I would've felt emasculated if I hadn't been so impressed.
Mel: It wasn't that bad.
Ivy: Yes, it was. How many razors did you go through to cut it all back?
Cameron: Be honest. You know you didn't use razors. You used chainsaws and weedwhackers.
Mel: How are you two my best friends. I must have really low self-esteem.
Ivy: Truly best friends are able to laugh at themselves and each other with equal joy.
Cameron: Don't you mean malice?
Ivy: Stupid autocorrect. Yes, I meant malice.
Mel: Lol. Honestly, when he said he liked the smooth look, I immediately knew I was a goner. I just didn't think you two would so gleefully call me out on it.
Cameron: We always find happiness in supporting the pursuit of your dreams, Mel.

If the dictionary added pictures to definitions, it would have a snapshot of my grandma and namesake, Evelyn Melanie Hirsch, to define "grandmother".

She still looked exactly the same today as she had when I was eight years old: a cap of white curls haloed her head, plastic clip-on earrings pinched her earlobes, and Velcro sneakers peeked out from the legs of her elastic-waist-band slacks. She limped a little from hip pain, but she was almost ninety. All in all, she still got around well.

She leaned back in her recliner with a contented sigh—until a neighbor-hood teenager drove down the street, radio blaring. She glared out the window, cursing "kids these days" more colorfully than my cousin who was an actual sailor.

Just because my grandma looked like the quintessential grandmother didn't mean she acted like one.

She turned back to me, her glare replaced with the sweet smile she usually wore when I was around. "Now, dear Melanie. Tell me all about what you've been up to. Have you grown taller? You have such long legs…"

Wait for it…

"…and you know young men just love long legs."

There it was.

"No, Grandma, I haven't grown any taller. I'm turning thirty this year, so no more growing for me."

"No need to remind me about the age of your uterus, dear. Soon it'll be as wrinkled up as mine." She pulled her crocheting onto her lap. "How are your parents doing?"

"I think Dad is in Houston, and Mom is in Tokyo. Or maybe Hong Kong?"

Since their divorce when I was around eleven, my parents had flung them-selves into their work. They traveled the world, made who knew how much money, and rarely reached out to me. Spending most of my childhood alone had taught me independence at a young age, leaving me with plenty of time for reading my favorite books over and over again. Ivy, more cynical than I was, theorized pitting their careers against one another was their favorite form of post-divorce competition. I just thought they were hiding from something. One another, loneliness, family, me, all the above.

Regardless, Dad didn't reach out to Grandma either, so she always asked me how he was, and I visited her on most weekends to hold together some semblance of a family.

"Oh, tell me about your sweet friend Ivy. What a dear."

"Ivy is doing well. She's still working at the registrar."

"Just at the registrar?"

"She says she likes it well enough."

She huffed. "That girl has more artistic talent in her dead ends than all those yahoos on my TV, and she settles for working at a college registrar?" Another string of curses, none of them too strong, so Ivy was still in her good graces.

"She's figuring things out. She hasn't always had a good support system."

Grandma jabbed her crochet hook into her yarn. "Well, that's true. You're her best support. You and that young man." She gave me a meaningful look. "How's our sweet Dr. Cameron?"

She always referenced him like that, "Our sweet Dr. Cameron." He'd only met her a few times, and he blushed every time she said it. He hated it. I loved it.

I smiled. "He's good. A full-time position opened up, so he's working toward that."

Her meaningful look continued. "A full-time position means he'll be ready to settle down soon. Any little lady in his life?"

"Not that I know of."

Again, wait for it…

"Sounds like it should be you."

"No, Grandma. We're just friends."

"No red-blooded young man hangs around a pretty girl like you for, what, fifteen years and only wants to be friends!"

Five years, to be exact.

"Grandma—"

"I ran around with my fair share of"—she glanced toward the doorway to check for Grandpa—"young men back in my day, and none of them would've been my friend for fifteen years if they hadn't wanted something a little sweeter, hm?"

"Grandma—"

"I say you give him a chance. When he asks you out—"

"He's never going to ask me out." I willed myself to be patient with her.

She pointed an arthritic finger at me. "I said *when* he asks you out, you say yes. You jump on him. Because a young man like him doesn't come around often." She squinted at me. "Unless you have something against him?"

"No, Grandma. Cam is a great guy."

She continued staring.

"I'm serious. He's great. He really cares about his students. Everybody loves working with him."

"What are you, interviewing him for a job?" She stabbed with the crochet hook again. "If I had a handsome young man like that around, and if I were your age, I'd have a lot more to say than some platitude about his students."

I laughed. "I'm serious. Cam is a great guy. He's just…" I hesitated. He's just what? Too kind? Too funny? Too good of a friend? Cameron checked all the boxes. But I'd put him firmly in the friend zone, and he seemed to think the same of me, complete with yellow caution tape. I'd never gotten the impression that he felt interest in me as anything more than a friend—and I didn't want someone who didn't want me back. Even if he was as wonderful as Cameron.

So I cleared my throat and said what I thought: "Cam is just a friend."

She harrumphed, but I continued before she could start hassling me or cursing out the neighborhood kids again. "Actually, my love life is kind of why I'm here."

She perked up. "You have a different young man in mind? Why didn't you just say so?"

I explained the experiment and ignored her skeptical looks. "So," I summarized, "I wanted to ask you to look over this list of dating advice from the 1950s and tell me what you think is accurate or not."

While she slowly read through the entire list, I looked around my grandparents' living room. Every inch of each surface was covered with family photos. I could hardly see any wallpaper—thankfully, because the little bit of the wallpaper that I could make out was hideous. All the end tables, sideboards, and buffets were cluttered with framed pictures of family and friends. Evelyn Melanie and Fredrick Carter Hirsch lived a full life, in sickness and in health.

Their marriage was a perfect romance novel. Graduating high school as sweethearts, sticking together through Vietnam and PTSD, loving me the best they could when my parents checked out, sharing any dessert they ever ordered at a restaurant. Grandpa always wanted the lemon squares, but he'd order the chocolate cake because he knew it was her favorite. I knew for a fact they still held hands any time they walked together in public. Their marriage was strong and beautiful and the opposite of my parents and exactly everything I wanted someday.

Her laughter, followed by cursing, interrupted my thoughts.

"What?" I said. "What's so funny? Is the list wrong?" If yes, well, I'd just made an idiot of myself for nothing. Nicely done, Mel.

She wiped her eyes. "Oh, dear Melanie. Love doesn't come from a to-do list. It comes naturally. It's a choice. You think I feel the same way about your grandpa as I did all those years ago when we first met? Or the way I did on our wedding day? Well, I don't. Back then, love was like Fourth of July sparklers in my chest. Right now, love is making him hot coffee and breakfast each morning even after we got in a fight the day before and he spent all night snoring in my ear, so I didn't get a blink of sleep."

The fairy-tale romance I'd been picturing dissolved. "What?"

"I love him. And he loves me. And there are still some fireworks, sure. But now it's more of a comfortable love. Love is a choice you make every single day. Rain or shine. Making that choice is what keeps the sparklers alive." She started laughing again. "You certainly won't find it on this to-do list. Of all the things—"

The front door opened, and Grandpa walked in, his nose red and dripping from the cold outside. "Hello, Melanie." He rubbed frost from his mustache. "Getting into any trouble these days?"

Grandma spoke before I could. "I'll tell you what she's up to. She's found herself a to-do list to find a husband! Ha! Can you imagine?"

He didn't even bother taking off his coat and hat. He stepped closer, leaning over the recliner to read over her shoulder, and the bark of his laughter joined Grandma's. I tried to explain that it wasn't a to-do list for finding a husband, it was a social experiment for a book.

Eventually, I sat back and let them laugh.

Love might be the practical, everyday, ordinary reality that Grandma described, interspersed with a few sparklers and a lot of choices, but I still hoped for some romance, too. Couldn't love be both daily routines and sweeping romance? Why did it have to be one or the other?

Let my grandparents and everyone else laugh, I shrugged to myself. Cameron and Dr. Schaaf could keep their skepticism, and Ivy could be a cynic about men being users. I would finish the experiment and write a book and maybe meet my own Cameron. I would prove them all wrong. I hoped.

CHAPTER 16

CAMERON

Cameron: "Tell him that the death rate of single men is twice that of married men." Mel! Please please PLEASE do this one.
Mel: Sometimes your support feels less than genuine.
Cameron: I am 100% genuine in my confidence that this would be hilarious.
Ivy: He's right. It would be hilarious.
Mel: I will report back posthaste.
Ivy: Wait. Seriously?

Selfishly, I didn't mind that Ivy had canceled on us again.

Tonight it was just me and Mel. I felt greedy for more time with her. Just us. Her attention fully focused on me. Well, sort of focused on me, because this was still a mancounter. But I would take whatever she was willing to give me.

When we'd met in the parking lot, Mel had announced she was "winging it." She didn't have a specific item from the list in mind. She wanted to do this "naturally." But she had still done her homework. She'd chosen the busiest sports bar in town on a night when two major basketball teams were playing. (Or maybe the sports bar was a consolation prize for me because she knew that I was less than thrilled about the list but that basketball and wings drenched in hot sauce were my weakness.)

Massive TV screens glowed too brightly in the dim lighting. Speakers blared commentators' insights about plays and scores. There was hardly room to move around the dining area. People crowded into every corner, around every booth. If it were summer, the retractable garage doors would slide overhead and open up more space, but that would be insanity in New England this time of year.

It was a place I normally would've gone to with Toby or with teammates in college. Overly crowded, overly energetic, and overly loud. A restaurant full of sports fans ready to cheer on their teams no matter the odds. Comradery at its best.

We settled into the last two empty seats at a high-top table near a window. We placed our orders with the tall brunette who clearly hated her job. ("Sorry," she said, "we're all out of wings tonight." Words that should never be uttered at a place like this.) Mel craned her neck to scope out the crowd. I forced myself to pay attention to my plate and not drip salsa on myself because we were sitting so close I could shift my knee an inch and touch her thigh. How many times could my leg bump hers before it became obvious that I was doing it on purpose? How many other times had I done something similar in hopes she would notice? Now that these mancounters were my competition, my feelings for Mel featured new urgency.

Jumbled questions filled my head. Why didn't she have a plan for tonight's Dating Debacle? She'd always had a plan before. Why was she breaking the pattern? Each time she lifted her drink to her lips, or wiped her fingers on her napkin, or uncrossed and recrossed her legs, I watched for clues about what was running through her mind. On a completely related note, she hadn't worn heels since that one glorious day at work, and my extremely disappointed self needed to know what she considered an event worthy of wearing heels, and how quickly could I make it happen?

And what about Ivy? Had she ditched us again because she knew about my feelings and wanted to give us time alone? Impossible. I was too good at hiding how I felt. Mel didn't notice. Why would Ivy? But if Ivy did suspect something, had she said anything to Mel?

"Want any more chips?" I nudged the empty nacho basket toward her.

"Sure, but I can get it this time."

I covered her hand with mine and pried her fingers off the basket. "Too slow."

When I came back with fresh nachos and salsa (and guacamole, because I knew one of the servers), Mel was trying to talk to one of the nearby men wearing a jersey. He halfway paid attention to her, but his eyes were mostly focused on the oversized TV screens hanging from the walls.

On one hand, I couldn't blame him. This game was expected to be good. On the other, I hated him for not appreciating Mel's attention when I'd been trying to get her to see me for five years. On the other *other* hand—yes, I'm out of hands —I mentally high-fived him for ignoring her so I could have more time with Mel.

He didn't stand a chance anyway. He looked like a gnome with a head way too big for his body. (No offense, man. All contestants in the Dating Debacle were my personal dartboard for petty insults.)

I perched on my seat, pushing the nachos and salsa between us. "I ordered us some wings, too. They'll be up in a minute."

"But the server told us they were out."

I shrugged. "I knew someone."

"Of course you did," she said, smiling.

Gnomeo's team scored. He fist-pumped so hard he nearly fell out of his seat, even though the points wouldn't put his team in the lead.

Mel shifted out of the range of his fist-pumping and a little closer to me. I awarded him another mental high five for his lack of self-awareness and motor control.

I'd decided on a whim which team to cheer for since I wasn't a major fan of either one. The players pounded down the court again, and I knew the shot would miss as soon as the ball left the shooter's hands. I muttered it aloud without thinking, well ahead of the commentators and other fans around me.

"How'd you know that?" Gnomeo leaned over to peer at me.

"Know what?"

"How'd you know that would miss? You've called several shots like that, and you've always gotten it right."

I shrugged. "I played in college."

"He was really good. The best player on the whole team." Mel's chin lifted when she said it. (Was she bragging about me? How could I get her to do it again? Exactly how much could my chest swell without exploding?)

"Yeah?" Gnomeo's voice pulled my thoughts away from her. "Which teams do you follow?"

I named a couple, and he began rattling off basketball stats. What I knew in the sport's practical application, he knew in team and player stats. Gnomeo spoke enthusiastically, I would give him that, since he didn't even blink as his beer steadily dripped onto his shoe, probably soaking it through.

Happy to have discovered a fellow knowledgeable fan, Gnomeo divided his attention between me and the game, all but ignoring Mel. The more he talked, the more annoyed she looked. I don't think you could blame me for purposefully egging Gnomeo on with more stats that I knew would bore Mel to the point of no return.

Was it mature of me? No.

Was it necessary? Absolutely. One less man to contend with.

But I didn't expect Mel to pull my own joke on me.

When Gnomeo paused to take a breath for his next monologue of stats, she jumped in. "Speaking of interesting statistics, did you know that the death rate of single men is twice as high as the death rate of married men?"

Gnomeo gaped at her over his beer.

Mel gave me a subtle, smug look.

My eyeballs turned into pulsing cartoon hearts.

She'd stolen my joke (that I'd never imagined she would use, by the way) and made sure I was there to see it land. She'd been listening to my goofy ramblings Ivy always complained about. She saw me. Someone take me to a tall building, because surely I could jump it in a single leap right now.

I struggled to keep a straight face. Time to play along. "That's fascinating. How did they study that, exactly?"

She kept up the act like a pro. "Quantitative research, of course."

Gnomeo finally recovered, reaching around Mel to slap my shoulder. "I think she's hitting on you, man."

If only she would.

He stood. "Good luck with her. I need a refill."

In unison, Mel and I dropped our gazes. My face hurting from the restraint of not bursting into laughter. "I can't believe you actually said that."

"I couldn't resist." Mel turned to stare out the window, avoiding eye contact so she wouldn't lose her composure. "He was just going on and on."

"As much as you may feel like you're dying when you're forced to watch sports, *this* was not the best moment for that statistic."

"*Is* there a good moment for that statistic?"

"A wedding."

Finally composed, we faced one another again. Her cheeks were pink, her eyes a little glassy. She bit her lips like she was holding back another fit of laughter.

Soon my friend who promised us wings brought a heaping plate to our table. I didn't miss how she patted my forearm as she walked away, it was just that I couldn't tear my attention from Mel for more than a quick "Thank you."

Divvying up the wings between our two plates, I offered Mel some celery and ranch.

"How do you know her?" Tilting her head, she studied me with an expression I couldn't read. I knew all of Mel's expressions. Since when did she have a new one? Unacceptable.

"She graduated with my little brother."

"She likes you," Mel said.

"Not interested."

"What does it take to get you interested?"

I stared at her. Mel never asked pointless questions. Where was this going?

She tried to look noncommittal, but she was too pointedly looking everywhere but at me. "We've been friends for about five years. I've never seen you date anyone. Ever. Are you heartbroken over a high school romance? Are you just not interested in dating? Do you have a problem that I don't know about? If this is too personal, just tell me to stop..."

My problem had wavy brown hair and her name was Mel.

So much for leaping the nearest tall building. How could she not see me? I'd thought, just a moment ago, that she'd noticed me. She'd taken my joke—and made it better. I'd thought there was a connection. Clearly I'd read more into the moment than I should have. As usual between me and Mel. As usual for all the wishful thinking on my part. My stomach twisted.

Bracing one arm over the back of her chair and the other across the table in front of her, I leaned close. I intentionally filled her space, willing her to look at me, to see me, to understand what I'd been trying to say without words every time I left her a ridiculous note about Dr. Freisen's bowties. "I'm very interested in dating." *I'm very interested in you.*

She blinked but didn't shift away from me. "But you're always alone, so I thought maybe it was because—"

"I'm waiting." *Because I'm a fool over you.*

"For what?" I saw her lips form the whispered question, but the crowd was cheering too noisily to hear her voice.

"For the right woman." *For you. To see me. I'm right here. Open your eyes.*

Gnomeo chose that minute to return from the bar, his large beer frothing over and onto his shoe. (How could he still not feel that?) "Did you see that last shot? What a way to end the night!" He noticed how Mel and I were staring at one another. "Oh—sorry, man. Didn't mean to interrupt. Maybe I should go home and write my own list of depressing pickup lines, since it's clearly working for her."

It was working for her. Along with all her other quirks. I'd been a goner from day one. The frustration gnawed at me so strongly that I couldn't trust myself to stay calm. Now it paired with a sadness that pulsed in place of my cartoon heart eyeballs.

At his words, Mel's laughing eyes glanced at me like we had the world's best inside joke.

I leaned away from Mel and offered a tense smile to Gnomeo.

He was right. What a way to end the night.

CHAPTER 17

CAMERON

Mel: Apparently my neighbor decided my one-time offer to walk his Enormous Rex dog is a standing offer for the rest of time. Because he knocked on my door at 6:09 (!) this morning and handed me Horse's leash.
Ivy: I have several questions. One, is Horse the dog's actual name?
Mel: No. I've dubbed him Horse for as long as I have to put up with him.
Ivy: Two, were you fully clothed that early in the morning? (Any steamy ogling during the leash handoff?)
Mel: It's winter in New England. Of course I was fully clothed.
Ivy: Three, Horse belongs to a man? (Is said man a candidate for the list?!)
Mel: Yes, Horse's owner is a man. (Said man is very happily married to the most perfect woman of all time—no joke—and has two toddlers who cry in sync. So the answer is no.)
Ivy: Disappointing. Please wear a GoPro at 6:09 tomorrow so I can see Horse, his owner, and the most perfect woman.

Sitting at my desk, staring at the blank wall in front of me, I tried to think about anything *but* last night at the sports bar.

I had two more classes to teach this afternoon. Another meeting with a student between the two classes, and then maybe a quick lunch from the vending machine if I had a few seconds to spare. Answer an email from a student about tomorrow's exam. Check in with Renee, TA and part-time receptionist in our department, about the networking event tonight. Maybe dinner from the vending machine, too. Plus a note to Mel about Dr. Freisen's bowtie color for today: phlox.

Or maybe I'd forego the note for today, because what did my mind return to again and again? Last night.

Frustration gnawed at me. How many times had I flirted with Mel and she gave me zero reciprocation? How many cupcakes had I smuggled into the Fishbowl? How many times had I fixed her dinosaur of a laptop? And still nothing.

Maybe I wasn't the problem. Maybe it was her. Maybe she was playing clueless for the same reason I'd never told her about my feelings—because she didn't want to risk our friendship, either. She might've noticed my interest, but when she weighed the pros and cons, she decided that our friendship was worth more to her than any potential romance. I was just too good of a friend. She valued me too much to lose me. A little hurtful in one sense, but a little complimentary in another.

No way she simply hadn't noticed after all this time... Right?

I just didn't know anymore. Five years of waiting, wondering. And now, in my current mood, it felt like five years wasted.

It didn't matter anymore. My hands had automatically balled into fists at our conversation at the sports bar, and they hadn't quite loosened up ever since. Through all of my morning classes, my hands fisted. I'd even glared at Veronica when she batted her eyelashes at me through the Fishbowl glass. Now I sat in my office, stewing over the last twenty-four hours.

This wasn't like me. I needed to channel my frustration into something else. I needed to do something radical to put Mel out of my mind for good. Now was the time to take action before I lost my nerve. Enough was enough.

Finding Derek's grinning mug in my contacts wasn't hard. His avatar was a monster truck with his face superimposed on the windshield. (Yes, he'd sent the image himself, to all his friends and family, so they could see this gem every time he called.)

He answered on the first ring. "Cam, my man!"

Tucking my phone between my shoulder and my ear, I fiddled with the buttons on my shirt cuffs. I needed to think of this conversation as a Band-Aid and rip away the heartache and frustration in one go. I took a deep breath and exhaled the words in a rush. "I was wondering if you have any single coworkers I could meet."

It was so quiet that I thought I heard him swallow. "You're getting back in the game, huh?"

"I'm ready." Not really, but details were on a need-to-know basis.

My phone filled with sound. Mom gushed in the background, "Cam, this is wonderful." Dad said something about "funny timing." Trent and Samantha laughed about which of them won the bet. Skylar, eager to join the excitement, cooed along with them.

Derek's voice drowned out the background noise. "You're on speaker-phone, and everyone's here!"

I let my forehead thump onto my desk. Just what I wanted—a room full of witnesses listening in as I gave up on the woman I loved. They didn't know it. But I did.

"Thanks for the warning, Derek." My fingers curled inward. Why were they all hanging out like this on a weekday afternoon? "Hey, everyone. What are you all up to today?"

"Mom has tickets to the zoo," Samantha said. "So we're having a quick lunch before heading over. You said you couldn't make it, right?"

I'd been so swept up in work, I'd forgotten. "Sorry, I have classes and a couple meetings this afternoon."

Their chatter flowed through the speakerphone. "I need another fork," "Pass the rolls," "Who left the bottle opener all the way over there?" I could see it all playing out. Trent sitting with Skylar, who kept him wrapped around her finger worse than she did the rest of us; Derek sneaking a kiss with Samantha; Mom and Dad trying to keep the food moving around the table.

Samantha, as always, was the voice of reason, and she refocused on me first. Unfortunately. "Are you sure about this, Cam?"

I thumped my forehead on my desk a second time. Maybe my voice would sound more confident than I felt. "Why wouldn't I be?"

"I mean, are you sure you want *Derek* to be your matchmaker?"

"Hey!" Derek protested.

"Because if it doesn't work out," Samantha continued, "he will be obnoxious."

I grimaced. Wasn't he already a little obnoxious? Well-meaning, sure, but also obnoxious. "Isn't it already too late for me to back out?"

The sound of Derek's hands rubbing together carried through the phone. "I have just the girl in mind for you. Her name is Cheyenne. She's real great. I think you two would hit it off. She likes *Star Wars* and *Doctor Who*."

I stifled a laugh over the fact that Derek thought that's all it would take to interest me in a woman. "Thanks. Could you send me her number when you get a chance?"

"Just did. And if you look on my company's website, you'll see her picture, too. If you want to make sure or whatever."

What a way with words. "Thanks, Derek."

"Let me know when you text her," Samantha said. "So I can yell at this guy not to be too awkward about it at work."

I laughed through gritted teeth. "I will. Thanks. I need to get back to work, but enjoy the zoo for me."

I hung up in time to see a text notification from Mel pop up. I paused but decided to ignore it without reading it. She was probably just talking about the Dating Debacle anyway.

I added Cheyenne's number to my contacts app. Thumb hovering over the text icon, I hesitated. Maybe I should think about it a bit more before reaching out to her. Maybe I should sleep on it. Samantha was right. Did I really want Derek involved in my life as more than a vaguely annoying brother-in-law?

My computer pinged with an email notification. Eager for the distraction, I skimmed the message.

From: Keith Freisen
To: Cameron Whitacre
Subject: FW: Interview Request – The Courier

Good morning, Dr. Whitacre,

Please see Ms. Alma Torres's email below. She has reached out to you multiple times and also stopped by your office on various occasions to ask about scheduling this interview. Please advise.

Thank you,
Keith Freisen, PhD
Academic Department Chair
Computer Science and Information Technology

Not today of all days.

Noticing it was almost time for my first afternoon class to start, I slung my bag over my shoulder, juggled my coffee and phone, and locked my office door behind me. I screeched to a stop when I rounded the corner, quickly reversing away like a PAC-MAN ghost. Dr. Freisen and Alma stood just around the corner.

I didn't have time for this today.

I had classes and a networking event and a glitch in the biology department's printer that needed my attention and maybe a text to Cheyenne—

And all of this would be for nothing if I didn't do what the administration wanted. If I didn't do the interview and showcase my pain, then I wouldn't be gifted with the full-time position for all my heroic efforts. Because that's what it would be. After this article, I wouldn't have earned the full-time position, would I?

I peeked around the corner to see Dr. Freisen and Alma talking. She made an impatient gesture toward my door. He straightened his already-straight bowtie.

Now was the time to behave like I should. Just walk around the corner. Act like it was nothing. Stick my hand out and introduce myself to Alma. Not give away even a hint that I knew way too much about her student life because I'd done all the research necessary to avoid her. Run through the political and social niceties with Dr. Freisen.

I pictured myself doing all of it. I walked imaginary, charming Cameron Whitacre through each step, each word. I could fake this.

But my body wouldn't move. It was like years ago, when I just woke up in the hospital after the stroke, locked inside a body that wouldn't do what I told it to do. I knew I needed to take the proverbial plunge. But nothing in me wanted to walk up to Dr. Freisen and Alma. Reliving that moment, and so many of the moments after, was just...

Dr. Freisen gestured toward his office, and Alma fell in stride beside him, walking in my direction.

I scrambled back another few steps (PAC-MAN ghost-style again) to a random door and shut myself inside. At first I held my breath because of fear, and then I held my breath because of the smell. Bleach and ammonia filled the janitor's closet, and mops and buckets piled against the shelves, barely leaving enough room for me. My head bumped into the exposed lightbulb above me.

The footsteps in the hall echoed closer, the clip of Dr. Freisen's dress shoes a staccato next to Alma's clumping boots. I stood perfectly still.

Soon their footsteps faded, passing the janitor's closet and presumably stepping into Dr. Freisen's office.

I checked the time. I was late to class. I had no choice.

I cracked open the closet door. All clear.

Stepping into the hallway, I heard a muffled giggle. Renee stood behind me, eyes wide, biting her lips to keep from laughing. (She did that in class, too, when I made a nerdy joke.) Vernon was with her, frowning at me like I was a strange equation his genius brain couldn't compute.

Perfect.

They stared when I walked by and casually nodded a greeting. (What, hadn't they ever seen a professor in a janitor's closet before? Clearly they hadn't been here after hours, when Malcolm and Aki were both "teaching night class.")

Keeping my eyes focused on my feet, I walked the long way to my class, even though I was late. Anything to avoid that thirty-five-degree-angle office door and an overeager journalism student.

Checking the time to see exactly how late I was for class, I noticed my screen was unlocked—and my thumb was dangerously close to pressing Cheyenne's number and accidentally calling her. At least one thing had gone right for me today: I hadn't pocket-dialed Derek's coworker. I locked the screen and walked faster.

Tomorrow. I would text Cheyenne tomorrow.

CHAPTER 18

MEL

Mel: Do you know why Cam is always single?
Ivy: Oookay. Something on your mind?
Mel: When we went to the sports bar yesterday, his relationship status came up. And he said he's waiting for the right woman.
Ivy: Was this in the middle of a mom joke?
Mel: He was being serious. Like really serious. Kind of intense.
Ivy: So maybe he's serious. Maybe he's waiting for the right woman.

It was the best of times, and it was the worst of times, and no place demonstrated this better than the dimly lit bar Cameron and I stepped into. Laughter, clinking drinks, and celebratory voices came from tables packed with people; dismal, solitary silence came from tables with lone customers. In my experience, most bars were like this, but unlike other bars, this one was clean. Servers rushed to wipe down tables and sweep floorspace between customers. Behind the shelves of glass bottles, the mirror gleamed.

We maneuvered through the crowd and toward the bar.

I nudged Cameron's elbow. "Tell me again why you chose this place?" More like why he insisted this was the best bar of all time. It was an odd thing for Cameron to be opinionated about, in my opinion.

He leaned down so I could hear him. "It's a decent place"—I knew he meant *safe*, not *decent*—"and I know the crowd that works here."

"How? I've never heard you mention going out for drinks before."

"Would you have come with me if I had?" His mouth twitched into a half-smile. "It's because I'm too cool to go out for drinks. I'm so cool that I go out for Trivia Tuesdays."

At the bar, he nodded to the man behind the counter—who was built more like a bouncer and less like a bartender—and then ordered a whiskey neat for himself and my usual gin and tonic without needing to ask me.

The bartender reached his large hand across the worn counter. "Nice seein' you, Cam. Haven't heard of you comin' 'round lately."

"Work has been hectic. It should slow down soon, and then I'll be a regular again."

The bartender shook his head. "Nah, I don't believe that. I think you're just quittin' while you're ahead."

Cameron laughed. "How was your trip to the Keys?"

Of course he knew personal details about the bartender at his regular haunt.

I nudged Cameron again when the bartender turned away. "What's he talking about with you being ahead?"

He nodded toward a large wall covered with a hodgepodge of framed photos. "I told you, I come here for Trivia Tuesdays. My team is the reigning champion a couple years running now."

"I thought you were joking about Trivia Tuesdays. How have you never told me this before?"

He shrugged. "It never really came up."

"Because you didn't bring it up. Who's on your team?"

"Toby, sometimes his brothers, and a couple other people we've picked up along the way." He accepted our drinks from the bartender and handed me my gin and tonic.

For a moment I thought his fingers lingered on mine. Thanks, Grandma, for putting doubts in my head. Not that I needed her help when it came to imagining things with Cameron.

I stepped over to the wall to squint at the pictures. Miniature plaques displayed the year of each frame, and for several years in a row, Cameron, Toby, and their team held cheesy-looking trophies. Looking at his smile in the pictures, I could almost hear his laughter. I could also imagine his competitive spirit from his basketball days serving him well.

"I can't believe I didn't know this about you," I said.

"You and Ivy are welcome to join sometime if you want."

"I don't know that the two of us are trivia material."

He pointed to a picture, his arm brushing against mine. "Toby and I already make a good team. I know the computer, math, and nerdy pop culture trivia. He knows science, health, and history. We manage okay with geography between the two of us."

"So on your new dream team, I would know books and words, and Ivy would know art."

"We would be unstoppable." He grinned down at me, his eyes a darker blue in the dim lighting around us.

I blinked away. "Where is Ivy anyway?" I pulled my phone from my pocket to see a notification from her.

Ivy: Can't make it. Sorry! Knock 'em dead, Mel. But not literally. Not like that walnut fiasco.

Would I ever live that down?

Cameron also looked at his phone, reading the same group thread. "Guess it's just you and me."

I stared at the glowing screen of my phone. Cameron wasn't thrilled about this project, but he still supported me, tagging along as my wingman. I'd thought Ivy was on board—but now she'd canceled at the last minute again... Maybe she didn't feel as supportive as I'd assumed. Why else would she keep disappearing like this? Unless something else was going on in her life. And if that was the case, why didn't she tell me?

At least Cameron was with me tonight.

I cleared my throat. "Right. Well, tonight the agenda is 'Don't play coy.' Women weren't supposed to make the first move in the 1950s, so this would've been drastic advice."

"Not the dreaded initiative. It might make you promiscuous."

"Naturally."

"So are you going to flirt outrageously, see how many numbers you can get, call them, and make a spreadsheet to track how many people hang up on you?" His blue eyes skimmed the crowded tables and then peered at me. "If you take too much initiative with the wrong people, you might end up competing with Ivy's record for unsolicited nudes."

Ignoring the nudes comment, an image of Cameron unleashing his charm on a room popped into my head. "Why do I have a feeling that young Cam spent many college nights flirting with an entire bar just to see how many numbers he could get?"

"Why tell you that when I can keep the mystery alive?"

I smiled at that until my imagined scenario expanded. Cameron, at this bar every Tuesday, winning trivia games with his team, charming women with his cleverness and crinkling blue eyes, walking away with several numbers tucked into his pocket. Walking away with a woman.

Who was to say Cameron didn't continue his college adventures and wasn't still charming his way into a plethora of phone numbers? At least once a week he came here, where he could flirt and meet beautiful, intriguing people. Just because I hadn't seen him date anyone, like we talked about at the sports bar, didn't mean Cameron spent his nights alone.

Worse still, what if he came away with a number tonight?

Jealousy curdled in my stomach. I realized he was looking at me, waiting for an answer. What had we been talking about?

I sipped my gin and tonic. "Fishing for numbers isn't really my style."

"I could always try my flirting tactics on you. You'd be surprised how good I am."

The aching pit in my stomach shifted to butterflies so quickly that I almost choked on my drink. "You already have my number," I laughed. "There's no reward in it for you."

Leaning closer, his voice dipped a little lower. "I'm sure we could think of something."

I needed a beat to regain my footing. Sometimes an inkling at the back of my mind would question whether Cameron had feelings for me. But logic would always shut it down. He was kind and charming and teasing and the best-looking man I knew, but he didn't flirt with me, at least not in any serious way. This was Cameron. He joked in the face of anything serious.

"Just stay focused, okay?" I said and turned back toward the open room. "Maybe I'll buy someone a drink and see what happens. That's the opposite of coy, right?"

He looked away, his voice muffled against the rim of his whiskey glass. "Whatever you want."

I surveyed the bar. Some of these guys looked young enough to be my students at the university. How awkward would that be? Each group had a few defining characteristics, like the hipsters with their knit caps, or the white-collar workers with their loosened ties and unbuttoned suit jackets. A group of girls jostled us as they walked past, one of them wearing a "bride to be" sash. The bar door swung open, and a bearded man paused in the entrance.

I nodded toward his silhouette in the doorway. "How about him?"

Cameron gave him a skeptical once-over. "Since when do you like beards?"

"There's a first for everything. The list is about trying new things, right?"

We watched Beard take off his coat, hat, scarf—and go through the distinct motions of removing a ring and slipping it into his pocket.

Cameron cleared his throat. "Trying this new thing might make you a homewrecker, Mel."

I scowled. "Never happening. Some rules are meant to be broken, and some aren't."

He hid his smile behind his whiskey glass.

I watched Beard swagger to the bar, order a drink, and slide into conversation with one of the bachelorettes. He leaned closer, eyes spending more time on her low-cut shirt than on her face. She twirled her hair around a manicured finger.

As Beard leaned closer to Bachelorette, a man to his left came into my line of sight. How had I not noticed him before? He was supermodel gorgeous— hair in a perfect quiff, just the right kind of five-o'clock shadow. And it looked like he was alone. The bachelorettes hadn't noticed him yet since he was tucked into the corner.

If I was going to take a swing and risk a miss, I might as well make it really big, right?

"Got him."

Cameron's suspicious glance darted over the crowd. "Who?"

"Next to Married Beard."

"In the seventies sweatsuit?"

"No, the other guy."

"With the David Beckham hair?"

"David Beckham's hair is great, but this is a style called a quiff. I'm going in."

"Shouldn't you watch for a minute to make sure he isn't hiding a wedding ring?"

Okay, so less-than-thrilled Cameron was coming out to play.

"He's not wearing one," I said, "and if I don't move now, I'll miss my chance. The bachelorette party is on the prowl. Here, take my drink."

I power walked to the bar until I came within a few feet of Quiff, slowing until I angled my body between him and Beard. I should've thought of a good opening line before making it this far, but it was too late now.

"Hey. How about I buy you a drink?"

He glanced at me for a beat before looking straight ahead again. "I'll never turn down a drink."

The bartender materialized behind the counter. "'Nother gin and tonic for you, ma'am?"

"That'd be great," I said. "And another beer for him." I rested a hand on Quiff's shoulder.

The bartender blinked at me and glanced toward the wall of framed photos where Cameron stood. He clearly recognized me from our earlier conversation. "Comin' right up."

I turned more fully toward Quiff. *Don't be coy. Don't be coy.* "So, tell me—"

He craned his neck at an odd angle, tilting his head. It was a familiar gesture—the one all of us use to look in a mirror and check the hair on the backs of our heads. He picked at a single strand that was already perfectly in place. Is that why he'd been looking straight ahead this whole time, hardly even glancing at me?

Distracted, I lost my train of thought and had to start again. "Do you come here often?"

I wanted to kick myself. Was it possible to be any less original? Sure, I'd gotten sidetracked with the hair gawking, but still.

He couldn't spare any concentration from his hair to notice my cliché. "No, this is my first time here. Heard this place had some IPAs I hadn't tried before."

The bartender placed our drinks in front of us and then vanished again.

"IPAs, huh? I don't know much about the beer scene, but I've heard there are some great local breweries around here."

"I've toured all of them a couple times. They're good for something local. But it's hard to compete with the flavors of true IPAs."

"I've heard one of the local breweries might be expanding to a second location." My voice grew more hesitant as I watched him pose for a selfie with his new bottle of beer, courtesy of me, the woman he hardly acknowledged. "So maybe they'll...branch out...some."

"The one on the south side?" he said, now tapping on his phone screen.

"Um, yeah, that one." Hopefully Cameron wasn't seeing any of this.

Picking up his beer, Quiff turned toward the windows across the room, where the dark street turned the glass into a reflective mirror of everything in the bar—including his bicep flexing beneath his shirt as he took a drink.

Okay, I took it back. Now I hoped Cameron was seeing all of this. I flicked a glance in the mirror behind the bar and caught his eye. He was laughing into his whiskey glass. I bit my lip.

Quiff turned back to me. "The brewery on the south side will need to step up their marketing if they're going to make it. Their social media following isn't nearly enough to grow the way they want."

I nodded with fake interest. "Are you in marketing?"

"You could say that." His supermodel grin may or may not have been meant for me. Since he was looking at his own face reflected in his beer bottle, I honestly couldn't tell.

This conversation was going nowhere good. I could play coy or not, but I didn't want to waste time. I downed what was left of my gin and tonic and tried to think of an exit line. "Well, it was nice—"

The bartender materialized. "'Nother gin and tonic?"

"Um—"

"No, thanks," Cameron spoke from behind me. "I think we're good." He turned to me, the corners of his eyes still crinkled from laughter at Quiff. "Unless you'd rather stay?"

"No, I think I'm good here."

Through the reflection behind the bar, Quiff eyed Cameron and then me. "Thanks for the beer." He went back to tapping on his phone screen.

Cameron shoved his hands into his pockets as we left the bar. "I thought he was going to start kissing his reflection."

"Like in those eighties teen movies?"

"Exactly like those."

"I couldn't even carry on a conversation with him."

"You mean carry on a conversation with yourself?" He laughed.

We walked under glowing streetlights. Cameron's bar was nice, I'd give him that, and it was in a quaint part of downtown. The brick buildings cast long shadows. Local storefronts and restaurants stood out, their bright windows lit up and welcoming.

He cleared his throat. "You know, Trivia Tuesday is way better than what you experienced back there."

I pulled my hat lower over my ears. "That's okay. I'm a mere mortal and don't have your genius-level brains."

He scoffed. "I'm not that smart."

"Yes, you are. You've got too much of that nerdy GQ thing to convince me otherwise."

"Nerdy GQ?"

"You know"—I made a vague gesture with my hand and took slow steps toward my car—"like how you can dish out *Firefly* references, but you still know how to wear a suit."

He laughed. "Thanks, I think?"

"It's a compliment." I watched my breath fog the air in front of me, felt the steam of it on my cheeks. "It just makes you a bit intimidating sometimes."

"I'm not intimidating."

Surprise lifted my brows. "Yes, you are. If you weren't so nice, I never would've had the guts to be friends with you when we first met."

He frowned at me in the darkness between the streetlights. "Maybe I'm the one who needed guts to be friends with you."

"We both know that's not true. I'm average. And you would know just how average if you tried playing trivia with me."

"Not true." He said it with authority, like anyone who thought otherwise was highly suspect.

I shook my head and watched our footsteps on the snowy sidewalk. His longer strides were slower than my shorter ones. He'd adjusted his normal pace so I had no need to rush alongside him.

He pulled his hands from his pockets, tugging at his sleeves. "Were you really that intimidated when you first met me?"

"Definitely."

"I just can't picture it. You're such a go-getter."

"Oh, please." I laughed. "You walked into the room, all business casual and charming everyone—"

Now Cameron laughed. "I think that second gin and tonic went to your head."

"Ask Ivy. She knows how daunting you are. If you didn't go out of your way to be such a Care Bear and a team player, nobody would have the guts to be friends with you."

"That's funny, because I was the one who was intimidated by you when we met."

I elbowed his side. "Now *that's* funny."

"I'm serious." And he was. His words, simple and upright, shook a verbal finger in my face.

"What could possibly be intimidating about me? Every day I'm surrounded by professors with PhDs and lists of published pieces longer than my arm. 'Intimidating' is the last word people would use to describe me."

He rested a hand on my arm to turn me toward him. "You have ambition. You're passionate about your students. And you"—he removed his hand, glanced away—"look the way you do."

I patted at the waves that were probably puffing out in a frizzy tangle from under my knit hat. No wonder Quiff had hardly looked at me. "You mean my crazy hair?"

"No. I mean…" He tugged at his sleeves again, then stared at me without pretense and said, "You're beautiful. It's intimidating to talk to someone as ambitious and beautiful as you are."

I blinked. Cameron thought I was beautiful? Of course I'd snooped on his social media profiles, so I'd seen old pictures of his college girlfriends, and they were gorgeous. He'd had women like that hanging on his arm, and he still thought I was beautiful? My chest felt warm and fuzzy.

He swallowed audibly before teasing, "Don't let it go to your head though."

I scoffed. "That would be impossible with you around." Feeling fidgety, I checked the time on my phone and gestured toward my car. "Anyway, I need to be at work for an early meeting tomorrow. Dr. Schaaf must feel like ranting about Watergate again."

He walked around my car to hold the door open for me.

I paused before sitting in the driver's seat. "Thank you for coming with me tonight. I know you have a million things you could be doing instead."

He smiled down at me, his eyes crinkling. "Anything for you."

With the streetlights alternately highlighting and darkening his face, the shadows were too dark for me to read his expression. The inkling returned for a moment, and I wondered if maybe…

But he turned and walked away before I could be sure, his shadow gradually melting into the others along the street.

CHAPTER 19

MEL

Ivy: Please don't pretend to drown, Mel.
Cameron: What?
Mel: I would never follow the list that far.
Ivy: You pretended your car broke down.
Mel: In a public, well-lit parking lot. My life wasn't in danger.
Cameron: It was very much in danger. Remember the driver you met?
Ivy: Regardless, this is terrible advice. What if you pretended to drown and nobody noticed?
Cameron: You start swimming.

Of all the tasks on the list, one stood out to me as the most ridiculous: "Stow away on a Navy ship."

My gut instinct was a hard no. Just the thought of such tight quarters and the smell of that many sweaty people close together made me squirm. And that was even before thinking about the trouble I'd get into. I wasn't sure what national security looked like in the 1950s, but surely stowing away on a Navy ship had been a horrible idea at the time. And it was still a horrible idea today.

Cameron and Ivy agreed. All too happily, even if they did tease me about Navy sailors and prison time. So we modified it. Instead of a Navy ship, Ivy asked a rich friend of a friend—or someone like that—about getting invitations to a yacht party.

Maybe purists would fault me for modifying the list, but if they could do it better, they were welcome to stow away on a Navy ship and show me how it was done.

The three of us stood on the gangway, the icy New England wind slicing at us. The others in line ahead and behind us held themselves with the poise of wealthy people who had nothing to prove because they were already worth more than a small country. My university salary definitely didn't fit in here.

I'd warned Ivy we wouldn't blend in with such a crowd, but she insisted it would be "drunk businesspeople who couldn't tell a Rembrandt from a Monet anyway." Cameron and I also probably couldn't tell a Rembrandt from a Monet, but it seemed best not to mention that detail.

My phone vibrated. Another snapshot of Bora Bora filled the screen. *Mom: The view I woke up to this morning!* I felt a familiar prick of jealousy. Wouldn't it be nice, traveling like my parents did, relaxing by turquoise waters? Surely all the tension would leave my shoulders if I could just sit in the sun long enough.

At least we had a yacht party for tonight. Maybe I could pretend it was anchored in Bora Bora and not a frigid New England harbor.

The line gradually inched forward, far too slowly given how cold it was. Ivy whispered first to Cameron and then to me: "Let me do the talking." When she spoke to the security guard with the guest list, she rested a hand on his forearm and smiled through her electric-red lipstick and thickly mascaraed lashes.

Cameron and I exchanged looks. We'd seen her charm her way into extra fries or free drinks, but onto a yacht?

The guard, staring at Ivy, waved us through, and the New England winter transformed into an upscale tropical paradise. Palms and vines swayed in the heated indoor space, miniature umbrellas leaned on the rims of colorful drinks, servers in skimpy swimsuits carried trays high above their heads. The space was divided into thirds: a dance floor, an indoor swimming pool, and a bar and dining area.

This definitely beat the faculty and staff holiday party. Hands down. It might even be a good stopgap for Bora Bora.

A bit stunned, I followed Ivy toward the bar, where she mumbled something about needing to thank the host and then disappeared. For a moment, Cameron and I stood by the bar—which was a giant tropical fish tank—taking it all in.

He touched my elbow and nodded toward a wall. "Didn't Ivy paint that?"

He was right. Thick layers of bright paints were slathered over a canvas, in exactly the style that Ivy had done on commission a few years ago. How—

"Gin and tonic?" Cameron asked.

"Sure, sounds good."

He maneuvered closer to the bartender, his easy smile and friendly manners quickly earning him smiles from total strangers.

While Cameron charmed passersby, a man with perfect golden-blond hair and a slim-cut suit appeared next to me. He smiled with the bright ease of someone who'd had enough alcohol to lower his inhibitions but not enough to make him obnoxious—yet.

"I don't think I've seen you here before." He gestured at my face with his Guinness.

"I'm new here."

He grinned. "This is like a throwback to college days, huh?"

Not any college I'd ever been to.

"Right," I said, "those good ol' days."

"So tell me." He stepped closer. "Are you here for the business or the fun?"

Ivy hadn't mentioned which business all these "drunk businesspeople" were supposed to be involved in, so—"I'm here for the fun."

Guinness's smile took on an edge. "Excellent. Want to dance?"

Glancing around for Cameron and Ivy, I couldn't spot them. The lone bartender was busy with a large crowd, so Cameron would be a long while, and Ivy must've been tied up with the host. Besides, wasn't the point of being here to meet someone new? "Sure."

We moved to the dance floor at the edge of the pool, swaying with the bass. The light of the chandelier above us cast a glow over everyone and Guinness looked charming in the glass refractions, his golden hair glinting.

One hand still curved around his drink, he rested his free hand on my hip. He moved closer, in perfect rhythm with me and the music. Drunk businesspeople certainly had moves.

His lips brushed my ear. "You're beautiful."

It was nice, feeling charmed.

I took a breath to answer him with my own compliment—probably about his pretty hair—when my gaze locked on Cameron. He stood across the room, leaning one shoulder against an exposed pillar. I smiled at him, but he didn't return it. He just stared. My rhythm faltered. Tossing back the last of his drink —which actually might have been the gin and tonic he got for me—he moved through the crowd without the ease and friendliness he'd had earlier. No mischief lit his face. He didn't look away from me—not once—and I forgot that Guinness existed at all.

Cameron broke eye contact when he reached us, glancing at Guinness before opening his mouth to speak.

The crowd on the dance floor surged, jostling us toward the pool. Cameron's hands reached for me at the same moment Guinness let go of me. An instant passed as we fell into the pool, and then warm, chlorinated water surged up my nose. Even though I didn't stay under for long, I gulped breaths when my head broke through the surface of the water. The shock of suddenly being in the water, not to mention Cameron's actions, had left me breathless.

"Pool party!" someone yelled—it sounded like Guinness—and people jumped in at random. The water churned, and chaos reigned. The suits and tuxedos and gowns made a colorful kaleidoscope in the turquoise water.

Cameron grasped my hand underwater. "Are you okay?"

"Yes. Are you?" I sputtered around a wave of water when someone cannonballed next to me.

A man swam into view but I didn't recognize him until he spoke. The dim lighting of the chandelier was replaced with the harsh blue glow of underwater pool lights, and his golden hair was now flat against his head. He looked completely different. Wet Guinness was not at all attractive.

"Did you bring a swimsuit?" Guinness asked.

Irritation jabbed at me. Did I *look* like I was expecting a late-night swim? "No."

He grinned. "I don't mind."

And that was my cue to leave. I already felt disoriented from the surprise swim, but this? It wasn't his fault we were in the pool, or that he looked bad without his golden hair, but it *was* his fault for suggesting skinny-dipping at this exact moment.

Book note: The appeal of skinny-dipping relies entirely on the context.

I turned away and followed Cameron to the edge of the pool, moving through the water in that vaguely weightless slow stride I'd seen Grandma use in her water aerobics classes. He climbed out first and then turned to offer me a hand.

I looked up. *Oh.*

Mr. Darcy at the lake had nothing on Cameron emerging from the pool. Clingy, wet clothes; rivulets of water streaming down his chest; his cowlick sticking on end even as it dripped. Frantically looking away, I took his hand. I couldn't let Cameron see me staring—he'd never let me live it down.

He easily pulled me from the water. "I'm not sure what happened back there."

Back on the dance floor, two men stood in the middle, security guards holding them back while they strained to throw punches.

"Looks like a scuffle," I said. My gaze darted around, torn between my eagerness to stare at Cameron and dread that he'd notice my gaze.

He handed me a towel from a lounge chair. He looked around as we dried, thankfully not seeming to notice that I was facing inner conflict. My gaze pulled toward him again, but I didn't want him to catch me, so I tried to look away. Then again, if this was my only chance to stare, then maybe I should stare to my heart's content. Maybe I should've flirted with him at his Trivia Tuesday bar. Maybe tonight could've gone so differently.

Just friends.

"Is he coming?" Cameron said.

It took a moment for me to realize he meant Guinness. "I don't think so."

His lips quirked. "Not your type?"

"No." *Maybe you're my type.* I squashed the thought as quickly as I had it.

We agreed to find Ivy. I let him lead the way so I could commit a little more Cameron-turned-Mr. Darcy to memory, and we eventually ran across her dancing with a man in a fancy suit, looking as natural as her painting in the hallway did with its perfect framing and lighting.

She noticed us and walked away from the man without a second glance. For a moment, his shoulders slumped as he looked after her. But soon he shrugged and turned to another woman.

"I heard someone fell in the pool," Ivy said, "but I wouldn't have guessed it was you two."

"Mel's man of the moment was there, too. I'm sure we can blame him for it somehow." His smile turned teasing.

"Ian punched Auguste in the nose for dancing with his girl."

I blinked at her. "How do you know that?"

"Networking."

"Is that how your paintings got here?" Cameron said. "I've noticed two already."

"That was a long time ago." She turned away. "Let's go find you some dry clothes."

Ivy led a winding route through the dance floor, past the bar, and into back hallways with dim lighting and sharp corners. It was more maze than yacht. She opened a side door to a medium-sized bedroom and gestured toward the huge closets, their doors standing open.

"My friend's crowd tends to forget their clothes when they party at her place," she said. "You don't want to know the details. She has them cleaned and then keeps them here until a charity donation can be made. You're welcome to any of it."

I shifted my weight in my soggy shoes. "This feels weird, raiding a stranger's lost and found closet."

"Didn't we just crash a stranger's yacht party?" Cameron teased.

He had a point.

Cameron took the first shirt and pants he could find. "Good thing she cleans these first, right?"

Ivy laughed. "She doesn't clean them. She has them cleaned. That distinction matters in this world."

I fingered a wool coat. It felt soft and expensive. "We saw you dancing with someone. What's he like?"

She rolled her eyes. "I was just killing time. You two want to stick around for longer or call it quits?"

Cameron looked at me. "It's your list, Mel, so it's your call."

"Ivy, did you want to dance more with—"

"Definitely not. He was too gropey."

I tugged a top and skirt from a coat hanger. "Okay. Let's go."

"When we get to the security guard, I'll do all the talking."

Cameron studied her. "Ivy, are we not really supposed to be here?"

She laughed, her red lipstick framing a perfect smile. "It's fine. Just change your clothes, and we'll go."

The door closed softly behind her. Only then did I realize there wasn't a bathroom, just this medium-sized bedroom and its oversized closets. I glanced around the suddenly small space. We were supposed to change our clothes where, exactly?

We stared at one another. I tried not to think about Cameron's wet clothes, or his strong grip when he pulled me from the pool. I tried not to notice the way the low bedroom lighting darkened his eyes. I failed.

Cameron cleared his throat and pointed toward the opposite side of the room. "This corner is mine. No peeking, got it? I can't risk jeopardizing my modest reputation."

A laugh caught in my throat. I floundered for something clever to say as he strode the few steps away. When he saw me still staring, he twirled his finger in the universal "turn around" gesture. I turned. Curious to see if he was watching to make sure I didn't endanger his "modest reputation," I glanced over my shoulder to glimpse him pulling his shirt over his head in a single movement. When I blinked in surprise, he'd already worked his wet dress pants halfway to his knees.

I turned around so quickly that I almost ran my face into the wall. But on that wall was a framed photograph in black and white, and its glass mirrored Cameron's corner in a hazy reflection. A reflection of a completely pants-less Cameron.

Lean muscles and skin and—

Focus, Mel. Stop drooling.

As quickly as my shaking fingers could, I slipped out of my soaked dress and pulled on the dry skirt and top. If I'd had more mental wherewithal, not to mention privacy, I would've wrung out my bra and panties, but not here. Not now.

My eyes—the traitors!—wandered to the glass again. The borrowed jeans were too big for him, hanging loose on his hips, showing a strip of his boxers, so when he half-turned and pulled the dry shirt over his head—

Were those actual *pecs* on Cameron's chest?

And were those...miniature cartoon Albert Einsteins on his boxers?

"Let me know when you're decent."

His voice snapped me out of my ogling. I took a moment to collect myself before I said, "Decent."

I faced him with what I hoped looked like a normal smile on my face, and we opened the door to find Ivy standing in the hallway.

The three of us wove our way across the deck and toward the exit. Even more people had joined the crowd while we were rummaging through the huge closet. The "drunk businesspeople" made it difficult to move around. Maybe stowing away on a Navy ship would've been a better idea. At least the people would've been sober. Maybe.

At the top of the gangway, Ivy gestured for us to walk in front of her. I glanced back to see the security guard frown at her when she strolled by. I kept walking. The longer we were here, the more out of place I felt. Cameron's question, "Are we not really supposed to be here?" came back to me.

We reached the polished boards of the pier and started toward the dimly lit shoreline when a gruff voice called to us.

"Hey! You!" A few heavy footsteps sounded on the gangway and then halted. "Ivy Lunden!"

From behind me, Ivy shoved my shoulder with more strength than I expected from her lanky limbs. "Faster!" Her long legs wobbled in her heels as she hurried down the polished boards.

After exchanging a brief, wide-eyed look, Cameron lengthened his strides, and I tried to keep up in my own heels.

Cameron glanced behind us. "Was that part of the plan?"

Cameron didn't sound winded at all, but then again, he wasn't power walking in high heels. Apparently his Mr. Darcy physique wasn't just for show. Maybe I needed to start working out with him. I instantly vetoed the thought.

We piled into Ivy's car. She started the ignition, and even though no guards were in sight, she peeled away from her parking spot.

"Ivy?" Cameron spoke first. "What—"

She laughed, her face lighting up like I hadn't seen in too long. "We should definitely crash yacht parties more often!"

"Crash?" I echoed. "How did that guy know your name?"

"I was kidding when I said we were crashing it earlier." Cameron's stunned words didn't faze her. "I thought your friend got us in?"

She rolled her eyes. "Don't take everything so literally, Cam. Relax." Her eyes flicked to mine. "It's too late to worry about it now anyway."

So we actually had crashed a yacht party. Great.

One positive was that I'd gotten a new perspective of Cameron, his pecs, and his Einstein boxers. Or was that a negative? The lines felt blurry, but nestled into the warmth of Ivy's car and watching the lights of the dock fading behind us, I couldn't bring myself to regret any of it just then.

CHAPTER 20

MEL

Mel: Back to Cam's love life for a second. How will he meet "the right woman" if he doesn't even try? He never dates.
Ivy: Cam is beyond me. He could be with any girl he wants.
Mel: That's my point. He checks all the boxes. Does he have a defect that we don't know about that scares women away?
Ivy: A defect other than puns?
Mel: Aw, his puns are cute. A little lame, but cute.
Ivy: If you think that, then maybe you're the right woman for him.
Mel: Very funny.

"Which mancounter should I try next?" I shoved my laptop and a few folders into my work bag. "Maybe 'go to a high school reunion'? That could be an adventure. Or maybe I should 'change careers for a government job.' Because it's definitely a good idea to base huge career decisions on the hypothetical off chance of meeting my soulmate."

Silence. I turned to see Ivy glued to her cell phone—again. Why was she always on her phone these days? Was she trying a new dating app? Had she met someone?

Before I could call her out on it, Cameron strolled across the lobby. I noticed he wore that easygoing smile he always had at the end of the workday, like he didn't have a care beyond drinking a beer at our Monday game night tonight. They'd been good sports about the list—we all needed a break. Especially me, struggling with too many pool-related memories of Cameron at the yacht party.

He stopped in the doorway. "So I heard it finally happened."

Ivy didn't look up from her texting. "What happened?"

I stared at him. "Don't even."

Setting aside her phone, Ivy grinned in anticipation. "Now I *really* need to know."

Cameron kept a straight face. "Mel found some extra theater tickets to the university production."

"Impressive, Mel," Ivy said. "Those extra tickets are like gold around here."

He cleared his throat. "Then Mel asked Vernon to go to the play with her."

The only sound was Ivy's gasp. "No," she murmured. "Mel? Please tell me you didn't."

I tried for a nonchalant shrug. "I thought it might help to smooth over the walnut thing. I didn't know, okay?"

"How could you not know? He came to the last three holiday parties with his boyfriend."

I spread my palms in surrender. "I wasn't aware of that at the time, okay? Can we please just drop it?"

Judging from Cameron's smile, he was enjoying this way too much. "Like drop it as quickly as he let you down? Because I heard it was lightning speed. Ivy and I can't drop this that quickly. Nobody can drop anything that quickly."

Ivy frowned at me. "I'm going to set aside the fact that I don't understand how you didn't know, and instead I'm going to ask if you're okay?"

"I'd be better if we stopped talking about this."

Cameron laughed. "Come on. It's funny."

I shook my head and tried to think of a way to change the subject. There had to be a way I could get out of this conversation. "You weren't there."

"But I've heard all about it," Cameron volunteered with a grin.

Equal parts exasperated and amused, I crossed my arms over my chest. "How do you always hear the campus rumors first? Do you have the whole university wire tapped?"

"It's not my fault I'm charming and irresistible." He smiled.

"Details, people, details," Ivy complained.

Reliving one of my most embarrassing moments was not something I wanted to do tonight. Yet another mancounter failure for the book. "I'm not friends with either of you anymore," I muttered.

Cameron rubbed his palms together like he was warming up for an athletic event. "Okay, here's what I heard. Our darling Mel had these theater tickets in her pocket all day, not thinking anything of it. There was a community outreach event in the café in Montgomery Hall, so she stopped by to check it out. While she was at the event, she noticed Vernon. She made one of the worst decisions of her life, walked up to him, and asked him to go to the play."

"I had good intentions," I insisted, even as I watched as the picture Cameron painted unfolded in my mind. "Like I said, the walnut thing."

Cameron waved a hand to shush me. "So Mel asks him to the play while he's standing right next to his date for the event."

"No!" Ivy gasped.

"Yes!" Cameron was having too much fun leaning into the drama of his story.

I piped up. "I thought they were just friends."

Unfazed, Cameron continued. "So then Vernon was confused because he thought everyone knew about his boyfriend. His boyfriend was confused because he also thought everyone knew. Mel was confused because she was the one person who didn't know. Then Mel asked a second time if he'd like to go to the play."

"It was loud in there," I protested. "I thought he didn't hear me the first time."

"So then Vernon proceeded to explain to Mel, politely but in very clear terms, all the ways he's very happy with his current boyfriend."

Ivy turned sympathetic eyes to me. "Was it a public scene?"

"Extremely," Cameron said.

I rested my forehead on the desk in front of me, remembering the faces of my colleagues, Dr. Schaaf, my students that I tutored... "Someone please kill me."

Cameron continued. "The best part is that Mel felt so bad that she sold him the theater tickets so he and his boyfriend could go to the play together."

"Wait." Ivy's chair squeaked as she shifted. "You *sold* them?"

I could practically hear Cameron's teasing grin. "You greedy little capitalist, Mel."

I kept my head on the desk. "I tried to give them to him, but he felt so sorry for me that he insisted on paying me."

A beat passed as Ivy put the pieces together. "So that post Vernon shared about enjoying the play tonight...?"

Cameron laughed. "You were gifted a post of those two extremely handsome men on your feed thanks to Mel's capitalist ventures."

"I really did try to give him the tickets," I mumbled, lifting my head.

He turned his blue eyes to me, the corners crinkling in amusement. "Isn't it at least a little funny?"

Ivy bit her lip, a gesture that she always used to hold back a laugh. "It is kind of funny. Not as funny as almost killing Vernon with walnuts, but awfully close."

I fought back my own smile.

"We should make a new list." Cameron began counting on his fingers. "One, walnuts kill. Two, beware of coworkers' current relationships."

Ivy grinned. "We'll have several more to add by the time you're done with the list, Mel."

"Don't worry. We won't fail you." He straightened his shirt collar in exaggerated self-importance. "We are your faithful scribes."

Unable to hold back any longer, I smiled. "Okay, hearing it all again, it's a little funny."

"Who else don't you know about, Mel?" Ivy tapped a finger on her lower lip. "Cam, we need to protect her from her own cluelessness."

I laughed outright. "I'm not *that* bad!"

"I have some hard news for you." Cameron faced me in mock seriousness. "Ellen and Elton John."

I rolled my eyes. "Everyone knows about them."

Ivy laughed. "Everyone knows about Vernon!"

"Or so we thought," Cameron added.

"I'm just sad you gave him those tickets," Ivy said.

He pretended to cough the word "sold," and Ivy laughed.

I smiled at their antics. "The whole thing was a bust. No tickets. No date. Endless embarrassment. Now I try not to think about it. Except you two keep reminding me."

Ivy's lips twitched with the effort to hide her smile. "Sorry. We'll stop."

Cameron grinned, folding his arms across his chest. "Speak for yourself."

"Very funny, Cam," I said. "Don't think I won't retaliate. I see you at work every day."

"But will we see Vernon? Which of our unsuspecting coworkers will you target next?"

Laughing, I stood from my desk. As much as it was a little funny now that it was over, I felt like a failure—again—and wanted to share a peaceful Monday night with my two best friends. Was that too much to ask?

I reached for my work bag. "Anyway. Enough of this. Just let me pack—"

"Dr. Whitacre!" Alma's call was almost shrill. "Finally! Dr. Whitacre!"

CHAPTER 21

MEL

Ivy: My personal favorite from the list so far: "Hide your diploma." Some things never change. Men will never want a woman with brains.
Cameron: Sometimes I worry that you two forget I'm a man.
Mel: You're the exception to the rule.

Alma scurried toward Cameron, her combat boots skidding to a stop next to him, the weight of her enormous bookbag almost toppling her over, but again, she somehow recovered. She defied physics, I was sure of it.

"Dr. Whitacre, my name is Alma." She offered a handshake. "I'm a student writer for *The Courier*, and I've been trying to reach you about that article."

If I hadn't known him for the last five years, I might've missed the way he looked at her: like she was Charlotte Lucas, and he was Elizabeth Bennet, and she'd just told him that she was engaged to Mr. Collins. His expression was horror tinged with dread. Then Cameron shook her hand, and the look was gone.

Maybe I'd taken the Cameron-turned-Darcy thing too far.

"Hi, Alma. Pleased to meet you. Sorry we've been playing a bit of tag. I'll get back to you tomorrow about when we can interview—"

"What about right now?" she interrupted. "I'm free tonight."

"I have plans." He gestured toward me and Ivy. "But maybe—"

"You can do the interview now," I said, giving him a questioning look. "We can wait for you and start our usual Monday night a little later than we'd planned."

"No, we don't have to reschedule. This interview will take a long time, won't it, since I'm like the feature topic, right?" He flashed a good-humored grin at Alma. "So we can touch base tomorrow and—"

"The interview should take about thirty minutes," Alma said, "so now is perfect." Her bookbag nearly shook the room when she dropped it next to the front desk. In seconds, she whipped out her phone's voice recorder, a notebook, and a pen.

"It's really not necessary to do this now—"

"First and last name and official job title. Just for the record." Alma angled her phone toward him.

He frowned and tugged at the cuffs of his sleeves. "Cameron Whitacre. Computer science adjunct professor and director of IT services. But I like to call myself computer science mind-bender and IT department wizard." His eyes didn't crinkle when he smiled.

Alma interrogated him with standard questions about his education and background, and Cameron answered with more goofiness than usual, even by his standards. ("What, you think I'll try to pad my résumé and say I got my degrees from Oxford? Joke's on you, because I already hacked Google to pad it for me." "Raised by my father, mother, and bossy older sister who thought she was my second, better mother.")

Alma shifted in her seat. "I understand you decided to transfer colleges after about two years of undergrad. Why?"

"Just needed a change."

I'd been faking doing some busy work, and Ivy had been tapping on her phone, but we both froze at her next question.

"Did it have anything to do with your stroke?"

This student had the subtlety of a nuclear missile. She didn't know Cameron, so she couldn't know how closed off he was about that part of his life—but bringing up such a personal topic should have called for all the more tact on her part. Hadn't any of her professors taught her the social codes of an interview?

His sharp tone belied his casual posture. "Don't all of us need a change sometimes?"

"That doesn't really answer my question."

"Since when is it against interview rules to answer a question with a question? Politicians do it all the time."

She paused the recording. "Look, Dr. Whitacre. They assigned these profiles to lots of students. But I specifically asked to write about you. Because I believe that a profile about an overcomer is inspiring."

I looked at Ivy.

Ivy looked at me.

We both looked at Cameron.

He sat completely still. "I'm not a human-interest piece."

"You're right. And I won't write about you like that. Because the second reason I asked to write your profile is because I have experience with someone who felt like their story owned them until they wrote it down and made it tangible so that they could own it themselves." She looked down at her boots. "It's not overwhelming anymore. It's just a piece of paper with some ink spots."

I took it back about her not understanding the social codes of an interview. Alma knew exactly what she was doing.

Cameron stared at her. His face was expressionless except for three lines between his eyebrows. It was almost visible, the way his usual shield of humor fell away. I'd never seen him without that protection before. He looked vulnerable and a little sad.

Alma pressed "record" on her phone again. "Did transferring colleges during your undergrad years have anything to do with the stroke?"

His chest wasn't moving—was he even breathing? The only sign of life was a muscle pulsing in his temple. He looked down at his hands, tugging at his cuffs again. When he spoke, his voice was a whisper. "People never talk about what it's like in those first moments. You come to, and there's so much noise and light. All these doctors and nurses poking and prodding. And then you realize your body doesn't move when your brain tells it to. It's terrifying. Almost as terrifying as when it first happens, when you feel that break between your brain and your body. But when it's actually happening, there's this thought that it's just a nightmare. Or a fluke. But then you wake up hours later, and you're still like that..." The laugh that huffed from his lips sounded flat, not at all like the Cameron I knew.

He cleared his throat. His eyes fixed on his hands, the floor, the office plant, anywhere but on Alma, Ivy, or me. "I didn't just transfer colleges. I dropped out because I spent a few years in rehab. I had to relearn how to live, basically. I stayed with my parents. My mom had to feed me by hand every day. Wipe me like I was a baby all over again. Not much is more embarrassing than that to a twenty-year-old guy. I was the star basketball player at my college, carrying my team and even winning a championship. And then, in a split second, I was a heap of bones that couldn't even twitch a finger on my own." He half-smiled. "Feel free to leave those details off the record."

I swallowed the ache in my throat. I'd known the vaguest details about the stroke, but I hadn't known exactly what it had done to his life. Imagining young Cameron, full of the idealistic energy that I saw in my students each day, facing this kind of hardship—my chest squeezed.

His twitchy fingers had moved from his cuffs to dig at a fingernail. "I was lucky enough that my arm movement came back relatively quickly, but my legs took longer. By then my college friends and teammates were graduating and moving on with their lives. And I couldn't even walk. So I cut them out of my life. That's one of my biggest regrets, I think, isolating myself."

The left corner of his mouth quirked into a half-smile. "Anyway, my physical therapist wouldn't let me quit. He's the only person I know who's more stubborn than I am. He pulled me—no, he *forced* me out of it. He wouldn't let me stop. He still keeps an eye on me to make sure I'm not slacking off. We work out together almost every day now. He's good people."

I couldn't wrench my gaze away from him. Cameron looked new somehow. Less goofy sidekick. More human, more real. The silence felt delicate, like a poorly timed breath would shatter the momentum he'd built.

Alma's voice was softer than it had been before. "Do you still struggle with depression?"

"Sometimes."

She allowed for a pause before saying, "When did the stroke happen?"

"Just out of the blue when I was walking to class on a Tuesday. I'd had a headache for about a week, and it got worse every day, but between finals and basketball training, I didn't think anything of it. Then, walking to class, my ears started ringing, my heart was racing, and I felt too hot. The nausea hit next. When my left leg went numb, I tried to tell a friend that something was wrong, but my words were so slurred that he couldn't understand me. I ended up passing out on the sidewalk. When I woke up, I'd already spent two nights in the ICU."

"Are there any residual side effects from the stroke?"

"I have a little numbness in my cheek. And my smile is crooked."

His smile was crooked? His smile was perfect. He was always smiling. How could he be self-conscious about it? Unless it was another barrier, like his jokes.

When he didn't continue, Alma said, "What inspired you to keep going?"

"Toby." Cameron's face relaxed. "He can be incredibly annoying. It was an irritating method at the time, but it worked."

"He's your...brother?"

"No, this is Toby Azumah. Then-physical therapist, now-friend."

Ivy dropped her phone with a muffled thud against the cheap carpeting, and she mumbled a quiet apology.

Alma continued, unfazed. None of Cameron's words seemed to make her emotional in the least. Her lack of tact gave her nerves of steel. Meanwhile, I was a mess of half-held breaths and watery eyes, barely managing to stay upright at my desk.

"So Toby, and not your family?"

He hesitated. "Sometimes the love from family isn't what you need. They were going to love me no matter what. And I'll always be grateful for that. But sometimes you need people who will push you a little harder to become a better person."

"How did other people treat you after the stroke?"

"With pity. Like they thought I was fragile. I hated it."

My mind frantically sorted through memories of my time with Cameron. Had I ever treated him like he was breakable? How punishing that must feel for him, an independent, intelligent person who'd had to work twice as hard for his life to look as normal as anyone else's. But it was Cameron's life, and this was his story, and I couldn't look away.

"Do people still treat you differently now?"

"Not as much. Until they hear about it, anyway."

Her voice softened. "Another reason not to talk about it."

He shrugged. "I just want to build the life I want, like anyone else. I don't want my stroke to define me."

"So what did people do that was most helpful for you? Like what parts of your support system were most valuable?"

He thought for a moment, his eyes shadowed by the dark frames of his glasses. "This wouldn't be true for everyone, but for me, the most helpful people—other than Toby being a bully—just gave me space. They let me grieve for my old life, which is something I still struggle to move past some-times. They let me build something new for myself."

His eyes lifted to mine. The veneer he presented to the world was gone. This was just Cam, weaknesses and strengths, scars and hopes. And he was looking at me.

My chest felt cottony and warm again, but underneath the softness was the jagged, broken weight of his story. We blinked in unison.

The moment splintered when Alma paused the recording. "I think that's it." Moving quickly, she tucked her phone into her pocket and slung her enormous bookbag onto her shoulders. "Thank you, Dr. Whitacre. I really appreciate it. I'll let you know if I have any further questions as I write the article over the next week or so."

He nodded.

Alma clomped away. Without her, the silence around us felt thick, almost gelatinous, as I tried to force my brain past Cameron's story and back into working order. No wonder he kept this part of his life private. Sitting in the corner, Ivy looked as stunned as I felt. She kept popping her knuckles. Over. And over.

My eyes burned with tears. I wanted to cry for twenty-year-old Cameron Whitacre, for everything he'd lost, for everything he'd rebuilt over the years. I wanted to hug him and tell him how incredible he was.

Cameron tugged at his sleeves. "I think I'll just head home tonight."

"No game night?" Panic surged through my chest. He couldn't leave. Not when he'd said all that. He couldn't just walk away and expect us to have Monday night without him. I wanted to be there for him, not send him home alone.

He wouldn't look at me as he turned toward the lobby. "See you two later."

Ivy remained quiet. I sat numbly, thinking of Cameron all alone in his silent condo, surrounded by screens, and I thought of how he'd said the most helpful people gave him space. But right now he was asking for the last thing I wanted to give him. He needed space, but I ached to smother him with my mismatched pillows and throw blankets and vanilla candles. A Moscow mule or *Star Wars* movie. Anything to lift that slump from his shoulders.

CHAPTER 22

CAMERON

From: Alma Torres
To: Cameron Whitacre
Subject: RE: Interview Request – The Courier

Dr. Whitacre,

*Thank you so much for our interview earlier! I know you were a bit nervous,
so when I finish writing it, I'll send it to you so that you can read it before we
send it to press. If you have any suggestions for improving the article, just let
me know!*

Thank you again,
Alma

As soon as the door to my condo closed, I leaned against it, slumping all the
way down to the floor. A beer from the fridge sounded perfect. But the thought
of moving? Not so much.

Alma was the definition of overeager. It was obvious in her emails, but in
person? Her questions had sliced until there wasn't much left of me. She'd cut
through my nonchalance like it was nothing. I felt naked.

And Mel and Ivy had been there to see it. Ivy wasn't that big of a deal. Her opinion didn't matter to me as much. But Mel? Why couldn't Mel have left it alone and backed me up when I tried to sidestep Alma's interview? The resentment I'd felt toward Mel after the mancounter with Gnomeo had lessened over time, especially since I'd had a new set of feelings about Mel after we'd changed clothes on the yacht. The sound of her wet dress dropping to the floor had kept my pathetic imagination overactive for days. But now my hurt was back in full force. Fine, friend-zone me—but don't sacrifice me to *The Courier's* Emperor Palpatine-in-training.

Alma's rationale for the article sounded like something Toby would say. Write down the pain to make it more manageable. What a load of motivational mumbo jumbo.

Really, I should call Toby. He'd be here in an instant. We'd talk it over. I'd feel better after hearing his metaphors for pain and life (even if I mocked him through every word of it, diffusing awkwardness and clinging to the last few scraps of my emotional dignity).

But I couldn't keep using him as a crutch. His support was great. I needed it more than I wanted to admit. But someday I would need to deal with this rawness on my own. Avoiding the subject had worked pretty well for the past decade, but apparently the lifespan on that coping mechanism was coming to an end.

My phone screen glowed in the darkness, showing the time. I'd give myself five more minutes to wallow, and then I'd pull on my sneakers and go for a run. It would snap me out of this. While I distracted myself with a run, I should also distract myself by texting Cheyenne. That was one way to deal with my irritation with Mel, right?

But instead I sat there, picturing the life I wanted. The full-time position. Maybe sell my condo and buy a house. I could have a dog. Might as well cut Mel out of the picture—but maybe some other girl would come along at some point. We'd have that white-picket-fence life. And it would be good. Life was good.

Who was I kidding? It'd been how many days, and I still hadn't texted Cheyenne since that speakerphone mishap with my family. Mel was, by default, the only one in the picture because I couldn't manage to take the first step to moving on.

I mentally went through the motions of tapping on the icon for my contacts, searching for Cheyenne's number, texting her. *Hi, Cheyenne. My name is Cameron, and my brother-in-law, Derek, told me he thought we had a lot in common and would hit it off. I wondered if you'd be up for meeting for a coffee or drinks sometime in the next few weeks?* Straightforward, friendly, without being aggressive or creepy. Maybe we'd meet somewhere, get to know one another. Maybe we really would hit it off.

I felt even more queasy at that thought.

I locked my phone screen. Three more minutes to feel naked and raw. Then I'd pick myself up.

CHAPTER 23

MEL

Mel: Have I got a story for you. I took a wilderness survival class this week-end. Did you know people wear sunscreen even when it's snowy outside? A LOT of sunscreen.
Ivy: Yes. Welcome to pasty life.
Mel: But this guy wasn't that fair skinned. And the sunscreen was just in one thick stripe down the center of his nose. And he was barefoot.
Ivy: In the snow?!
Cameron: Please tell me both of his feet are like the legendary Mr. Deeds foot.
Mel: No Mr. Deeds feet.
Cameron: Hobbit feet?
Mel: Just normal, human-looking feet. That apparently don't feel a thing.

The list said to "draw, paint, or knit outside an engineering office or school." Art was beyond my skillset—that was Ivy's world—but I could read a book on a park bench like nobody's business. With sunshine and no wind, it was a beautiful day to read outside. So what if it just happened to be immediately outside the front door of the engineering building on a day when a guest speaker was giving a presentation, and engineers from around the city would be there? It was a happy accident.

That morning, I took extra care getting ready. I tamed most of the frizz out of my wavy hair—something I usually reserved for only special occasions—and wore my cutest hat and scarf set since I'd be sitting outside in the cold. I came prepared with my largest thermos full of hot tea. I hadn't accounted for the chill the park bench would send through my layers when I sat down, but such was the cost of husband hunting.

Honestly, the hardest part was deciding what book to bring with me. Ivy had tried to help.

"What about nonfiction?" she'd asked over the phone last night. "Engineers are logical, practical people. Maybe they would like a nonfiction girl."

"But what kind of nonfiction? Not everyone is a Wendell Berry or Annie Dillard fan, even though everyone on planet Earth should be. This book will be at the core of my meet-cute. It needs to set the tone for our hypothetical relationship."

"Something...engineering?"

"You've seen my bookshelf. I don't do engineering books."

"Oh, please. You do all books. Don't you have a book about the first submersible? Allen?"

"It's Alvin, and yes, I do have that book." I'd pulled it from the shelf. "But it's the only book like this on my shelf. Is it false advertising to act like I read books like this all the time?"

"Aren't *all* of your mancounters based on false advertising?" She'd mumbled something to someone in the background before returning to our conversation. "Let's think about the original advice from the article: paint in front of an engineering building. So maybe go a totally different route. Something artsy. Isn't poetry the painting form of writing?"

My poetry section suddenly felt too large to choose just one. "Are we thinking Pablo Neruda, Mary Oliver, Edna St. Vincent Millay? What about going old school with Elizabeth Barrett Browning or Christina Rossetti? What about tragically beautiful with Anna Akhmatova?" I'd audited a Russian literature course with Luca Kroft a few semesters ago, begging Ivy to sign me up before his classes filled. Offering to buy her margaritas for the next six months had been more than worth it.

I could almost hear her eyes rolling over the phone. "Now you're in too deep for me. I know better than to tell you how to choose your poetry. But do you think Neruda is a good idea? His lascivious love poetry might get you some attention, but those poems are liable to start steaming up your glasses, and then all the engineers won't be able to see your pretty eyes."

"Fair point. Neruda might get me booked for public indecency."

So I'd settled for a basic collection of poetry. The best of all poetry worlds I could choose from.

I cracked open my book. It was all going according to plan: look cute, arrive fifteen minutes before the presentation was scheduled to end, read book. But I couldn't focus.

My mind wandered again and again to Cameron's interview a few days ago. I couldn't imagine how he'd lost everything and started over again. Relearning to walk when he should've been in his prime years? I could imagine how he'd respond to that assessment—"Who says I'm not in my prime years now?"—but I still couldn't recognize the Dr. Cameron Whitacre I knew now with the hospital patient he'd described. I imagined twenty-year-old Cameron waking up, terrified. Struggling through rehab. Watching his friends move on with their lives with infinitely more desperation than the jealousy I felt toward Always Cheerful Lisa. Isolating himself and then rebuilding his life to where he was now, with his work and fan-club students and bachelor condo.

Cameron was a real-life hero.

The morning after the interview, he'd been his cheerful, charming self at work. Like nothing had happened. But now that I'd glimpsed behind his charisma, I could see it for what it was—a wall constructed out of humor, firmly locked in place to protect him from pity.

Soon engineers began streaming out of the building. Eyes fixed on my book, I watched people out of my periphery, taking mental notes.

First. The engineers were mostly men. Not a surprise, since I knew the women in STEM statistics like any other working woman, but it was still a shock to actually see it for myself in terms of human bodies and not percentages written in an article. It was almost physical, the force of seeing so many more men than women leaving the building. Wouldn't statistics be more impactful if they always included a visual aid?

Second. Was there a uniform for engineers? No wonder there were stereotypes about bland suits and laptop backpacks. Even the few women followed the trend. Did they all shop at the same bland, androgynous place?

Third, and most worrisome for my experiment. They were all consumed by their own worlds. Almost no one looked around long enough to notice the fresh snow that had fallen during their hour-long presentation, let alone a woman sitting alone on a bench. They walked with their eyes fixed to their phones, or their phones fixed to their ears, or their footsteps fixed to follow the groups of friends and colleagues they'd attended the lecture with.

I didn't expect Prince Charming to throw himself at my feet, but I did expect at least someone to glance in my direction. Instead, not a single person even looked at me, let alone stopped to talk. So much for assuming this would be one of the easiest mancounters on the list.

Was this what the world was coming to? Was it so difficult to catch someone's notice? Maybe I should've worn brighter clothes. Or maybe fewer clothes.

The steady flow of engineers dwindled to a handful here and there. I waited patiently, pretending to read for several moments. Nobody stopped. I listened to the sound of their dress shoes, refusing to be obvious but planning to leave as soon as the sidewalks thinned out.

The sound of familiar laughter made me look up. Cameron. What was he doing here? He walked with a few others I didn't recognize. Of course he'd managed to break through the cell phone barrier. The group laughed with him, and they waved goodbye as they parted ways, probably having exchanged numbers and summer plans. It was a mystery to me, how Cameron always did this, charming total strangers with his humor and messy cowlick.

As he turned toward the parking lot, he noticed me. Head tilted to the side, he wandered over. "Hiya, Mel."

"Hiya, Cam. Want a seat?" I patted the park bench next to me.

He sat, his knee bumping into mine. "Aren't you cold?"

"A little, but it's not too bad."

"Don't you have somewhere warmer to read"—he angled his head to look at my book cover—"*The Oxford Book of English Verse*?"

"Sure, but if I park myself outside the engineering building, maybe someone will fall for my womanly wiles." I wiggled my eyebrows at him, hoping for suggestive but probably just coming across as clownish.

"The list. Of course." His smile was too small to crinkle his eyes.

"What about you? Why are you going to engineering presentations?"

He shrugged and toed the snow-dusted gravel at our feet. "Networking. There's a good amount of overlap between the IT and engineering departments. Maybe it'll help with the full-time position."

"They'd be stupid not to give you the job."

"I don't want them to give it to me. I want to earn it."

I frowned. "You've already more than earned it."

When he smiled at me, his expression held something I hadn't noticed in him before, and I couldn't quite place it. "Do you remember when we met? Both of us new hires on orientation day?"

"Of course. You were in my icebreaker group."

"After the morning session, you were trying to carry all of your books and notebooks and pens at once. Without a bookbag. You dropped a few binders.

So you handed your armload of books to me, and then you picked up the ones you'd dropped, and then we walked to the parking lot with you carrying two flimsy binders and me lugging eight massive textbooks and manuals."

I grimaced. "No way. It was only three." I had no idea how many books it was, because all I could remember was his handsome face and kindness. And he remembered my cluelessness.

"You were too distracted to notice."

"Hopefully I wasn't *that* obnoxious and cocky." I tried to laugh.

"No. You were passionate and full of life." He still smiled at me with that indefinable look.

I looked away, using my toes to dig a trench in the gravel at our feet. I'd been so certain then. But here I was, five years later, still working at the tutoring center—still just dreaming. Only the dreams were in black and white now, not 3D high-def. Somewhere in there, I'd lost my optimism.

Cameron continued. "What I instantly loved about you was that you knew what you wanted in life, and you weren't backing down. You were unstoppable."

Unguarded—that was the expression in his eyes. For only the second time since I'd known him, I was seeing Cameron without his humor shield. The gregarious bravado he kept up was gone, just like during the interview. His jokes were his walls, carefully arranged. But this new sincerity changed him. The handsomeness Ivy had mentioned shifted to something more intriguing. And right now, Cameron was looking at me like I was special to him.

What had we been talking about?

We spoke at the same time, overlapping our words.

"Look, Mel—"

"Cam, I wanted—"

He gestured for me to go first.

Now this felt awkward.

"I just wanted to say that we don't look at you any differently than we did before. You're the same Cam we know and love."

He blinked at me, his shoulders rising and falling with a deep breath. His lips parted. "I hope—"

A voice spoke from a few feet away. "You forgot, didn't you?"

Cameron jumped.

I spilled some of my hot tea down my leg. "Ivy! Don't sneak up on me like that."

"I've been stomping through this gravel for yards. I wasn't sneaking up on anyone." She crossed her arms. "You never met me at the Bluesy Bean. You're supposed to give me all the details from the engineering mancounter."

I blotted my soaked leg with my scarf. "You're right. I forgot. Sorry."

Her eyes darted between me and Cameron. "What's wrong with you two?"

"Nothing," we both said too quickly.

"Let's go to the Bluesy Bean." I stood and tugged on her arm. "Want to come, Cam?"

But he was already walking in the opposite direction. "I have plans with Toby. Maybe next time."

We parted ways, and I told Ivy about the doomed decline of humanity—or maybe just engineers—and its complete lack of awareness toward single young women on cold park benches in front of public buildings. But really, I was thinking about Cameron and what he might've been about to say.

CHAPTER 24

CAMERON

Mel: I'm wearing a Band-Aid and not a single person has asked what happened. The list lied.
Ivy: It's those laws I keep telling you about. They're called HIPAA.
Mel: It's not a HIPAA violation to ask about a Band-Aid! Or to send an email about food allergies!
Cameron: Ahem. I noticed your Band-Aid and asked what happened.
Ivy: Yeah, give Cam some credit.
Mel: Sorry, Cam. Thank you for asking after my Band-Aid.

What had I been about to say to her?

I sat at the poker table, cards in my hands, but I was thinking about Mel on that park bench, poetry book in her hands, cheeks pink from cold, pretty brown eyes looking at me, long legs crisscrossed. If I time-traveled back to that moment, what would I say?

All I knew was in that split second before we talked over one another, I felt out of control. Like the last five years of pressed-down feelings just bubbled past the breaking point. I wanted more (so much more) than friendship with Mel. I had to admit, even if only to myself, that Cheyenne (whoever she even was) wasn't for me, which was why I'd deleted her number from my phone earlier tonight. Mel was for me.

Maybe that's what I'd been about to say. Or something along those lines. "Have dinner with me" or "It's been five years and you've given me no hints that you feel like I do, but I adore you" or "They say the gift for a five-year friendship anniversary is true love."

It was always a little painful to be around Mel, but I'd never before come so close to blathering about my feelings.

It was Alma's fault. I'd felt raw since the interview a few days ago. She and her annoying article had razed the emotional dam I'd grown to rely on.

Luckily I hadn't said anything. Luckily I had a few hours before seeing Mel at work tomorrow. I had time to rebuild my dam and regain control.

Even as distracted as I was during poker, I tried to go easy on Toby (I really did) but he was not hard to read. The poor guy never stood a chance. Toby and I preferred video games, but his brothers liked the higher stakes of poker—maybe because Toby always lost his stakes in poker. He was too guileless to play the game well.

His brothers had already gone home to their wives for the night, so it was just the two of us at his apartment, playing a few final rounds of Texas Hold 'Em. An ace, queen, six, and two threes were on the table. Toby frowned at his cards, and I tried to act like I didn't know exactly what he was thinking.

When I first met Toby, he'd been a reminder of everything I'd lost. He was young, successful, and caught the eye of every girl in the therapy gym. He moved with effortless grace.

I'd hated him. And told him that to his face.

His response: "Hate me all you want. Just give me another two reps."

I later learned (overhearing a conversation between his coworkers at their literal water cooler) that his boss had told him he should give up on me. That I was a lost cause. That he should exchange me for more pleasant, lucrative clients. He hadn't listened.

That was exactly why I'd just told him about the interview with Alma. I'd tried to explain it in a neutral tone. I wanted to talk about it without any drama, with someone who was used to cutting through all the complicated mess of politics and management.

"...And then Freisen said that if I didn't go through with the article interview, my name would be knocked down a few pegs on the list of potential hires for the full-time position."

Toby gaped at me, effectively pausing the game for the moment. "He said that?"

"Using management speak, yes."

He cursed under his breath.

Navigating to my email on my phone, I showed him Alma's latest message. Sure, it was nice of her to say thank you, even though it was probably routine for these interviews, but the way my breathing eased when I'd read that she would send me the article before going to press? The spunky student was growing on me.

"You'll send me a copy of the article, right?" Toby said. "We can burn our copies together in a massive bonfire. Or in a barrel. Whatever you want."

Maybe I shouldn't have told him.

"It'll be a fluff piece," I said. "Probably just filler content for the actual paper."

"Sure, that's probably it." His tone was far from convincing.

He refocused on the game, his index finger tapping his cards. His tell. He felt good about his hand.

"All in," Toby said.

I turned my cards over. When he saw my full house, he threw his cards down in disgust. Seemed that my guess about him having two pairs was right. I gathered up the small pile of our fake money that we'd used since his brothers left—coupons for the best gourmet grilled cheese dive in town, Take It Cheesy.

"I'm done playing poker with you," he said. "You've *got* to be playing dirty."

I laughed. "Don't cry just because I'm finally better than you at something. Enjoy that humble pie with a good attitude."

He ignored me and opened another beer.

"Considering we've been playing for coupons tonight, and I know you still have more stashed in your kitchen drawer, you have no right to take this so hard," I said.

"Don't mess with my coupons. They're sacred." He began doodling in the condensation on his beer. "But back to your debut in *The Courier.* I have to admit, this student sounds like she did a good job with the interview. The article might surprise you."

"Or it'll be another sappy story for elderly college board members to cry over while they eat Sunday brunch."

He shrugged and sipped his beer. "I think she's right. Maybe having it on paper will help you feel some sense of control."

"She said sense of peace, not control." Though I could do with some control right now.

"Same difference. Most of us feel peaceful when we have more control. It's just semantics. My point is, there's a lot more to alternative therapy than people realize. Art therapy, writing therapy, music therapy. Physical therapy isn't the only way to deal with pain anymore."

I thought of the therapist my parents had tried to take me to when my depression was the worst. He'd been so fresh out of grad school that I'd been a mystery to him. Those sessions hadn't lasted long. It turned out that Toby's optimistic force was all I'd needed.

"I think you should see this as a good thing," he said. "Yes, their methods suck and are borderline HR violations, but you need more closure on this. More perspective."

"And you need to find a new source for more coupons. It looks like I'll be eating well this week."

He smiled. "This is exactly why I don't play for actual money. Your cheating is beyond me."

"It's not cheating. It's called having people skills. You should try it sometime."

He pointed a finger at me. "You're not distracting me. I have one more thing to say about this article."

"Yes, Mother."

"You can't control how people treat you or see you. But you can control how you respond to them. You choose how to respond to the way they treat you. Is it messed up that they pretty much forced you to do this so you could be considered for the full-time position? Yes. But now you can choose what to do from here."

He was right. He was always right with his "you can do it" and "be the change you want to see in the world" pep talks. But it didn't make it any easier, thinking of people reading an article that focused on the worst part of my life. Maybe they'd start looking at me closer. Maybe they'd even notice the crookedness in my smile when they hadn't before.

I resisted the impulse to rub my hand over my mouth. My own tell. A habit I'd broken long ago. Now, without my emotional dam, it fought back to the surface.

I cleared my throat. "So it's all mind over matter."

"Exactly."

"Thanks, Confucius. Now if you could rustle up a few more coupons, we'll see if you can mind-over-matter your way to winning a game of poker for once."

CHAPTER 25

CAMERON

Ivy: I can't get together tonight. Something came up. I'll make up for it next Monday night!
Cameron: Are you okay?
Ivy: Yeah, I'm fine.
Mel: We'll miss you!

I stared at my phone. *We'll miss you.* Did that mean Mel was still coming over? Without Ivy? For the first time ever?

I sat bolt upright on my sofa. Urgency and anxiety struck me like Mel hadn't already been here a dozen times before (always with Ivy). All of the cleaning I'd done earlier was no longer enough. Mel was coming over. Alone.

Like an elementary student who'd received a birthday party RSVP from the most popular kid at school (not that I had any personal experience with that, of course), I ricocheted around my condo. Everything was just wrong. I already cleaned more for Monday nights than I did any other time. But it didn't matter. When I saw a shadow of lint on the carpet, I picked at it; when I noticed a dirty plate in the sink, I hid it in the cabinet because she could be at my door any second; when I saw that the photos Samantha left behind weren't perfectly symmetrical, I straightened the frames.

Everything was still wrong.

Should I put on some music? What would I even choose? The yacht party floated through my mind, specifically Mel on the dance floor, and then Mel in wet clothes, and then the rustling sound of Mel changing her clothes just a few feet from me—

No music.

Giving up on my condo, I threw my shirt in the hamper and pulled another from the closet. This would be the first real time I'd spent with Mel since that interview with Alma. And since my broken dam nearly let loose my feelings on a cold park bench. Anxiety had already been seesawing against my rational thinking all day, and that was when it was Mel and Ivy coming over together. But now, with just Mel?

The new shirt was too green. Another shirt. It was too blue. Another shirt. It was too red—

A knock at the door.

Mel.

The red would have to do.

I paused in the bathroom for a quick teeth check. (Broccoli bits always show up at the worst moments. It's a scientific fact. I'm sure of it.) Wetting my fingers, I tried to straighten my hair. No luck. And now I noticed that the squeeze in my chest was plainly obvious on my face.

Definitely not okay. I took a slow, deep breath. Then again. Ready or not.

She smiled at me when I opened the door. She was all pretty brown eyes and flyaway curls and comfort. Absolutely lovely. Absolutely Mel.

My teetering world tilted back upright on its axis.

"Hiya, Cam."

"Hiya, Mel."

She stepped inside, shrugging off her snow-flaked coat. "It's too bad about Ivy. Wonder what's up with her."

"Her mom's health isn't doing too well."

She frowned. "Since when?"

I shrugged. "A few weeks now, I think. Or at least that's when I found out."

"How did you find out?"

"She seemed worried lately, so I asked if she was okay, and she said something vague about her mom. She didn't want to talk about the details. At least not at work."

She frowned, more to herself than at me. "I didn't know any of that."

Needing to do something with my hands, I took the covered plate from her. "What's this?"

She toed off her snowy boots. "You smuggle me cupcakes, I make you snickerdoodles. Well, snickerdoodle bars, specifically. I meant to make another apple pie but ran out of time."

"These look great, but I already have stale Oreos in the kitchen. Now I have a big decision to make."

She followed me into the kitchen, but I still heard her quiet laughter.

I shot her a look over my shoulder and noticed her grinning at my collar. "What?"

"Your shirt is inside out."

First too red, now inside out. *You're a real lady killer, Cameron Whitacre.*

Without thinking, I set the snickerdoodles on the counter, yanked my shirt over my head, turned it right side out, and pulled it back on. "Better?"

Only when I saw her wide-eyed look did it occur to me that I probably shouldn't have done that. Or maybe I did exactly what I should have. I would do it again if she would keep looking at me like that.

She cleared her throat and reached up a hand. "Now you've messed up your hair."

My instincts fought to lean into her touch, and my logic fought them right back. Friends didn't nuzzle other friends like a cat nuzzles a hand. I knew that. I just needed to remind myself, that's all.

Stepping back, she gestured a hand at my torso. "All that working out is paying off. Looking to impress the girls, Cam?"

I shrugged and did my best Schwarzenegger impression. "Just working to counteract these snickerdoodles."

Note to self: "snickerdoodles" is not a good word to say when speaking in a terrible Austrian accent.

I jammed a cookie bar in my mouth before I could say anything else idiotic, like *Just trying to catch your attention. Been at it for about five years now. Is it working yet?*

"That was awful." She laughed. "You're lucky Ivy wasn't here for it. She'd never let you live it down."

I grinned and turned toward the sink. "Well, The Rock doesn't have an accent, so I can't really imitate him."

"Fair enough." She opened a cabinet. "Do you have any bowls for this salsa you set out or—" She held up the dirty plate I'd hidden moments before she knocked on my door. "Do you consider this plate to be clean? Because it's not."

"Uh, I got distracted." I shoved it under the faucet.

She laughed. "I know you have this whole 'bachelor' reputation to live up to, but still. Please tell me it's not your new dishwashing method? Hiding your dirty plates in the cabinet?"

"Don't knock it till you try it."

"I definitely won't be trying it."

The more she teased me about the plate, the more tension left my chest. She hadn't brought up the stroke. She hadn't asked what I'd been about to say on the bench. The inside-out shirt, the messy hair, the dirty plate. All things she would've teased me about before.

We were still us.

Feeling more relaxed, I watched her glance around my apartment. It never changed every third Monday she and Ivy were here (still bare walls, still multiple screens), but Mel always looked for signs that I was domesticated. Clearly I wasn't, as proven by the dirty plate.

"You have such a nice condo," she said. "I wish you'd do something more with it."

I bit into another snickerdoodle bar. "Pillows and paint colors are beyond me."

"I think you're perfectly capable of figuring out pillows and paint colors. You just keep up the bachelor vibe as part of your master plan to lure single women into your life."

I opened a beer and handed it to her. "The only thing my bachelor vibe has done is inspire my overbearing sister to stuff coupons to department stores under my front door. So my master plan backfired."

She flashed a challenging grin. "So if I brought over a candle, you'd light it in here? Get rid of that leftover takeout smell?"

"I'll have you know I haven't ordered takeout for two whole days. Just for you."

She wrinkled her nose and grinned, teasing. "The fact that it lingers for so long is somehow worse. But thank you for trying?"

I laughed. "Fine. Bring your vanilla candle next time."

If my condo smelled like her all the time...I swallowed.

Her brown eyes lingered on me. "How did you know it's vanilla?"

I tried for nonchalant but probably toed the line of indifference instead. "I can read a label."

"You're...unexpected, Cam."

Good thing she didn't know all of the other things I noticed about her apartment. Or about her. Like the shadow dipping into the valley of her collarbone. Like the precise angle of her chin nudging upward to sip her beer. Like the wispy strands slipping from her ponytail.

The kitchen peninsula separated us, so I leaned across it on my elbows. My voice was raspy when I spoke. "Exactly how am I unexpected, Mel?"

She looked away. Her shoulders rose and fell with a breath before she answered. "What you said in the interview. I didn't know all that. About the stroke."

Well. That wasn't the direction I'd hoped this would go.

I straightened away from her. "It doesn't really matter."

"Of course it matters."

And now for my third snickerdoodle of the night—and we weren't even thirty minutes in. Anything to keep myself from talking.

"Look," she said, "I can see this makes you uncomfortable. So I'm not going to push it. I just want to say that I think what you did—the interview with Alma, the entire recovery and rehab process you went through, how honest you were about all of it…"

Reaching across the peninsula, she rested her hand on mine. Her palm felt smooth and chilled, cooling the back of my hand. My jaws stopped working the snickerdoodle mid-chew, and I stared at our crisscrossed fingers. How could I find a way to warm her hands without overstepping her boundaries?

"You're incredibly strong, Cam. Even when you don't feel like you are. I hope you know that about yourself."

There was that rawness again.

Too soon, she withdrew. "Anyway. That's all I was going to say on the bench a few days ago, and that's all I'm going to say about it now. If you want to talk about it, I'm here. Otherwise…" She mimed locking her lips shut and throwing away the key.

She busied herself filling a plate with chips and salsa and snickerdoodles, rambling something about having a movie night because she needed a break from the Dating Debacle. Not that she called it that. I busied myself obsessing over her words, especially "incredibly strong," and—more importantly—wondering what I could do to get her to hold my hand like that again. Did I dare? Maybe Toby was right. Maybe I'd been an idiot, hiding behind the pain and fear, all in the name of rebuilding my life to keep busy.

The rawness made me feel reckless.

She called to me from the sofa. "Are you picking the movie or am I?"

"Definitely me. Your movie taste is terrible."

"Is not."

"Is too." Giving up all pretenses of not devouring the cookie bars before the night was over, I carried the entire dish of snickerdoodles into the living room. "You consistently choose movies that are rated three stars on IMDB."

"IMDB doesn't know everything."

"It knows movie ratings. That's kind of its thing."

"But IMDB doesn't know what I like. I do."

"And you like terrible movies."

She threw a chip at my face, missing by several inches. It landed next to the shadow of lint on my carpet.

"And you have terrible aim."

She laughed. "Now that I already know."

I watched her more than the movie. No matter what I picked, her in-movie commentary made the story even better. I couldn't count how many times I'd listened to guys complain that their girlfriends or wives drove them crazy talking through a movie, but I could listen to Mel's quips all night.

For once it paid off to have only my couch for living room seating. We sat facing one another, my legs on the outer edge of the cushions, hers on the inner, one of my legs pressed against hers from hip to ankle. Snack plate on her lap, wavy hair falling over one shoulder, she sat wrapped in a throw blanket—the only one I owned, since I'd bought it just for her to use when she came over. When she offered to share the blanket, of course I said yes.

I thought of her wide-eyed look when I fixed my shirt. What had she been thinking? Nobody had seriously caught her attention for a long time now. Not that she'd ever dated like Ivy did. Sure, she had the Dating Debacle, but nothing serious was coming of it. Maybe *I* could catch her attention after all.

What would it be like, I wondered, to move a little closer? To put her empty snack plate next to mine on the coffee table? To tuck that haphazard curl behind her ear and lean in and brush my lips against her neck—

What if I started with a foot rub? No. It might come across creepy to rub feet while still in the friend zone. Not to mention it was too cheesy.

What if I put on a horror film? I imagined her moving closer during the scary parts—and then rolled my eyes at myself. Mel laughed at horror films for their "unrealistic predictability." She would never move closer during scary parts. And that move was just as overdone as a foot rub.

Maybe—

"Want another drink?"

I startled. "No, thanks."

"Are you okay?" She laughed. "You're so jumpy tonight."

I didn't answer, watching her walk to the kitchen.

When she came back, she shifted lower on the couch, taking up more than half the space, but since it brought more of her even closer to me, I wasn't about to say anything. Holding my breath, I rested a hand on her shin, feeling her warmth even through the blanket. She glanced over and smiled at me. I breathed again.

Maybe, just maybe, I had a chance. Maybe, just maybe, I should take it.

CHAPTER 26

MEL

Mel: The list says to associate with women who are more attractive than I am because they might have some leftovers. Ivy, you're gorgeous. Got any leftovers?
Ivy: None that aren't garbage humans.
Mel: Any chance of them having grown up since you dated them?
Cameron: Great idea. Leftovers always taste better after a few days at the back of someone else's moldy fridge.
Ivy: Did you just call my love life a moldy fridge?

The three of us had different levels of experience with clubbing. I'd never been a big fan. Ivy regularly went to clubs on her dates. Cameron had the most experience, but he was quiet about his earlier years of being one of the popular college athletes, vaguely referencing them but never giving us any details. We had disagreed on almost everything—which club to go to, what we should do when we got there, whether we should drive or Uber—but the one thing we had agreed on? Going on an eighties-themed Thursday night.

Ivy and I had cobbled together our brightest clothes from our closets and some legwarmers from her gymnast neighbor. Too much hairspray and a few layers of gaudy eyeshadow later, and we thought we looked pretty good.

Cameron laughed when he met us outside the club. "You two are taking this more seriously than I realized."

"And you look like you came straight from work," I told him.

"Because I did come straight from work."

I stepped forward to muss his hair and undo his buttoned shirt so his plain white undershirt was visible. I started at the top, my fingers brushing underneath his chin, and worked my way down to the last button at his waist.

Stepping back, I surveyed my work. "Since you're wearing jeans and men's fashion doesn't change a lot, that'll do."

When he didn't answer, I looked up. He was unblinking, all his attention focused on me.

Oh. Had I just unbuttoned…? My mind flooded with images. I tried not to think about the actual *pecs* that I'd seen on the yacht when he changed clothes. Pecs that I'd just brought one clothing item closer to naked by undoing his button-down. And now my thoughts ricocheted between his wet clothes at the yacht party, and exactly how close I'd stood next to him in his kitchen last Monday when he'd stripped off his shirt with zero warning.

Willing my face to a normal temperature—and my brain to normal behavior—I looked everywhere but at him.

Ivy plopped a worn-looking fedora on top of his head. "I figured you wouldn't care about dressing up. So I came prepared. You actually look good, Cam."

I forced myself to refocus. "Very eighties Johnny Depp," I agreed.

He blinked his gaze away from me and straightened the hat. "I'd rather be Jack Sparrow Johnny Depp, but I didn't dress for that either."

"It wouldn't fit eighties night," Ivy said.

He scoffed. "Who says it's 1980s and not 1780s?"

"He has a point." I laughed.

We stepped inside. The club was bigger than I expected…and louder. Lights strobed across the room. Bodies swayed to the beat of Michael Jackson. The dim lighting gathered shadows in corners and booths, making me squint. It smelled of alcohol and sweat and cheap bar food.

"Find us a table?" Cameron had to shout in my ear so I could hear him over the bass. "I'll get us some drinks."

Ivy and I wandered through the club, her steps altering to match the rhythm of Guns N' Roses.

She chose a small table just the right size for the three of us. "I've never seen an eighties night so packed."

"You've been here before?"

"A few times."

I nudged her shoulder with mine. "And you didn't take me with you?"

She didn't meet my eyes as she looked around the club. "I actually worked here for a bit."

"Seriously?"

"You know me, always working to save money." She nodded at the crowd. "I bet I would've made more in tips if I could work the crowd like he does."

Cameron held three drinks overhead, smiling and nodding at every person he passed along the way. Each bystander grinned and laughed like he was a long-lost friend.

When he finally reached our table, he set our drinks in front of us. "One margarita for Ivy, one gin and tonic for Mel, and one whiskey for me."

We chimed our thanks.

Ivy eyed our surroundings. "Okay, Mel. What's on the list for tonight?"

"'Stand in a corner and cry softly.'"

Cameron scoffed. "And what's that supposed to do?"

"Hopefully some nice young man asks me if I'm okay," I said. "It's like a way to break the ice. I think." Actually, I'd been trying not to think about it all day. I felt exposed at just the thought of crying in front of strangers.

Ivy laughed. "Pity is certainly one way to get attention."

"More like someone will think you're vulnerable," Cameron said, oddly echoing my thoughts.

Not that I would admit that.

"We've already talked about this," I said. "Scumbags are everywhere. I'll be fine. That's why you two are here." I patted his shoulder. "You can help fight off weirdos."

Cameron pointedly looked around the club. "But there are so many to choose from."

Ivy licked salt from the rim of her margarita. "I hope you've been practicing your fake cry. Now's your chance to win your Oscar."

"I actually have been practicing my fake cry, thank you very much." I stood and collected my drink and purse. "And wouldn't it serve you right if I met a guy named Oscar tonight?"

"Touché." She laughed, and Cameron grinned.

"Wish me luck." I darted off to the last empty table, this one in a quiet corner. Technically, the list said to stand in a corner, but this was close enough.

Once seated, I crossed my legs under the table and did exactly as I'd practiced in front of my bathroom mirror at home. Yes, I really had practiced my fake crying. I slouched my shoulders and let my lip wobble when I sipped at my drink. I brought up mental reels of the saddest things I could think of: *The Notebook, Marley & Me,* Fantine and Éponine in *Les Mis.*

I wasn't sure what I expected. Would people ignore me if they saw me, too uncomfortable with my tears to talk to me? Or would they be so distracted by the strobing lights and eighties hits that they would overlook me completely?

Regardless of what I'd expected, I didn't need to wait long.

"Are you okay?"

Her hair wasn't just blond, it was white blond, and it practically glowed in the odd lighting. To go with the eighties theme, her hair was teased into a halo that stayed stiff when she moved. I hardly noticed her neon lipstick and shoulder pads—her hair was that glorious.

I hoped my smile looked sheepish. "I'm sure I look like a hot mess."

Blondie rested a hand on my forearm. "It's okay. We all need a good cry sometimes. Love life trouble?"

"Isn't it always?" Not quite a lie, not quite a truth. I was here because of my love life, in a way, so…

"Let me guess. You came here to forget, but seeing all the couples having a good time just made it worse?"

I shrugged. Also not quite a lie. Seeing couples have a good time always did make me feel that twinge of envy. I just hoped my newfound friend didn't hurt my chances of a man stopping by my table.

She nodded sympathetically. "It'll all be okay." She draped an arm over the back of my chair and leaned closer. "As my last girlfriend always said, 'Love is worth the pain unless you're the one who just got screwed.' Or something like that."

My thoughts scratched like a record player with a stuck needle. Girlfriend? I glanced at her body language, gauging how close we were sitting, how her hand was still on my forearm, how her other arm was on my chair, and how she'd just made it very clear that she was single. This…wasn't exactly what I had in mind when I decided to fake cry in a corner.

I started to speak, stuttering over my words, when Blondie smiled and leaned away. "It's written all over your face that you're not my type. I get it. But if you ever change your mind"—she winked—"I'm here every eighties night."

She melted into the dancing crowd.

Book note: never make assumptions.

My gaze instinctively went to Cameron and Ivy's table. They were both

160

grinning at me over their drinks. Of course the one time in my life a girl hits on me, the two of them are witnesses. I bit back my own smile even as I almost wished Cameron and his crinkly blue eyes would look somewhere else.

Let them laugh. I'd already wasted a whole can of hairspray and palette of neon eyeshadow, not to mention my time and my friends' time. I refused to give up. I slouched a little more, trying to regroup for a second attempt.

Before I could force a new round of fake tears to roll down my cheeks, a man wearing the quintessential denim suit—blue jeans and blue jean jacket—danced up to my table. Then around my table. Then around my chair where I sat. Denim pulled out the chair the girl had just left and turned it so he could straddle it, well within what most people would define as personal space. The last time I'd felt so aggressively invaded was when my cousin's schnauzer, er, schnauzed her way underneath my skirt.

Apparently looking even remotely sad did the trick. The list was right.

I purposely avoided eye contact with Cameron and Ivy. If I could see their grins over Denim's dance moves and suit, I would lose my sad act completely.

Book note: looking sad gets their attention.

"Hey," Denim said, doing that upward nod that seemed innate to so many men.

"Hey."

His shoulder was damp when he nudged me, proving the denim suit was too warm for his dance moves. "You okay?"

I started to speak, but he didn't wait for my answer.

"A pretty girl like you should not be sad in a corner, all alone." I couldn't place his accent. Maybe Dutch? "You should be out on the floor." Still seated, he demonstrated some moves, his face lit up with a smile.

Guessing it was something a self-respecting 1950s woman would've said to a dance offer with so many hip thrusts, I said, "I don't really feel like it."

"Aw, come on, of course you do." Another nudge from the damp shoulder.

I had to shout over the music. "Your accent—I can't place it. Where are you from?"

"Germany. The original homeland of dance clubs and eighties nights. You know, diskothek?" His overeager, lit-up smile did make it difficult to stay fake sad.

"I've never been to Germany."

"You should come with me sometime," Denim said, clearly oblivious that it wasn't a normal invitation for a first conversation. "Have you heard of teledisko?"

I shook my head.

"They are phone booths turned into mini dance clubs. Pop in a coin and boom! Music, lights, all the works. I go home every few months. We should go together. Teledisko is much more...intimate...than this."

He leaned closer, and I leaned away. Maybe I needed to be a bit more 1950s—or a bit lonelier—for his eagerness to be appealing instead of aggressive.

As I was moving to stand and return to Cameron and Ivy's table, a hand on my shoulder pressed me back into my seat.

"You're making my friend uncomfortable."

Above us stood a Magnum P.I. lookalike. He was a young Tom Selleck with dark hair, Havana shirt, jeans, and a self-assured smile that turned cold when he looked at Denim.

Denim, still ever eager, stood and moved away, his palms stretched outward. "Hey, man, I did not know she was with anyone." He flashed another smile at me. "If you are ever lonely and want an adventure, Germany is calling."

At least Magnum hadn't ruined Denim's enthusiasm for a good diskothek.

Magnum sat next to me. "How long were you going to put up with that guy?"

I shrugged. "He was entertaining."

"If you like needy puppies, sure, he was perfect."

I felt a little bad for laughing. Sure, Denim was odd, but he didn't deserve to be made fun of. A negative point for Magnum, I mentally noted.

Magnum leaned back in his chair. "Sitting here all alone like this attracts the crazies." He nodded toward my drink. "Need a refill?"

"Maybe in a minute."

Magnum was more of a conversationalist than my other two encounters. He was an architect, working his way up at a firm in the city. His hometown was in the Midwest. He liked living in the city, but he was excited to go home in the next few months to meet his newborn nephew. This was his first eighties night—he liked it enough that he might come back next week.

Maybe there was something to this crying-in-a-corner idea. Sure, Blondie and I were batting for different teams, and Denim had been a little, well, overt, but Magnum was friendly, charming, and normal. He showed potential.

As we talked, he kept his eyes focused on me, genuinely interested in what I said. His attention never strayed from our little table. I couldn't help my delight that the thumping bass and flashing lights, let alone the squealing sororities two tables over, never once drew his gaze away from me.

I thought of my imagined meet-cutes again. Hope stretched awake, catlike, in my mind, and I told it not to get ahead of itself. But still, the flattery of his attention and smiles had me daydreaming. For the first time, I began to think advice from the list could end in an actual relationship. Strange how the vulnerability of crying in public had paid off more than all the other advice I'd followed so far.

Book note…

He gestured toward the bar across the room. "Did you know they switch out the artwork and some of the décor to match the theme of the night?"

"Really?" Impressed, I craned my neck to look over my shoulder, but I couldn't see anything beyond the flashing strobe lights and twisting bodies.

"They have a Keith Haring and a Richard Prince that weren't there a few nights ago. They're just prints, definitely not originals, but I like that they made the effort."

"You know art much better than I do." Maybe he and Ivy would get along, and we could all be friends…

Two hands forcefully landed on the table, making me jump and sloshing my drink.

Cameron's face. I'd never seen him like this before. His skin was scarlet, his brow was in a single line, and a vein in his neck pulsed. I'd only ever seen him as goofy, laid-back Cameron. For him to be like this, something had to be very wrong.

"Hey, man." Magnum scowled at him. "What's your problem?"

When Cameron spoke, his voice was an octave deeper than normal. He annunciated the words slowly. "What did you put in her drink?"

Air rushed from my lungs. When…? How…? My mind stuttered to process the scene playing out in front of me. My emotions caught up much faster. Hurt, anger, and fear drowned out the small hope that had started growing just moments earlier. So much for vulnerability paying off with a quirky meet-cute.

I stood and faced Magnum too, placing myself side by side with Cameron. "Did you put something in my drink? Just now, when I wasn't looking?"

Magnum stood so quickly that his chair fell over. "What kind of accusation is that?"

"I've been watching you," Cameron said, "and I just saw you put something in Mel's drink. What was it, and how many others have you used it on?"

Magnum eyed Cameron, clearly sizing him up. While Magnum might have a little more bulk, Cameron was taller. And he was furious.

Magnum straightened his collar, muttered, "I don't have to put up with this," and then darted into the dancing crowd. Cameron followed.

Ivy touched my arm. "Are you okay?"

I nodded, struggling to force sound from my throat. "I never even noticed."

How embarrassing. I almost hadn't invited Cameron and Ivy tonight, thinking that I should try to do a few of these mancounters on my own. If I had been alone, met Magnum, sipped more of my drink after he drugged it, well, tonight would be going very differently. What if I had been alone?

"Cameron has your back," Ivy said. "Always. We both do."

"He mentioned something about the art at the bar, and I looked away without even thinking."

"It could happen to anyone."

That wasn't a reassuring thought. It was the opposite. I remembered Cameron's words, and I looked around the club. What if I wasn't his first of the night? What if there were other women from other nights? What if he had been doing this for...*years*?

My eyes focused on my drink. I picked it up, studying it like I thought I'd be able to see his guilt floating at the top. "It *could* happen to anyone. And it does."

She turned me toward the table she had been sharing with Cameron. "Cam will chase him down. When Cam comes back, the three of us can go home and relax, or we'll stop at the Bluesy Bean. We'll do something fun and forget this ever happened."

Ivy's modus operandi—distract and forget. But I knew I wouldn't forget. Sure, I hadn't put myself out there that much in the dating world, but I thought I was relatively street smart. Park under lights, be aware of your surroundings, check your backseat. I'd thought of myself as an independent woman who was making her way in the world, who was savvy enough to look out for herself without any help.

I didn't feel independent or savvy right now. I felt naïve and weak. For the third time that night, embarrassment colored my cheeks. Maybe Cameron's endless worries about my safety weren't just annoyances. Maybe they were valid. Now that he'd been proven right, I could already hear his "I told you so," and he would be perfectly justified in thinking I couldn't fend for myself.

Staring down at the table, I wondered how this would change my friendships with Cameron and Ivy. Would Cameron worry even more now? Would Ivy start fretting too? Would they still support the mancounters? Did I *want* to continue with the mancounters?

Cameron reappeared next to our table, breathing hard. "I couldn't catch him. He ran faster than I thought he would. And the crowd didn't help." He leaned down to study me, his hand on my shoulder warming me through my shirt. "Are you okay?"

I stared at the glowing exit sign above the door. "I'm fine. I just want to go home."

CHAPTER 27

CAMERON

Ivy: Thanks for picking up the Uber fee, Cam. Let us know if you need anything, Mel.
Cameron: I still vote that we unroll our sleeping bags on Mel's floor for the night.
Mel: Please stop fussing. I promise I'm fine.

It was only after I'd locked my door and collapsed on my couch that I let myself take my first deep breath in several hours.

Even staring at the ceiling, all I could see were images of Mel's terrified face.

Not to mention images of the man's hand as he spiked her drink. It was steady, practiced in a way that said he had made those same sly motions countless times. How many other women had he drugged? What had happened to them? Had any of them had someone watching out for them?

I felt like a failure for not being able to catch him. I'd underestimated his speed, the density of the crowd on the dance floor, the number of men dressed in obnoxious flowered shirts. By the time I'd reached the other side of the room and made it through the exit, all signs of him were gone.

I rubbed shaking hands over my face. Sleep wouldn't come easily tonight.

I should shower, go for a run, call Toby—something to take the edge off this adrenaline.

But I still felt the fury from the moment I'd realized what he was doing. That anger wasn't going anywhere anytime soon.

I forced another deep breath into my lungs and reminded myself that Mel was at home. She was safely locked into her apartment. Her eyes, wide and terrified at the club, had already shifted to a dazed expression by the time I'd left her place.

By the time I'd left? I almost laughed at myself, knowing it hadn't really been my choice to leave. Ivy had nearly dragged me from the apartment. I'd wanted to stay all night and make sure she was okay. I would've wrapped her in one of her dozen fluffy throw blankets and held her until she drifted to sleep and my hands stopped shaking. I would've lit every single one of the vanilla candles in her apartment. Whatever it took to make her feel better.

The only thing that had kept my feet moving out the door was my plan to go to the police. Not that they'd been able to help when I'd reached the station. Nor could I blame them. "No, officer, I don't know his approximate height, or weight, or even hair color because the lighting was terrible. No, I don't know his name. But I do know that he wore a flowered shirt, and drugging women seemed to be his regular hobby." They'd said that they would do what they could, but I knew the chances were slim.

My hand still shook as I dug my phone out of my pocket.

Cameron: You okay?

Mel: Please stop worrying. I'm fine.

I refrained from responding with what I wanted to say—*Really? So fine that you're glued to your phone and answering my texts in mere seconds?*—and settled for something a little less smothering. Something a little more like the Cameron she relied on as a friend and a little less like the real me who was worried sick over her.

Cameron: Well, I'm not fine. I stubbed my toe chasing after that guy. I might lose a nail. Just in case you were worried about me, too.

Mel: Lol. Of course I worry about you. So sorry to hear about your boo-boo.

A dozen lines about kissing boo-boos ran through my head, but now wasn't the time for that kind of teasing. Now was the time to give her the same space I'd so desperately wanted so many times after my stroke.

I hadn't meant to say it.

Big clouds of air puffed up from our mouths as I ran next to Toby. Brilliant snow crunched under our running shoes and glittered under the early sunlight. The clarity that comes with running first thing in the morning—and the kick of starting off the day with endorphins—helped to start smoothing out some of my rough edges from the night before.

Still, after staying up most of the night worrying about Mel and fuming at myself for not running fast enough to catch the guy, I was in a quiet mood. The most I'd said was asking Toby to add more speed work to our training plan. The next time Mel needed me, I wouldn't let her down.

Toby agreed, saying he'd add sprints to next week's schedule and then proceeding with an extremely detailed description of his newest patient, an older man who could do perfect celebrity impressions. Then again, the celebrity impressions may not be that good. Sometimes Toby's optimism was a little, well, unrealistic. Surely it was an endless pressure, having to be upbeat for patients all the time, but Toby was unstoppable. The man automatically thanked the bank ATM at the end of his transactions.

I just wished I could truly clear last night out of my head. I'd already been more preoccupied with Mel than usual, thanks to our Monday night with just the two of us. I kept turning over every detail in my mind. How her eyes had gone wide when I'd changed my shirt. How she fixed my hair. How she touched my hand and told me I was "incredibly strong" even when I didn't feel like it. Now I tried to focus on those memories. It was better than thinking about what had happened at the club last night.

Could Mel have feelings for me? Could she see me as more than her comfortable friend? If nothing else, maybe she thought I was attractive. She'd pointed out that I looked like I was trying to impress a girl. Had it worked on her? Maybe, if I did everything just right, I could nudge that attraction (however slight it may be) into something more. Most relationships start with thinking someone is good looking, right?

Not to mention she had told me that she didn't think of me any differently after she knew about the stroke. She still treated me the same. She hadn't put me on a pedestal like I was an inspiration. She hadn't tiptoed around me like I was fragile.

Mel was insightful. She had to know by now that my humor was a wall that I used to keep people at a distance (class-clown style). That I worked so hard to rebuild my life because the handouts felt worse than running basketball drills with a hangover. After five years of friendship, she knew my flaws and didn't seem to mind them.

She'd seen me. And she hadn't look away.

As our feet pounded against the pavement, my thoughts pounded in my head, gradually clearing to reveal exactly what I needed to do.

What better risk was there than the leap from friendship to something more? Who could I trust more than Mel to either take that leap with me and meet me halfway, or let me down gently and still be my friend?

So it just popped out.

"I'm going to tell her everything."

CHAPTER 28

MEL

Mel: How's your stubbed toe?
Cameron: I'm happy to report that I woke up with all my toenails intact.
Mel: Good! Now let's never talk about losing toenails again. It's gross. Unless you actually lose one. Then I'll tough it out and bring you clean socks. Or whatever you need for a lost toenail.
Cameron: Thanks! How are you this morning? I'm here if you need anything.

I'd paced my apartment well into the night. After Cameron and Ivy had finally stopped fussing—even though it was sweet and well-meaning—and left my apartment, I'd spent almost an hour showering and trying to wash away the bright eyeshadow and head full of hairspray and images of Havana shirts.

My shoulders had drawn toward my ears with tension. The inside of my lower lip was almost chewed raw. Finally, with some mindless TV for background noise, I'd fallen asleep at an odd angle on the couch. Now Friday morning light was filtering into my living room. I blinked at the brightness, grateful Cameron and Ivy had talked me into calling off work today.

It was a relief when my neighbor, the Perfect Man, knocked on my door and explained that the Perfect Woman and the Synchronized Crying Kids were sick with food poisoning, and Horse needed a walk. Perfect Man couldn't walk Horse and hold his family's hair back at the same time.

Even though I could've one-upped his bad day with my night at the club, I didn't want to talk about it. Maybe walking Horse would burn off some restlessness. So now I power walked Horse—or more like he power walked me—through the small park nearby my apartment, wondering about myself, the mancounters, my book, and everything in between.

In short, I was a mess.

What was I actually doing? What was the point of this whole experiment anyway? I'd had the horrible experience at the club; I'd somehow started walking Horse on a more permanent basis than I'd like; I'd nearly poisoned a coworker with walnuts; and a very old security guard escorted me back to a college basketball arena. Not to mention my near-death driving escapade. Can't forget that.

What did any of that say about dating today compared to dating in the 1950s? What did it say about the timelessness of love? It wasn't like I knew anyone who'd followed this list in the 1950s—how would I know whether their experiences differed from my own? There were too many variables. It was impossible to know. This idea was flawed from the start.

I'd wasted my time and energy, and my friends' time and energy. Through all the mancounters, I'd felt scared and embarrassed more than any other emotion. Especially since Cameron and Ivy had witnessed almost every cringeworthy moment. How much longer would they commit to wasting their time like this? How much longer could my ego keep taking blow after humiliating blow?

Then again, why bother with any of this at all? Why not give up? I thought of going back to my quiet life—listening to Dr. Schaaf's latest conspiracy theory, spending Monday nights with Cameron and Ivy, envying Always Cheerful Lisa on Instagram.

Going back to that life sounded...well, less than ideal. For years now, I'd felt like a failure as a writer. What was a little more added embarrassment, especially when it could be my big break? Was pursuing this idea with the mancounters, with all the accompanying fear and shame, worth it to get what I really wanted?

Maybe men and women used each other all the time, and with the mancounters, I was just using men the same way I complained about them using women. Maybe all of us were the reason twenty-first-century dating was such a mess. Maybe none of us knew what we wanted, and so we took our frustration out on everyone we tried to date when they failed to measure up—through our own fault as much as theirs.

Then again, the list was an experiment and not an exact science. Following the dating advice was more about the experience and writing about it than it was about the actual results. Or so I could convince myself as long as I didn't think too much about my secret hope for a real romance.

I didn't even know anymore.

Keeping pace with Horse, I told myself to stop thinking and just enjoy the snow-covered ground and the way it sparkled in the early sunshine. Several others were out walking their dogs. They smiled and nodded, the good weather lifting everyone's mood. A group of teenagers started a snowball fight.

The mancounters had consumed me. I'd missed out on sights like this, regular Monday nights with Cameron and Ivy, and staff meetings without EMTs and ambulances. Maybe Cameron was right. Maybe I was losing myself and should stop the entire idea. There were other things I could write ab—

The snowball exploded on my face. Freezing pins needled into my skin and up my nose, caking my eyes shut. I spluttered and fumbled to clear the snow from my face without dropping Horse's leash. My eyes were just clear enough to blink again when a large hand took Horse's leash from me.

"I don't want to startle you," a man's voice said, "but I'll just stand here with your leash until you're ready to take it back. Those kids didn't even say sorry, did they? Just ran off."

The voice sounded genuinely upset on my behalf, but I was more concerned about getting my bearings so I could sic Horse on those kids. I blinked enough to make out Horse's happily clueless face. Forget it. That big softie would never sic anything but a tennis ball, and even then he'd probably lose.

"You okay?"

I blinked until green eyes, blond hair, and a friendly smile came into focus. "Yes, I'm okay. Thanks." I grasped Horse's leash again.

"Not even Hawkeye could've seen that snowball coming."

"Felt more like an ice ball," I muttered, still wiping my face with mittened hands.

He winced. "The kids got carried away. They still should've apologized though."

"Maybe they're embarrassed enough to be more careful next time."

"Have you met any teenagers lately? They don't get embarrassed about anything."

"There should be a law against snowball fights this early in the morning." Listen to me, grumbling because my bad mood was carrying over from last night into today. That's what I got for barely sleeping, for following this list in the first place.

"I'm Marcus, by the way." He stuck out a gloved hand. "And this is Cap." He gestured to the golden retriever carefully sniffing at Horse.

"I'm Mel," I said, "and this is...this is Horse."

His laugh was instantly one of my favorite things. It was big and explosive, a bark that tilted his head back and shook his shoulders. Unlike Magnum's façade last night, this laugh was impossible to fake.

"Horse?" he said. "I mean, he's big, but surely he's done growing by now?"

I laughed with him, more caught up in his own response than Horse's nickname. "He's my neighbor's dog, but they had a"—it was probably too early in the morning to bring up food poisoning symptoms—"a family emergency, so I'm walking him for them. They told me his name, but I think 'Horse' suits him better."

We watched the two dogs circle and sniff. Horse was much younger than Cap, whose white muzzle and slower movements put him at a disadvantage to Horse's dark fur and clumsy almost-puppy antics.

"That was nice of you to help out a neighbor." He grinned down at me. Marcus seemed so...normal. He wore normal winter clothes (no Havana shirt), he was a normal age (no offense, security guard), and he had a normal dog. His green eyes and smile were bright and friendly, and his blond hair reminded me of surfers and sunny days at the beach.

I needed normal.

Marcus shifted on his feet. "So, do your neighbors need Horse back any time soon, or would you like to join me for morning coffee? There's a place down the street that's pretty good. And they allow dogs."

Book note—

No. Enough with the mental book notes. I needed a break from the experiment for the next twenty-four hours. Just the thought of setting aside the list and all the pressure I'd been putting on myself, even for a few moments, made my breathing a little easier for the first time since last night.

No crazy pickup lines. No shenanigans. Just normal people walking their dogs and sharing coffee. I could go back to the list later.

I smiled up at him, feeling the tension begin to ease from my shoulders. "Coffee sounds great."

CHAPTER 29

MEL

Mel: "Prove to him that you're fun even on a cheap date. Remember not to overdo it!"
Cameron: All my dates are cheap dates. Welcome to adjunct life.
Mel: Do they mean not to overdo how cheap I am or how much fun I'm having on the cheap date?
Ivy: How cheap you are. There's no such thing as too much fun on a date.
Cameron: There are some public records that disagree.
Mel: Cam?! Do you have an arrest record from a wild date?!
Ivy: Tell us everything. Right now.
Cameron: I'm deeply offended that you think it's from just ONE wild date.
Mel: Spill it!

If "hope is the thing with feathers / That perches on the soul,"—thank you, Emily Dickinson—then I was a penguin stumbling around with the full 80,000-feather package. Maybe I even had the upgraded feather package. Whatever that looked like.

Marcus texted me.

Multiple times.

From Friday morning to today, Sunday afternoon. He didn't waste time or play games.

Marcus was normal. More than that, Marcus seemed, well, perfect.

While we'd sipped overpriced but delicious coffee that morning, he'd been charming without any of the flash that usually turned me off. He was down to earth, sincere. We'd covered the small talk about jobs, families, etc., and surprisingly enough, we had similar hobbies and interests.

He'd even tried to pay for my coffee, smiling and frowning at the same time. "I always pay for the meal when I'm with a woman."

"This isn't a meal," I'd said. "It's just coffee."

And now, his most recent text. *Marcus: About that meal I want to buy you...what are you up to tonight?*

Now for the fine-tuned balance of deciding how eager was too eager. Should I play hard to get? None of my mancounters had progressed this far.

But was this a mancounter? I'd agreed to coffee with Marcus while telling myself I needed a break from the experiment—a break for just twenty-four hours, which had come and gone. As much as I'd needed a rest, I couldn't help my near obsession with the project.

I justified Marcus as a mancounter easily enough. First, walking Horse was part of the list. Second, running into Marcus was a meet-cute Nora Ephron herself could've written. Third, seeing Marcus beyond our meet-cute would give me something substantial to write about. Romantic hope was alive and well in my mind, but I stifled any potential feelings because this was all for my book. Definitely just my book.

Staring at my texts, I settled on: *No plans for tonight. What do you have in mind?*

Regret hit me instantly, sending my many-feathered hope fluttering far away. Why hadn't I tried harder to sound flirty? How flirty was too flirty for a man you'd just met?

I didn't have to wait long for his reply. *Marcus: Tonight it is. We can meet at Armand's at 7:00 and walk the river after, if it's not too cold.*

Armand's was the Harrods of fine dining in our entire state. Fair trade, organic, farm-to-table, delicious, and expensive. A college friend had gone once for her internship, and they'd wrapped her leftovers in the shape of a chubby little triceratops. Not a swan, like normal swanky restaurants. A triceratops.

I knew Marcus worked in finance, but could he afford Armand's? Color me impressed.

I typed my reply. *Mel: Never been to Armand's, but I've heard it's amazing. See you at 7!*

. . .

Ivy hadn't answered any of my texts, so I settled for the classic standby, the little black dress, after overthinking what Marcus would wear, what people usually wore to Armand's, and the kind of signal I'd send if I dressed up too much or too little. You know, normal first-date worries for a totally normal woman going out with a totally normal man.

Marcus, in what looked like a tailored suit, waited for me inside the restaurant doors, where he stood at the hostess' station, smiling at me. "You look nice." He set his stride to match mine. "Our table is over there."

I could feel the warmth of his hand at my lower back. "You look nice, too." *Hi, I'm an aspiring writer, and all I can do is regurgitate your words back at you.*

He tucked in my chair as I sat. A server placed a bread basket and water glasses on the table, and I sat stiffly as she spread a napkin over my lap. Marcus ordered a bottle of wine with smooth sureness. No fumbling over French for him.

I smiled at a memory of Cameron from a few years ago, when Ivy had brought wine on a Monday night, and he'd over-exaggerated his own comedic mispronunciation. I would love sharing dinner with Cameron at Armand's.

But I wasn't with Cameron. I was with Marcus, and here, in candlelight and a tailored suit and ambient music, he looked nothing like the dogwalker I'd met in a puffy winter coat at six in the morning. He looked perfect, each hair in place. It was intimidating—and put a few goose bumps on my arms, too.

"How's Horse?"

"Huge as ever. He pulled me into a snowdrift this morning. I'm sure we looked like a cartoon."

He frowned. "Your neighbor's family emergency isn't over?"

"It's a little more complicated than that." I laughed. "I'm happy to walk him for now. It gets me moving a little earlier in the day if nothing else." It was probably too soon to bring up the mancounters and explain all the weirdness that came with them.

"It's nice of you to help out your neighbor." He leaned back in his seat. "I've been thinking about your job since we talked about it over coffee. Why be a writing tutor? What about, say, journalism?"

"That's easy. I'm a writing tutor because I believe in teaching others to tell their stories. And I'm waiting for my big writing break, like a lot of writers. Journalism isn't really my style—I'm more into books than news."

"So instead of 'The truth shall set you free,' your life mantra is 'The story shall set you free'?"

"In a way. It's more like we walk around in our daily lives wearing these masks of what we think we're supposed to be and what we're supposed to do. We put on a show or go through the motions. But stories can get to the core of something in a way that few other media can. Like, for instance, a lot of fantasy or sci-fi books show the flaws or corruption in our world, but they change the angle so that we're forced to understand the truth in ways that we don't see in our everyday lives."

My nervous goose bumps faded as I grew more comfortable. "Stories also show the beauty in something so that we appreciate it differently. Like, for instance, *The Lord of the Rings*. Tolkien shows horrors, but he also shows courage and friendship. He does it through a fantasy world that seems so different from ours, but we can still relate because the basic concepts are the same. Or take *Pride and Prejudice*. It shows the way pride can destroy relationships and also the beauty of love once assumptions are set aside. Both Tolkien and Austen write about worlds that are completely different from ours, whether they wrote fantasies in Middle Earth or romances in Regency England, but they're still stories about the same things that worry us today. Good versus evil. Truth versus deception. They show us what really matters at the core of life."

"So you're the next Tolkien or Austen?" His tone was sincere, curious, not at all belittling or mocking.

I fingered the condensation beading down the side of my water glass. "Or I'm the next Malcolm Gladwell. I'm working on something now. I'm still in the research stage—it's like a social experiment. But it's top secret. I would tell you, but then I'd have to kill you."

He smiled. "That escalated quickly. And it makes me think I'm part of this social experiment."

Book note: It's good to be a little mysterious.

I grinned at him over my wineglass. "I'll never tell."

He laughed that same way he did on our first morning together—head thrown back, shoulders shaking—that was completely out of place in fancy Armand's, and it was still one of my favorite things. He didn't have a fake laugh for formal events.

The server materialized next to our table. While Marcus ordered our meals—perfectly pronouncing every foreign word on the menu—I glanced around the restaurant again. Crystal glasses and candelabras, china dishes, phantom-like servers. A woman two tables over wore an actual fur animal draped over her shoulders. The entire setting had put me on edge when we first sat down, yet Marcus had put me back at ease by bringing up a topic he knew I was passionate about. It reminded me of something Cameron would do.

When was the last time I talked to anyone about my writing like this? I couldn't even remember.

Marcus spent the rest of the evening deftly maneuvering the conversation to comfortable topics or entertaining, self-deprecating stories about himself and his family. He paid for the meal—I stayed happily ignorant of the price on the bill—he helped me into my coat, and when he noticed me burrowing my hands into my pockets while we walked along the river, he insisted I borrow his gloves.

We were walking back to my car when he began packing a snowball together. "We should track down some teenagers. You can be the Punisher and avenge yourself."

I laughed. "Well, I did consider siccing Horse on them in the heat of the moment."

"That would only work if you wanted him to cuddle them to death." He threw the snowball and squarely hit a slim tree trunk.

"Show-off," I muttered.

He laughed and started packing another snowball, even though his hands had to feel numb without any gloves. "This is more like goofing off than showing off."

"I mean you have actual aim. I have terrible aim."

As I was speaking, his second snowball hit exactly the same spot on the same tree trunk.

"It's not that hard," he said. "I'll teach you."

The list had said to learn to play poker. But what about learning how to aim? Surely that counted.

Book note: The point was the man, not the game.

"Fine. Teach me how to hit something."

"First step, make your snowball. Pack it tight. No, make it tighter, like this. Good. Now stand like this, with your front shoulder pointing at your target. When you throw, you'll take a step forward to move your weight from your back leg to your front leg. And lift your elbow above your shoulder"—he reached around me to adjust my arm—"like this."

I tried to focus on his directions and not his touch. His palm brushed my thigh, his hands maneuvered my hips through the back-leg-front-leg movement. He reached both of his arms around me to adjust my elbow and shoulder angle. My goose bumps were back—and not because of the cold.

"Now keep your eyes on your target and throw."

My snowball sparkled as it flew through the night air, the streetlights making it glisten as it sailed past the tree trunk. Miss.

Scooping up more snow, Marcus walked me through it once more. Again his touches guided me into position, stepping closer when he readjusted my elbow-to-arm angle this time. My snowball missed again, but it was a few inches closer this time.

"It would help if we had an actual baseball," he said. "Then you could use a four-seam grip. Better physics that way."

"How do you know all this?"

He passed me another snowball and threw his own, again squarely hitting the same spot on the same tree trunk. "I grew up with it."

I threw again, nicking the edge of the tree trunk this time. Arms lifted above my head, I jogged an exaggerated victory lap around Marcus in the snow.

Laughing, he tossed an arm over my shoulders, tucking me against his side and walking toward the parking lot. "Great shot. My work here is done."

"Your work is far from over. Barely nicking a tree trunk doesn't count as mastery."

"If only I'd started off with a better student," he teased.

I drew us to a stop by a parking meter, regretting that I'd lose the warmth of his arm around me. "This is me."

Ivy's embarrassing striptease story echoed in my mind. He'd paid for dinner, he'd listened to me talk about myself. That's what her last date had claimed would earn him a striptease. Marcus did seem too perfect. There had to be something wrong with him. Maybe this would be it.

He shoved his hands in his pockets. "I almost offered to pick you up tonight, but I had plans on the other side of town earlier today."

"I didn't mind meeting you." I pulled off his gloves. "Thanks for lending me these."

"You're welcome." He studied the gloves in his hands for a moment before looking up, his eyes serious in the streetlight. "Thanks for tonight. We should do it again sometime soon."

I held his gaze. "Yes, we should."

The smile that stretched across his face was instant and sincere. "Good." He held open my car door for me. "More snow is coming tonight, so text me when you get home, if you don't mind."

"Sounds good." I hesitated before stepping into my car. Our date had been wonderful. I didn't want to ruin it with a misjudged kiss—it wasn't worth the risk of making it awkward. Even if he was perfect. In reality, the fact that he was perfect made me hesitate even more. Sharing an ill-timed kiss with, say, Cameron would be vastly different from embarrassing myself with Marcus.

Then I thought of the list, of taking chances even when the sensible thing would be to walk away. So, well, why not?

He leaned closer at the same moment I did, and our lips met in a soft press. His hand cupped the back of my neck with perfect pressure, letting us deepen the kiss for a few moments...

He broke away with a grin, his fingers lingering on my cheek.

I smiled and stepped back toward my car. "Thanks again for tonight."

After I settled in the driver's seat, he closed my door and waved as he backed away. He was still smiling when I looked in my rearview mirror and turned onto the main street. But then again, I was still smiling, too.

What a perfect date.

It would've been more perfect with Cameron.

I mentally rolled my eyes at the intrusive thought. Well, obviously. Everything was better with Cameron. But I couldn't have everything, and I couldn't have Cameron.

I willed myself to keep smiling for the whole drive home.

CHAPTER 30

CAMERON

Mel: FRIENDS! I just had the most perfect date!

Ivy: Details. Now.

Mel: His name is Marcus. He took me to Armand's for dinner. AND he paid for it. And then we walked the river. And he's nice. And just perfect.

Ivy: Armand's is impressive, but you know how I'm skeptical. Concrete examples, please.

Mel: He gave me his gloves on the river walk, even though he was making snowballs with his bare hands and had to be freezing.

Cameron: Snowballs? Is he 12 years old?

Mel: He helped me with my terrible aim. I *almost* hit a tree.

Ivy: Okay, so he has Mr. Deeds hands instead of Mr. Deeds feet. (We all know you were thinking it, Cam.) More examples, please. You know I take your love life seriously.

Mel: He asked me to talk about myself. And then he listened.

Ivy: Okay, so he's a decent human being. I'm sorry if I'm extra negative, but I'm still rattled after the club. Your mancounters are starting to make me nervous. How did you meet this guy?

Mel: We met when I was walking Horse yesterday morning.

Ivy: Isn't walking Horse on the list?

Mel: It is, but it's like the most normal thing possible on the list.

Ivy: True. But I'm still skeptical.

Mel: He's going out of town for a few days because of work, so he's meeting me for lunch at the cafeteria next week. You get to meet him!
Ivy: Good. I will haze him. (Also, he took you to Armand's and you're taking him to the cafeteria? Hilarious.)
Mel: I'm classy like that. And I want him to meet my two best friends. What if the outdated advice is onto something after all?

I was too late.

Mel had met someone. Some fancy man who could spend a few hundred dollars on a first date at Armand's but still be up for sharing lunch with her at the university cafeteria. (So he was wealthy but not snobby.)

He let her borrow his gloves even though Mel never complained, so he must've noticed her hands were cold all on his own. (He was attentive and kind.)

He tried to help her with her terrible aim. (He was patient and at least a little athletic.)

He was generally a good person.

Half of me burned. I'd let Mel borrow my gloves, hat, and coat countless times over the last five years. I'd taught her things, like answering her basketball and IT questions. Between regular life and college debt, I couldn't afford Armand's, but I'd picked up her coffee bill at the Bluesy Bean and other places countless times.

The other half of me crumbled to pieces. What did this guy have that I didn't? Other than money, obviously. But Mel wasn't someone who cared about money. Was she?

I'd been the best friend I could be. I'd been supportive of her mancounters even though I hated them. I'd been the shoulder she literally cried on several different times. I'd set aside my feelings for her so that I could be exactly what she wanted from me—just a friend. I'd waited for her.

This Marcus also didn't have the baggage I carried. She'd never have to listen to him stumble through an interview, or notice his crooked mouth when he smiled, or wake him up from nightmares where he relived a stroke. My hands fisted.

Now I'd have to listen to her gush about him. And I'd have to watch them together at the cafeteria. What if they were *together* together? What if they ended up in love, and I had to watch from the bench?

I reread her texts. She sounded gushy. Head over heels. Twitterpated. Whatever you called it, I hated it.

Mel had met someone. She liked him. He liked her.

Toby had been right all along. I'd hidden behind excuses. I'd played it safe. Focusing on rebuilding my life, on work, on just being friends until Mel showed signs of wanting something more. On trying to be normal.

And now? When I was finally brave enough to take a leap with our friendship? When it finally felt like the timing was right?

I was too late.

CHAPTER 31

MEL

Ivy: I'm really sorry to ditch at the last minute. Something came up. I'll make it up to you.

The words glared so brightly on my phone screen that I had to squint in the early morning light.

The text was part of our private thread, so Cameron wouldn't know I was planning to try another item on my list today: joining a group hike. Only for a writing project would I get up before dawn on a weekend to go for an early morning hike. The ad online promised an "out of this world" sunrise view at the halfway point. It had better be "out of this world" for how much coffee I'd needed to be awake enough to drive.

I should text Cameron to ask if he could come along at the last minute. But I could already feel guilt seeping in if he wasted a weekend morning on me. If he knew I'd done a mancounter alone, he would be kind but worry would cloud his eyes, especially since the Magnum nightmare. But it was early—the before-dawn-on-a-weekend kind of early—and I was a little tired of my friends' hovering since the eighties night. I just needed to do this myself.

After sending a quick text to Marcus, I tucked my phone into my pocket, climbed out of my car, and trekked into the dark outdoors. I wished I could tuck my guilt into my pocket, too. Marcus and I weren't exclusive by any means, but it still felt strange to have hopes about him while I continued to follow the list without him knowing about it. No, it didn't feel just strange. It felt hypocritical, playing games with people this way while I hated when people played games with me. I told myself to channel my inner Ivy feminist. One date didn't mean he had any claim on me or my time, right?

My footsteps, crunching on the frosted grass, silenced when I reached the trailhead. The registration list had shown twenty names, but there were only six other people, two of them men, standing by the sign.

I confirmed my name with the guide, Aleia, a woman with two long braids poking from her cap. She wore a neon vest over one of those outdoorsy coats stuffed with emu feathers, or something like that. I stepped back when she spoke more loudly to the rest of the group.

"Thanks for coming, everyone. It's cold enough that we might not have anyone else show up. It's their loss because they'll miss out on a gorgeous view this morning. Be sure to give them a hard time about it later. We don't get many clear days like this at this time of year."

Heads shook in pity ("Not many chances for a morning like this") and mouths tilted in superiority ("I told him not to have those other two drinks last night").

"At the end of the hike," Aleia said, "we'll stop at the cliff for that view. You'll have a few minutes to snap some pictures, take a breather, anything else you might need. I have coffee thermoses in my pack"—she patted her bag, which was almost large enough to rival Alma's—"so we'll be able to warm up with some hot drinks and then hike back here. Let me know if you have any questions."

Feet shuffled into a shape that was more or less a line, hands readjusted caps and gloves, and then we were off. And by "off" I mean we trudged through the crunchy, frozen grass and onto crunchy, frozen trails.

Aleia set a grueling pace. I thought I was relatively fit, but apparently my walks around campus and on the treadmill at my apartment's gym weren't enough to cope with this terrain and the extra weight of my heavy winter gear.

With just two men on the hike, the pickings were slim.

First was the man on the trail just ahead of me. He was fully invested in the curvy blond hiking in front of him. His random comments on the trees, or rocks, or temperature in the valley versus on the mountain did nothing to gain her attention. Valiant effort, though.

My only other option looked about thirty, and he wore a name-brand coat and name-brand shoes with nearly an inch of tread. When another group of hikers passed us with miniature speakers blaring music, he sighed loudly enough to earn side-eye from them.

"Makes it hard to enjoy the morning peace, huh?" I said. The cold air felt colder when I realized that I just disturbed his morning peace myself.

Tread's voice sounded like a guru, like he would be more at home wearing a linen robe as he sauntered down a mountain to enlighten his followers. "We all have our own versions of what a peaceful world looks like. For some, it means a quiet morning hike. For others, it's hard rock on a loudspeaker."

I turned back to the trail. Did he put me in the quiet hike or hard rock category? More like annoying bystander, probably.

He spoke again. "Technology and preset social standards unfortunately make it easy to become disconnected from one another. Accepting that lack of connection and becoming complacent are the real dangers."

I thought of the engineers leaving that conference glued to their phones and only Cameron noticing I even existed. The students I tutored who thought "LOL" was an appropriate way to conclude a research paper. The time I spent scrolling through social media, not realizing an hour had passed while I scowled about Always Cheerful Lisa and others like her. "Sure, I can see that."

"The only way to rise above the cultural norm is to reconnect with our truest selves and then with one another."

"Like self-care?"

"Not just any self-care. But the self-care that fills our wellsprings so that we can fill others' wellsprings. It's a full circle." His hands, encased in name-brand mittens, drew a circle in the air.

What was it about Tread that reminded me of something I couldn't quite place?

I shrugged. "I guess I can see that."

The biting air pried at the spaces between my hat and scarf, my gloves and sleeves. When I tucked my nose and mouth into my scarf for a little extra warm, my eyelashes gathered beads of moisture and blurred the edges of my vision. Whoever thought winter hiking in New England was a good idea?

At least the conversation was distracting, so I asked, "How do you fill your wellspring?"

Even his sigh sounded Zen. "I go on hikes like this every morning."

"Even during the workweek?"

"Especially during the workweek. That's when it's more important than ever. And I meditate for an hour every day."

I tried to calculate the time he must spend driving to the trails, hiking the trails, meditating... "So when do you get up in the morning?"

"Three."

Good thing he was hiking behind me and couldn't see me nearly trip over my jaw dropping to the ground. "What time do you go to bed?"

"Seven."

There was nothing wrong with hiking, or meditation, or wellsprings. But getting up at three and going to bed at seven? His lifestyle didn't allow for date nights—or really anything outside of work and filling his wellspring. And if Tread got married and had kids? How would those ever fit between his self-imposed tidy little margins?

He was still speaking. "...I think our real purpose as human beings here on earth is to become fully realized within ourselves and then help others to do the same."

I snapped my fingers, but my gloves muted the sound. "That sounds familiar. Have you read a book about this?"

"Actually, I wrote a book about this. *Thirty Days to Living at Peace with Yourself, Others, and the Natural World.* Have you read it?" There it was. The very un-Zen and un-guru tone of pride in a job well done. Good to know he was still human.

Now I regretted bringing it up. "Not exactly. But I've heard about it."

Oh, I'd certainly heard about it. Great-Aunt Hildie had sent it to Grandma as a sincere but misguided effort to help Grandma stop cursing. But Grandma liked to curse. And Grandma liked to fight. Great-Aunt Hildie couldn't have been prepared for the brutality of Grandma's "return to sender" note. She'd also been unprepared for Grandma's onslaught of holiday and birthday cards— all of them with some variation of swearing—over the next several years, which could've been avoided if Hildie had stopped sending other self-help books. Actually, the obscenity-filled card battle might still be waging. All over a self-help book.

This wasn't a story I could tell Tread. Fortunately, just then we stepped from the wooded trail and onto an open plateau at the peak of the mountain. Murmurs of "The others really missed out today" echoed through our group.

I turned to Tread, but he was already doing a sun salutation on a flat rock at the edge of the mountain. A short distance away from him, a couple from a different hiking group leaned close to one another for a selfie. Their cheeks pressed together. They turned to watch the sunrise, holding hands.

Aleia stepped toward me, her warm breath clouding around her head. I took a steaming tin cup from her. My thumb traced the logo of the guide company along the rim. The cups were souvenirs to take home with us.

"Enjoy," Aleia whispered, keeping the peace for everyone else taking in the view.

"Thank you. And thanks for the hike," I said. "It's been fun."

"You're welcome. Is this your first time—"

Tread, apparently finished with his sun salutations, interrupted. "Do you have any soy milk?"

"No," Aleia said. "Just the cream and sugar packets I left on my bag under the tree over there."

"Regular dairy cream and white sugar?"

"Yes."

"Not even almond or coconut milk?" Again with the un-Zen tone.

"Just dairy creamer."

"Does it bother you"—his guru voice was back—"that you're hiking in this beautiful wilderness and then feeding people unethically sourced cream and processed sugar?"

Her customer service was flawless. "I'm not the one who handles ordering supplies for the company, sir. If you'd like to leave some constructive feedback, there's a form on our website. We always welcome new solutions and ideas."

Tread nodded. "I think I will. Thank you."

Book note: Don't tolerate someone who don't walk the talk.

Aleia and I enjoyed the view in silence, sipping our coffee. Too soon, we formed an almost-line and meandered along the trail toward the parking lot.

While Tread darted to the front of the line to continue pestering Aleia about milk and sugar, I hung back. Tread, in his quest to become his fully realized self, was, to put it kindly, a jerk. He and Quiff struck me as similar in the way they talked about themselves and other people. Quiff couldn't have cared less about me because he was too worried about his hair and selfies; Tread was more concerned with the appearance of connecting with people than he was with treating people, like Aleia, decently.

Quiff and Tread reminded me of the people that Ivy found so frustrating in the dating world. They couldn't be more opposite from Cameron, who put genuine effort into connecting with others. No matter who you were, you felt special when Cameron focused his attention on you.

I tucked my hands deeper into my pockets, telling myself that this wasn't a failed mancounter, even if it felt like a failure, because I could still add this experience to my book. Maybe I would organize the chapters according to the most common pitfalls. This one could be *Self-Care Gurus and Selfie-Addicts Make Selfish Dates*.

Move along, people. No failure to see here.

I had just settled into my car, willing the heater to warm up faster, when my phone vibrated with a call.

"I heard someone went rogue."

Cameron's tone was lighthearted, but I still heard the concern—or was it disappointment? I also heard the sleepiness in his voice. He must've just woken up. His morning voice was…

I shouldn't be thinking about Cameron's morning voice. I shouldn't be imagining him still in bed, his phone propped between his ear and a naked shoulder, his comforter skewed at an angle to let soft, early light dance across those actual *pecs* I'd seen on the yacht. Who knew, maybe he slept in those boxers with the miniature cartoon Albert Einsteins.

Just friends.

I cleared my throat. "Good morning to you, too, Cam. I guess Ivy told you."

"She did. And then you didn't answer your phone."

"Sorry, Mom, I didn't have any service in the wilderness. I promise I'm okay."

"It's not weakness to have a wingman," he said.

"I know it's—"

"Even Tom Cruise had Goose."

Did he really just reference *Top Gun*?

"Even Captain Kirk had Spock. Even Sherlock had Watson."

"Okay, I get it—"

"Even Mulan had that sassy little dragon voiced by Eddie Murphy."

I laughed. "Okay, I get it. You and Ivy are being supportive as I take a stab at potentially living my dream. Thank you."

"And even that Eddie Murphy dragon worried about murderers in the wilderness sometimes."

"He did?"

"No clue. I haven't seen the movie in forever."

I smiled, warming from my slowly heating car and from our conversation —this was so much better than talking to Tread. "We can watch *Mulan* next Monday night."

"Back to my point. You know I like hiking. I would've gone with you regardless of the list, as long as you wanted me there."

"You would've?"

"Why didn't Marcus go with you?"

I fiddled with my car's heat settings. "I didn't ask him."

"Did you tell him about the list?"

"No."

"Are you going to?"

"Probably at some point."

Honestly, I hadn't thought that far. We'd just met. It was one date. He'd been traveling for work all week. We texted. But it was hard to tell where this was going. That was sensible reasoning, right? Right. Not at all selfish like Quiff and Tread.

He cleared his throat. "Which trail did you take?"

"Creek Run Pass."

"So you went to the peak and saw the frost at sunrise?"

"How did you know? Have you done it before?"

I pushed away an image of Cameron cuddling close to a girlfriend for a selfie, their smiling cheeks pressed together, holding her hand while they watched the sunrise.

"A couple times with my sister when she was doing some wilderness certification. It was ages ago now. But the view was amazing."

Cameron and his imaginary girlfriend went up in imaginary smoke. I shouldn't feel so much relief that he watched the sunrise with only his sister.

The distinct sound of a coffeemaker beeped in the background. So he wasn't lounging in bed, but those boxers might still be in the picture.

"Anyway," he said, "I'll let you go. Just tell me the next time you're doing something fun. If you want company."

Maybe it was all these half-naked Camerons floating around my head. Maybe it was the quiet of my car in the silent parking lot. Or maybe it was the comfort of his voice in my ear after I felt like a failure yet again. Regardless, the intimacy stirred me to say something a little closer to my deeper feelings than what I normally would say, even with him.

"Cam?"

He paused, only his breath filling our connection. "Yeah?"

"Are you saying you want to be the Mushu to my Mulan?"

"I already am."

His answer was automatic, natural, like he didn't need to think about the words before he said them. I didn't even have a chance to hold my breath in anticipation. Still, I smiled. Maybe, someday, possibly—

I shut down the thought before it could go any further and send me into more senseless daydreams.

CHAPTER 32

CAMERON

From: Alma Torres
To: Cameron Whitacre
Subject: RE: Interview Request – The Courier

Dr. Whitacre,

Attached below is the article. Please let me know what you think of it within the next twenty-four hours (sorry for the short turnaround!) and we can discuss making changes if you have preferences. We'll go to press—only if you're happy with it—within a few days.

Thank you again,
Alma

Cameron Whitacre: Computer Science & IT
By Alma Torres

Several years ago, a sophomore student was walking to his Tuesday class when his left leg went numb and a headache that had been growing worse every day suddenly turned to razor blades inside his skull. He collapsed, passing out from the pain. Later, he woke up in the hospital and learned he would need to rebuild his entire life because the unthinkable happened. He had just survived a stroke.

Today, this student is now a professor at our university. He is arguably the most popular professor on campus because of his approachability and patience, his genuine goal for all his students to succeed.

This student turned professor is Dr. Cameron Whitacre, adjunct professor of computer science and director of the IT department. In the years spanning the distance between that fateful Tuesday and today, he has achieved remarkable feats.

Academically, Dr. Whitacre graduated at the top of his high school and college classes. He earned fellowships at top universities. He has received several academic and teaching awards, not to mention grants for research.

More important than book knowledge, however, is Dr. Whitacre's real-life knowledge. Recovering from the stroke took years of intense therapy and grit.

Before the stroke, Dr. Whitacre had a normal life. Growing up, he was "raised by my father, mother, and bossy older sister who thought she was my second, better mother." In high school, he earned good grades and played multiple sports. His true talents shone on the basketball court. When he graduated, he was offered several basketball scholarships. He chose a nationally recognized college, quickly making a name for himself as their best player within the first few months of his freshman year.

All of this changed after the stroke.

He dropped out of college to devote himself to rehab. He moved in with his parents, who became his 24/7 caretakers.

The road to recovery was long. Young Dr. Whitacre was fortunate that his arm movement came back "relatively quickly." His legs were a different matter.

"I started thinking that I would never get my legs back... That's when the depression hit."

One of the biggest hurdles was the difference in how people treated Dr. Whitacre as a "stroke victim." He hated that people would look at him with pity, "like they thought I'd break in two at any moment."

This did not help his battle with depression. Watching his friends graduate and move on was the proverbial salt in his wounds.

Fortunately, he had a few good people in his strong support system who stuck with him and encouraged him through every step of the rebuilding process.

His "then-physical therapist, now-friend," Toby Azumah, was instrumental, motivating him to keep going. At the time, Toby was "incredibly annoying," Dr. Whitacre said. "I was willing to do anything to get him off my back...he's the only person I know who's more stubborn than I am... He wouldn't let me stop."

Toby Azumah, physical therapist at Better Movement, remembers this a little differently. "Cameron is, to this day, the most challenging patient I've ever worked with," Mr. Azumah said. "But I can also honestly say that he's had the most success. It's not often a person can go from a near-death stroke, being completely incapacitated, and transform their life into something totally new."

Dr. Whitacre appreciates his support system even now. "The past can feel heavy. But sometimes the future feels heavy, too. Just being with people who love you, and loving them back...makes the heaviness a little lighter."

Ivy Lunden, registrar staff, is good friends with Dr. Whitacre. "Students practically swarm my desk each semester to get into his classes. I even had someone try to bribe me with wine and chocolates."

Melanie Hirsch, writing tutor at the tutoring center, said, "Dr. Whitacre is an incredible professor and an incredible friend. His compassion, his kindness, and his expertise in his field are unrivaled. I couldn't ask for a better coworker, and I couldn't ask for a better friend."

Today, Dr. Whitacre brings his life experiences into the classroom, particularly in the way he interacts with students. He endlessly encourages growth and critical thinking. Just like he learned during his rebuilding process, "sometimes you need someone who'll love you while they also push you to be a better person." He shows students that they're valued while he urges them to reach their full potential. Whether he's teaching one of his computer science classes, troubleshooting technology in the IT lab, or grading papers in the smallest office ever seen, he is a critical part of the solid infrastructure that makes up our university.

The hard work won't stop anytime soon. His determination and can-do spirit are contagious in his classroom, on campus, and in the community. Nothing—not even a one-in-a-million stroke—can stop Dr. Whitacre from making our campus a better place.

From: Cameron Whitacre

To: Alma Torres
Subject: RE: Interview Request – The Courier

Alma, thank you for sending the article. You're quite the wordsmith to turn my jumbled interview into this masterpiece. If only you could've described me as handsome and dashing (despite my crooked smile). But since that's too much creative license for journalism, I approve the article as is. Onward to press.

Thanks,
Cameron Whitacre
Computer Science Mind-Bender (Adjunct Professor) and IT Department Wizard (Director)

CHAPTER 33

CAMERON

From: Keith Freisen
To: Cameron Whitacre
Subject: Courier Article

Dr. Whitacre,

Congratulations on your profile in The Courier. I just read it late last night. I know you were hesitant to take on this task. I appreciate you stepping outside your normal realm of expertise for this.

The article is a testimony to Alma's writing, to be sure, but it is also a testimony to your own strength of character. Even before the article, I believed you were an asset to this university, its students, and the community. I know the others on the hiring committee now believe the same. As ever, I will advocate for you taking on the full-time position as soon as possible.

Regards,
Keith Freisen, PhD
Academic Department Chair
Computer Science and Information Technology

My Mel was laughing at something Marcus had said. They stood in the sandwich line at the cafeteria, people streaming around them as they clearly enjoyed their own little world.

Her laughter wasn't a polite "that joke was mediocre, but I'll laugh to be nice" kind of laugh. It was a real Mel laugh, with her head tilted to the side, her dark waves swaying. If I listened closely enough, I could probably hear it through the background noise of the busy cafeteria.

My gaze shifted from Mel's beautiful laugh to Marcus's hands. Didn't he respect the fact that he was at Mel's workplace? He'd been all hands since they met at the front door. Every minute he could, he touched her in some way. The small of her back, her elbow, her hand when they exchanged looks.

Was this what hate felt like? Because this felt very much like how I imagined hate would feel. But it was tinged with something else, too. Something that clouded over my burning frustration and smothered it with regret. How could I have been so foolish and waited so long? It would've been better to have tried and failed than not try at all. And now…

This was childish of me. From what I knew, Marcus was a good person. Even now, in his fancy suit that drew all the students' eyes to him (just like I'm sure he'd intended) he moved through the cafeteria with her like she was the center of his universe. He was good to Mel. From her texts alone, she was giddy with the new world she saw through her heart-shaped Marcus glasses.

They were at the fountain drinks now. I had a clear view of her face as she angled her chin to look up at him, her eyes bright in a way that they never were when she looked at me.

I stabbed my fork at my food, mindless of exactly what I was eating. I didn't want to think about the article, but I didn't want to think about this, either. In fact, I had planned to tell Ivy and Mel about the article over lunch today, back when I'd thought it would be just the three of us. But with Marcus around? Forget it.

Ivy's voice, a droning white noise in my ears, stopped.

I snapped to attention. "Sorry. Were you saying something?"

She rolled her eyes at me. "For someone so smart, you're such an idiot."

"I'm pretty sure that's not what you were saying."

"For years I've sat here and watched you wait for Mel to fall in love with you. But you've never even tried."

Wait. She knew? What had given me away? How long had Ivy known? Not that it mattered. I already had Toby all over me. And I had my own thoughts and feelings battling it out in my head and chest. Ivy really didn't need to join the fray.

Best solution: play dumb.

"I don't know what you're talking about."

She leaned closer. "You're too scared to take a chance. And you disrespect yourself and her by making the decision for her."

"I never made a decision for her."

"You do every time you look at her like she's the Georgia O'Keeffe to your Alfred Stieglitz and still you never tell her how you feel."

"The who to my what?" Her art references were always beyond me.

"I said, you're an idiot. You make the decision for her by never even giving her the option. By not even asking her if she's interested in you."

She frowned at me, and all the tension in my chest moved to my posture. She was right, in a way. But so was I. I had my reasons for staying in the background, and they were good ones.

"Let's say you're right—hypothetically. If I'm so obvious that you figured this out, then why hasn't Mel? Maybe she knows and doesn't want to risk ruining our friendship."

Ivy's face softened. "Come on. You know her just as well as I do. Mel is...Mel has some blind spots."

I frowned at her.

"You know it's true," she continued. "She's not meanspirited about it. She just doesn't always notice things like most of us do because she puts all her attention on whatever that one thing is that she's after in that one moment."

I couldn't deny that. Her focus and resilience were just two of the things I loved about her. She saw what she wanted, and she went for it, and once she had it, she never let go. I wished I were more like that, that sure about life.

But Ivy didn't mean this in a positive way.

Mel and Marcus were still at the fountain drinks, and she was so happy to talk with him and stare at him that she didn't notice the students trying to get their own drinks. Marcus was the first to realize they were holding up the line. So he touched her arm (of course) to guide her out of the students' path.

I stabbed at my plate again. "I was going to tell her last week. But then she sent those texts about her date at Armand's, and I just..."

She made a scoffing sound in her throat.

None of my plans mattered anymore anyway. "I can't ask her now."

Mel and Marcus made their way across the cafeteria to our table. She walked in front while he clearly appreciated the view. (Wouldn't I do the same if I had the chance?) But the look on her face, with that lightness in her step...

"Look at her," I said. "She's...incandescent."

"They barely know each other."

"But they both look like all they really want out of life is to get to know each other."

How could I take that happiness from her by telling her I loved her now of all times? I'd had five years to do something about it.

"I guarantee that if you asked her out right this second, she would say yes, even if Marcus stood right next to her when she did it."

"You don't know that. She thinks he's *perfect*. Remember?" I muttered to Ivy just before Mel and Marcus were close enough to hear me.

Mel set down her plate and began the introductions. "Ivy, this is Marcus. Marcus, this is Ivy, registrar staff by day and artist by night."

Ivy rolled her eyes and focused on Marcus. "Nice to meet you. Welcome to the magical world of the cafeteria, where all the drama unfolds and the tuna casserole tastes different every time they make it."

Mel gestured toward my side of the table. "Cam, this is Marcus. Marcus, this is Cam, computer science professor and IT department director."

I stood to my full height, topping Marcus by a couple of inches. I offered a close-lipped smile. "Hey."

"Nice to meet you." Marcus shook my offered hand, his smile stiffening because I may or may not have squeezed his fingers too hard.

"Cam, sit over here on my side." Ivy pulled out a chair. "Make room for Marcus."

"Thanks, man." Marcus smiled as he settled next to Mel.

Mel picked up her fork. "Tonya says there are double-fudge brownies for dessert today. A fresh batch will be out in thirty minutes."

Ivy reached for the ketchup. "Tonya talked to you?"

Mel smiled (no, *beamed*) at Marcus. "It was all him. He charmed her."

So he was also the kind to charm the perpetually moody cafeteria worker who always wore purple eyeliner and fluffy orange Crocs. The best I'd gotten from Tonya was an extra cookie once. It had been stale. So it probably didn't count.

Marcus draped an arm over the back of Mel's chair.

My hand clenched around my fork as I imagined casually leaning across the table and stabbing it into his shoulder.

A corner of his mouth lifted with smugness. "Tonya wasn't that bad."

Mel nudged his shoulder (the very one I'd mutilated in my mind). "She went from hating you to thinking you're worthy of the inside scoop about dessert. That's a big jump in the space of one conversation. Especially for Tonya."

Fortunately Marcus already had a mouthful of sandwich and couldn't grace us with another insight into Tonya not being "that bad."

"So what do you do, Marcus?" Ivy said.

"Finance."

She scrunched up her nose. "Too vague. Are you in corporate finance or startup finance?"

"Former corporate, current startup."

So that was how he could afford Armand's. I hoped the FBI and IRA were raiding his swanky mansion at this very moment.

"Feeling shabby with the commoners these days?" I said.

He reached for a napkin. "Hardly. The startups are growing quickly. I have to travel more, but it's worth it to watch these new businesses take off."

"Next week he's going to Miami." Mel grinned like it was the most exotic place she'd ever heard of.

Ivy sighed. "I'd love a sunny day at the beach."

Marcus flashed his perfect smile. "I'll be there over the weekend, too. You're all welcome to come visit if you want."

A Miami vacation with Marcus? Maybe I could bury him up to his neck in sand.

"I wish I could." Ivy circled a finger over the rim of her plastic cafeteria cup. "I have too much going on right now. Mel probably can though."

My chest seized up. Mel and Marcus in Miami for a weekend? Alone? She'd probably wear a bikini, and they'd probably share a hotel room, and they'd probably— Wait. How many nude beaches were in Miami?

"I can't," Mel said. "My grandma's birthday is this weekend."

The seizing in my chest eased up. "How's your grandma's hip doing?"

"It hurts a lot more in the cold, but she gets around okay. She still curses at the doctor every time he mentions a hip replacement." She smiled at me. "Thanks for asking. That's sweet of you to remember."

If I were sweet, I wouldn't be thinking of all the other non-shoulder places I'd love to stab Marcus with my fork.

Ivy kicked her pointed shoe into my shin.

I angled my legs away from her.

Marcus sipped his water. "I'll be back in Miami next month. Maybe we can all go then. What about you, Cam? Want to join us on our hypothetical vacation next month?"

How had I been roped into this Miami idea? The last thing I wanted to see was Mel walking hand in hand with Marcus along a beach. I already had to choke down my food while his arm draped across the back of her chair. How much more of this could I sit through?

Not much, apparently, because a dark slip of hair curled around the side of Mel's face (not even anywhere in her way, for the record), and Marcus reached over to tuck it behind her ear like it was the most natural thing for him to do. Her cheeks pinked.

My fork clattered too loudly onto my plate, my chair nearly toppled when I stood too quickly, and my voice was too stiff. "I need to head back to the office. Some new software came in, and I need to test it before we send it out to everyone." I tried not to rush too obviously as I slung my messenger bag over my shoulder and took my half-full plate.

Mel's shoulders sagged. "So soon? We just got here."

"Yeah, sorry, busy day," I mumbled.

Marcus sent that perfect smile my way. "It was great to meet you, Cam."

"Likewise."

I fled.

CHAPTER 34

MEL

Mel: They had memes in the 1950s! "Mail him a cartoon for an inside joke."
Cameron: This also qualifies as GIFs.
Ivy: Don't you two have a whole separate thread where you just send GIFs
back and forth instead of having an actual conversation?
Cameron: We do.
Mel: We invited you, Ivy, but you rejected us.
Ivy: I can only handle so many of Cam's Jack Black GIFs.
Cameron: There's a certain finesse to entire conversations in GIFs. I guess you
just can't have everything.

Since Ivy had to stay late at work, it was just me and Cameron in the stacks at our local indie bookstore, Between Two Covers. It was easily one of my favorite places of all time. The store always had something new, even putting the larger corporate bookstores to shame with how well the owner could predict a little-known title that would make it big within a few months. If there was something here, and you hadn't heard of it yet, it was almost guaranteed you'd know all about it soon. At first glance, books and records towered haphazardly in stacks, but if you looked closer, you could decipher an organized chaos that helped you find exactly what you wanted—and also find new books you hadn't known you would love.

We were supposed to be looking for my next "victim"—as Cameron put it —but he was spending more time tugging at the buttons on his shirtsleeves than anything else.

We paused at a large area filled with comic books. I recognized the biggest names. Thanks to Marcus, who had just flown to Miami this morning, I knew a few of the more obscure ones, too. Not that Marcus needed to know I was using his comic book interest as a way to talk to other men without him knowing.

My stomach dropped at the thought. What was I doing? Maybe Cameron was right. I should tell Marcus about the experiment. But what if he wasn't okay with it, and what would I do if I had to choose between a man who seemed perfect and a writing idea that might—

I couldn't think like this right now. For a distraction, I gestured at the comic book section and asked Cameron, "Do you ever read these?"

"Sometimes. You?"

"No. They just seemed like something you'd like."

He grinned. "What does that mean?"

"You seem like someone who grew up reading Marvel comics, so you would know all the backstories and Easter eggs that I always miss in the movies."

"Someone like him?" He nodded toward a lanky teenager sitting cross-legged on the floor, a stack of comic books next to him. The teenager slowly turned a page, clearly reading the books at the store instead of buying them to read at home.

"Exactly like him," I said.

"Sorry to disappoint. I was a jock in my high school years." He smiled down at me, the corners of his eyes crinkling.

I tried to imagine Cameron as an athlete in a jersey and not a professor in a button-down. I always forgot how different his pre- and post-stroke lives looked. I hoped to camouflage my thoughtlessness by tugging a comic book from the shelf.

Glancing into the aisle again, I noticed someone else partially hidden behind a stack. Extremely tall, extremely good looking. Maybe I could try out list item "tell him he's handsome."

"He's the one."

"The high schooler?" Cameron sounded appropriately horrified.

"Of course not. The guy behind him."

I watched Cameron study him for a moment, his blue eyes cataloguing each detail he could see from this distance. Of course Cameron was better looking than the man reading the comic books—but maybe I was biased. I knew Cameron so well I could recognize his footsteps in a busy hallway and pick out his laugh in a noisy room. Surely knowing someone so well made them more subjectively attractive.

A thought smacked into my brain. Why not tell Cameron he's handsome? Technically, it would fulfill the list. The imaginary scene played out in my mind: I'd tell him he's handsome, he'd look surprised and dodge the compliment, I'd insist, and he'd tighten his humor-shield into place to make a joke about me being so desperate that everyone was starting to look handsome. I'd feel shot down, and I'd wonder whether I *was* desperate to keep allowing myself to think about Cameron like this.

That sounded just like us. No matter how many of my daydreams starred Cameron, I would just be a sidekick in his superhero saga. I didn't wait to hear his opinion about the tall stranger.

"I'm going in." I sounded more confident than I felt, my mind still half-wondering about Cameron.

I walked past the stranger, pretending to peruse the covers while I watched him and noted the comic book he held. The title said something about X-Men. At least I knew a little bit about them from the movies. The more obscure titles I ran my fingertip over were well outside my limited knowledge of Marcus's superhero references.

Clearing my throat, I began to say "Excuse me, could you recommend a comic book for a beginner Marvel fan?" but I didn't make it past "Excuse me" because he turned to look at me and—I'd never seen someone so handsome in my life. He was celebrity-level handsome, or somebody else well beyond my league. People this attractive actually existed off the silver screen?

An irrational thought muddled its way through his good looks. Sure, he'd been reading an X-Men comic, but maybe he was the actor for the next superhero movie that I just didn't know about yet?

Book note: Comic books aren't just for high schoolers.

"You're really handsome." My voice sounded as stunned as I felt. It had been my plan to tell him he was handsome, but, well—this certainly was not my smoothest moment. I'd imagined saying it with a bit more finesse.

He smiled as if he'd never been told that before. "You're pretty, too," he said.

"Thanks." Did I sound gushy? I felt gushy.

Closing his comic book, he fully turned toward me. His cologne wrapped around us, enveloping us away from the high schooler and Cameron standing just a few yards away. His gaze moved over my face. Hopefully I didn't look as flabbergasted as I felt.

"I'm Mel," I managed.

He continued smiling. "Nice to meet you, Mel. I'm Evan. But, you know" —he tucked the X-Men comic back onto the shelf—"you can call me Clark, if you want." He leaned closer. "But only if you let me call you Lois."

CHAPTER 35

CAMERON

Mel: Cam, if I stumbled when I walked into a room that you're in, would you notice me?
Cameron: Is this your way of telling me you need me to take you to the ER because you tripped and cracked your head open?
Mel: No. It's from the list.
Cameron: In that case, I would definitely notice you. And I would think that you're clumsy and my insurance policy can't afford you.

I have a handful of preselected favorite moments in life. When my dad handed me the keys to Granddad's old Chevy. When I was voted MVP of my high school basketball team for my junior and senior years. The first steps I took after all those months of physical therapy.

But the look on Mel's face when Wannabe Clark Kent offered to call her Lois? That nearly topped them all.

Her jaw dropped open. Her eyes widened. Her face turned bright pink.

"Like...Lois Lane?" she croaked.

He nodded, grinned, and leaned closer, clearly thinking that line had done him some good. (No, Clark, that line would never impress a woman who doesn't have tickets to Comic Con.)

"That's not really my kind of thing," she said.

He frowned. "You don't like Superman? How could you not like Superman?"

"He's too perfect. Nobody wants to be with someone who's so perfect. And all the stories are basically the same. He's the picture of justice, the villain finds some kryptonite, he needs to save his loved ones, the end. It's always all about the kryptonite."

His voice rose defensively. "That's not true at all. He's—"

Mel interrupted. "It's just not my thing."

Clark Kent frowned, studying Mel as he jammed his hands into his pockets. He cleared his throat. "Fine. What if you call me Bruce and I call you Rachel?"

It took my own superhero effort not to double over with laughter.

"I'd rather not." Mel's tone was polite but firm.

"You don't like Batman either?" He let out an exasperated sigh.

"He's too dark."

"Superman is too perfect, and Batman is too dark? This isn't going to work." Shaking his head, he walked past me, mumbling something about women not appreciating quality literature.

I stared at the comic books on the shelf in front of me like they were the most fascinating things I'd seen since the latest Alan Turing documentary.

Mel stepped next to me, her cheeks still pink. "Did you hear all that?"

"Hear what?"

She frowned, and I swallowed back the urge to smooth my thumb over the crease on her forehead. (Marcus would probably do it without a second thought.)

"That guy. He just…"

"He just what?"

She bit her lip. "You know what? Never mind. It just didn't work out."

My jaw tensed with the effort to keep a straight face. "Not into the superhero scene, Lois?"

She was so preoccupied with what Clark had said that it took a moment for the name to register. When it did, she punched me in the arm.

"Hey." I laughed and pretended to rub a nonexistent bruise. "Cut it out, Selina Kyle. Or how about Jean Grey?"

She laughed then, too, the crease on her forehead melting. (I did that. I melted that crease. And I didn't even need my overly touchy hands, *Marcus.*)

"You have to admit it's funny," I whispered. "Possibly the funniest one you've met yet."

"I get that people are into roleplay or whatever, but there was absolutely no buildup to that."

"Right," I said. "All action and no thought. Kind of like a Superman plot?"

"Very funny."

The teenager sitting on the floor shot us a glare over his comic book. I took Mel's elbow and steered her toward the exit.

"But seriously, you don't like Superman?" I held the door open, and we stepped into the glow of evening streetlights.

She shrugged. "Not really. I mean, I get that he has inner conflict, and I get that his weakness is kryptonite. But he doesn't really have any human, relatable flaws. Or at least not relatable to me."

I jammed my fists into my pockets to stop myself from warming her hands with my own. I doubted Marcus would appreciate another man helping Mel with her cold hands. I also doubted he would appreciate this whole mancounter, but it was none of my business. Or so I kept telling myself.

I cleared my throat. "You're forgetting his biggest weakness of all."

"What's that?"

I feigned shock. "Surely you know."

"No." Now she was curious, fully turning her eyes away from the snowy sidewalk and toward me. "What's Superman's biggest flaw?"

Leaning close, I whispered, "His mother's name is Martha."

She frowned. "I don't get it."

"Haven't you seen *Batman v Superman*?"

"No," she laughed. "Maybe *you* should date our friend Clark Kent."

"Nah. I don't think the name 'Lois' is a good fit for me."

I fully deserved that punch in the arm, too.

CHAPTER 36

MEL

Mel: "Never tell him how much you spend on clothes."
Cameron: That's right. Get married first and then slap him over the head with
your shopping bills. Bam! Healthy marriages since the 1950s!

The plan had been for Cameron and Ivy to meet me at the Bluesy Bean after
work. We would catch up, figure out plans for the next mancounter on the list.
I'd arrived much too early on purpose. Cameron had a late class, and Ivy had
something to take care of at home first, and I wanted time to look over the list
before they arrived.

The snow had finally stopped a few hours earlier, turning the day from a
gray snow globe into a sunshiny freezer. Every person in the dining area sat
with their hands cupped around a steaming mug of warmth. Even though most
Northerners knew not to complain about the cold—complaining just made you
think about it more—we still fought against the frigid temperatures with hot
drinks and thick socks.

I'd ignored a notification from Mom—vacationing in Santorini now—in
favor of texting Marcus, sending a picture of the Bluesy Bean full of bundled-
up customers.

Mel: Don't you miss this?
Marcus: Miami is looking better and better!

Mel: I'm sure it is. Thanks for rubbing it in.

He'd sent a photo of a pink and orange sky, rippling waters, and the arching back and fin of a dolphin peeking between the waves. I could almost feel the sand between my toes.

Mel: Jealous!

Marcus: It's paradise. The only thing missing is you.

While I'd texted him and waited for my coffee, a man about my height had stood next to me. His business casual slacks were topped with a winter coat and a thick cap. His smile had been much too happy for a weeknight evening. I'd liked him immediately.

Now, almost thirty minutes later, I couldn't even remember how we'd started talking in the first place. We'd settled at a small, round table near the pastry display and eased into comfortable conversation, him drinking his Americano and me sipping my decaf. Maybe my grandma was right about the most natural connections happening organically. I should have a chapter about it in my book. Something about choosing organic for food *and* for relationships.

The timing of running into my new companion, Gil, just after texting Marcus wasn't lost on me. Even without anyone but me knowing, I felt guilt settle into my stomach. I did my best to ignore it.

Ivy had arrived before Cameron. Seeing me sitting with Gil, she'd chosen a table next to ours, quietly pulling off her gloves and coat to wait for Cameron.

He hadn't been far behind. Unlike Ivy, who'd been discreet, Cameron had slowly removed his coat while watching us closely enough that Gil had noticed, giving him a "mind your own business" look.

All I knew was that I felt more comfortable with Gil than I had with just about any other mancounter—other than when I met Marcus, of course. His happy smile was just one piece of his happy personality, and I'd found my own mood lifting to meet his.

Once Cameron had walked toward the barista, I tuned back in to hear my new friend cheerfully complain about the family drama that unfolded at his brother's recent wedding.

"…but the real treat was my great-aunt, who went around asking everyone how long they expected the marriage to last."

"You're kidding?" I laughed.

"I wish. If people said they thought the couple was a perfect match, she said she agreed that the marriage would last forever. If they said the couple was less than ideal, she said she gave it three months."

"Did your brother ever find out?"

He nodded, a lock of reddish hair falling over his brow. "He tried to get her to stop, but she just laughed, told him to drink more champagne, and moved on to the next person."

Cameron returned to the table next to us. He whispered to Ivy, who shrugged and pushed her half-eaten pastry across the table to him. Guilt brought me down from my good mood with Gil. I'd made plans with my friends, and now I was sitting here with someone else.

"I'm not for or against marriage one way or another," Gil said, "but I'm all for eloping somewhere quiet. Just the officiant, me, and my girl."

The list floated into my mind, like it usually did these days. By now, I had it memorized. I could picture it, complete with bullet points, indentations, and Times New Roman twelve-point font. *I'm thinking of...*

"I'm thinking of getting married." I said it nonchalantly, noncommittally, quoting the list like it was the most natural thing for me to do.

Cameron's coffee sloshed onto their table.

"Oh? Are you engaged?" Gil's eyes darted to my bare ring finger.

"No, I just think about it a lot." I cleared my throat to stall, unsure of what to say next.

Grinning, Gil quirked an eyebrow. "Are you saying I'm in the running?"

"Would you like to be?" I hoped my smile looked as flirty as the ones I'd seen Ivy toss around.

The thought occurred to me that I might be getting his hopes up for nothing. Well, not nothing, but for my own selfish interest in writing my book. I squashed the thought just as quickly as it popped into my head. Just because these mancounters were designed with my book in mind didn't mean I wouldn't connect with someone at a deeper level, like I had with Marcus. The experiment wasn't selfish because, essentially, it was like regular dating. Meet someone, get to know them, see what happens. And like regular dating, Gil might be vaguely interested, but it was simply that—vague interest. Just because I would probably write about Gil didn't mean I was cold-hearted. Right?

His gaze turned serious. "In that case, you should know I'm very family oriented."

I smiled. "Is this your nice way of saying you still live with your mother?"

He laughed. "No. I mean my family is everything to me." He pulled his phone from his pocket, opening his photo app. "Here, you can see them if you want." He slid his phone toward me.

Looking down, I stared into the eyes of a chubby angel, complete with rosy cheeks and a pink hairbow magically fastened to an otherwise bald head.

"She's precious!" I summersaulted through some numbers to piece together a vague timeline. How old was Gil, and how old was the baby? Was he divorced, or a widower, or a single dad? "You must be very proud to have such a beautiful daughter."

"I am very proud, but she's not my daughter. She's my granddaughter."

My gaze ricocheted between the chubby-cheeked angel and his dark hair and wrinkle-free forehead.

He smiled. "It throws off most people. I'm forty-three. My ex and I had my daughter in high school. It wasn't the plan to start a family so young, but I wouldn't trade her for anything."

I nodded, swiping through a few photos of a smiling baby, several of them including a young woman with a carbon copy of Gil's cheerful smile. The baby's mother, Gil's daughter.

"My daughter got pregnant about two years ago," he said. "The father didn't want kids and walked away. So now I have my darling granddaughter. Raising my daughter was the best part of my life, and I didn't think it could get any better until I started helping to raise my granddaughter, too." His smile was sweet and sincere, the kind good people reserved for the ones they loved most.

As sweet as it was, I channeled my inner Cameron and did some quick mental calculations. This meant Gil's daughter was nearly my age. I tried to imagine my dad striking up a relationship with a woman my age—or any father figure striking up a relationship with a woman his daughter's age.

I uncrossed and recrossed my legs, swiping through more photos, thinking of how my parents' phones were filled with screenshots of work projects. Would they have endless pictures of my kids on their phones someday?

"Your family looks so happy," I said.

"They're my pride and joy, as cliché as that sounds," he said. "We're a close-knit family, and we've gone through some tough times together. I think that's why family is so important to me. We can't survive without them, you know?"

"Friends and family," I echoed, my thoughts on the table next to ours, my grandma cursing the neighbors through the open window, my grandpa smiling at her antics with that glow on his face. "Doesn't get much better than that."

"What about you and your family?" He put his phone back in his pocket.

"I'm not as close to my family as you are with yours." I laughed to keep it superficial, but he wasn't having it.

"May I ask why?"

I hesitated. The thought of telling him about my parents' divorce after he'd just gushed about his own family—it didn't feel right. The light in his smile was brilliant compared to the way my family was the opening and closing lines of a book. Connected, related, but vastly separated.

Words from the list hit my tongue before I could think through the consequences. *Tell him you're...*

"I'm adopted."

Ivy's fork, stacked with a bite of quiche, clattered to her plate, eggy bits sticking to their table. Cameron sat motionless, his coffee mug halfway to his lips.

"I haven't met many people who were adopted," he said, eyeing our strange neighbors and their klutzy table manners.

I nodded. "My adoptive parents were great. I don't have any complaints."

"Can I ask about your birth parents?"

Considering I wasn't really adopted? Considering he was being open about himself and the people he loved, while I sat here and outright lied to him? I swallowed the remorse sticking in my throat. "Actually, I'd rather not talk about it."

He nodded, his expression a little sad, clearly wishing my family were more like his. I wished the same, if I were being honest.

We entered our first uncomfortable silence of the evening. I could almost see Gil's mind debating whether an adopted kid would be a well-adjusted adult and a good addition to his own family.

He smiled. "I'm sorry to go, but I need to get home."

"Right, of course. You have a family to get home to. It was great meeting you."

"Nice to meet you, too." He stood. "Maybe I'll see you here again sometime."

"I'm a regular," I said, "so maybe you will."

Book note: Spare yourself some complicated feelings and just tell the truth from the start.

Did that mean telling Marcus the truth, too?

When the bell above the door chimed that Gil had left, I shifted over to Cameron and Ivy's table, bringing my coffee mug with me and hoping to leave behind my guilty feelings. Maybe we could just ignore that I'd held up our evening plans for so long.

Cameron rested his hand over mine. "I'm hurt you never told us you were adopted."

With my other hand, I stole a bite of brownie from his plate. "I'm hurt you only left me one bite of your brownie."

"He seemed nice," Ivy said.

"Did you hear about his family? I'm glad they're his pride and joy, but I can't imagine being with a guy whose daughter is about my age." I cringed.

She nodded. "She would probably find it awkward, too."

"You don't say." Cameron moved his plate farther away from me.

"Some people are probably fine with it," I said. "I just don't think I could do it."

The corners of his eyes crinkled. "Imagine if you two had kids. He'd have a kid and grandkid the same age. Or your four-year-old step-granddaughter would call your newborn baby 'aunt' or 'uncle.'"

Ivy wrinkled her nose, and I grimaced.

"Well, he definitely doesn't get my vote," Ivy said.

I traced the handle of my mug. "He'll make someone very happy someday. Just not me."

"So the manhunt continues." She wiggled her eyebrows. "How many mancounters have you done on the list now?"

"A lot," I said. "I've been keeping notes on everything."

"Have you started writing yet?" Cameron asked.

"No, but I have everything in my head. I have a few angles that I've been brainstorming, just nothing solid yet."

"Let me know if you need a strong feminist perspective," Ivy piped up.

"Or a strong man's perspective," Cameron said. "We are the prey in this whole predatory scenario, you know."

Ivy rolled her eyes. "This isn't *National Geographic*. The prey doesn't get a voice."

He shrugged. "That's up to the writer to decide."

I nodded. "He has a point. I have told him several times that he's our token male in this experiment."

"Our 'token male'? His ego really doesn't need that."

He grinned. "With all your ribbing, my ego needs all the love it can get."

I laughed, but Ivy waved him away. "Enough about your ego. We're your wingpeople, Mel. Tell us what's next on the list."

CHAPTER 37

MEL

Mel: So basically the list expects women to be perfect at all times. Like it says to ask him about the women he didn't marry so that I can avoid the mistakes they made.
Cameron: Don't be a normal, flawed human being, Mel. He might dump you for it.
Ivy: Standards of female perfection haven't changed much, huh?

YouTube contained multitudes. I knew this. Most people in the twenty-first century knew this. It was one thing to fall into the stereotypical wormholes of adorable kittens and baby goats, celebrity interviews, and comedians. But this? Endless YouTube videos about toupees, toupee bases, "thin skin" toupees, "v-looped hair"... It was a world I'd never known existed.

Multitudes indeed. Walt Whitman had no idea.

My last tutoring session had ended an hour ago, and without any other appointments scheduled on the calendar, I'd filled the rest of my shift with research for the list. My eyeballs felt reshaped to the YouTube logo—that's how deep I'd gone.

According to the list, I needed to *make and sell toupees, because bald men are usually single.* Definitely not something I'd ever thought I would spend time researching. But, hey, writing opens new doors all the time. Right?

When I'd texted the group about it, Ivy had sent several laughing GIFs in a row, and Cameron had replied with a *Seinfeld, anyone?*

Mel: I'm hit or miss with Seinfeld episodes. Which one is this?

Cameron: The one where George wears a toupee. Chaos ensues. How do you not know this?

Mel: I can't picture George in a toupee.

Cameron: I have so much to teach you.

Mel: Okay, fine, next Monday night will be a Seinfeld night. We'll watch that episode. Deal?

Cameron: Seinfeld is like potato chips. You can't watch just one.

Mel: Then we'll have a Seinfeld marathon. Better?

A *Seinfeld* episode sounded perfect right about now. A belly laugh would snap me out of my YouTube-coma.

Footsteps echoed in the empty lobby. Cameron was walking toward the exit. At my wave, he detoured toward the tutoring center.

He leaned a shoulder against the doorjamb. His blue eyes shone with half the brightness they usually did. His button-down and dress slacks were wrinkled, and his messenger bag hung limply from a slouching shoulder. Even his cowlick seemed to droop.

"Hiya, Cam. You look exhausted," I said. "Why didn't you go home earlier? You don't have a night class on Fridays."

"There was a compatibility issue with some new software. I needed to take care of it." He grimaced with a stifled yawn. "Why are you still here?"

"Lauren took some PTO for a long weekend."

"Well, don't stay too late." He shifted away from the doorjamb.

"Do you have any plans this weekend?"

His eyes narrowed. "Who's asking?"

I scoffed. "Since when are you coy about weekend plans?"

"Are you asking because you want me to be a toupee model? Because in that case, I'm extremely busy. I bought some avocados this week, and they are going to be ripe between 7:15 and 7:30 Saturday night. I can't miss it."

"No, I don't need a toupee model." I laughed. "I need someone to teach me about golf."

He looked down, tugging at his shirt sleeves. "Why not ask Marcus? He seems like someone who'd have a country club membership."

"He's in Phoenix this weekend. And he can't come with me. This is for the list."

He blinked at me one, two, three times, a tidy line deepening between his eyebrows. "Why are you still doing the list if it's already served its purpose? You met Marcus. You like him. You're dating him. The list is over."

I frowned. Why was Cameron always voicing the doubts I didn't want to say? "It's not over. Meeting Marcus hasn't changed anything about my writing plans."

"Does Marcus know that?"

I glanced at my laptop screen, still open to a YouTube tutorial titled "DIY toupee template." "I haven't had a chance to explain it to him yet, but he'll understand. He'll probably think it's funny."

When Cameron spoke, his voice had a new edge to it. "He won't think it's funny."

Now it was my turn to blink at Cameron. "He won't mind."

A sharp laugh burst from his throat. "I saw how he looks at you, Mel. He likes you. A lot. He'll mind that he clearly thinks you two are dating while you're meeting random strangers as a social experiment."

I prickled with defensiveness. What was his problem? Cameron knew what these mancounters meant to me—a new future for myself. He knew that this was my chance to make something of my writing, to build a career that actually went somewhere. I'd been a writing tutor for years. Promotions weren't an option for me, unlike Cameron, on the brink of his full-time position. How could he discourage me from doing this right now? Didn't he see how important this was, how it could be my big break into living my dream? At some point, I'd explain it, and Marcus would be fine with it. Marcus and I hadn't even discussed whether we were exclusive yet. It was fine.

"Why are you so worried about Marcus?" I wanted to add *You barely even spoke to him when you met him,* but that seemed too petty to say aloud.

"I'm not worried about Marcus. I'm worried about you."

I rolled my eyes. "I told you I'm not losing myself and I'm not in danger. I want to finish the list. I'm no quitter."

Another sharp laugh. "Nobody would ever call you a quitter."

"Then what are you trying to say?"

The muscles in his jaw twitched as he opened, then closed, then opened his mouth again, finally settling it into a thin line. "You and Ivy are always talking about men using women. Demanding stripteases after dates, whistles when you walk down streets, ghosting after a few dates. If you're not serious about Marcus, you need to tell him. If you're still meeting men while you're seeing him, you need to tell him. If you don't, you're just using him."

I closed my laptop more forcefully than necessary. "I'm not using him. He's a mature adult. He'll understand that this project could open up new opportunities for me. Writing this book could change my life." The defensive prickles were full-grown porcupine quills now. "What are you really saying, Cam? What's your problem?"

"I'm saying that I just—" He let out an exasperated sigh. "You and Ivy are right. It's selfish when people use other people. And I just—"

"So you think I'm selfish?"

He raised his voice. "I'm saying that sometimes you get really focused on something, which is a good trait to have, but"—his voice lowered to normal volume again—"but it makes you a little...narrow-sighted."

"You mean selfish." I folded my arms across my chest.

"No, I mean when you're focused on something like you're focused on this list, you lose perspective on other things. Like what other people might think or feel." He gestured vaguely with his hands. "Like right now. You're not taking Marcus and his feelings into consideration. And Ivy. Have you asked Ivy about her mom?"

I'd fully intended to ask Ivy about her mom. To ask about the way she was glued to her phone, or the times she canceled Monday nights or asked to meet at my apartment or Cameron's condo instead of her house. I'd meant to check in with her. To see if she was okay.

But I hadn't. Every time we were together, we talked about other things. Like a session I'd just had with a student whose entire paper didn't have a single punctuation mark, or how Dr. Schaaf's sweater was so covered in coffee stains that it looked more coffee than sweater, or what my next steps were with the list, or... Shame twisted in me.

Cameron was still talking. "That's all I mean. Your focus is awe-inspiring, but that same determination sometimes costs the people around you."

He tugged at his shirt sleeves. "I'm not saying you're selfish, I'm saying it's like whatever you already have is never enough for you. It's like you're so focused on that one thing that you miss what's right in front of you." A deep breath lifted his shoulders. "You're so busy looking somewhere else for happiness and love. But everything you're looking for is...right here."

As he talked, his voice gentled. His tone was one of concern, not anger.

But there's this thing about defensiveness—once the quills are up, there's no bringing them back, no matter how kind Cameron's blue eyes might look or how gentle his tone might sound.

"And what about you?" I demanded. "Since we're picking on flaws tonight."

He opened his mouth to interrupt, but I continued.

"Do you think people don't notice how you use your class clown persona and lame jokes to keep everyone at arm's length? You don't accept compliments, you don't want Alma to write about you, you never want to be serious. Because being serious takes vulnerability. And you're too cowardly for that."

I regretted the words the instant I said them. But I was too proud—selfish? —and too hurt to apologize right then. What he'd said cut deep. He'd plucked out a flaw and shone a spotlight on it. My bruised heart squeezed, sharp quills just waiting to be unleashed if he brought up another flaw, real or perceived.

Cameron stood there, his face expressionless. But his eyes? All of the emotion he could've worn on his face was held in his blue gaze as he stared at me. His feelings were too much for me. I looked away.

The silence felt enormous. His whisper filled it just the same. "Melanie. I just want you to be happy."

I sensed more than saw his lean shadow pace the short distance through the lobby and out the exit, toward the parking lot. The quiet in the Fishbowl felt pained, so much so that I glanced at the carpet as if I would see my words shattered on the floor. Instead, my eyes landed on the place where Cameron had stood when he'd done the interview with Alma. He'd revealed more of himself that day than I'd ever seen before. And now he'd gently revealed something of me. He'd done it with the concern of a friend. And I'd recoiled and lashed out.

Cameron was good people. One of the best. He'd never want to hurt me. He didn't senselessly cause pain. If he thought I was being selfish, if he thought I didn't appreciate what was right in front of me, then he was probably right. Even when the most annoying students plagued him, even when staff meetings lasted for all eternity, he didn't speak badly of anyone. For him to be willing to say these things to me meant that it must be true.

If Cameron saw me as selfish, if Cameron cared enough to tell me, then I was selfish. Plain and simple.

I'd never asked Ivy about her mom. I'd never asked Cameron for more details about the full-time position or Alma's article or how he felt about either one. I hadn't thought of much outside the mancounters in a long time.

And to call him cowardly? He was one of the bravest people I knew.

My hands shook as I wrapped my laptop cord, shoved my timecard into the punch clock, and flicked off the lights in the Fishbowl. I held back my tears until I safely locked myself into my car. But just barely.

Multitudes indeed, Walt Whitman.

CHAPTER 38

CAMERON

Ivy: Here's a bizarre 1950s gem: "When he takes you to dinner, only order your steaks rare."

Student papers and test Scantrons littered my desk. I had a system, I really did, but a larger office would've been handy right about now.

Without meaning to, my eyes drifted across my desk, lingering on Mel's last scribbled note from a few days ago: *Eburnean (Freisen). Grape jelly (Schaaf). I had another student raving about you today!* My gaze settled on the article in *The Courier*. The photo from my university ID, pixelated in black and white, returned my stare. Next to it, my name was printed in bold font.

Kindness.

Determination.

Can-do spirit.

Was that what people really thought of me? The article made me sound so different from how I saw myself. It's a surreal thing to see what other people think of you in physical print. In this case, a good surreal thing. Or maybe they just hadn't been willing to say anything bad when they knew I would read it later.

I hadn't realized Alma would interview anyone else in my life. Toby, Ivy, and Mel hadn't mentioned it. Had Alma tried to contact my family? Had they avoided her like I'd always asked them to avoid reporters when the stroke first happened?

My inbox was filled with so many emails about the article that I'd stopped reading them, instead creating a filter that sent all of them to a specific folder that I would take care of later. Their congratulations were too overwhelming for me to deal with right now. (Except for Dr. Freisen's email. I'd studied his over and over, trying to read between the lines of his management-speak in case there were any details I'd missed about the full-time position. When I started googling cipher methods to see if he'd emailed in code, I knew I'd gone too far.)

All that aside, it was Mel's quote that haunted me the most right now. For the last five years, she'd never called me anything but "friend." She'd made that more than clear. And she was with Marcus now. Obviously they were head over heels for each other. I needed to accept that we were only friends. And I did. For the last few weeks, I'd been trying my best to give Mel space for her new relationship with Marcus while I sorted through my feelings. My only weak moments had been when I'd given in and gone to Between Two Covers and the Bluesy Bean. I couldn't stay away. I craved her too much.

Did she really believe I thought she was selfish? That wasn't what I'd meant at all. She wasn't selfish. Selfishness implied a certain mean intention behind it. Nothing about Mel was mean. I didn't think any less of her for her unbreakable focus.

I'd only been trying to explain to her that the life she had was a good life, with good people. I'd wanted to ask her to stop trying to find happiness some-where else. Her happiness was right here. *I* was right here.

But that's not how it had played out.

Even though I knew it was her knee-jerk reaction to call me cowardly, I knew she was at least partly right. I did hide behind humor. I did orient my life around rebuilding normalcy to make up for what I'd lost. I chewed on my lip, thinking of my crooked smile.

She didn't even know the worst of it, that I'd avoided telling her about my feelings for the last half-decade.

You don't accept compliments, don't want Alma to write about you.

True on both points. The way I squirmed when I first read the article was testament enough.

Being serious takes vulnerability. You're too cowardly for that.

I'd been too cowardly to confess my feelings until it was too late and Marcus was on the scene. Fear of losing her friendship had paralyzed me. But now that same fear urged me into motion. Now I knew how it felt to lose Mel.

I'd spent the last few days without her in my life, and the emptiness left behind was so barren that I was willing to take her friendship over nothing at all. I'd been sick with the knowledge that I'd hurt her, that she wouldn't leave me notes about Dr. Freisen's bowties, that I couldn't smuggle cupcakes to the Fishbowl.

Before I'd been too cowardly, but now I was brave enough to try to fix what was left of our friendship.

Like the article said, I'd rebuilt my life. If I could do that, I could patch things up with Mel.

Picking up my phone, I navigated to our private text conversation, separate from the group thread. My fingers slowly tapped out a message.

Hey. I'm sorry about the other night. I've been giving it a lot of thought. Can we discuss over coffee at the Bluesy Bean? My treat.

No. I couldn't send her that. It was too vague. And too formal. I deleted and tried again.

Hey. I'm sorry about the other night. It's just that I've been in love with you for years, and you never see me like that, no matter how much I try to get your attention, and I need to tell you all the reasons we'd be great together. I know you just met Marcus, so it's bad timing, but I can't stand by anymore. Please—

No way I was sending that.

I deleted again.

Hey. I'm sorry about the other night. I've been giving it a lot of thought—

But all I can think about is your brown eyes, and how your wavy hair would feel between my fingers. And the way you're the first person I want to tell when I get good or bad news. And how much it means to me when you laugh at my jokes or steal my nachos at basketball games. And I think you don't see me. Or the relationship we could have.

—and you're right. It's your decision whether to tell Marcus about the list. I overstepped.

My fingers paused over the digital keyboard. This is what she wanted. If I'd made it this long, I could make it through forever being just friends. Even if Marcus was there. (But no promises that I wouldn't imagine stabbing him with a fork.)

Forgive me, friend?

If I really loved her (and by the tattered feeling in my chest, I did) then I could do this.

Just before I sent the text, a notification lit my screen. It was an email from a student, asking about the assignment he'd just bombed.

The notification brought me back to reality. What was I doing? I couldn't text Mel about this. I needed to talk to her in person. I wouldn't let this delay be stalling, either. I would find her, and I would talk to her, and we would be friends. If that was what she wanted.

Please let that be what she wanted.

I refocused on my office. The black-and-white pixels of my staff photo still stared at me. I ran my thumb over the headline, holding the newspaper over my desk trash can. At the last minute, I stowed it away in a drawer instead.

See, Mel? I could take a compliment. Sort of.

Mel may be looking for happiness in all the wrong places, but so was I. I was looking in the past, at the life I could've had, at the ways I should've told Mel I loved her. And now, where I spent all my time looking at what was impossible. If Mel was guilty of missing what was right in front of her, then I was guilty of it, too.

I slipped my phone back into my pocket. I would get that full-time position. I would apologize to Mel in person. Our friendship would go back to normal. I would finally, absolutely, completely leave behind any mixed feelings I had about my old life and what could've been.

The life I had now was a good one. I'd rebuilt it. And I would keep rebuilding it into what I wanted. And maybe I'd rebuild it with someone by my side someday. But whatever happened, as long as I had a choice, Mel would be a part of it, even if she was just a friend.

But for now, it was eight o'clock and time to start another late night of work.

CHAPTER 39

MEL

Ivy: Have you asked anyone you know whether they know eligible bachelors?
Mel: I asked a couple coworkers a few weeks ago. Their answers ranged from
"Why else do you think I'm single?" to "If I did, I wouldn't be stuck with the
deadbeat back home."
Ivy: Ouch.

It was eight o'clock, and I'd had it with everything.

The 1970s punch clock Dr. Schaaf was so attached to was broken, so all of our timecards were messed up for the last few days, which added up to several extra hours of work to sort it out. Rumors were circulating about the French tutor who'd apparently been handing out cheat sheets for midterms. We had a leak in the ceiling, so now there was a bucket that drip-dripped annoyingly every few seconds. And the scheduling software was down, so students, professors, and tutors were in mass chaos over assignments and paperwork.

And underlying it all was a whispered chant in my mind: *Cameron thinks I'm selfish.*

Normally, I would've asked Cameron to fix the scheduling software. Normally, he would've dropped whatever he was doing and immediately come to my rescue. And normally, I wouldn't feel this tension inside, knowing that Cameron thought so little of me.

Instead, Vernon—who was fully recovered from his near-death via apple pie—was the IT personnel who'd come to my rescue. And poor Vernon, after awkwardly eyeing me and the tutoring center as if I'd hung walnuts from the ceiling, was at a loss for how to fix the software.

"I can call Dr. Whitacre and see if—"

"No!" I'd practically shouted it the instant he'd reached for his phone. "I mean, isn't there something else you can think of that could fix it? What about...deleting the browser history or cookies?"

Not that those suggestions would do any good. I was definitely not an IT person. But I was desperate to avoid Cameron. I still blushed in humiliation every time I thought of our last conversation.

Now Vernon was clicking at my computer and calling the software company—both things I could've done myself anyway. I sat at an empty table, stacks of ruined timecards in front of me and the drip-dripping bucket beside me. And all I could think about was Cameron.

In the last five years, I'd never gone a full twenty-four hours without talking to him—text, email, or in person. And now I'd gone more than seventy-two hours without talking to him or hearing from him in some form.

The gaping hole this left was uncomfortable, to say the least. Excruciating would be the more accurate term.

How was he? Had he heard the rumors about the French tutor? Did that one student from his 8:00 a.m. class turn in her assignment on time, or had she forged another doctor's excuse?

More importantly, what did he think of the article? It'd been waiting for me in my staff inbox first thing this morning. Alma had done an excellent job. I loved it, even if I squirmed as I read it, remembering how I'd called him cowardly when he was anything but. Did Cameron see himself as a strong person like the rest of us did? Did he regret being forced to open up about the stroke and depression in an article that all of his coworkers would read?

I replayed our argument for the umpteenth time. He was right. I hadn't been a good friend to him or to Ivy.

I'd known Ivy had been distracted lately. Had I ever asked her anything beyond superficial questions? No. I should've pushed her to tell me why she didn't want Monday nights at her house anymore. If it had to do with her mom's health—and Cameron had mentioned it did—then Ivy was more stressed than I could imagine. No more talking about the list with her until she told me what was really happening in her life. That was that.

I should've asked Cameron about the full-time position more often. Maybe

I could've helped him with his extra workload. I knew how Scantron machines worked, and I knew how to enter grades into our software. I should've made him an entire apple pie all for himself. I should've talked less about the list and my plans and given him more space to tell me whatever he wanted to tell me about himself.

That was my biggest regret. Cameron was wonderful. I should've treated him like he was wonderful, not a commodity to be used for my own immediate needs.

Did he still want to be friends with me? Who would want to be friends with a selfish person? Or was it selfish to worry about what he thought of me?

The timecards glared at me. The bucket drip-dripped. Vernon acted like I wasn't there.

I had to fix this. I had to prove to Cameron that I wasn't selfish. I had to prove it to myself, too. I could argue with him or make excuses for myself, but none of that mattered. What mattered was that Cameron was right. I needed to change. Whatever it took.

First step, text Ivy.

Mel: Girl! We need to hang out. I'm sorry I've been wrapped up in the list. Want to come over to my place for dinner this week and catch me up on all things Ivy?

There. Cheerful, friendly, apologetic, and reaching out. All in one. Except for one last thing—

And by dinner, I mean an entire meal of brownies and ice cream.

No way she would say no to that.

Ignoring a notification from Marcus, I moved on to my second step, text Cameron.

Hey. I'm sorry about the other night. You're right. I lost sight of what mattered most. I'll explain the list to Marcus. And I'll be less selfish. Forgive me, friend?

No. That wasn't right. It didn't say nearly enough, and that last sentence felt wrong. I deleted and tried again.

Hey. You're right. I've been selfish. Forgive me, friend?

Even worse. That last sentence still bugged me. For being a writer—or wannabe writer—this text felt beyond my skills.

Vernon turned toward me and stood, eager to leave. "Got it. It should be good as new. Need anything else?"

I set aside my phone. Apologies were better said in person, right? Not that I was stalling. This definitely wasn't stalling. This was practical.

I thanked Vernon, ushered him out the door, and settled at my desktop to try to undo the mess of the last few days. The mess as far as work was concerned, at least.

CHAPTER 40

MEL

Ivy: The list says to stand in a public place with a lasso. I can already hear your cowgirl jokes from here, Cam. Stop it.

It's called ghosting. I'd heard about it in the dating world—from Ivy, among others—but this was my first personal experience with it.

First came the questions. Why didn't Marcus text back? I was counting on him to distract me from how much I missed Cameron. Where was Marcus when I needed him? He'd gone out of town for work again, but he was back by now, unless his trip had been extended, which wasn't likely.

Second came the worries, which were also a good way to distract myself from Cameron. Had something happened to Marcus? Was he hurt? Every outlandish scenario from Hollywood blockbusters became a way for me to give him the benefit of the doubt. Maybe he'd been in a wreck and had amnesia, or maybe he'd had a family emergency and was dealing with relatives squabbling over a vast inheritance, or maybe he'd defected from Russia in a nuclear submarine, Sean Connery-style. Anything was possible. Anything that gave me a reason to excuse his vanishing act and hope he'd text or call or show up at my door.

Third came the anger and sadness. I ricocheted between the two with surprising speed. The anger: how dare Marcus waste my time and then disappear on me when I needed him to reassure me in my moment of Cameron crisis. How dare Marcus not give us a chance beyond a handful of dates. The nerve he had, to seem so perfect and act so charming and then just disappear. The audacity, to take up my valuable time and energy when he was clearly a waste of a human being. The sadness: surely something about me had been a deal breaker. I thought we'd had the start of something special but now I could see I'd been wrong. My walks with Horse felt lonely. My mancounters felt more and more pointless. All my doubts about the list were coming true.

Since we hadn't been involved for very long, the Marcus-shaped hole in my life was small enough that I filled it quickly and easily. It was nothing compared to the Cameron-shaped canyon splitting my heart in half.

Everything felt wrong, wrong, wrong, and Marcus was only a small part of the wrongness. The rest of it was Cameron. It was all his fault for making me doubt myself. His fault for being right. Because now I couldn't stop thinking about him. Or maybe I'd always thought about him this much, and now that our friendship felt strained, I noticed it more—or it bothered me more. Because now I inspected each action and word for selfishness, each thought that even hinted at any discontent I felt. Every time I noticed anything even remotely related to *Seinfeld*, or apple pie, or basketball, even trivia, or any other memory we'd made during our friendship, I thought of him. So, basically, I thought about Cameron all the time. But I couldn't bring myself to seek him out and apologize to him because, really, where would I even start?

Well, not everything felt wrong, because Between Two Covers felt very right, even if I'd last been there with Cameron on a mancounter. I walked through the doors and lost myself in the row after row of shelves.

My hand paused above a thick book designed for the sole purpose of looking posh on a coffee table. Unless you were an artist who knew what you were looking for in each photograph. Unless you were looking for a gift for such an artist because you were trying to be less selfish.

Ivy used to make the most amazing sculptures. Maybe it would inspire her. Trying to remember the last time she looked inspired, I realized I couldn't think of it. Maybe this book would help. Our dreams wouldn't survive much longer if we didn't act on them. But maybe Ivy already had the book.

Pulling out my phone to text Ivy a photo of the book's cover, I noticed a new message from her.

Ivy: My mom fell. We're at the ER. I'm freaking out and need someone to check on Van because my neighbor just called to say he's stuck on her roof. Help?

I was still processing her message when Cameron texted.

Cameron: I'll rescue Van and set out fresh cat food and water for him. I'll meet you at the hospital after. Anything I can bring you from home?

I smiled. Cameron would always jump at the chance to help out. Then I twinged with guilt. But now wasn't the time for regrets or self-centered thoughts.

Mel: Be at the ER in a few minutes.

I made a quick stop by the Bluesy Bean for two of Ivy's favorite pastries and a coffee or tea for the three of us. ERs were no place to mess around when it came to comfort food, and I was glad I came prepared. Outside of a few others in the waiting room, it was just Ivy and me, huddled in a row of chairs. Cameron was still chasing down Van.

Ivy slumped in her chair. The nurses had taken her and her mom to a private room in the back of the ER, and now that "Mom is tripped out on morphine anyway," Ivy had stepped out to the waiting room to visit for a few minutes. Thankfully it was a small ER, so the nurse hadn't minded.

"I'm sorry," she said. "I'm sorry for ruining your weekend. I was worried about Van with how cold it is, and then Mom, and then I couldn't think of anyone else, and I'm sorry—"

I rubbed a hand on her back. "It's okay. I'm here because I love you. You can always call me for anything."

Ivy slumped even farther back in her chair, gripping a pastry in one hand and a thermos of chamomile tea in the other. "She was finally getting a little bit better. I just...I don't think I can handle taking care of her much longer, you know? But if I put her in a nursing home, she'll hate me, and I'll feel guilty, and I just—"

The doors to the waiting room slid open. Cameron strode through. My chest filled like a balloon, my stomach plunged through the nondescript linoleum floor, and my face heated with embarrassment and uncertainty. This was our first interaction since our fight. How would he act around me?

He looked good. Cowlick still messy, eyes still incredibly blue behind his dark-framed glasses, his shoes leaving tracks of snow across the entryway carpet. He carried a bag of pastries and a carrier of drinks from the Bluesy Bean. His expression shifted from concerned to relieved (when he saw Ivy) to hesitant (when he saw me). A beat passed, maybe two, and then his mouth formed into a smile. It was small but sincere. Just that one tilt of his lips, and a smidge of my humiliation lifted.

Cameron placed the cups and pastries on a small end table and crouched in front of Ivy. "What do you need? Is there anything I can do?"

"Just having you both here is more than enough." Her eyes were watery. "Thank you."

"Of course," he said, resting a hand on her knee.

I stared at his hand on her jeans, wondering. My cheeks flushed with a new tension, the same I'd felt in middle school when Isabella Guitierrez won the science fair and I came in second.

It was getting to me, this restlessness I'd been feeling since arguing with Cameron. It was messing with my head—or more like my heart. I curled my fingers into fists, nails biting half-moons into my palms.

Just friends.

A nurse walked into the room, her posture slouched with exhaustion from what was probably a twelve-hour shift. She said the name like a statement. "Ivy Lunden. You asked me to come find you when the doctor was ready to see your mom."

Ivy bolted from her seat and nearly tripped over a chair in her rush to follow the nurse.

Watching Ivy disappear down the hallway, I swallowed. She'd been the last buffer between us. I'd never felt uncomfortable being alone with Cameron before, but now I itched for an excuse to run away. I needed to be here for Ivy, so I couldn't just leave, no matter how I felt.

I glanced around the quiet waiting room, reluctant to make eye contact with Cameron. The other people kept to themselves, absorbed in their own worries and vending machine snacks, giving me nothing to think about but my worries.

Was Cameron mad at me? What would I do about it? Would we keep up appearances for Ivy since she was already suffering, or could we go back to being normal? Why hadn't I just put on my big-girl panties and apologized before now, when the humiliation had grown unwieldy with time? Why did it matter so much?

Cameron cleared his throat with a quiet hum. "Everything will be okay. With Ivy and her mom."

I stared at the floor, unable to meet the pressure of his blue gaze. "I hope so." I pulled at loose threads at the hem of my sweater. "Poor Ivy would be devastated if anything happened to her mom, even if they fight all the time."

The threads on my sweater become my sole focus. The way the separate strings twined together, each a different color that felt more solid together than they did apart. The texture softened and pulled between my fingers. I tugged on it a little harder.

He didn't say anything. Why didn't he say anything?

I blinked away from the thread to peek up at him. No humor lit his face. I couldn't look away, even though staring at him made something dig at my chest and stick in my throat. I willed my tears to dry up before they spilled out and made me look foolish and puffy-faced.

When he spoke, his voice was nearly a whisper. "We'll be okay, too, I hope? You and me?"

My pause before I answered was intentional. I remembered what he said a few nights ago, and I saw all over again that he was right. *Everything that you're looking for is...right here.* Right in front of me. Even in the face of Ivy's worry and my fear.

An emotion curled in my chest, filling the Cameron-shaped canyon with a feeling stronger than relief, deeper than friendship.

Rebellious tears streamed defiantly down my cheeks. I rushed to wipe them away.

"I hope so," I said, and then corrected it with, "Yes," because I wouldn't know what to do without him in my life, and because saying it aloud felt like a promise.

The apprehension slid from his face. The corner of his mouth tilted upwards. "Good." And then he made his own promise: "We'll be okay."

CHAPTER 41

MEL

Ivy: "Promise him no mother-in-law trouble." My future man is in for a surprise because my mom's a treat. Maybe I can prevent them from meeting until after we're married.
Mel: He's an idiot if he doesn't think you're worth it.
Cameron: I second that.
Ivy: Thanks. I really needed that today.

The doctors said Ivy's mom had a broken ankle, giving Ivy even more caretaker responsibilities. As the following weeks brought more snow and ice, Cameron and I helped her as much as we could. I made meals, and he brought her takeout. He shoveled her driveway after each snowfall, and I spread salt on her sidewalks. We did our best to cheer her up. When my schedule allowed, I sat with her mom to give Ivy a break.

Cameron somehow still found time to smuggle me cupcakes at the Fishbowl. He always smiled, he always asked about my day, and on the surface, everything about our friendship stayed the same. But it was all different now. I felt it. And I wondered if he too noticed how the terrain had shifted beneath our feet and changed the undercurrent of how we interacted. There was a hesitancy between our words. We behaved like new acquaintances, not best friends.

The only time our interactions felt normal these days was when Cameron and I talked via our group text with Ivy. His joking made me feel like nothing had changed at all. Case in point, a conversation from when Ivy took a few days off work to be with her mom.

Mel: Ivy, I left some frozen meals at your house. Van glared at me from the top of your fridge. (How does he get up there?)

Cameron: Don't mind Mel, just committing your average breaking and entering.

Mel: It doesn't count if I leave food. Everyone knows that.

Cameron: Cats defy physics. Everyone knows that.

Ivy: You two always make me smile.

Cameron: Comic relief is my specialty. Not sure about Mel's. Maybe it's crime?

Mel: Frozen meals are my specialty. Much cooler than your specialty. (It's not a crime to leave frozen lasagna at a friend's house.)

Cameron: Literally cooler. (Get it?)

Ivy: Again, if you have to ask whether someone got it...But he might have a point, Mel. Van only glares from the top of the fridge when he's feeling suspicious of someone.

Cameron: The correlation of his fridge-perching and your breaking and entering is too strong to ignore.

Mel: Correlation doesn't equal causation. Van loves me!

Cameron: He never sits on the fridge when I'm there.

Ivy: I hate to admit it, but he may be right, Mel.

Mel: I'm driving back to your house to take back those frozen meals now.

Then again, in the moments after I reread and overanalyzed text after text, I found myself thinking the awkwardness intruding on our friendship might just be me. His messages sounded so normal that my fears had to be imaginary, right?

That other, stronger emotion from the hospital waiting room hadn't dissolved, but I wasn't brave enough to let myself name the feeling. I refused to think about it, especially when the feeling was strongest, like when Cameron smiled at me from the doorway of the Fishbowl, or when we made quiet eye contact across the cafeteria. Instead, I kept busy, dividing my thoughts between Ivy and my book.

The mancounters, as much as so many of them had felt pointless, began taking fuller shape in my mind. I outlined chapters. I combined narratives of my personal experience with research about social and cultural values that had changed since the 1950s. The book continued shifting, but I enjoyed the process. Even though I still wasn't at the point of putting a solid plan into action, I experimented to see where the story would take me.

Late after work one night, I locked the door to the Fishbowl and listened to Ivy's voice filtering through my phone's speaker.

"I'll pick up the cat food," I said. "Please stop worrying about Van. You have enough going on."

"It's just hard to accept help when I've been on my own for so long."

"You're not a burden, if that's what you're worried about. Everything will be okay." I echoed Cameron's words a lot lately. They felt natural.

"I really can't thank you enough," she said. "I've always known I could count on you, but you've really come through for me. It means more than I can say."

My apology for earlier weeks stuck in my throat. Ivy was dealing with a lot —now wasn't the time. "I just wish I'd stepped up sooner."

"I was keeping this all pretty close to the chest. You couldn't step up if you didn't know about it."

My keys tapped against my thigh with each step I took closer to the parking lot. "But I get too focused on my own"—I gestured with a hand even though she couldn't see—"whatever, and then I miss what's happening with other people and their lives. I'm trying to grow out of it."

"Don't give it a second thought." Ivy's voice was more forceful than I'd ever heard it before. "You never settle for anything less than excellence. It's a good thing. I wish I were more like you in that way. I settle too much."

I scoffed. "No. You're fabulous exactly as you are, Ivy. Don't try to be like me." My mouth was still open, ready to tell her everything about Marcus ghosting me, and my fight with Cameron, and how I felt about it all. But I closed my mouth instead. Ivy had enough on her mind. She didn't need to hear about my own woes, too.

I unlocked my car. "I'll pick up the cat food and some Take It Cheesy sandwiches. Let me know if there's anything else."

Ending the call and tossing my bag into the front seat, I noticed a familiar shadow slanting along the sidewalk.

"Hiya, Mel."

"Hiya, Cam."

And there it was, that pause where there would've been familiar comfort and now there was a shift of feet and a jingle of car keys.

The glow of his phone illuminated his face as he checked the time. "I thought the Fishbowl was open until eleven."

"With exams next week, we shortened our hours. Students have fewer papers, more studying. And Ivy needed some stuff."

He tugged at the wrists of his coat sleeves, his eyes following the motion of his hands. "I thought maybe you had a date with Marcus."

Another pause.

It was a peace offering of sorts. Even if we'd been friendly, not like before, but relatively friendly, he'd never mentioned Marcus. He didn't go out of his way to be rude, but the very fact that he didn't go out of his way to be friendly was about as close as Cameron ever came to snubbing.

Might as well just say it.

"Marcus isn't really in the picture anymore."

His fingers stopped tugging. His head shot up. "What?"

"He ghosted me." I shrugged, hoping to come across as indifferent. "Typical twenty-first-century dating, right? Wonder if they had the same problem in the 1950s. Ghosting would've been so much easier then, without cell phones and social media." I let out a humorless laugh. "It could be a chapter in my book."

He stood motionless. The parking lot lights glazed over his glasses, so I couldn't read his expression. "How are you?"

"I'm fine."

"How are you really?"

"I'm fine, like I said. He was too perfect anyway. That kind of perfection isn't sustainable, and it would make me crazy. I'm too weird for a life like his."

"But when you talked about him...you sounded really happy."

I stared down at my feet. With the toe of my boot, I scuffed against a piece of ice, gradually chipping away at it until it flaked into pieces. "I think I was more hopeful than happy. If that makes any sense."

When I looked up, he may or may not have been staring at me, his glasses still opaquely reflecting the streetlight. His lips were parted, his breath puffing into clouds that quickly vanished.

He could have been thinking anything right now. He could have been thinking about how he hadn't liked Marcus anyway, so no loss there. He could have been thinking about what he'd said to me—about never being happy with what I have—and how this was more proof that even when I was faced with absolute perfection, I still hadn't really been happy. He could have been thinking about the cafeteria's sketchy tuna casserole. It was impossible to know.

Before our argument, I would've teased him for being mysterious and not sharing his thoughts. Now I hesitated. Now the exact feelings I'd worked so hard to ignore began to gather in my chest. I struggled to shove them back.

Not being with Marcus didn't change anything. Cameron and I would do what we always did—Cameron being Cameron and me lecturing myself about noticing his blue eyes and smiles.

I cleared my throat. "Anyway. Ivy is waiting for me. The great tabby cat Van Gogh won't be kept waiting for his favorite treats."

"You buy him treats?"

I saw it as the favor it was: asking about Van so I could stop talking about Marcus. I could've hugged him for it.

"Of course I buy him treats."

"He's already a prima donna."

"A super cute prima donna."

"Do you buy treats for Horse, too?"

I ducked my head to hide my smile. "Maybe."

"Softie."

I looked up to grin at him. "I can't resist a cute face, what can I say?"

I reached out to jokingly pat his cheek and infer that he had a cute face, too, but it came across all wrong. My palm touched the angle of his jaw, molding to match the curve of his smile. His skin felt warm. His slight stubble felt prickly.

His grin dropped away.

Uncertainty had me holding my breath. I moved to withdraw my hand and step back.

But instead of breaking contact, he stepped forward, his own hand covering mine, keeping my palm pressed to his cheek. The shift changed the light, clearing his glasses so I could see his blue eyes. They were focused on my lips. That was the only warning I had before he dipped his head.

What—

How—

This was the rightness that had been missing with Marcus. It was right here, my palm on his jaw, his hand covering mine, our lips pressed together in a soft slide of skin and feelings. Something clicked inside me with his mouth on mine.

And then the simple touch was over. He scrambled back, his eyes again blocked out by the streetlight. He patted all his pockets like he was looking for something. Fumbling for words, he muttered nonsense, "need to go" and "keys" and "see you later," and practically ran for his car.

I stood there until fresh snow began falling, melting when it landed on my flushed face. My fingers tingled with cold. What time was it?

I started my car and tried to remember how to drive the quarter-mile to the local grocery store for Van's cat treats.

What had just happened? And what did it mean?

CHAPTER 42

CAMERON

Ivy: "Go to and from the airport in a bus." Lol. What a valuable investment of someone's time.

That kiss could mean the end of life as I knew it.

I thumped my forehead against my steering wheel. I hadn't even left the parking lot. I'd locked myself inside my car and agonized. How long had I been sitting here, stuck inside my own head and feelings? Long enough that the cold gnawed at any exposed skin. But even that discomfort wasn't enough to break me from my thoughts and urge me home.

Just one moment of no self-control may have cost me everything. It certainly cost me my sanity for the foreseeable future. Because now I knew exactly how Mel's lips felt on mine. Smooth and soft. I knew my chest could split open at each rib just from that one kiss.

How would I not think about those delicious details when I next saw her? How would I ever make eye contact with her again without remembering—

This was bad. This was very bad.

Not that I'd thought it was bad in the moment. Not that I'd thought about anything at all. When her hand had touched my face, I'd lost all self-preservation. I'd felt propelled forward, pulled to her like I was caught in a tractor beam. In that moment, there wasn't any other option.

But I should've been able to think of other options. I should've been able to act casual. I'd been faking casual for a long time now. Why hadn't I stuck to the plan?

Step one of acting casual: don't bring up Marcus.

First mistake: I'd brought up Marcus.

I'd tried to be supportive—or at least indifferent—about Marcus being her boyfriend, or whatever he was. I wouldn't have guessed that he would ghost her.

I tried to piece together when Marcus had disappeared. She was still doing the list (as far as I could tell). She'd seemed different lately, but she always seemed different since our argument, so I'd thought nothing of it beyond my usual worries. I'd never thought Marcus was the reason she was less bright when she walked into a room.

Step two of acting casual: don't think about Mel being single.

Second mistake: I'd thought about Mel being single.

Usually when she talked about Marcus, her face lit up. She'd tuck her hair behind her ears in a happily flustered gesture I knew well. But this time? Her voice was flat. She couldn't hold eye contact. Her hands stayed pushed deep inside her pockets.

I should've been happy she was free again. In some ways, I was, because my stomach finally lifted from the soles of my feet, where it'd sat in dejection since I read her first text about him and their "perfect date." But instead, my mind fixated on her sadness and how helpless I was to do anything to help her feel better.

Step three: keep physical distance.

Third mistake: I'd kissed her. *Kissed her.*

All my years of trying to subtly show my feelings, of watching her for signs that she reciprocated, and then I spontaneously kissed her. So much for subtlety. I'd savored every moment, too, even her fingertips grazing my temple, the heel of her hand pausing along my jawline.

That kiss was...well. Earthshattering for me. Less so for her. She'd stiffened when our lips met. But could I blame her? I'd practically launched myself at her.

Thankfully the kiss had just been a peck. Imagine if I'd kissed her like I really wanted to kiss her for all these years. That would've been so much worse. Or better, depending on your perspective.

The worst mistake of all, though, was how I'd left her afterward. I should've stayed. Explained. Confessed how I felt. Or, you know, said *anything at all* instead of running away.

The sheer panic of that moment—I blamed it on all my other mistakes that added up to one colossal blunder, like a butterfly effect, building and building until it was beyond control. There was no other way to explain it. Each error led to the next, then the next, and then I was fleeing the scene like a criminal.

So many missteps in a matter of seconds. I'd finally made marginal progress at rebuilding our friendship after our argument. And now this.

How could I ever face her at work tomorrow when I knew the feel of her lips on mine?

There was no more acting casual for me.

CHAPTER 43

MEL

Ivy: Mel, was that you I saw slipping on the icy sidewalk outside the registrar building? Are you okay?
Mel: I really hoped nobody saw that. I'm fine. The ice is just extra slick today, lol.
Cameron: We keep a first aid kit in Freisen's office. I can bring it upstairs if you need it.
Ivy: Just don't trust Cameron to stitch you up. Remember when he tried to get you to mend his loose buttons? If he can't sew buttons...
Cameron: Hey. I can unwrap a Band-Aid like nobody's business.

I'd slipped because I was running late. Because I was avoiding Cameron. Because avoidance is the best way to deal with these hot and cold feelings you get after your best friend kisses you and then runs away from you as if you taste like swamp scum. And because I thought I'd glimpsed him at a distance, I'd lost my footing on the icy sidewalk, and— It was all Cameron's fault.

Everything was Cameron's fault these days. He was the reason I was distracted at work and sent the wrong student reports to the wrong professors. He was why I'd run out of conditioner last week and went without it for three washes and turned my hair into a nuclear frizz bomb. It was because of

Cameron that I was now at the grocery store, picking out a bag of chips and chanting "conditioner" over and over to myself.

I willed myself to focus. But my mind was preoccupied, frayed between Grandma's words that *love happens naturally*, Cameron's words that *everything you're looking for is right here*, and *conditioner*.

Maybe Cameron was right. Maybe I was using men the same way Ivy and I always complained about men using women. It was just one massive experiment, wasn't it? Acting out these strange scenarios to see if men would notice me. Flirting like I was actually interested in them. Playing with any potential emotions they might feel about me—not that I flattered myself that their interest in me was anything more than passing, but still.

No, that wasn't entirely true. I wasn't against the chance of meeting someone through the list. Marcus was a perfect example. Had I seen a future for us? It had ended too soon to tell. Had I enjoyed spending time with him? Definitely. Had he known he started off as an item on a list? No, and I'd balked at the thought of telling him. I should've been honest. He'd had the right to know why I'd been walking Horse in the first place. To know I'd continue with the list even as we went to Armand's.

So that brought me full circle, right back to "Maybe Cameron was right." Maybe I needed to put a pause on the mancounters and reevaluate exactly what my purpose was in all this.

Not to mention the kiss. What had he been thinking—

Frustrated, I grabbed a bag of chips and stomped to the checkout line.

Only after I got home did I notice what was missing. I'd forgotten my conditioner. Again.

That was also when I remembered it was Monday night. How could I forget about Monday night? It had been a tradition for years, ever since we became friends as new hires at orientation.

Seconds after I remembered, Ivy let herself in and curled up in her normal seat, wearing her usual all-black. At first she looked as confused as I felt. She glanced around for the drink I typically had ready and waiting for her at her seat by now.

She blinked at the empty coaster on the coffee table and then looked up at me. "Are you okay?"

Not at all.

"I'm fine." I dug into my kitchen for vodka, ginger beer, and limes. This called for alcohol.

When she spoke again, she was next to me, leaning her hip against the kitchen counter. "You don't seem fine."

250

"How's your mom?"

She rolled her eyes. "Still crazy. But she's gone a few days without trying to convince me of some imaginary condition she's about to die from, so that's a win. No fake heart attacks for a few days now. Things I never thought I'd say."

"She'll regret all this if she ever does have a heart attack someday."

Ivy snorted. "You're telling me."

I felt her eyes on me while I plunked ice into copper mugs—thank you, thrift store—and measured out the ingredients. If I kept ignoring her...

"Something is definitely wrong with you. Is it Marcus?"

I stirred Ivy's Moscow mule and handed it to her. "Marcus is out of the picture."

She choked on her first sip.

"He ghosted me." Glancing at the clock, I calculated when Cameron probably left work, what time he'd be here, unless there was traffic, because in that case— Wait. What if he didn't show up tonight?

Ivy managed a croaky "what?"

Oh. We'd been talking about Marcus.

I shrugged. "I really don't have any more details than that. You know how it goes. He was there. Now he's not. The end."

"I thought he was really into you."

"I thought so, too."

The clock now read 7:09. Was Cameron not coming? We hadn't spoken since the kiss. What if he felt too uncomfortable or embarrassed? I'd been uncomfortable enough to avoid him at work. What's to say he hadn't been avoiding me, too?

"And you...you seemed really into Marcus."

"I thought so, too. I don't know." Should I tell her about Cameron? She still didn't know about the kiss or our argument. Unless Cameron had told her. But he wouldn't do something like that. Would he?

"Is this why you haven't seemed like yourself lately?"

Instead of meeting her gaze, I studied the way the bubbles from the ginger beer fizzed around our ice cubes. "How do you mean?"

"You've been quiet. Less bouncy."

"I'm bouncy?" I grimaced. "Please don't tell me I'm one of those perky people that we hate and this is your nice way of telling me."

She laughed. "I couldn't be friends with you if you were perky."

"Good. I was worried for a minute there."

Now it was 7:12. What if—

A firm knock at the door.

I splashed my Moscow mule down my sleeve. Apparently, on top of my short-term memory loss about hair conditioner, I'd regressed to a klutz in the last few days. Also Cameron's fault.

I tried to walk normally as I covered the short distance from the kitchen to the front door. Ivy already knew something was wrong. I needed to just be...normal. Like I normally would be normal. Just normal.

Cameron blinked at me when I opened the door. His hair was tidy, except for that cowlick, and he carried his usual chips and salsa. But his posture was too straight. His smile was a beat too late and a hint too stiff. His eyes moved over my face like he was taking stock of me the same way I was taking stock of him.

He was uncomfortable. So was I.

At least we matched.

"Ivy's in the kitchen with your Moscow mule," I said, and then kicked myself for bypassing our normal greeting. "If she hasn't already finished it off."

His posture softened a fraction. "I was hoping this would be a Moscow mule kind of night."

My eyes—the traitors—caught on his lips, and when I managed to look away, I saw his blue gaze fixed on my lips, too.

Maybe we both needed a drink.

Ivy called from the kitchen, "Cam, did you know Marcus ghosted her?"

"She may have mentioned it the other day." He handed me his chips and salsa, and I gingerly took them since I couldn't risk brushing his fingers with mine.

"I'm missing all the news since I'm stuck at home with my mom," Ivy complained. "I can't wait to be back next week. What else am I missing? You two better not be holding out on me because you're worried about distracting me. I need to be distracted."

Cameron shrugged out of his coat and hat, toeing off his shoes. "Dr. Freisen wore a different colored bowtie today, so there's that."

I pulled bowls from the cabinets. "He broke his yellow Monday tradition?"

"Good riddance," Ivy said. "It's not even a pretty yellow. Of all the yellows in the world, that's the one he chooses. I'm glad he got rid of it."

"I didn't say he got rid of it." Cameron stood at the edge of the kitchen. "It might still be in his closet. But he's changing which days of the week he wears certain bowties, and that's a lot for him."

"He hasn't changed an inch the whole time we've known him." I bent to pull extra napkins from below the sink, willing myself not to notice how naturally Cameron leaned against the cabinets.

"Wonder what brought this about," Ivy said.

Cameron shrugged. "Probably just some new quirk."

She pointed a finger at him. "You should dig deeper. Ask around. Find out what's happening."

"It's really not a big deal—"

"Can you hack his computer? I feel like that's something you can do."

"Well—"

"Maybe you'll find some skeletons in his digital closet," she said, "or emails from a new lover. Or blackmail from the mafia. It could be anything."

I frowned at her. "How much TV have you been watching while you've been stuck at home, Ivy?"

She gestured, her Moscow mule sloshing in her mug. "Give me some credit. Changing his bowtie color is the Dr. Freisen equivalent of having a crisis."

The corners of Cameron's eyes crinkled. "Good thing you're coming back to work next week, Ivy. You need to get out more." His lips quirked into a teasing smile.

I needed to stop noticing his lips.

"Can't argue with you there," she said. "What juicy news do you have for me, Mel?"

I stacked the napkins, one by one, into a swirling pattern. "Nothing much." Other than an argument, then a kiss, then avoidance. And now Cameron was leaning against my kitchen cabinets, eye corners crinkling. Had my kitchen always been so small?

"Any interesting developments with the list?" Ivy said.

The list. Probably the last thing Cameron wanted to hear about.

"No," I said. "I think I might start writing soon. I think I know the direction I want to go."

"Tell us."

I fumbled for a spoon longer than necessary. "It's still just a vague idea taking shape, but I'm picturing sort of a combination of research and narrative. Mostly narrative because I think that's what'll grab readers' attention."

Ivy nodded, her blue eyes blinking at me over her copper mug. "Good. What else?"

What else? I'd been incredibly lonely without talking to Cameron at work this week, that's what else.

My hands had nothing left to do, so I stared into my own Moscow mule, my fingers tracing the condensation droplets. "I think the narratives will show that dating has drastically changed since the 1950s, but that doesn't mean love has changed all that much."

"So dating advice has an expiration date and love doesn't?" Ivy said.

Cameron shifted against the cabinet. "But if love is timeless, aren't the basic principles of finding love also timeless?"

"I remember you bringing that up earlier," I said, "and it's a good point. The whole goal was answering a question: If love really is timeless, then aren't the basic principles of pursuing love timeless, too? And all the questions that come with that: Do we actually know more about men and women today than they did a few decades ago? Is the 1950s dating advice still applicable?"

I fussed with the napkins a little more. "I do think love is timeless, and I do think the basic principles of finding love are also timeless. When you break it down, the list is really just encouraging single women to put themselves out there more."

Ivy snorted. "By stowing away on a battleship? And learning how to make wigs? And pretending to break down on the side of the road?"

"They are terrible ways of getting out there," I admitted, "but all they're really saying is if you want to meet someone, you need to leave the house. You need to be willing to fail or make a fool of yourself if you want to experience love."

Just like true friends would be willing to make fools of themselves and damage friendships by pointing out flaws in hopes of helping their friends be happier. Just like Cameron did for me. Unless—

Ivy reached for a chip. "So love is timeless, the principles of finding love are timeless, and we just need to put ourselves out there more? Basically, you're telling me that I need to give my dating apps more time. But I really hate my dating apps."

My mind struggled to focus while also wondering whether...if...maybe...

"No, I don't know that dating apps are the way to do it. Sure, you're putting yourself out there, in a way, and in some really rural areas or for people who have insanely busy careers, that's the only way to do it. But if you're putting yourself out there physically, taking a dog for a walk, joining a hiking group, going to eighties nights on Thursdays, love happens more organically."

Thanks for that, Grandma.

"But," Ivy said, "my dating app has algorithms and whatever it is that nerds like Cam invent to make people like me feel like I have a chance."

Cameron grimaced. "Nerds like me who develop apps like that are the last people who should be put in control of anyone's love life."

"Well, that's reassuring," she muttered.

He shrugged. "Just saying."

I smiled. "I don't have all the details worked out yet, especially with dating apps, because some people meet and get married and live happily ever after thanks to those apps. But I think in those cases people are actually looking to meet someone, not just serial date an entire city from the comfort of their sofa, ghosting people after barely giving them a chance."

Thanks for that firsthand knowledge of ghosting, Marcus.

Ivy reached for another chip. "My love life agrees with you."

"I might interview some people who would've dated in the fifties or grew up around then. Their firsthand accounts would be more helpful than reading articles and books like I've been doing. My grandma told me the other day that true love is a choice that happens in daily life. I think she's right, in a way."

"Your grandma is my hero." Ivy sighed.

I watched the bubbles in my mug. "After the initial infatuation wears off, we choose to be with the people we love. We live our normal, everyday lives, and in our normal, everyday choices, we choose to make someone a priority."

Like bringing me cupcakes. Like repairing the glitches in my tutoring software. Like caring enough to tell me when I'm hurting myself instead of just standing by and watching me self-destruct.

Ivy was still talking about her dating app—something about the number of unsolicited nudes she receives in a single week—and Cameron laughed at her description of one picture in particular. "What did he honestly think a nude selfie in his grandmother's bathroom would get him?" Then Cameron looked at me, the corners of his blue eyes crinkling, and the longer I stared at him, the more his smile and crinkly eyes faded into a stare of his own. That tidy line creased his brows as he studied me. I held my breath, seeing beyond my friend to something more, watching him watching me. I just—

I knew. I'd been looking for someone to sweep me off my feet. I'd been looking for a brooding bad boy or a dashing Prince Charming. I'd thought a forever relationship would look passionate and dramatic and fiery. And I felt sure love with him would be all these things, if we just gave it a chance.

Cameron was right. I'd been looking for love out there when he was right here the whole time. Right in front of me.

Ivy touched my arm, but I couldn't look away from Cameron.

"Mel, are you okay?"

I blinked. "Sorry. I need to pee."

I fled, closing the bathroom door to the sound of Ivy's "Good to know exactly what you're doing in there, Mel." Their voices lowered to a murmur.

I pressed my back against the wall and stared at myself in the vanity mirror.

For a long time, I didn't move, mentally watching everything I thought I knew about Cameron turn inside out and upside down. My perception wasn't just tilting on its axis. It was off its axis and in an alternate universe.

Cameron loved me.

No, no, that was too much of a jump.

Cameron wanted to be more than friends. There was no other explanation. My mind's eye fast-forwarded through our years of friendship, especially the last few months, when I came up with the mancounters and how he was only minimally supportive. But mostly, my mind's eye zoomed in on just now.

Friends didn't stare at their friends' lips. It simply wasn't a thing.

He'd kissed me in the parking lot. The kiss—in the context of the cupcakes and the tech repairs and his unwavering presence in my life—made much more sense. It was spontaneous. He hadn't meant to kiss me, that had been painfully obvious. And then he ran away, probably upset with himself and terrified of my reaction.

He'd had every right, because just look at my reaction. I'd done everything I could to avoid him ever since.

How deeply was I wrapped up in my own world to miss that such an amazing man was standing right in front of me, wanting more than just friend-ship for— Wait. How far back did this even go for him? How self-centered must I have been to just now see what Ivy had been hinting at all this time?

Speaking of Ivy, she had to know. All her little comments about "Have you ever noticed how handsome Cameron is?" and "He's so good with people" and "He really cares about his work and the college, you know?" The times she'd told me to ask him out, and I'd thought she was teasing. Why hadn't she been clear about it?

Okay, so Cameron at the very least liked me as more than just a friend. And, like me, presumably he didn't want to risk our friendship to try for some-thing more. In his mind, if he asked for more but I said no, our friendship would be weird forever.

But what if we both wanted more? What if it wasn't just him?

I turned on the faucet to feel the shock of cold water rushing over my hands. I needed to snap out of this. Cameron and Ivy were here right now, sitting in my living room, drinking Moscow mules from my thrift store copper mugs.

Cameron wanted me. And I wanted him. But how would we take the next step? Exactly what steps did people take to transition from friendship to something more without jeopardizing what they already had?

CHAPTER 44

CAMERON

Ivy: Let me know if you want to shop for new glasses, Mel.

Mel: Is this your nice way of telling me I need my prescription changed? Am I squinting?

Ivy: No, I'm helping you. According to the list, "Men still like women who wear attractive glasses." So if you want an updated look, let me know.

Mel: I almost always wear contacts, so this doesn't apply. But as an occasional glasses-wearer, I find it vaguely insulting. "Still"? Come on.

Cameron: You already look good in your glasses, Mel.

Sometimes I imagined Toby was secretly Tony Robbins in disguise. I pictured Toby's dark skin and close-cropped hair transforming into Tony Robbins's angular jaw and graying stubble. (How hard would it be to make a deepfake of Toby's voice coming from Tony Robbins's head? I knew people in tech. I could make it happen.)

In this case, even as Toby lost to me in *Street Fighter II*, he still encouraged me. "You're doing great." "Kick a little higher next time." "Where are your catlike reflexes, Blanka?"

The man was literally coaching me to beat him.

He set down his controller and leaned back on the sofa. "You're on a winning streak tonight, man."

Which was surprising, given how distracted I'd been. Mel had been avoiding me since the mistaken kiss. It was impossible to track her down at work. I'd dropped off cupcakes at the Fishbowl again yesterday. Still no Mel in sight. Her work bag and laptop had been there. I briefly wondered if she was hiding under a desk, but I didn't want to embarrass either of us by looking.

The only time I'd seen her since the kiss was at her apartment on Monday night. When she'd answered the door without our usual greeting, I was tempted to bolt back to my car. (A perfectly reasonable solution, right?) Thankfully Ivy kept the conversation moving. But when Mel stared at me for so long, I couldn't stop myself from hoping that maybe, just maybe... Her face had turned a little pink, and that was curiosity in her eyes, right? Or was I dreaming?

Then she'd taken that unusually long bathroom break. I'd started to worry that she was sick. Once she'd rejoined us in the kitchen, she'd shifted with restless energy. ("Do you need a refill?" "Here's an extra napkin, just in case." "If you're hungry, I can heat up some frozen lasagna.")

Ivy had given me a look and then suggested we move to the living room where we could relax, but comfortable seating hadn't helped Mel. She'd offered us extra throw blankets and brought out new vanilla candles—and between it all, I'd repeatedly caught her staring at me before darting away again.

I'd tried waiting for Ivy to leave first so I could talk to Mel, but with an early morning class and a forty-five-minute drive from Mel's place, I had to leave. Not that I'd been able to sleep when I got home anyway. I'd stayed awake most of the night, puzzling over Mel's pink cheeks and frenetic movements.

Now we were back to our game of Mel avoiding me. I hated it. I was almost desperate enough to try to solve the mystery of Dr. Freisen's changing bowtie colors. Maybe if I taunted her that I knew the answer, she'd finally come out of hiding. It would mean fueling Ivy's strong opinions about the color yellow, but it'd be worth it.

I set down my controller. "How could I not be a winner with your endless pep talks?"

He grinned. "You know you love them."

"It's true. I do."

"And you know you're awesome."

That was a stretch, but I shrugged it off.

He stared at me, his brows drawing together. "Are you feeling okay?"

"Why? What?"

"You never accept even the most generic compliment without some kind of 'your mom is awesome' comeback."

I sipped my beer. "That's not true."

"It's absolutely true. You deflect all. The. Time."

Great. Now Toby was on my case, too. "I'm not that bad."

"You are. Most of your jokes are awful."

"I'm funny. You're just jealous you're not funny."

"You're funny *maybe* forty percent of the time."

That couldn't be right. "My students laugh at my jokes."

"Because in the fifty minutes you have them under your spell, you control their futures. Of course they laugh at your jokes."

That was a valid argument. But I still thought I was funny. "You're bringing me down. What happened to your pep talks?"

He laughed and kicked my leg off my coffee table. "Don't mock my gift."

Toby stood and meandered down my dim hall to the bathroom. I unlocked my phone and tapped through my emails, texts, WhatsApp, Facebook, Instagram, Twitter, and LinkedIn until I was out of options. Nothing from Mel. Our nearly daily messages for five years had trickled down to meager exchanges through the group thread only. It was torture.

If she freaked out this much over a barely there kiss, imagine if I'd told her how I felt.

Toby's bare feet padded back up the hallway. When he opened the refrigerator door for another beer, the fridge's automatic light brightened the semi-dark condo and cast Toby's exaggerated shadow along the wall and ceiling.

Maybe it was the beer, maybe it was the dim lighting, maybe it was the comfort of knowing Toby and his Tony Robbins tendencies. Maybe I was just an idiot like Ivy said.

"I kissed Mel."

His shadow froze, its warped arm poised to bring a beer to his lips. The next instant, he was close to me on the sofa (too close, breaking that unspoken man code of leaving an empty cushion between us) and leaning ever closer. "Say that again."

I shifted away as much as I could. "I kissed Mel."

"And?"

"It was a mistake."

"I don't believe that. Tell me what happened."

So I told him, leaving out the details that made me sound pathetic.

When I finished, he said, "Why'd you leave? Why didn't you stay and see what she would say?"

"Weren't you listening? She stiffened up like—like—I don't even know what. It doesn't matter. She wasn't happy about it, that was obvious."

"She was probably just surprised. It's not like you gave her much warning."

I stalked to the window and looked at the dark street. "I couldn't stop staring at her lips the second she told me that Marcus was out of the picture. How much warning did she need?"

"You've been playing the friend-zone game for five years. She needs more warning than a few minutes of creepy staring."

I glared at him.

He snorted. "I'm saying you haven't given her much reason to believe you see her as more than a friend. Then suddenly you jump her like a hormonal fourteen-year-old? She just wasn't expecting it."

I turned back to the window, my fingers picking at my hoodie sleeves. "My point is, now she's avoiding me. This whole time I didn't want to damage our friendship. And now I did exactly that."

When he didn't say anything, I turned toward him. "What?"

"I didn't say anything."

"You're always saying something. Why aren't you saying anything now?"

"You won't like it."

"Since when does that stop you?"

He leaned forward, his elbows pressed to his knees. "She's avoiding you because she feels uncertain. Humans like labels, categories, systems that help us make sense of the world. You've changed the label of your relationship with Mel. So she's hiding from you until you man up and make it clear what you want. She needs to know where she fits in your life."

My laugh sounded hysterical even to me. "You want me to waltz up to her and say, 'Hey, Mel, you're the only woman I think about night and day'? When she obviously hated that kiss?"

"Don't be dense. I'm saying you need to be clear about what you want. Ask her to coffee. Take her to dinner. See what she says. If she says no, then you explain that you hope nothing changes between the two of you being friends, and then you accept it like a man and move on."

I rubbed a hand over my mouth, for once not bothering to fight the old habit.

"But," Toby said, "if she says yes, you wine and dine her like your life depends on it. Because your life *does* depend on it. I've had to listen to you mope about her for five years, and if you blow this, I'll bury you myself."

"Maybe I should just follow her lead," I said. "I don't want to make her more uncomfortable—"

Toby strode the short distance between us and jabbed at my chest with his index finger. "You fought for your new life. All those years ago, all this time. You fought your way back from nothing. *Nothing*. Why won't you fight for her?"

He was right. As always. Of course. But I couldn't admit it so easily.

"It's more complicated than that," I said.

"No, it's not. It's very simple. Either you two live happily ever after or you watch her find her happily ever after with some other guy."

"She was freaked out with just a kiss."

"But if you take her to coffee and explain, like I said, so she can re-label your relationship, she'll be fine. It's her natural human reaction. The point is, you need to fight to have Mel as more than your friend."

Sometimes I hated Toby Tony Robbins.

He punched my shoulder and turned back to the sofa. "Now let's get back to *Street Fighter*. I'll beat you this time. I can feel it. Not that you aren't doing great, because you are. Just be sure to block those low kicks."

CHAPTER 45

MEL

Ivy: "Don't let your parents talk to him like he's your husband." Hey, look, overbearing parents are timeless.
Mel: My parents are never meeting any man in my life before I'm engaged to him. Not that they care.
Cameron: I've met your parents. And your grandparents. And some extended family, too. Looks like I'm in the running.

I didn't have time to avoid Cameron today. And yet, here I was, tucked into an alcove in the library basement, willing myself to stop breathing so loudly. Who decided to put the restrooms in the basement, next to the IT department, exactly where it was impossible to avoid running into him?

His footsteps echoed in the empty hallway, coming closer and closer. Something jingled with each step, probably his car keys in his pocket. He paused to greet a student, and I nearly sighed at the sound of his voice. Pathetic, I know, but I hadn't heard it almost all week, and I missed him. I'd been busy begging off lunches and ducking into doorways.

Soon Ivy would track me down and demand answers. She'd only tolerated my weirdness for this long because she'd been distracted with her mom. But I couldn't deal with her questions right now because I had so many of my own. What did our feelings mean for us? Should we give it a chance? What if he didn't really want to give it a chance and had merely been swept up in the moment? I mean, he's a man, and I'm a woman, so maybe he just hadn't kissed anyone for a while, and I was the closest person. What if I had misread everything?

His footsteps began again, and then there he was, passing by without a glance in my direction. Just like I'd wanted. But a part of me wished that my plan would fail and he'd turn my way just by chance.

He looked good. His messenger bag hung from his shoulder. His head bowed over his phone. That cowlick stuck out, refusing to be in professor mode like the rest of him.

Waiting until all sounds of him disappeared, I mentally reviewed his schedule. He'd probably just left from checking his adjunct mailbox like he did every afternoon around this time. He had a weekly staff meeting in a few minutes. He would go to class immediately afterward.

So when he walked from the meeting to his class, I would hide behind a plant in the Fishbowl.

A dozen things waited for me at my desk, and none of them could wait. Tutoring sessions, reports for professors, administrative work for my boss, reorganizing the schedule because a tutor recently quit, and the book, always hovering at the back of my mind.

I left my hiding spot and tiptoed back to the Fishbowl. Feeling my phone vibrate in my pocket, I glanced at it while climbing the last few steps from the basement to the library lobby.

Cameron: Cupcake delivery. Where are you?

My steps stuttered to a stop.

He stood in the doorway of the Fishbowl, one hand in his pocket, the other holding a napkin wrapped around a gourmet cupcake. He looked directly at me, smiling stiffly like he had on my doorstep on Monday night.

All that evasion for nothing.

I couldn't run now. He'd seen me. We'd made eye contact. I had no excuse. He had that look on his handsome face—

I walked forward, enjoying the sight of him in the late afternoon sunlight even while I tucked my hands into my pockets. "Hiya, Cam."

"Hiya, Mel." He held out the cupcake. "Since you skipped lunch again today."

"Thank you." Accepting the cupcake and keeping my eyes on the swirling chocolate icing, I didn't look at him as I walked past. Hopefully he didn't ask where I'd been for lunch. *Oh, you know, just eating cold leftovers in an empty study room in the library, hoping I wouldn't see you. But also kind of hoping I would see you. You know what, just don't ask.*

He followed me into the office. "The meeting was canceled today. Dr. Freisen was out sick, and he didn't want anyone to run the meeting while he's gone. You know how he micromanages. So there are lots of cupcakes downstairs if you want more." His tone turned teasing. "I can bring them up so nobody asks questions when you trespass into IT territory."

I tried not to think too hard about how many cupcakes he'd brought me over the years, about how clueless I'd been. "Is Freisen okay?"

"He'll be fine. It's just a head cold."

"Good."

I watched him fuss with his shirt cuffs. One of the hardest things over the last few days had been stopping myself from obsessing over his every word and action from the last five years. Every cupcake, random comment, joke, Monday night—there was a lot to obsess over. And now he was here, in person, and I studied his every word and action like I was Hercule Poirot solving a murder on the Orient Express.

"Are you okay?" Cameron said.

I blinked. "I'm fine. You?"

"I'm fine," Cameron echoed, and then he stopped tugging at his sleeves and fully turned toward me. "Actually, no. I'm not fine."

"What's wrong?"

Did they not give him the full-time position? Because nobody deserved it more. The nerve they had, turning him down. He'd worked—

"You've been avoiding me. And I hate it."

All of the anger I'd felt toward administration morphed into shame. I stared at the cupcake I'd set on my desk. "I've been busy—"

"You're bad at lying. It's a compliment. But please don't lie to me."

Now shifting my stare to a stack of paperwork, I willed myself to say something normal. Definitely not *I don't know what we are, what to call us, and what it all means, and I feel stupid, and I wish we could take a chance, but I don't even know where to start.*

"We need to talk," he said. "About the other night. In the parking lot." A partial laugh broke from his throat. "Or really, whatever you're willing to talk to me about, because I miss you."

I blinked up at him. "You miss me?"

A tidy line formed above the bridge of his nose. "Of course I miss you."

My whisper slipped through my lips before I caught myself. "Why are you doing this?"

"Doing what?"

"Why do you bring me cupcakes?"

"Because I want to." His tone said it was a silly question for me to ask. But he was looking at me like his cupcake deliveries meant—

The office phone rang. My hand shook when I rushed to answer it, almost tripping over Veronica's empty receptionist chair. It was a commuter student who couldn't log in to the scheduling software from home. Her password wasn't working; her paper was due by midnight tomorrow; her rural-area internet kept shutting down ("SAT Systems is supposed to be here next month," she said). I scheduled her appointment for the morning and explained what she would need to bring for her tutoring session. I'd given the same spiel millions of times. But I hoped I sounded halfway intelligible because my mind was completely overwhelmed with thoughts of Cameron watching me.

As soon as the receiver clicked into its cradle, the phone rang again. I mumbled an apology to Cameron and took a message for Dr. Schaaf about rescheduling his flight to a conference four states away.

Why had Veronica chosen today of all days to call in sick? And why did I always feel the need to fill in when someone was out? The combined pressure of multitasking and Cameron's presence was too much.

I hung up from the second call and grumbled at my scrawled sticky note. "Why am I even doing this?"

"Because you're extraordinary." He said it instantly, like it was as obvious a fact as him being the best player on his college basketball team, both verifiable by Google. That same line reappeared above the bridge of his nose. "You're resilient and determined and extraordinary."

I hadn't felt resilient lately. I'd felt raw and uncertain about myself, him, us —whatever "us" even meant. About everything.

So I laughed instead of crying. "Now *that's* funny."

He stepped into my space, his proximity nudging me into the filing cabinet at my back. No hint of a smirk-shrug now. He was serious.

"You're extraordinary," he said. "Life kicks you down. People stand in your way. You never let them win. You never stop." His gaze caught on my lips. "You see what you want, and you go after it."

I swallowed, my throat thick, my vision filled only with his blue eyes. "So do you," I managed.

He slowly shook his head. "No. I see what I want, and I pretend to go after it, but I always hold back, just in case..." Blinking his gaze back to mine, he took a single step back. "I'm not resilient like you, Mel. I'm not good at bouncing back."

Did he want me to read between the lines? Was he holding back any feelings he had for me because he was afraid he wouldn't bounce back if I rejected him? Like I could imagine ever rejecting him.

Or had he not bounced back from the fact that I'd been so stunned by our kiss that I'd frozen up?

His voice was more breath than whisper. "So what do you say?"

"About what?"

How dare he wear a shirt that made his eyes even bluer and made my focusing even harder.

His lips twitched. "Talking tomorrow night. We can go out, if you want, or go to your place, or mine. I have a night class coming up or else we could meet sooner."

Oh. That. "Okay."

His smile was instant and genuine. He withdrew, backing toward the doorway. "Tomorrow. Meet you in the lobby after work, around seven. We can figure out where we go from there." He backed through the door, and he was still smiling when he turned around to walk forward through the lobby.

I released a shaky breath. Until I realized the silence he'd left behind didn't feel like a relief. It felt like excitement.

Tomorrow night. So we could talk about the parking lot.

I needed Ivy. Stat.

CHAPTER 46

MEL

Mel: Emergency. Can you come to my apartment? I'll provide the junk food.
Ivy: Definitely. My neighbor can come over to watch Mom.
Mel: You're the best.
Ivy: It's what friends are for. Should I bring wine?
Mel: Already have a box of merlot.
Ivy: A box? That bad, huh?

"I *knew* you were holding out on me!" Ivy threw a candy wrapper at my face.

I threw one back. I missed. "I just didn't know how to talk about it."

We sat on my couch, stress-eating our way through several kinds of candy and the partial ice cream pint from my freezer. But it wasn't helping. I was still stressed, and not even Ivy's company and my vanilla-scented candles were helping me to relax.

"Start over at the beginning," she said, "and give me more details."

So I started at the beginning, or what I considered the beginning, with Cameron telling me I was selfish, and how I'd been trying so hard to change. (The true beginning started the day we met, but she didn't need to know that.) She sighed consolingly, but her overall silence confirmed what Cameron had said about my selfishness. If I hadn't been so distracted with other, more important events, I would've been hurt. How long had she thought of me that way?

But the other, more important events at this moment were that kiss (Ivy fist-pumped in the air) and my revelation on Monday night (she grinned maniacally at me) and my conversation with Cameron in the Fishbowl (she squealed).

When I finished, she was silent. Patience wasn't something in my repertoire, especially not now, so I nudged her. "Well?"

"It's about time. You two make me crazy."

"So you knew this whole time? Why didn't you say anything?" My hand itched to throw a second candy wrapper at her face, but I knew I'd miss again.

"I did say something. Several times over the years, in fact. But I didn't push it because I didn't want to be caught in the middle. You're my best friends. I didn't want to matchmake and have it ruin the three of us together. You two needed to do this on your own."

"I feel so stupid."

"About that. I honestly can't believe it took you this long to notice."

I refilled my wineglass. "Thanks a lot."

"I'm serious. He's been pining after you since you two met. I also honestly can't believe it took him this long to finally do something about it."

Since we met? Could that be true? Five years of cluelessness when I could've been with Cameron, aka Mr. Darcy's Lake Scene? What a waste.

"How did you know?"

Ivy rolled her eyes. "How did you *not* know? He's so attentive to you it's ridiculous. He asks about your grandma, about your day at work, about some obscure movie you watched or book you read literally years ago. He gives you all those cupcakes. And did you not see how much he hated Marcus? Oh, and his reactions to the mancounters?"

Her words stacked into an impressive argument. But, unwilling to accept I'd been so stupid for five whole years, I hedged. "I mean, he wasn't super supportive of the list, but he was worried about safety more than anything else."

She twisted open another piece of candy. "First of all, not true. Second of all, he was worried about safety because he was worried about *you*." She punctuated "you" by throwing the wrapper at me. "He hates the list. He barely participates in our conversations about it. We have to drag him along with us every time. And he makes sarcastic comments about it every step of the way."

True. The only one he'd been remotely okay with was the apple pie, and even then, he'd seemed annoyed. Or maybe he'd only been remotely okay with it because he loved apple pie.

"Remember how he made jokes about Marcus being twelve years old?" Ivy said.

All of this had been happening right in front of my face for five years. That's how long it took for J.K. Rowling to outline Harry Potter and Always Cheerful Lisa to become a famous author. That's how long it took me to notice Cameron.

"I've been really self-centered, haven't I?" I said it more to the throw pillow on my lap than to Ivy.

She shrugged. "I think you've been so determined to see him as only a friend because you're scared. But he's also been too scared to be honest about *his* feelings. So between the two of you, you were destined to take forever to be together."

My fingertips skimmed the soft edges of the throw pillow. I thought of how many times Cameron had probably sat on this couch, holding this pillow, pining over clueless, selfish—

"But now that it's finally happening," Ivy said, "I'm thrilled."

"You don't know that it's happening."

"What else could he want to talk about? He did say he wanted to talk, right?"

"Yeah, but he was so vague," I said. "He might be trying to put us back on the friend track. Like 'It was a mistake, I'm sorry, I shouldn't have kissed you in our workplace parking lot, let's just be friends forever.'"

Her face twisted in frustration. "You can't honestly believe that."

I gestured with my wineglass. "You can't deny it's a possibility."

"It's a one-in-a-million possibility."

I shook my head. "It's still a possibility. So I still need to plan for the worst."

She ripped the comforting throw pillow from my lap. "No planning for the worst. We're planning for the best. I've been watching his sad puppy eyes for years, and I'm sick of it. If he tries to back out of this, don't let him."

I snatched the throw pillow back, clutching it to my chest. "Do you hear yourself? I'm not going to force him into a relationship that he clearly has doubts about. Why else has he waited so long?"

"All of his doubts are just insecurities about himself." She wagged a finger at me. "Don't you dare let him run away before telling him about your own feelings, too."

She clearly thought that this was a done deal, that Cameron and I were about to ride away into a blazing sunset as the romance novel ended. But what if we weren't?

I cleared my throat and stared at the pillow instead of looking at Ivy. "I just...don't know."

Her pause was so heavy I could feel it weighing on my shoulders, pressing me further down into my confusion and fear. When she finally spoke, her voice was a thin whisper. "What do you mean you don't know?"

"I mean—I just—I don't even know. I just feel so confused. I really care about him. He's a great friend. He's a wonderful person."

"And...?" She nudged me with her foot since I wouldn't look at her.

"I've spent my whole life picturing love being a certain way. Like swooning and starlight and singing angels."

She scoffed. "That's because you read too many romances."

Yes, I'd learned about romance through books more than I had in real life, but the list was supposed to help with that. Or so I'd thought. Clearly it wasn't helping me at all.

"My point is," I said, "I've always dreamed of finding a Mr. Darcy to my Elizabeth Bennet. A John Thornton to my Margaret Hale. Cam and I aren't a classic love story. How do you become more than friends when 'friends' is all you've ever been? There's no timeless model for the next step."

"What do you mean you two aren't a classic love story?" Ivy said. "Are you saying that because you haven't fainted into his arms, you think you don't love him?"

"Elizabeth Bennet never fainted into Mr. Darcy's arms."

She rolled her eyes. "But Margaret Hale fainted in John Thornton's arms. Don't pretend you haven't made me watch these movies way too many times. And don't distract me."

"I just—I guess there was a kind of lightning bolt moment on Monday night, when it hit me that he has feelings for me. But I don't know what it would look like for us to be more than friends, and I don't know that either of us want to risk our friendship."

Just friends. The mantra taunted me now, keeping me stuck.

Ivy began ticking questions off on her fingers. "Have you missed him like crazy?"

All those silent days without talking to Cameron or hearing from him, and all the times I hid from him, and all the questions I had about Dr. Freisen and his bowties simply because it was something Cameron had noticed.

"Yes."

She lifted another finger. "Who's the most attractive man you've ever seen in your life?"

His dark hair and that silly cowlick. His button-downs—always a little wrinkly—and his blue eyes, crinkling at the corners when he laughed and widening in shock after he kissed me in the parking lot.

"Cam."

"Who's always there for you no matter what, and you're always there for him?"

With each mancounter from the list, he'd been there. When I read a book of poetry outside the engineering building, and when the eighties night at the club ended in disaster. Always him. Guilt needled me. Was I there for him the same way?

"Cam."

"What—"

"I get it."

"Do you? Because you may think this is something sudden, but it's definitely not sudden for Cam. And, if you're honest, it's not sudden for you either. I've caught you checking him out when you thought nobody was looking. I've heard you sing his praises to students and faculty and even your family."

She wasn't wrong. I regularly bragged about Cameron until I brainwashed everyone in my life into adoring him like I did.

Loving him like I did.

"You know," Ivy said, "it's not Darcy's brooding mood or wealth or handsomeness that ultimately win Elizabeth's love. It's his goodness. And you and Cam love each other's goodness. So just get married already."

My eyes bulged cartoonishly. "Married! You're really jumping to conclusions."

But now that she mentioned it, what would it be like to be married to Cameron, with his humor and warm hands and morning voice—

"Dating is about getting to know each other," Ivy said, "and you two have been getting to know each other for five years. I'm counting that as five years of dating. So marriage is the next logical conclusion."

"You're crazy!" I flung the pillow at her, and since pillows are much larger than candy wrappers, it landed squarely in her face.

She flung it back at me. "Maybe. But you two could use some crazy. You know I'm right about the 'loving each other's goodness' thing."

Considering I didn't know anyone with as much good-heartedness as Cameron, yes, she was right about that.

Ivy set our wineglasses and candy on the coffee table, standing and stretching her arms far overhead. "So now that we have that out of the way, what are you wearing to meet Cam for coffee tomorrow night? He'd probably be just as smitten with you if you showed up in your ratty pajamas, but I think you should look stunning. Let's attack your closet for something that'll make his jaw drop."

CHAPTER 47

CAMERON

From: Mary Holcomb
To: Cameron Whitacre
Cc: Aisha Jassim; Gerard O'Leary; Keith Freisen
Subject: Application: Full-Time Computer Science Position

Dear Dr. Whitacre,

After serious review and consideration, we would like to offer you our sincere congratulations on being accepted to the full-time position of Computer Science Professor.

We chose you for the position because of your outstanding academic experience and career. The final difference that tipped the scales in your favor was the sheer number of positive student reviews you receive each year and auspicious input from your department chair, Dr. Keith Freisen.

There were many applications for this position, which is why our hiring process was much more lengthy than usual. We appreciate your patience in this matter.

Please review the attached documents and let us know if you have any questions or concerns.

Sincerely,
Mary Holcomb
Associate Dean

From: Keith Freisen
To: Cameron Whitacre
Subject: RE: Application: Full-Time Computer Science Position

Excellent news. My warmest congratulations to you on your new position and all the future opportunities that this will allow. The university could not have chosen anyone better.

Regards,
Keith Freisen, PhD
Academic Department Chair
Computer Science and Information Technology

From: Cameron Whitacre
To: Keith Freisen
Subject: RE: Application: Full-Time Computer Science Position

Thank you for your kind congratulations and for putting in a good word for me. I truly appreciate it.

Thanks,
Cameron Whitacre
Computer Science Mind-Bender (Adjunct Professor) and IT Department Wizard (Director)

From: Keith Freisen
To: Cameron Whitacre
Subject: RE: Application: Full-Time Computer Science Position

You are very welcome.

May I suggest you reduce the volume of your celebratory exclamations. Your voice is carrying through the hallway even though your office door is closed.

Regards,
Keith Freisen, PhD
Academic Department Chair
Computer Science and Information Technology

From: Cameron Whitacre
To: Keith Freisen
Subject: RE: Application: Full-Time Computer Science Position

Sorry about that.

Thanks,
Cameron Whitacre
Computer Science Mind-Bender (Adjunct Professor) and IT Department Wizard (Director)

From: Keith Freisen
To: Cameron Whitacre
Subject: RE: Application: Full-Time Computer Science Position

Dr. Whitacre,

There is no need to apologize for celebrating good news.

Regards,
Keith Freisen, PhD
Academic Department Chair
Computer Science and Information Technology

From: Cameron Whitacre
To: Mary Holcomb
Cc: Aisha Jassim; Gerard O'Leary; Keith Freisen
Subject: RE: Application: Full-Time Computer Science Position

Ms. Holcomb,

Thank you for this opportunity! I'm excited to join the team in a full-time capacity. I will review the hiring documents and be in touch if I have questions.

Thanks,
Cameron Whitacre
Computer Science Mind-Bender (Adjunct Professor) and IT Department Wizard (Director)

CHAPTER 48

MEL

Mel: I might puke. Wish me luck.
Ivy: Always. (To the luck. Not the puke.)

Walking past Cameron's office hadn't been my intention. We were supposed to meet in the library lobby. But I hadn't seen him one time all day—not even in passing—and I worried that he wouldn't show up, or that he'd text and cancel, or that I'd text and cancel because I was sick with nervousness.

Basically, I was a worry wart. I couldn't take it anymore. I needed just a touch of reassurance. That was it. Nothing more.

Without thinking about it, at 6:45 my feet took me on a meandering route to the IT and computer science department.

The hallway was dim, but light from Cameron's office cast a bright rectangle across the floor. He was there. He hadn't played hooky on me after all. My stiff shoulders relaxed.

I stepped closer to the rectangle, peered through the doorway—and froze.

The smallest office in all of history looked like Dorothy's tornado had swept through it seconds ago. His papers were scattered across his desk. All the books from his shelves were stacked into leaning pillars on the floor. His trash can overflowed with paper plates, napkins, and an empty Bluesy Bean pastry box.

Cameron was on his hands and knees, facing away from me as he pulled more papers from cabinets and file drawers.

While I appreciated the view, I had important questions. Firstly, "What happened?"

His head thumped against the shelf above him. Still on his knees, he turned, further mussing his cowlick as he rubbed what would surely be a sore spot. "Hiya, Mel. You're early."

"Hiya, Cam. I'm not that early. It's only a little before seven. What happened?"

He stood from his kneeling position, smoothing his dress pants as he straightened. "I decided to reorganize."

He wasn't wearing his glasses. This was one of the few times I'd seen him in contacts instead, and without the dark frames of his glasses frames and with the background of his navy shirt—

I blinked away and gestured at the mess. "So reorganizing means unleashing an apocalypse?"

His eyes crinkled. "I promise it's organized chaos." His fingers tugged at his long sleeves. "It's because I have some news. I got the job."

My smile was so big it hurt. "The full-time position?!"

"Well, you know, the ultimate genius position was already taken by Albert Einstein, so I settled for—oof!"

I didn't give him time to finish before I lunged across his cluttered floor and hugged him as hard as I could. "This is wonderful news! When did you find out? Why didn't you tell me right away? Have you told anyone else?"

Cameron settled his arms around me. His laughter echoed into my ear that I pressed to his chest. "Word got around the department really quickly. It's been a crazy day or I would've told you sooner. I just didn't want to tell you about it in a text."

"This is too perfect! Have you told Ivy?"

"I didn't want to tell her in a text, either. But I could hardly wait to tell you. I went to the Fishbowl an hour ago, but you were in a session, so Lauren shooed me away. You were the first person I thought of sharing the news with."

Out of all the people he knew, colleagues, mentors, friends like Toby, his family... "I was the first?"

"Of course."

My chest warmed. "We should do something to celebrate."

"We both love the Bluesy Bean," he said. "I wouldn't want to celebrate anywhere else."

I snorted. "Nowhere else? This is a big event. You're finally getting everything you want."

"Mostly."

Those two syllables hung above us, a door opening into something new.

He paused long enough that he drew my glance to him. His gaze wandered over my face like it had last Monday night at my apartment—slowly, purposefully. His thumb drew a leisurely circle between my shoulder blades. My thoughts shattered.

I swallowed. "We can go to that steakhouse—"

"No. The Bluesy Bean with you is perfect. Unless you want to make us some Moscow mules at your place, of course."

There was no need for us to be hugging for this long. But I didn't want to pull away, and he didn't look like he wanted to, either. His blue eyes studied me with this look like—like—

We needed to talk before I raced too far ahead of myself, of him, of whatever this was.

I withdrew and cleared my throat. "My place it is. We can order whatever food you want. Are you ready to leave, or do you need more apocalypse time in your office first?"

He grinned. "I'm done apocalypsing for today. Let me grab my coat."

Even though I teased him that nobody would think there was anything valuable in an office that looked like such a disaster, he smiled and turned the lock when we left.

"Should I bring anything?" he asked. "I can stop at the store on my way."

I watched his fingers shuffle between his car keys. "No, I have everything for drinks."

As we turned away from his office, he briefly touched his hand to the small of my back, and it felt right with him in a way it never had with anyone else.

I struggled to focus as we began the climb up the stairs toward the lobby. "So you'll start your new position next semester?"

"Yeah, I'll get my new schedule then, and they'll let me know about—"

I was so busy noticing the way his arm brushed against mine as we walked that I almost didn't notice the man standing in the lobby. If Cameron hadn't broken off mid-sentence, I might have walked right past him. Instead, I blinked up at Cameron to see him staring ahead, wide-eyed. I followed his gaze.

Marcus stood in the library lobby.

CHAPTER 49

CAMERON

Ivy: I'm texting you privately to let you know that tonight is important. Make it count.
Cameron: Hello to you, too.
Ivy: If you screw this up, I'll make you regret it.

Marcus couldn't be standing in the library lobby. It was impossible.

He was supposed to be sunning on a beach in Miami, or wining and dining some other woman he'd met at some other park, or running from the IRS. He wasn't supposed to be looking at his phone, standing a few yards away from me on the night I hoped to win Mel's heart.

I blinked once. Twice. No, he was still there.

I looked at Mel. Lips parted, eyes wide, she clearly hadn't expected to see him. That knowledge didn't stop the punch to my gut or the crushing feeling in my lungs. I couldn't seem to take a deep enough breath.

If only I'd thought faster on my feet and rushed the two of us out the door before she'd noticed him.

Mel spoke first. "Marcus?"

Looking up from his phone, his face split into that beaming smile I hated. "Mel! I texted and called when I saw you weren't at the tutoring center. I thought I'd missed you."

You did miss her. You know, weeks ago, when you disappeared?

Mel blinked. "I went downstairs to meet up with Cam."

I couldn't move as I watched Marcus stride up to her and take both of her hands in his. "I'm sorry I didn't answer your last texts and calls. Work was crazy, and I just got back into town this morning. Let's go get some drinks and catch up."

My chest tightened even more. Mel's surprised face now included a crease on her forehead. I could practically see her mind sorting through his words and thinking of her own.

Old habits instinctively pushed forward, forcing their way through the boulders in my stomach. Marcus was Mr. Perfect. I could walk away, give them space, let them make up. They would go for drinks at a fancy place where Marcus would leave a generous tip, and they'd walk hand in hand back to his shiny car, and maybe they'd end the night at his fancy mansion.

She'd been happy with him before. I could let her be happy with him again.

But I remembered the way she'd looked after telling me he'd ghosted her, just before I surprised both of us by kissing her in the parking lot. She'd stared at the pavement and shoved her hands ever deeper into her pockets.

Mel hadn't been happy then. I'd felt desperate to do something, anything, to erase that look from her face. I would hate myself if she ever had that look on her face again when I could've done something about it. This was my chance.

My jaw clenched. I stepped forward, taking a breath to explain that Marcus needed to walk away and never come back and hopefully fall on that ice patch outside the main entrance on his way out. Whatever I needed to say to make him leave Mel before he hurt her again—

Mel pulled her hands away from his and took a step back. "No, thanks. I have plans tonight."

Her gaze found mine, and the boulder in my stomach dissolved.

Marcus took it in stride. "What about tomorrow? I'm in town until the weekend—"

"No." She shook her head and took a half-step closer to me. "I'm not inter-ested in starting this up again, Marcus."

That half-step was all I needed. I stepped closer to her, my hand automati-cally at her waist. I stood as tall as I could, glaring down at Marcus from my four-inch advantage over him, just like I'd wanted to glare when I first met him in the cafeteria.

His gaze darted between us. "Are you sure, Mel? I—"

"She said no." Was that my voice, all growly like that?

She shifted closer to me again. "I'm sure."

He blinked at us. Marcus was a man used to getting what he wanted. But he wasn't leaving here with My Mel.

Apparently seeing that in my face, he raised his palms and backed toward the main entrance. "I understand perfectly."

I stood for a moment, watching Marcus walk through the glass doors. I relished the feel of my hand on Mel's waist. Hopefully I hadn't overstepped. She hadn't really needed me to speak up. She could've handled it herself. But I'd wanted to let her know I was right next to her if she needed me. I was always here if she needed me.

Marcus disappeared into the darkness.

CHAPTER 50

MEL

Ivy: I have positive vibes about tonight. Remember: kiss first, overthink later.

We stood in silence for a few minutes. My mind and feelings had scattered even further at the sight of Marcus—and at what he'd said. Why had he even bothered? Did he really think I'd try again after he'd so obviously ghosted me? How naïve it would have been of me to go running back to him, regardless of where I stood with Cameron.

Speaking of where I stood, Cameron's arm still curved diagonally around my back and ended with his hand at my waist. He'd done that when Marcus hadn't backed off. Ivy would probably laugh at him for thinking I needed backup, but I appreciated the gesture. It had anchored me.

Marcus showing up had been unexpected. Like I wasn't already worried enough about my "talk" with Cameron tonight. The earlier tension still weighed in my stomach.

Cameron cleared his throat. "Are you okay?"

I nodded. "I'm relieved to have some kind of closure, actually."

He frowned. "I would've preferred that he never showed his face again, but I guess that wish can come true starting now."

I smiled and looked into his worried eyes. "I hated the open-ended disappearing act. This is better."

Turning for the exit would've been the natural thing to do, but I hesitated. It would mean losing his arm around me.

Cameron made the first move, stepping toward the glass door and holding it open for me. We walked into the cold night air. Our steps were slow along the freshly shoveled sidewalk.

My worries settled into every thought. What would he say? What would I say? Would everything change or stay the same? Would it be better or worse?

"I've been trying." My statement was so inadequate for what I meant.

His fingers fiddled with the cuffs of his jacket. "What?"

"I've been trying. To be less selfish."

His hands stilled. "Mel, I never meant—"

"No, it's a good thing you told me. Friends help friends become better people. I needed to hear it. And you did it just in time, so I could be better for Ivy when she needed me."

"But I didn't—"

"So let's pretend this is like a student-professor review. Tell me how I'm doing." The vulnerability of what I said didn't fully hit me until it was too late. I wanted to know, and I didn't.

"This isn't why I asked to talk with you tonight."

I focused on our footsteps turning the corner toward the parking lot. "I've been trying to be a better friend to you, too. So tell me. How am I doing?"

In his pause, the salt on the sidewalk crunched under our feet.

Just say something already, Cameron. Anything.

He stopped walking. "Friend? That's it?"

I paused to face him. Once I looked up, I couldn't look away. He was leaning forward, his posture curled toward me. His gaze was magnetic.

When I didn't say anything—couldn't say anything—he spoke instead. Softly. Gently. "Mel, I never thought you were selfish. I thought you were unhappy. I worried about you. And...I was jealous. Of Marcus."

"That was jealousy?"

"Jealousy. Rage. Hatred. Take your pick."

"Oh" was all I could manage as I remembered how his knuckles had whitened around Marcus's handshake in a hard grasp. How he'd withdrawn into his work. The distance had grown because we were both too scared and stubborn to take a chance. Not to mention his defensive stance in the library lobby just a moment ago.

"I just wanted you to be happy." He shifted a little closer. "Forgive me?"

"Of course." Not forgiving Cameron had never even occurred to me as an option.

His posture relaxed. "Samantha always tells me I get overly protective of people I care about, so I guess I showed it in a weird way there."

"So you don't hate me?" I meant for it to sound lighthearted, teasing, but instead it sounded neurotic and childish.

"I could never hate you."

That didn't mean he wanted me as more than a friend. Maybe Ivy had it all wrong. And so did I.

I turned my gaze back to the concrete. I toed at a particularly interesting grain of sidewalk salt and maneuvered it around a small patch of snow.

"Hating you has never been the problem." He reached over to brush the back of my hand with three fingertips. "It's the opposite."

I stopped messing with the salt grain. I'd always thought the romance novels had it wrong—how could a person's surroundings completely melt away?—but now my surroundings did just that. The few students meandering along the sidewalks, the remaining cars in the parking lot, they melted. All I could see was Cameron's blue eyes and messy cowlick. All I could feel was the nerves in my stomach and his fingertips on the back of my hand.

His voice was low. "I shouldn't have done that. Kissed you like that."

My heart fell to my stomach, and then both my stomach and my heart fell to my feet. His face and tone made his regret clear. I thought of bolting for my car in the parking lot, but that much movement felt impossible with my weighted feet.

"It wasn't right, to launch myself at you like that without any warning," he said. "I don't blame you for reacting the way you did."

He was letting me down gently. Next he would tell me that my reaction had been the right thing to do, and he liked me only as a friend and nothing more, and everything would go back to the way it had been for the last five years. Only it couldn't go back for me. I had this mess of new feelings that I didn't know how to live with if he wasn't living with them, too.

I looked back to the sidewalk, with its tiny salt grains isolated against the dark concrete.

"It was wrong of me to do," he said, his fingertips pressing a little more firmly against my hand, "because you deserve better. Because I want to be the one who gives you better than just a spur-of-the-moment kiss in a parking lot."

He paused long enough that his words registered in my worried brain, drawing my gaze back to him.

"Mel, I've felt more than friendship for you ever since the day we met. If friendship is all you want, then I'll be the best friend I can be for you. But if there's even the smallest chance, even a one-in-a-million chance that you can see us being something more than friends—"

Was he saying what I thought he was saying? Did he mean—

"I want to be so much more than friends with you, Mel."

My breath caught. More than friends with Cameron? That meant even better than Monday nights and weekday lunches and staff meetings. It meant holding his warm hands, and kissing his adorable smile, and feeling—

He stepped a little closer, settling his whole palm against the back of my hand. "Melanie Hirsch, I love you."

It settled against my chest, warming into me. *He loved me.*

I doubted I would ever breathe again. This was more than I'd hoped for. I'd thought we'd confess our interest in being more than friends. This was even better.

His words came in a rush now. "You don't have to say it if you're not sure. I realize this is probably a shock, and I probably shouldn't have just said all that, but I can't keep going without at least trying, so I'm putting myself out there, I'm taking a chance, and it's a chance I'm willing to take with you. I've had five years to think about this. I don't want you to tell me that you love me just because you feel pressured or caught off guard. If you need time to think it over, that's okay. I can wait."

Cameron paused, shifting his weight from foot to foot. His half-laugh sounded stiff when he said, "Just please don't make me wait another five years until you say something."

I blinked up at him. "All this time, I kept telling myself to see you only as a friend because I thought that's all you saw in me. I didn't want a one-sided romance." I stepped a little closer. "I told myself I only felt friendship toward you because I expected love to look a specific way. But love looks all kinds of ways, and it can grow over time before I realize it's happened. Just like us." I turned my hand to link our fingers and press our palms together. "I love you, Cameron Whitacre."

His eyes widened. "You do?"

"Yes."

"You're not just saying that to stop my rambling?"

I shook my head. "No."

He stepped closer, grasping both of my hands in his. "I love you, Melanie Hirsch."

I smiled and also stepped closer. "Let's keep saying that for the next several hours."

"Or longer."

My hands shook so much that I almost missed that his were trembling, too. I looked down, enjoying the sight and feel of his fingers wrapped so tightly around mine. Looking down a little further, our shoes touched toes. He stood directly in front of me.

His thumb rubbed a slow circle over mine. "Are you really sure?"

"That I love you?" I smiled up at him. "Of course. Are you?"

"I've had years to be sure of you."

I squeezed his hands tighter. "All these years? Why didn't you say anything?"

His gaze moved over my face, our hands, my hair. "Toby says I've been standing in my own way. A very existential Macbeth situation, apparently."

"Your Toby sounds very wise, even if a little too Shakespearean."

"And Ivy threatened my life."

"Ivy talked to you about this?"

Cameron shrugged. "Not about tonight, specifically, but about me being a lovesick idiot, yes." Reaching into his pocket, he scrolled through some texts Ivy had sent him earlier that day. "See for yourself."

Ivy: If you screw this up, I'll...

I smiled at her words. "Oh, Ivy."

"We should probably tell her."

Yes, we should probably tell Ivy and Toby and Grandma, and they would all be too smug for their own good. But for now, it should be just the two of us, not noticing the dark sidewalks and parking lot around us.

I traced the pad of my finger across his knuckle. "Let's not tell anyone just yet."

After tucking his phone back into his pocket, he idly coiled one of my wavy strands around his finger—winding it, releasing it, winding it again. His other hand still held mine, like these extra touches were the most natural things in the world.

"It's such a relief to finally say all this out loud," he said.

"Is this why I've never seen you date anyone?" I had so many questions but this one came to mind first.

"Yes."

"But I've dated a few people since we've met."

"I could tell they wouldn't last," he said. "But Marcus had me worried."

The pad of my thumb moved to wander over his nail, enjoying the smoothness. "All for nothing."

"Your list had me worried." His tone sounded like a confession.

I smiled. "It was more about the book than the men."

Now he pressed our palms more tightly together, like he was testing out how it felt to touch my hands in all the ways he'd been waiting for. "But you were still meeting a lot of people, and the more you met, the more likely the chances that you'd be with one of them and not with me."

"Then you should've said something earlier."

Cameron considered me, his eyes slowly moving over my face and settling on his hand still winding and unwinding my hair. "I think we needed the list. We spent more time together outside of work. It forced me to get moving." He grinned. "And it also helped you see that no one can love you as much as someone who has already spent five years of his life feeling crazy about you."

Warmth in my chest spread through my limbs, all the way to my feet. Winter in New England? I couldn't feel the cold at all.

CHAPTER 51

MEL

Ivy: I'm going to take your silence as a sign that good (meaning SEXY) things are happening. Right?

Cameron hadn't stopped touching me since that first brush of his fingertips on the sidewalk. When the streetlights flicked on, his arm curved around me, and we only managed a few steps into the parking lot before we stopped again, too busy talking and touching to remember where we were. One moment his fingers would press against mine, the next they wound through a wayward wave of hair. He was making up for the last five years of friends-only touches.

I loved it. All of it. The touching, the freedom to watch his face as he laughed over how annoying Toby had been about the two of us, the joy of running my fingers through his cowlick to mess it up even more and make him smile at me.

By the time we finally reached my car, it was late, and the parking lot was nearly empty. I stepped onto a curb and turned to face him, putting us at eye level. We were just inches apart, but I didn't step back.

I hoped for a kiss. More than a peck this time, please and thank you. That first peck had been too quick, and I'd been too shocked to enjoy it. I couldn't wait to enjoy the next one, our first *real* kiss. Couldn't. Wait. With how he kept staring at my lips, I knew he was thinking about it, too.

"With the job and the girl," I said, "you've finally gotten everything you want."

He smirk-shrugged. "Mostly."

Those two syllables again, opening the door wide to more than *just friends.* A whole new world waited on the other side. I felt breathless just thinking about it, and each shallow pant brushed the front of my coat to his.

"What else do you want?" I whispered.

Standing this close, with our hands at our sides, his fingertips barely brushed mine. "Surely you know by now."

I leaned slightly forward, the rasp in his tone drawing a taut line that tugged me closer to him. The steam from our breaths mingled into a single cloud around us in the darkness. "I think I could guess."

His gaze was direct and meaningful. "And?"

"And why not...just go for it. If the list has taught us anything, it's that fortune favors the bold."

His eyes flickered to my lips for a moment. The pause was short-lived. Slowly, slowly he leaned in, studying me as he closed the remaining breaths between us.

At first his lips were chaste, but before I could wonder whether Cameron would settle for just another peck like before, he shifted and drank me in. Tasting, giving and taking, teasing—his kiss said that he'd thought of this for five long, long years and now was the time to try all the kisses at once.

I felt everything Cameron in his kiss. His hesitancy and his hope, his years of waiting, his restraint. All this without any other physical contact. Only our lips touched. He was giving me space.

But we'd already had five years of space.

I linked my arms around his neck and tugged him closer. He reacted instantly, pressing his hands into my back, pulling me into him.

The kiss expanded to all my senses. My skin tingled where he held me. His quiet sigh roared in my ears when I tightened my arms a little more. I'm sure if I opened my eyes, I would've seen extra galaxies in the night sky, but I was too distracted with so many other sensations.

We broke off the kiss, breaths panting. I blinked him into focus, enjoying that his eyes stayed closed, like he was savoring the moment. He pulled in his bottom lip with his teeth, and he smiled a Cheshire grin. I waited until Cameron's eyes opened, just so I could see how his smile grew when he looked at me.

He touched his forehead to mine and tightened his grasp on the back of my coat. "Please tell me I'm not dreaming this."

I laughed because I had too many feelings to hold inside. "You're not dreaming this."

Another laugh—until he kissed me again. And again. And again.

We didn't notice the big, fluffy snowflakes until they began sticking to our eyelashes. When we did finally become aware of them, we grinned and kissed through those, too.

Standing there, wrapped up together underneath the streetlights, I felt the quiet, sure, steady love that I hadn't even known I needed. He'd swept me off my feet in his own Cameron way. Everything I ever wanted was standing right in front of me.

EPILOGUE

MEL

Mel: Are you in your office? I have a surprise for you.
Cameron: Are you the surprise? Are you naked?
Mel: No. Cam. We're at work in the middle of the day. How could I be naked?
Cameron: Come to my office and find out.

It is a truth universally acknowledged that when a woman loves a man, she brings him his favorite apple pie on his busiest workday, just to cheer him up.

Students hurried through the hallways of the IT and computer science department, their arms filled with wires, laptops, monitors, and books. Everyone in the computer lab focused with laser intensity on their screens. It was completely unlike the relative quiet of the Fishbowl at the end of the semester.

I lingered outside Cameron's open office door. He was talking on the phone, facing away. I already knew my favorite navy button-down would make his eyes even bluer. He needed a haircut, and his cowlick was more out of control than usual. A ceramic mug—a gift from me last year, complete with a pi/pie design on the side—sat on his desk, full of pens. A framed photo leaned next to it, displaying a picture of the two of us with an award I won for my first book. A gold band on his left hand caught the overhead light.

When the administration asked Cameron about moving offices, he'd said he liked this one just fine, but if they could find a different storage spot for the cleaning supplies and Christmas decorations, it would be much appreciated. He kept his desk tidy these days, clear of spare tech and papers. He said it was my neatness rubbing off on him, but he'd perched me on his desk often enough that I knew better.

Something in my chest shifted. It felt too good to be true, delivering a pie for Cameron before walking upstairs for another tutoring session, and then leaving work early to talk to my agent about my second book. This was my life. And I couldn't ask for anything better.

Cameron hung up the phone and noticed me immediately. He stood and pulled me into his office, closing the door behind me. "Hiya, Mel."

"Hiya, Cam." I set the pie on his desk. "Just in case your meeting runs long into lunch, I made your favorite."

Taking my hands, he backed into the chair behind his desk and then pulled me onto his lap. "Thank you."

"You're welcome."

He tucked his face into my neck. "I knew I smelled something delicious."

My skin tickled at his kiss. "The pie has cinnamon. That's what you're smelling."

His finger tucked under my chin and turned me toward him. The corners of his eyes crinkled. "I wasn't talking about the pie."

I moved to give his arm a playful shove but somehow ended up kissing him instead. It was a regular theme in our relationship; I would be going through a perfectly normal routine, and then we'd be kissing. It was a recurring plot device that I didn't mind one bit.

"Isn't your first meeting in a few minutes?" I managed between kisses.

"I'll be fashionably late." His fingers busied themselves taking out the pins in my hair.

I broke away for breath. "You're incorrigible."

His lips drifted along the length of my neck. "You mean insatiable."

The phone on his desk rang.

"Shouldn't you answer that?"

He nipped my ear. "I'm busy."

"I came here to help you by bringing you pie, not make you late and end up with a lecture from Dr. Freisen."

He sighed and leaned back, pulling fingers of one hand through my hair and answering the phone with the other. The call was short, his eyes on me the entire conversation. As soon as he hung up, he kissed me again, murmuring that a lecture from Keith would be worth it.

* * *

Cameron

Every night with Mel meant coming home to throw pillows and fluffy blankets, vanilla candles, and the patchwork of furniture that came together when we combined our homes. In the winter, it meant curling under those fluffy blankets with movie marathons; in the summer, it meant sitting on the balcony and watching the city lights. It meant cozy. Comfort. Absolutely us.

It also meant sex. All. The. Sex. Mel was worth every minute of pining celibacy I'd endured over the last five years.

I jogged up the stairs to my old condo (now *our* condo), mentally running through our plans for the night. My dream team for Trivia Tuesday would have its big debut tonight—Toby, Ivy, and the two of us. We would crush the competition. I could feel it.

I opened the door to see Mel wearing nothing but a bra, panties, and her wedding ring.

"Hiya, Cam."

"Hiya, Mel."

"Eyes up here."

"Nah. I'm good."

She laughed and walked down the hall to our bedroom. Naturally I followed her, passing the framed pictures on our walls: our wedding, some vacations, Mel's book launch. I made a mental note to buy another frame this week so I could hang an article Alma had written for *The Courier* about Mel's book being a bestseller. My empty, boring condo didn't feel so empty and boring anymore.

Her attention was on the closet. "What can I wear tonight that's really comfortable but still looks good on me?"

"Nothing."

She slowly turned from the closet, her eyes wide with hurt. "Nothing? Ouch."

I wrapped my arms around her, nuzzling into her brown waves. "No. I mean *nothing*."

She laughed at my suggestive tone. "I don't think our teammates would like the change in dress code."

Making her laugh was one of my favorite things. Kissing her was a top favorite, too. I started at the space behind her ear and worked my way down to her shoulder before she stopped me.

She pulled away. "You're going to be an awful trivia team captain if you make us late for our first game."

"Trivia Tuesday doesn't sound like much fun right now," I said.

But she was right. Trivia Tuesday first. We could pick this up later.

I turned away to let her dress in peace and to ensure my own self-control. "Fine. Put some clothes on. Break my heart."

I waited for her in the living room, texting Toby to let him know we would be on our way in a few minutes. Her footsteps echoed behind me. I looked up and gave her sweater and jeans a brief once-over.

She frowned at me. "What's that look for?"

Synchronizing our steps down the stairs, I took her hand, just like her grandparents always did.

"*Nothing* would've been better."

ACKNOWLEDGMENTS

What a dream come true! I'm in awed gratitude that God brought this opportunity into my life.

Reader, thank you for welcoming *Book Smart* into your life and, hopefully, into your hearts. May Cameron and Mel always remind us that true love is timeless.

Thank you, Smartypants Romance, for such a warm welcome! Penny Reid, Brooke Nowiski, Fiona Fischer, and all of the Smartypants Romance authors - thank you for patiently answering my endless questions and making *Book Smart* possible.

Thank you to the East Palestine Memorial Public Library and the Friends of the East Palestine Memorial Public Library. You will always be my home library.

Thank you to my college mentors, Dr. Jensen, who encouraged me to make that first trek to the Writing Center, and Dr. Summers, who hired me as a writing tutor. I'll always remember your kindness.

Thank you, Mrs. Masters, for teaching me to embrace my voice and creativity. I still have your notes!

Christina Fleischer, I cannot thank you enough for being just a DM away. You inspire me more than you know. (How amazing is it that both our dreams came true?!)

Thank you to my alpha (and beta) reader, Kymberly Krogh, for reading multiple drafts of *Book Smart* and intervening with much-needed pep talks. Alphas forever!

Thank you to my team of beta readers: Jessica Fergen, Dawn Koontz, Glade and Kelsey Pennington, Karen Sutherland, my husband, and my parents. Thank you, Grant Garden, for your willingness to lend your voice to Cameron's experience. *Book Smart* is a much better story thanks to all of you!

Special thanks to Vince and Melissa Winner for being beta readers, for supporting me through the most stressful yet exciting part of my life, and for fangirling with me over all things Smartypants. (Okay, the fangirling was more Melissa than Vince, but still.) I love that you allowed one of your clever, romantic quips to make a cameo appearance in Cameron and Mel's relationship. And thank you for making one of my all-time favorite memories: a surprise champagne toast after I finished my book!

Endless thanks to my Rupp family for supporting my lifelong obsession with reading, books, and big writing dreams, especially when those dreams felt further away than ever. There were many times I doubted my writing would ever go anywhere, but you always believed there was more to come. Thank you!

Thank you to my Pennington family for listening to my ramblings and encouraging me to ignore naysayers. "You have nothing to lose" - and you were right!

To my family, friends, and mentors who have supported me throughout the years, thank you. You are too many to name, but don't think I've forgotten you! I wouldn't be writing this without your guidance. You'll never know how much you helped me through the writing process!

Last but most of all, thank you to my husband, Gregg. You supported me through every high and every low, made a valiant effort to teach me poker, and brainstormed mancounter ideas. From the very beginning, when you encouraged me to submit my book proposal, to the final draft, you never let my doubts get the best of me. I love you!

ABOUT THE AUTHOR

Amanda Pennington lives outside Louisville, Kentucky with her husband in their fixer-upper house. When she's not writing, Amanda loves traveling, running, and reading anything within reach. More information is available at www.amandacpennington.com.

Facebook: https://www.facebook.com/amandacpennington
Instagram: https://bit.ly/3r5fWn2
Newsletter: https://bit.ly/3qielLI
Twitter: https://twitter.com/seeamandawrite
Goodreads: https://bit.ly/3fdsvHH
Pinterest: https://bit.ly/3tm3uT0

Find Smartypants Romance online:
Website: www.smartypantsromance.com
Facebook: www.facebook.com/smartypantsromance/
Goodreads: www.goodreads.com/smartypantsromance
Twitter: @smartypantsrom
Instagram: @smartypantsromance
Newsletter: https://smartypantsromance.com/newsletter/

ALSO BY SMARTYPANTS ROMANCE

Green Valley Chronicles

The Love at First Sight Series

Baking Me Crazy by Karla Sorensen (#1)

Batter of Wits by Karla Sorensen (#2)

Steal My Magnolia by Karla Sorensen(#3)

Fighting For Love Series

Stud Muffin by Jiffy Kate (#1)

Beef Cake by Jiffy Kate (#2)

Eye Candy by Jiffy Kate (#3)

The Donner Bakery Series

No Whisk, No Reward by Ellie Kay (#1)

The Green Valley Library Series

Love in Due Time by L.B. Dunbar (#1)

Crime and Periodicals by Nora Everly (#2)

Prose Before Bros by Cathy Yardley (#3)

Shelf Awareness by Katie Ashley (#4)

Carpentry and Cocktails by Nora Everly (#5)

Love in Deed by L.B. Dunbar (#6)

Dewey Belong Together by Ann Whynot (#7)

Hotshot and Hospitality by Nora Everly (#8)

Love in a Pickle by L.B. Dunbar (#9)

Checking You Out by Ann Whynot (#10)

Scorned Women's Society Series

My Bare Lady by Piper Sheldon (#1)

The Treble with Men by Piper Sheldon (#2)

The One That I Want by Piper Sheldon (#3)

Hopelessly Devoted by Piper Sheldon (#3.5)

It Takes a Woman by Piper Sheldon (#4)

Park Ranger Series

Happy Trail by Daisy Prescott (#1)

Stranger Ranger by Daisy Prescott (#2)

The Leffersbee Series

Been There Done That by Hope Ellis (#1)

Before and After You by Hope Ellis (#2)

The Higher Learning Series

Upsy Daisy by Chelsie Edwards (#1)

Green Valley Heroes Series

Forrest for the Trees by Kilby Blades (#1)

Parks and Provocation by Juliette Cross (#2)

Story of Us Collection

My Story of Us: Zach by Chris Brinkley (#1)

Seduction in the City

Cipher Security Series

Code of Conduct by April White (#1)

Code of Honor by April White (#2)

Code of Matrimony by April White (#2.5)

Code of Ethics by April White (#3)

Cipher Office Series

Weight Expectations by M.E. Carter (#1)

Sticking to the Script by Stella Weaver (#2)

Cutie and the Beast by M.E. Carter (#3)

Weights of Wrath by M.E. Carter (#4)

Common Threads Series

Mad About Ewe by Susannah Nix (#1)

Give Love a Chai by Nanxi Wen (#2)

Key Change by Heidi Hutchinson (#3)

Educated Romance

Work For It Series

Street Smart by Aly Stiles (#1)

Heart Smart by Emma Lee Jayne (#2)

Book Smart by Amanda Pennington (#3)

Smart Mouth by Emma Lee Jayne (#4)

Lessons Learned Series

Under Pressure by Allie Winters (#1)

Not Fooling Anyone by Allie Winters (#2)

Out of this World

London Ladies Embroidery Series

Neanderthal Seeks Duchess (#1)

CPSIA information can be obtained
at www.ICGtesting.com
Printed in the USA
LVHW031955110422
715892LV00007B/1264